"WHY HAVE YOU BEEN AVOIDING ME?" ATHENA DEMANDED. "WHY, QUENTIN?"

He was silent, holding her close and slowly rubbing her cheek with his. When the song ended he took her by the hand and led her to the small morning room off the kitchen. He turned on the light and bent down to stoke the fire before placing another log into the fireplace.

She leaned back against the table in the middle of the room, her arms folded across her chest. He turned to her and walked slowly to where she stood and ran his hands up and down her arms, staring deeply into her eyes. He kissed her gently, his hands warm on her bare skin. He kissed her mouth and her chin, her cheeks and her neck, her shoulder, before moving to her mouth again.

"Why, Quentin?" She would not be put off. She wanted an answer, even while her knees buckled and her heart pounded and she wanted him to keep on kissing her. . . .

MARIAH STEWART

A DIFFERENT LIGHT

POCKET BOOKS

New York   London   Toronto   Sydney   Tokyo   Singapore

This book is a work of fiction. Names, characters, places and
incidents are products of the author's imagination or are used
fictitiously. Any resemblance to actual events or locales or persons,
living or dead, is entirely coincidental.

An *Original* Publication of POCKET BOOKS

POCKET BOOKS, a division of Simon & Schuster Inc.
1230 Avenue of the Americas, New York, NY 10020

ISBN: 0-671-86855-1

First Pocket Books printing November 1995

10 9 8 7 6 5 4 3 2 1

POCKET and colophon are registered trademarks of
Simon & Schuster Inc.

Cover art by Franco Accornero

Printed in the U.S.A.

Heartfelt thanks to two women who, as teachers, motivated me through their belief in me and who, as friends, helped me to believe in myself. . . .

Edna Dey—who told me that I *could*—
and
Eleanor Shuman—who told me that I *would*—
someday be the writer of books.

Sleep in heavenly peace.

M.S.

Acknowledgments

There are so many people to thank for all the good and happy things that have happened to me over the past few years. Certainly at the top of the list—for this book and every book—is my agent, Loretta Barrett, who is everything that an agent should be: caring, smart, funny, dedicated, professional, and *always* on my side. My editor, Linda Marrow, who opened the door onto *someday* for me, and who is sooo good at what she does (and who does it with such great humor that it doesn't feel like work). Kate Collins, assistant editor, who answers my questions, keeps things moving, keeps me in the loop, and is just such a joy to work with. And, of course, Joan Sanger, who taught me how to write a novel.

Thanks, too, to Carole Spayd, who bought a copy of my first book, *Moments in Time,* every time she saw it on display because she just couldn't walk past it, and who showed up at almost as many of my book signings as I did. Likewise, Helen Egner, who brought the champagne, and who was, I admit it, right again. Cherie Christakis, who graciously and patiently tutored me in just enough Greek to give *A Different Light* a distinct flavor—*Hilea efharisto.* A thousand thanks. Gail Link, who cheered me on, taught me the ropes, and showed me how to avoid hanging myself with them. Joan Galvin, who bought copies of *Moments in Time* for her entire family and many of her friends, and who, I believe, was single-handedly responsible for the book selling out in more than one bookstore. Nolia Scott, who made sure that everyone knew when I had signings. Jo Ellen Grossman, who has known me forever and loves me anyway, and whose love and friendship have been part of my life for more years than either of us likes to admit (okay, Stephen, you too).

Special thanks to those many readers who took the time to write a note or card to let me know how much they enjoyed *Moments in Time.* It was an absolute thrill for me to learn that so many people loved Maggie, J.D., and their family. I'm hoping you'll love this book every bit as much.

Last—but never, as they say, least—my parents, who stuffed their Christmas cards with my bookmarkers and who made certain that the bookstores in New Jersey kept selling out; my daughters, Katie and Rebecca, for, well, just for being Katie and Becca; and my husband Bill, who is learning how to cook so that I don't have to.

M.S.
P.O. Box 481
Lansdowne, PA 19050

A DIFFERENT LIGHT

1

The first light of day softly invaded the room through lace curtains nudged aside by the dawn breeze, a remnant of the storm which had passed through in the early morning hours. The sweet scent of lilac wafted upwards from branches weary from their stubborn struggle to remain erect against the heavy downpour, branches which now sagged backwards against the brick and stucco house like tired old ladies on park benches. The heady fragrance drifted through the window with the poking sunlight, coaxing the sleeping woman to open her eyes.

Long slender legs stretched towards the end of the mattress while bare arms reached up and over to rest upon the headboard. Athena Moran opened her eyes and stared miserably towards the window through which the soft yellow rays of sunlight had begun to dance.

Encouraged by the forecast for rain the night before, she had prayed it would continue into the morning and with luck, perhaps even last the entire day. Kicking back the thin blue blanket, she peered out the window, hoping to see the sun peeking from some dark clouds about to burst forth again in a torrent.

She grimaced as she looked upwards through the trees. The blue May sky was unblemished, and even at this early hour, the sun was beginning to dry up the residue of the storm. It would, in all likelihood, be a perfect spring day.

Damn.

It was exactly the type of morning her daughter would call a "happy to be alive" day. She wondered how long it would be before Callie bounced in to make that very pronouncement.

Sitting on the edge of the bed, Athen sighed and ran her long fingers through a cascade of straight black hair. With the passing of the storm, her only excuse to avoid the annual Woodside Heights Memorial Day picnic had been snatched from her.

"Mommy! Look! The rain stopped!" Nine-year-old Callie danced into the room and pulled the curtains all the way back. A splash of gold spilled gleefully across the green carpet, mocking Athen with its cheerfulness.

"I looked, sweetheart." For Callie's sake, Athen forced a geniality she did not feel, knowing her daughter had eagerly awaited this day for the same reason she herself had dreaded it.

"So what time?" Callie asked as she skipped back towards her room to dress. "The picnic starts at eleven . . ."

"Well." Athen pondered whether it would be better to go early and leave early, or go late . . .

"Can we go right at eleven?" Callie pleaded anxiously.

"We have a few other things to do today, Callie . . . ," she began hesitantly, trying to buy time before making a commitment she would be unable to break.

"What other things?" Callie stuck her head back in through the open doorway.

"Well, we have to go see your grandfather . . ."

"We can do that on our way to the park. We can have breakfast right now and go see Grampa and go right to the picnic." Pleased with the agenda, Callie ran off to dress.

It's just a picnic, Athen told herself. You've gotten through worse days than this over the past months. She grabbed her robe from the foot of the bed and headed towards the bathroom for a shower, repeating to herself, "It's just a picnic . . ."

The Memorial Day picnic sponsored by the city fathers every year at Enid Wood Memorial Park gathered together all the city employees—past and present—along with their families, for a day of fun and games. As daughter of a former, much-loved city councilman, Athen had attended every year for as long as she could remember. And, as wife of a city police officer, she had served willingly on various committees over the past twelve years.

Her father's stroke three years ago had ravaged his mind as well as his body. Paralyzed and deprived of speech, he now sat lost in a world of his own definition, confined to a wheelchair out at Woodside Manor, a small private nursing home on the grounds of the old mansion once owned by the Wood family. It was never easy for Athen to sit and chat with her father's old cronies, especially on this one day each year, when memories of Ari Stavros in his prime abounded and his old friends would make a special effort to share their favorite recollections with her, as if she needed to be reminded how witty he had been, how clever, how devoted to the city and in particular to the Greek community he had served for so long.

If facing her father's cohorts had been difficult, this year, she knew, would be endlessly more painful. This year she would attend as the widow of the town's only police officer killed in the line of duty in over twenty-two years.

John Moran had been an enormously popular figure in the Woodside Heights Police Department. Street-smart and well-educated, handsome and affable, he'd been dubbed "Lucky" by the local press for his daring in the face of the dangers which had seemed to increase steadily as the drug traffic had begun to flow from New York City, a mere thirty miles away. The new bypass off the interstate had made it so much more convenient for the runners to zip into this small northern New Jersey city, make their connections, then zip back onto the highway towards New York or Washington. More often than not, when the dealers hit the city limits, John Moran was waiting for them. He'd made more drug-related arrests than anyone on the force, and had been heralded for his tenacity, his bravery.

One night in January, on the corner of Marshall and Oak, John's luck had run out. A carefully planned drug bust had been aborted when a small child stepped out of a corner market directly between the undercover officers and the dealer. John had leaped without hesitation from behind a Dumpster to knock the youngster out of the line of fire when the dealer pulled his gun. The young boy had scooted away from the scene with no more than a scratch on his elbow. John Moran lay facedown on the concrete, blood gushing from a huge hole in the back of his head.

The city had afforded Johnny a hero's funeral, with representatives from every law enforcement department in the state of New Jersey. The press had had a field day with the story, and for weeks Athen could not leave her house without being photographed. The slain officer's widow had been pure marble, blinking back tears which never fell in public, not even when her sobbing daughter had clung to her as John's body had been lowered into the ground. Photographs of a dry-eyed, stony-faced Athena Moran, stoically comforting her in-laws, gently consoling her husband's partner, were picked up by the national wires and appeared in almost every major newspaper across the country.

For all her stalwart facade, those close to her had despaired, knowing John's death had devastated Athen to her very soul. The once dancing gray eyes were mirror now only to the void within her, the dazzling smile only a memory. Her fiery beauty had seemed to evaporate, leaving her face drawn and tired, a telltale sign that the tears which had been so impassively held back in public had been wept in solitude every night for the past five months.

She had cut her ties to all but those most intimate, had gone nowhere she hadn't needed to go. Her life revolved around her daughter and her father. Messages left on her answering machine went unanswered, those left with Callie were never returned. In her heart she knew there was a life to be lived, decisions to be made about her future, but she was unable to face them, and so she did not, telling herself that time would heal her, trying to believe it would just happen, that one day she would wake up and be whole again. She recognized the self-deception for what it was, but was powerless to move beyond the spot where she stood.

Until that cold January day, even Athen's social life had fairly revolved around John. Her one night out every other Monday had been with the wives of his fellow officers—dinner, gossip, support. Since John's death she had gone but once. The fear in the eyes of the other women, some once as close as sisters, had taken her aback. To them she was a reminder of what could happen, her shattered life a taunt that theirs, too, could as easily be destroyed. She had read their minds in an instant . . . there but for the grace of God . . . and she had never gone back, the fear in their eyes warding her off as a cross would cause some evil thing to retreat into the shadows in a grade-B movie. She had gone home early, seeking the safety and comfort of her home, and had lain awake all night cursing John for having left her and taking her life with him.

Stepping from the shower and reaching for a towel with which to dry her hair, she tried to calm herself. Were it not for Callie, there would be no thought given to this annual event. Athen knew that her daughter had counted the days, eager to see the sons and daughters of city workers she'd known since birth. Separated by neighborhoods and different schools, some friends she saw infrequently, but always she could look forward to Memorial Day to renew old friendships, play games, swim in the lake. Athen silently prayed that Callie, too, would not feel set apart from the other children as she herself now felt from their mothers.

Pulling on a short soft yellow cotton knit dress, a long T-shirt type thing, she cinched it at the waist with a wide green belt and sat on the edge of the bed to tie multicolored thongs of leather sandals around her slim ankles. She reached for a straw hat and tied the ribbons under her chin slightly to one side, and stepped back to look critically at herself in the mirror for the first time in months.

She was pale, almost haggard, and she knew it. Removing the hat, she stepped into the bathroom and turned the light back on. She wound her hair up into a soft twist and secured it with some pins. Better, but not great. On a whim, she snapped a piece of dried baby's breath from a wreath which hung on the bathroom wall, and tucked it into the back of her hair. She rummaged through a basket of makeup that had sat unused for months and found blush, a pale lilac eyeshadow and mascara. When she had finished, she stepped back to take a look.

The merry widow I'm not, she told herself, but I'll be damned if Callie's going to that picnic with a woman who could pass as her grandmother.

2

Athen parked the car at the far end of the lot, back near the trees that would shade the small vehicle from the sun. Not quite eleven, the temperature was already into the eighties, the humidity rising.

"Mom, look . . . Grampa's on the patio." Callie took off towards the back of the white-columned Georgian mansion, running up the grassy slope, all legs in white shorts and white sneakers. She waved a greeting to Lilly, the nurse's aide, a large black woman of gentle touch and gentle humor, and sat on the bricks at the feet of the old man in the wheelchair.

Only six when her grandfather had suffered the first stroke, Callie would never, Athen knew, remember him as the strong giant of a man he once had been. Nearing the place where he sat silent and imprisoned, Athen lamented that the once-broad shoulders upon which she had ridden as a child were now so small and slumped, the hands which had lifted her into the air now lifeless and pale.

"Pateras," she addressed him formally, with respect, in Greek. "I've a letter from Demitri."

She kissed the top of his head and pulled a chair closer, taking the thin white pages from the neatly addressed envelope. She read the letter from her father's brother, who had never left their homeland, first in Greek, then in English, wondering if anything at all got through to him. She chatted, a one-sided conversation with her father, a few words with Lilly, then sat wrapped with him in his silence as she watched Callie feed the ducks which had gathered at the edge of the pond.

Lilly left them and Athen confided her fears and anxiety to her father, telling him in a tearful whisper how she had prayed for strength to get through this day, how the emptiness inside her had seemed to widen, not diminish, as time had passed, how her life, except for Callie, had no meaning, no direction.

"I guess you felt like that when Mama died," she spoke softly, not expecting confirmation. "I don't remember what it was like for you then, only what it was like for me, I was so little . . . but I remember you kept going. Kept working and going to meetings . . . I remember the nights Aunt Helena stayed with me when you went out. How did you have the strength to go out, Papa? How did you go back into a world she had left?"

There would be no response, she knew, nor any recognition that he had heard or understood. The dark brown eyes—so like Callie's—flickered briefly. If indeed there had been a message there, its meaning was lost to her. The man who had been both mother and father to her since she was five years old no longer existed. Her guardian, her champion, who had so carefully and lovingly sheltered her from the world's dangers, could shelter her no more.

She sat quietly, watching a black speckled caterpillar inch across the bricks, waiting for the enormous lump in her throat to dissolve, forcing herself to regain control. Lilly appeared to announce lunch, and Athen kissed her father goodbye, telling him she'd stop back tomorrow, and would bring him all the news from his old friends.

Callie greeted her mother's beckoning call with a loud "Yahoo!" as she dashed from the pond to the parking lot. Athen's stomach churned as she pulled out of the drive, knowing this would be a very long afternoon.

* * *

Athen was certain that the fact that Diana Bennett was the first person she saw upon arriving at the park was an omen of just how bad the day would be.

"Hey, Mrs. Bennett. Hi!" Callie called to her as she jumped out of the car.

"Hello, Callie. Good Lord, Callie, you've grown another two—make that three—inches since I've seen you." Diana smiled fondly at the young girl. "We've missed you out at the academy. Aren't you taking lessons anymore?"

"Mom said I can start riding again in the fall, maybe. I hope so. How's Brady?"

"He's a lonely old horse without his favorite rider, Callie," Diana told her solemnly.

"Tell him I'll be out to see him. I miss him too." Callie's sadness at having suspended her riding lessons over the past few months was evident. She brightened then a bit, adding, "We just came from seeing Grampa."

"Oh, shut up, Callie," Athena muttered silently as she prepared to exit the driver's side. "Just shut up . . ."

"How is he this morning?" Diana's face tensed slightly.

"He's okay. The same," Callie told her. "Hey, Mom, there's Julie . . . hey, Julie, wait up . . ."

Callie sprinted across the asphalt, turning back once to wave. "See ya, Mrs. Bennett . . ."

"Hello, Athen," ventured a cautious Diana.

Ari Stavros's mistress faced his daughter from across the back of the car.

"How are you holding up these days?" Diana asked with what appeared to be genuine concern.

"I'm fine." Athen opened the trunk and appeared to be engrossed in checking the contents of Callie's beach bag—the carefully folded swimsuit, the towel, sunscreen . . .

"I'm sure this is difficult for you. To be here, I mean . . ." Diana began hesitantly.

"I'm fine." Athen slammed the trunk with more vigor than was necessary. How could Diana possibly know . . .

"Look, if you need a refuge, if things get tough, I'll be here . . ." The blond woman made an attempt to offer her hand.

"I'm fine, Diana. Really," Athen insisted, averting her

8

eyes to the left as another car pulled in to park next to her. Finding herself oddly relieved to see an old friend of John's behind the wheel, she turned her back stiffly on Diana as she greeted the newcomers. When she turned back, Diana had gone.

It had not been as bad as she had anticipated, she reflected later in the day. There had been some tense moments, some tears shed reluctantly, but all in all, everyone had seemed happy to see her. Had anyone been uncomfortable in her presence, they had cloaked it well behind warm smiles and outreached arms.

She sat alone on the small mound of grass, not quite a hill, overlooking the playing field where the children's games were being set up. Searching the gathering crowd, she found her daughter in the midst of a group of young girls pairing off for the sack race, bending down to tie their legs together much as she herself had done so long ago. Unconsciously her tongue sought out her front tooth, capped since that Memorial Day when she was twelve, when Angie Gillespie's foot, tied to Nancy Simpson's, had collided with Athen's face as they had fallen together in a heap. . . .

Lost in reverie, she did not hear the approaching footsteps until it was too late.

"Would you look at that bunch?" Diana Bennett sat down beside her on the grass and nodded to the group of men gathered not fifty feet away, set off slightly apart from those who had flocked around the picnic tables. "Our fearless leaders. Defenders of the city. Rossi's sitting on that beach chair like Caesar at a field maneuver. Surrounded by all his little generals. The man who would be king . . ."

Athen smiled wanly as the feeling of being trapped washed over her. She had no desire to engage in conversation, personal or political, with this woman. She turned her attention to the white-haired man in the dark glasses and the Mets cap.

Dante Rossi, the mayor of Woodside Heights and its undisputed political kingpin, was seated in a folding beach chair—provided, no doubt, by a thoughtful and devoted employee so that the boss would be spared the discomfort of perching on the edge of backless picnic benches with the peons all afternoon—while his closest advisors stood around him in a cluster like the palace guard.

"And look at Harlan Justis—that's City Solicitor Justis, of course." Diana nodded towards the tall thin man as he took several steps towards the picnic table closest to him and lifted a tiny infant from the backpack a young mother was struggling with. "That son of a gun is playing the crowd, look at him. Campaigning. Now check out Rossi, watching Justis . . . look at his face . . . Someone had better remind old Harlan that no one's a candidate until I say he's a candidate!" Diana effectively mimicked the mayor's gruff tone.

"Candidate for what?" Athen heard herself ask.

"Mayor, of course." Diana opened her purse and pulled out a cigarette, then fumbled in her pockets for a lighter.

"What do you mean? Rossi's been mayor forever . . ."

"It only seems like forever." Diana laughed. "But actually it's been only eight years. Look at those meatheads. Circling like sharks around a capsized boat. Just waiting for Rossi to give one of them the nod for the big chair."

"But Rossi's still mayor . . ."

"Not after November, he won't be." Diana exhaled white smoke and leaned back on one elbow.

"Is he retiring?"

"Sort of. Forced retirement. City charter says four consecutive terms max. This is Rossi's fourth term."

"Oh." Athen stole a sideways glance in Diana's direction.

It was as close as she had ever been to the woman with whom her father had kept company for so many years. How many? Athen didn't know for certain. Ari had never discussed Diana with his daughter, had never mentioned her name. It had been John who had first informed her of it, talking about his father-in-law's relationship with the young woman as if Athen had known all about it. She had not. For some reason she still did not understand, she had been shocked that her father had taken up with a woman who was but six years older than Athen herself. She wasn't certain if she'd been jealous because her father had found someone to fill his hours, or if she'd been offended because it was a part of his life he would not share with his daughter.

"What a sorry group," Diana went on. "They all want it so badly they salivate every time they get within ten feet of that office, bending over backwards to please Rossi these days . . ."

"Why?" Athen studied the woman's face surreptitiously. Diana had those bee-stung lips which were so in vogue these days, crystal blue eyes, long dark lashes, a peaches and cream complexion. Her short blond hair curled around her face in ringlets. She was very pretty, Athen conceded, though the very opposite of her mother, who had been olive skinned, hair and eyes as dark as night . . .

"Because whoever he picks to run will win."

"But won't there be an election?"

Melina Stavros had been a tiny doll of a woman, small boned and fragile as a butterfly. Diana was soft and rounded, though an athlete all her life. Tennis, riding, she even played softball on the city's intramural team. Athen had watched her play one time, when the police department had played city hall. Melina had been a hothouse flower, chained to her home by the heavy braces borne on both legs, unable to walk without crutches, unable to climb the steps.

"Elections mean nothing in this city, Athen. It's a one-party town. Dan Rossi is the party. He'll choose his own successor."

"You mean whoever he picks will win? Automatically?" And Diana's so . . . contemporary, wearing makeup and smoking cigarettes, a CPA. Mama was a page from a novel out of the past, old-fashioned in her ways and in her dress, beautiful in her simplicity . . .

"Yup. Oh, there'll be an election. But Rossi could run Lassie in this city and the party faithful would vote for the dog." Diana stubbed the cigarette out in the grass. "And each one of those little mutts wants to be Rossi's dog. If he has a favorite, though, he hasn't let on."

"Why doesn't Rossi just name a successor then?" If Melina had been candlelight, Diana is sunlight on an open field . . .

"What? And put a premature end to all this butt-kissing?" Diana laughed heartily. "My guess is that Rossi doesn't want to give it up. Pure and simple. Afraid if he tells someone they'll be the next mayor, they'll start acting like mayor. Rossi loves it all too much. He loves the power."

"But he'll still be head of the party, right?" Diana talks politics like one of the boys . . .

"Not the same." Diana shook her head. "My gut tells me if Rossi could find a way to hold onto it all, he would. He's a crafty bugger, I'll give him that . . ."

"How could he do that if the charter says four terms?" Melina's realm had never extended beyond her own front door . . .

"Good grief, Athen, didn't you learn anything about politics from your father?" Diana chided good-naturedly, blue eyes twinkling.

"No." Athen had hoped her father would not be mentioned, and was uncomfortable now that he had been. "I've never been particularly interested in politics."

"That's what brought us together, Ari and me. I was just starting out in the finance office, Ari was already on the city council . . ." She stopped, realizing that Athen had deliberately turned her face from her. "You don't really want to hear about that, do you?"

"No," was the abrupt response.

"Why? Are you afraid I have something of him that you don't? And even if I do, what has that taken from you, Athen?" Diana spoke quietly, but there was anger beneath the soft tone. "I have loved that man for eighteen years, Athen—that's right, since the time you started college. I have stayed in the background and never intruded into your life. Not when Ari had the stroke—not when John died and I wanted to comfort you, because I know just what you've lost . . ."

"You have no idea what I've lost, Diana . . ." a waspish Athen snapped.

Tears welled in Diana's eyes and began to stream down her face. "You think that I was just a diversion for a lonely widower, don't you? That I was nothing more to him than an evening's companion? You do, Athen, I can see it in your eyes . . ."

The blond woman stood up, the enormity of her pain very much evident in every line on her face.

"How old are you now, Athen? Thirty-five? Don't you think it's time you grew up?"

Stung and surprised by the outburst, Athen watched with flushed cheeks as Diana fled in the direction of the parking lot.

3

She had remained on the spot, wrapped in embarrassment at having caused such unexpected anguish. While not wanting to know the details of her father's relationship, she had no desire to intentionally hurt Diana. And Diana had been right. Athen had assumed that her relationship with Ari had been strictly fun and games, that he was slightly embarrassed by it and so had never involved Diana in any way with his family. Ari had attended his daughter's wedding unescorted, had spent every holiday, every birthday, with Athen and John, though he had always, she now recalled, departed immediately after dinner.

Diana's quiet declaration of love had left her disconcerted. Had Ari returned that love? For the first time she wondered if her failure to offer her father the option of bringing a guest to share Christmas or Thanksgiving or birthday celebrations had been a source of pain not only to Diana but to Ari as well. Had he been reluctant to ask Athen to share him with Diana, or was it Diana he had been unwilling to share?

When she became conscious of her surroundings, the children's games had ended and Callie was running towards her jubilantly, proudly showing off the medals she had won that day, for swimming and for the pie-eating contest.

"Let me guess," Athen said wryly, "blueberry, right?"

"How'd you know?" Callie asked.

Athen laughed and pointed to the front of Callie's shirt.

"Oops." Callie giggled and rubbed at first one, then another of the purple stains.

"It's okay, honey," her mother assured her. "Look, it's getting late, Callie. Why don't you start gathering up your things . . ."

"Aw, Mom, it's not that late," protested Callie.

"It will be by the time you find everything and we get out of here. Go now . . ."

Athen stood up and brushed off the grass which clung to the back of her bare legs. She looked over towards the picnic grove, and saw that Dan Rossi was on his feet now, preparing to leave. She should go pay her respects, she told herself.

Walking towards him she caught his eye from thirty feet away and watched as a broad smile of recognition spread across his face. The old man abruptly ended the conversation in which he'd been engaged and walked to greet her, beaming broadly, his arms opening to enfold her.

"Athen, sweetheart." He embraced her warmly. "What a joy to see you. You are well? And Callie? And your blessed father—you must tell me how he is doing. Not a day passes that I don't remember him in my prayers. Come, walk with me a bit and we'll talk. I haven't seen you since . . . well, since that terrible day when John . . . God rest his soul . . . you're getting your checks on time? The workers' compensation, the pension . . . ?"

"Yes, everything on time, Dan. Everyone's been very helpful."

"God help them if they're not," he told her. "We take care of our own, that's a fact. You need anything . . . I mean anything . . . you call me directly, you hear? Not Mary Fran, you call me. Though of course soon enough Mary Fran won't be there anyway . . . you remember Mary Fran Ellison?"

"Sure . . . she's an old friend of my . . ."

"My right hand. Best assistant anyone ever had. Gonna be next to impossible to replace her."

"Is she retiring?" Mary Fran must be close to sixty-five, Athen recalled.

"Back surgery. Had a car accident last year, let them operate on her back. Worse now than she was before.

14

Anyone ever wants to operate on your back, Athen, you tell them to go to hell, hear?" They were nearing the parking lot, and Dan waved to a departing fireman and his family of young ones. "What are you doing with yourself these days, Athen? You back to school? Did I hear you went back to school?"

"I went back about three years ago. At night. I thought it would be a good idea to start on my master's. In education. I thought maybe I'd go back to teaching when Callie started high school. I quit when she was born, you know. I wanted to stay home with her, after having lost my own mother when I was so little . . ." Why am I babbling, she asked herself, a flush settling on her cheeks.

"Ah, but that was a tragedy, her dying so young. I've said it a million times if I've said it once, Melina Stavros was the most beautiful woman I've ever known. We all mourned her, Athen. Just as we all mourned your John. As fine a man as ever wore the uniform, no question about that. Ah, and your father . . . it breaks my heart . . ." Rossi pulled a white linen handkerchief from his pants pocket and wiped at his eyes. "So . . . you're back to school this fall, then?"

"Maybe not this fall. Maybe next spring . . . I'm not sure. When I'm ready . . ." She glanced away.

"Well, I'm a great believer myself in the importance of timing, you know. Always have been. Just don't put it off too long, dear. Not enough of life to waste a bit of it." He waved to a passing group, calling after them, "Good to see you. Glad you could make it."

They walked towards the spot where Athen had parked her car. Callie was nowhere to be seen.

"So what do you do with your time?" he asked directly, watching her face for a response.

"Not a whole lot." She turned to avert her eyes.

"That's not good, Athen. Not good at all. You're young, you've a whole lifetime ahead of you, my dear," he said gently.

"I know." She swallowed a lump. "But it's just so hard . . ."

"I know it is. Didn't I lose my own Madeline two years

15

ago? Don't I know how hard it is to go on? But you have to. Find something meaningful to do, Athen. Find a job . . . only thing that kept me going was the job."

"A job?" She laughed. "I couldn't handle teaching right now. Not even as a substitute. I'm at too many loose ends, Dan, it wouldn't be fair to inflict someone in my state of mind on a classroom full of children."

"It doesn't have to be teaching, Athen. There's plenty you could do, I'd wager, if you gave it some thought. And you should find something to fill the hours, honey. Get your life moving forward, it passes all too quickly as it is . . ." He stopped again to shake a hand or two. "Hey, there, Bob, Susan, glad you joined us. Sue, tell your sister we missed her today . . . Like I was saying, Athen, you should look into finding a little something to keep your mind occupied, you know, until you get your feet back on the ground again. Think about it. Anybody would love to have you on their staff, bright and pretty as you are. Love to have you myself." He stopped in midstride and grabbed her arm. "Now there's an idea. Why not come to work for me?"

"For you? Doing what?"

"Answering my phone, keeping the wolves from the door, keeping my day organized . . ."

"Dan, lately I can't organize my own days . . ."

"More I think about it, more I know it's just the thing for you. And for me. I need to replace Mary Fran, and there's no one I could trust more than you . . ."

"Dan, I can't replace Mary Fran. I have no office skills, I don't type very well . . ."

"Nothing to it." He dismissed her objections with the wave of a hand that was both beefy and arthritic. "Just like running a house."

"I'm not even doing that well these days," she told him. "Thanks, Dan, I appreciate the offer, but no, I don't think . . ."

"Don't give me an answer now, give it some real thought."

"Dan, I can't commit to something long-term right now . . ."

"Athen, we're not talking long-term." He laughed good-naturedly. "Since I'll be out of a job myself come November, chances are you'd be too. New mayor'll want his own right hand sitting outside that door, not someone loyal to his predecessor. No, darlin', long-term is definitely not an issue here. But it will get you out of that house and give you a change of scenery, which I suspect you need."

"Still, I don't . . ."

"Here's my car now." He motioned to the driver of a dark blue Cadillac inching its way through the crowd. "All I ask is that you give it some honest thought. . . ."

She nodded, then put out her hand to him.

"What handshake?" he chided. "Give the old man a hug, eh? There you go, now, great to see you. You think about what I said . . . you give me a call, hear? My love to your dad . . ."

And the whirlwind that was Dan Rossi disappeared into the back of the waiting Cadillac. The driver hesitated momentarily as the throng jamming the parking lot parted like the Red Sea to permit the vehicle to pass.

"Hey, Mom! Julie and Jessie are going to the ice cream parlor on the way home. Mrs. Myers said I could go if it's all right with you . . ." Callie called from five cars down.

"Okay, Athen?" Liz Myers stuck her head out the window. "We won't be long. We'll drop her off on the way home."

"That's fine. Thank you," Athen called back, motioning Callie to her and scrambling in her wallet as Callie ran to her with an outstretched hand. Athen handed her a five, reminding her that there'd be change.

"Thanks, Mom." Callie gave her an abbreviated hug and ran off.

The crush of departees descended upon the two-lane exit like ants jockeying for position on a discarded M&M. Athen waited patiently for her turn to pull out onto the highway. At the last minute, for no discernible reason, she changed her directional signal from left to right, and eased onto the road which led back through the park.

The air was cooler with the descent of the sun behind the trees and she opened the windows to let the breeze flood the car. She turned on the radio, still set to John's favorite station. KROC out of New York. Classic rock. Though jazz was more to her preference, she had never been able to bring herself to change it. She turned it off abruptly.

She drove absentmindedly for a few minutes, thinking how the day had turned out to be okay. Better than okay, she admitted. Except for that little to-do with Diana. She rounded a curve, braking sharply to avoid the opossum that had just stepped from the shoulder onto the asphalt. The animal froze, and Athen could see the sparks from tiny eyes peering over the mother's back. Careful, Momma, Athen told the frightened creature as she accelerated slightly.

Slowing down at the next bend in the road, she found herself at the back entrance to Woodside Manor. Might as well stop in for a minute, she thought, and say goodnight to Dad. Wonder what he'd say about Rossi's job offer . . .

She followed the dirt drive to the front entrance, and headed for the section of the lot closest to the building. For the second time in less than five minutes she slammed on her brakes.

In the first spot nearest the gate sat Diana's red sports car.

The motor running, her arm resting on the open window and her chin in her hand, she debated for only a moment before quietly turning the car around and heading for home.

4

The first harsh crack of thunder rattled through the night silence and the heavens came suddenly to life, a raucous opening act for the rowdy sound and light show about to begin in the skies above Woodside Heights.

"Mommy . . . !" Callie Moran stumbled through the dark, fleeing to the safety of her mother's bed.

"It's okay, Callie," Athen told her, patting the left side of the bed in answer to her daughter's unspoken question. "Come on in."

18

Callie snuggled in and curled up beside her, while Athen stroked the back of the child's head, her fingers caught here and there in the wild tangle of curly brown hair.

"I hate it when thunder does that," she murmured, "when it sneaks up on you in the night. Like it's waited up there in the sky all day till you go to sleep, so it can jump out at you in the dark and scare you half to death . . ." Callie yawned, and snuggled a bit closer. "Tell me again why we have thunder. And don't give me that stuff about the trolls bowling . . ."

Athen lay wide-eyed, staring at the ceiling.

"I don't remember," she admitted sheepishly. "I know it has something to do with positives and negatives, but right at this minute I can't seem to come up with it."

"Daddy would," Callie said quietly, "Daddy would remember."

"Yes, sweetheart," Athen whispered, "Daddy would know."

And John, of course, not only would have remembered, but would have delivered a fully detailed science lesson, even at three A.M. He would have thoroughly answered all Callie's questions patiently, until he was certain her understanding was complete. Athen had, on many occasions, marveled at his ability to explain nature's mysteries in a manner that the youngster's mind could visualize and comprehend.

Athen closed her eyes and tried to return to sleep, but the rain rushed against the windows like a giant hose held by some rain demon intent on torturing her with sweet memories. It had been a long-standing joke between Johnny and her that the sound of rain on the roof had always seemed to bring out her more amorous nature. Once, after an unusually emotional argument, she had stomped upstairs and slammed the bedroom door. She had gone to bed immediately and pulled the covers up over her shoulders, refusing to respond to his pleas for an opportunity to further explain his point of view. After she had rebuffed him for about the twentieth time, he had quietly left the room. Some minutes later she had been startled to hear the sound of rain, steady and rhythmic, beating against the roof. Curious, she tiptoed to the window and peered out, only to see John, the garden hose in hand, directing the stream of water onto the tin roof of the garage. At the sound of her laughter, he had looked up and grinned impishly.

"Come back to bed," she had told him, her anger forgotten, and he had . . .

Athen lay awake listening to Callie's breathing until she was certain the child was on her way back towards peaceful slumber. She lifted herself carefully, trying not to disturb the sleeping form curled next to her, then eased her legs over the side of the bed. The soles of her feet slid over warm fur. The dog's huge head snapped up to quickly identify the human body part which now dangled just slightly over her neck.

"Go back to sleep, Hannah." Athen leaned down to pat the dog's yellow rump, then walked quietly towards the doorway. Under one foot a soft rubber object squeaked. Hannah's favorite toy, a small orange hedgehog, lay right inside the door, close by, as always, to where Hannah slept.

Quietly she crossed the hall to Callie's room and closed the windows, proceeding next to the back bedroom. Hesitating only briefly, she turned on the light, averting her eyes from the sudden brightness. She stood in the doorway, surveying the remnants of the only home improvement project Johnny had ever failed to complete.

The wallpaper table still bisected the room, a sheet of paper, cut but not hung, held flat by a level at one end and a book at the other. The earplugs still dangled from his radio that stood on the ladder's shelf. He had finished two walls the day before he had died, had tried to finish a third on what was to be his last morning. Unsuspecting of his fate, he had risen early and proceeded to work on the room, the new guest room, in preparation of a planned visit from his sister, Meg, the following week. He had worked steadily through the morning, eager to finish one more wall before it would be time for him to stop and change into his uniform before reporting for the four to midnight shift.

Athen had not been there when he had left for work that afternoon, having a number of errands to complete before picking Callie up at the school bus and taking her to the library. She had run through the afternoon's itinerary a thousand times in her mind since that day. Which of her tasks might she have omitted to have permitted her to have been home to have said goodbye to him? The supermarket, where she'd stood in line for ten minutes, her cart filled with who could remember what? The drugstore, where she'd leisurely thumbed through magazines before making a selection from the paperback novels which lined the shelves of one aisle? Had she picked Callie up at three at school, instead of at the bus stop at three-thirty, would they have returned from the library before he had left the house? Where had she been when he had closed the door behind him that last time?

And had she arrived home in time, would she have known that it would have in fact been goodbye? Would she have kissed him more passionately, some unknown intuition gnawing at her to give him yet one more hug?

She had not said goodbye, had not kissed him. She had stood in the doorway watching his meticulous measure of the wallpaper before making the cut.

"Looks great," she had told him, "the room will be gorgeous. Certainly suitable for visiting royalty."

"Or at the very least, my sister." He had looked up from his work and grinned as he yanked the earphones off, letting them dangle across his broad chest. "Where're you off to?"

"Errands," she had replied, "then to pick up Callie for a very quick trip to the library so she can get one last book she needs to complete her social studies report."

"What's she doing? Something on American Indians? She talk to Meg?"

"Last week. Also talked Meg into taking photographs of the Indian reservations around Tulsa and mailing them out so she'd have them in time for her report, which is due before Meg's arrival. Callie figures this to be an easy 'A'."

Johnny chuckled, knowing his sister, who coanchored the evening news at a network affiliate in Tulsa, would gladly give her only niece more information than any nine-year-old would ever be able to assimilate.

"Well, hopefully, Meg won't get carried away and include some of Chief Tall-Pony's political speeches on the abuse of the Indians at the hands of the white man . . ."

"It's Tall-Horse, and he has historical documentation to back up . . ."

Johnny frowned, cutting her off with a wave of the paste brush.

"I know, I know. I heard it all before. I heard it all night Christmas Eve and all day Christmas Day. I don't need to hear it again. I'm just glad Meg's not bringing the Chief back with her this time . . ."

"His name is Grady and he's not a chief," she reminded him. "And frankly, I'd rather see Callie present the truth in her report . . ."

"Well, it'll be great to have the old Meg back for a few days instead of the political activist she turns into whenever he's around . . ."

"What makes you think she only turns it on for Grady's sake? How do you know she's not as deeply committed to Indian rights as he is?"

"Because I know my sister. Changes her causes every time she changes men. Been doing it all her adult life . . ."

Athen stood silently, watching as he climbed the ladder and pressed the paper onto the wall, expertly smoothing it out with the long flat brush, eliminating tiny ripples with his fingers, pushing it firmly into place with his hands.

"What d'you think? Think the room will be done by next weekend?" He stepped back to admire his work, deftly diverting from the subject he no longer cared to discuss.

"I would think so . . . it does look wonderful," she told him, knowing there would be no further discussion of Meg, her love life, or her crusades.

He had been right, of course. His younger sister, Athen's best friend since grade school, had always seemed to don the cloak—political or otherwise—of the man du jour. It had driven Athen crazy over the years, but Meg was Meg, and would most likely never change.

"The furniture will be lovely in here, don't you think?" she asked, shifting her weight from one foot to the other, visualizing for the one-hundredth time the way the room would look once completed.

The pale butter-yellow paper dotted with white roses would be the perfect backdrop for the bedroom set stored in the attic. They'd brought it from her parents' house right before it had been sold two years earlier, after Ari had suffered the second stroke and Athen had to face the fact that he would never leave Woodside Manor. The 1930s walnut bed, two matching dressers and two bedside tables had been polished and readied for the move, hopefully by the end of the week. The dressing table had long since been installed in the master bedroom, the dressing table before which Melina had sat every night, brushing her long black hair. It was one of the very few enduring memories Athen had of her mother.

"Do you need me to pick up anything for you?" A glance at her watch told her that she should be leaving if all her errands were to be accomplished in time to meet the school bus.

He stood on the ladder, looking down at her, singing along with the song playing through the earplugs.

"You say something?" He grinned.

"I said, can I pick anything up for you while I'm out?"

"Well, we're running dangerously low on Doritos . . ."

"Message received." She winked and turned to go.

"Hey, 'Thena," he called to her as she reached the top of the steps.

She went back to the room and stuck her head through the doorway.

"Wait up for me tonight," he had told her as he plugged the headset back on and resumed singing.

"You betcha." She'd laughed.

His voice followed her through the hall and down the stairwell. Standing now alone in the room where she had last seen him alive, she could for the briefest second see him as he had stood there, broad grin on his handsome face, widely spaced brown eyes, curly brown hair falling slightly onto his forehead.

"Damn you, John Moran. Damn you for dying . . ." She

spoke aloud to the apparition, tears flooding her face. "Damn you . . ."

The wind blew up again suddenly, sending a cold chill of rain into the room. She closed the window as the thunder began to roll with enthused vigor, the sky beyond the trees now bright as midday as lightning began a frenzied dance across the night sky. She turned the light off, unable to bear another second in this room. She leaned against the wall in the hallway, wiping her face with the hem of her nightgown.

A brilliant flash illuminated the entire house. A deafening crack followed, then a terrible tearing of wood. The house seemed to shake to the foundation, as if sitting upon an earthquake's fault. A crash like nothing she'd ever heard split the night.

"Mommy!" Callie screamed in terror.

"I'm right here, baby . . ." Athen went quickly to the bedroom, colliding with Callie in the doorway. "Lightning struck something very nearby, maybe one of the trees in the backyard . . ."

Callie clung to her in fright. Hannah howled as the sirens began to scream above the storm.

"Come on, Callie, let's take a look."

She turned on the hall light and they passed into Callie's room. Pulling aside the curtain at the window overlooking the backyard, they gazed down in horror. A tree had fallen, flattening most of the garage as it made its way to the ground.

"Daddy's tree!" Callie cried. "Oh, Mommy, it's Daddy's tree!"

Callie sobbed openly, distraught at this newest loss. The magnolia which Johnny had planted the day they had moved into the house fourteen years ago lay split right down the middle.

Lights flickering in the homes of their neighbors announced that most of the street had been awakened by the crash. The few who had slept through it were surely now being roused by the sound of the police cruiser as it rounded the corner at the end of the street.

"You okay, honey?" Athen caressed the trembling child. "You want to get your robe on and come down with me?"

"Why are the police here?" Callie, unwilling to be left alone, pulled her robe from the closet.

"I guess they want to make sure no one was hurt, that no wires were brought down . . ." Athen decided it would be just as fast to dress as it would be to find her own robe, which she rarely wore. She pulled on sweatpants and a sweatshirt just as the doorbell rang. Hannah, barking and growling, flew down the steps.

"Hey, Fred, come on in," Athen greeted the officer as she grabbed the snarling dog's collar and opened the door.

Fred Keller quickly stepped inside the entry as the water slashed behind him.

"You okay, Athen?" the short stocky officer asked anxiously.

"We're fine." She nodded. "But it looks like we lost one of our trees . . ."

"Any wires down?"

"Not that I know of . . ."

"We'll take a run out back and have a look . . . you got any lights back there?"

"On the porch. I'll turn them on for you . . ."

Fred went back out the front where he was joined by three other officers who were already heading up the driveway. Athen and Callie first turned on all the downstairs lights, then those on the back porch which illuminated the entire back of the house. John's magnolia had been split cleanly in two, one half smashing the garage, the other huge section demolishing the neighbor's fence.

Athen went out onto the back porch and surveyed the damage wordlessly. Callie wrapped her arms around her mother's waist and cried.

"Daddy's tree is gone, Mommy. And look, it smashed his garden, too . . ." She pointed across the lawn to John's prized perennial beds, covered now by the huge slab of wood.

Damn, cursed Athen silently, wondering what to do next. The tree would have to be removed, the garage rebuilt, the Sullivans' fence replaced . . .

As if reading her mind, Callie lamented, "Daddy would know what to do."

What would John have done? Athen pondered. When he'd finished cursing, he'd have called their insurance agent. And that would be her first move, first thing in the morning.

5

The sound of the slamming car door at the end of the drive announced the arrival of the insurance adjuster, right on time. She peered out the window as the chubby young woman started towards the front door. Athen was there to open it before she could ring the bell.

"Mrs. Moran?" The adjuster handed her a business card as she introduced herself. "I'm Susan Watson . . . Mr. Fisher, your agent, called this morning and asked that I come out first thing . . ."

"So he told me. Thanks for being so prompt . . . I guess you're pretty busy today." Athen ushered her into the house.

"We have the distinction of insuring a good portion of the city's homes, at least in this part of town." Susan followed Athen towards the kitchen. "And we've already received a week's worth of reports. That was some storm . . . mind if I use your phone? We're supposed to call in when we get to each stop."

Athen pointed to the wall phone and waited while Susan dialed and gave her location.

"Let's take a look," she said, trailing behind Athen through the back door and into the yard, where steamy fingers of mist rose like smoke from the wet grass, warming now in the sun.

"Boy oh boy," Susan whistled, walking in the direction of the garage, the front section of which now hugged the ground. She turned to Athen and grimaced. "I hope your car's not in there . . ."

26

"No." Athen nodded to the driveway.

"Can you get me a list of contents?" Susan walked towards the base of the tree, taking a steno notebook from the large satchellike purse which hung over her shoulder. "Be as specific as you can, brands if you know them, receipts if you have them, if not, where and when you purchased things, how much you paid, as much information as you can . . . we'll do the best we can for you. And I'll have a contractor out by tomorrow morning to appraise the garage. We won't pay to replace the tree, but we'll pay to remove it and for the damage it's caused. Might as well go over and talk to your neighbor while I'm here . . ."

The adjuster started across the yard in the direction of the next property. She paused and looked over her shoulder. "It's a shame about the tree. Must have been a beauty. Gonna be hard to replace it."

Harder than you know, Athen thought sadly.

Two days later Athen peered through the kitchen window watching as the contractor's men worked to clear the debris. First they cut the remains of the tree into large chunks, a pang shooting through her when the chain saw first sang out, making the first cut. When they'd finished, the stump had been cut to the ground. Nothing remained but a pile of sawdust where the tree had stood, almost as if it had never existed.

In her mind's eye she could still see the sapling John had proudly planted. Dripping with sweat from his effort, he had walked back to the porch where she had stood, hands on her hips, wondering why, with so much unpacking to do, he had chosen moving day to plant a tree.

"My grandmother always said the land's not yours until you plant something on it," he had told her solemnly.

She had smiled at his Irish sentimentality, pulling his wet face to hers to kiss him, tasting sweat and grime. He had laughed and used the back of her left hand to wipe away the smudge he'd left on her chin . . .

From the rubble, one of the laborers lifted out her prized bicycle. John had bought it for her five years earlier, when she'd become serious about her biking. She watched impassionately as its twisted frame was tossed up on the Dumpster. She hadn't ridden since that last sixty-mile race, back in the beginning of November, before the weather had turned cold, before her life had been turned upside down and things that used to matter lost their meaning. She had declined invitations from members of her bike club all through the spring. She had simply lacked the energy to join them.

"Hey!" she called to the contractor's assistant as he began to remove the debris from the garage, the battered walls of which now rested in the Dumpster.

Her hands raised in protest, she raced to the driveway, demanding, "Don't throw that out!"

The startled young man looked over his shoulder at her rapid approach. "Lady," he told her, "the insurance company will pay for new ones."

"They look fine," she insisted, and began to gather up the assortment of garden implements which had been dropped on the ground. "Any more undamaged?"

He disappeared into the shell of the garage and brought out a hoe, a short-handled shovel, a smashed bucket from which poked the shiny green handles of a transplanting trowel and a long, thin dandelion digger.

"You find any more of this stuff, you bring it to me, okay?" she instructed him.

She brought John's gardening tools up onto the porch and inspected them, surprising herself with her delight at having found them all intact, spreading them upon the wooden deck like newly found treasure. John had been passionate about his gardens, devoting hours to plot plans and soil improvement, nurturing the new plants he brought home every spring from Ms. Evelyn's little nursery up on the hill. In January he would anxiously await the arrival of the current nursery and seed catalogs, poring over the offerings until he had made his selections, carefully planning what he'd plant and where in the beds which outlined their property. When the weather had warmed, he'd set out, Callie always in tow, for Ms. Evelyn's nursery to make his actual purchases. Athen rarely accompanied them, having little interest in gardening beyond the spectacular bouquets he'd present her with later in the summer, when the yard would be ablaze with color from every angle and passersby would ring the doorbell to express their admiration.

She stared down at the tools of his leisure hours, the solid hardwood handles tipped in dark green enamel. Imported from England and made to last a lifetime, she'd ordered them from one of his catalogs seven years ago as a special surprise. After having found the catalog open to the page upon which they were displayed, first on the kitchen counter, then on the dining room table, then a few days later in the living room, she had taken the hint and called in the order for his birthday. He'd been more delighted than with any gift she'd ever given him.

She would present them to Callie as soon as she arrived home from school. It had been Callie who had worked by his side, digging, planting, weeding, learning, while Athen sat reading on the white wicker sofa which graced the back porch, her only function being to keep the gardeners supplied with cool drinks. Callie would be thrilled, Athen was certain, to have these precious reminders of her father.

At noon she went into the house and poked through the morning's mail. She straightened the kitchen for the fifth time. She looked around, seeking some small task with which to occupy herself. Laundry? Done on Saturday, there'd not be enough clothes in the hamper to justify the effort. She'd paid the bills on Thursday, shopped for groceries on Friday.

She sat down at the kitchen table and looked out the window at the view that seemed stark with the absence of the tree, wondering what to do with the rest of the day. With the rest of her life. When the tears began, she made no effort to wipe them away.

How had she spent the hours before he had left her? She could not remember. She had the same errands to run, the same number of meals to cook, the same house to clean. Now, with his passing, her life seemed to be nothing but huge chunks of time, waiting to be filled.

Even the leisure activities of her old life were no longer of any consequence. Biking seemed frivolous. Her painting required too much concentration. The Greek Community Center, where she had for years tutored the older residents as well as the recent arrivals in English, was an unwelcome reminder of happier times.

When Callie had been little, Athen's world had been defined by the needs of her child. She had loved those days, before Callie had started school, when the weather was the only restriction on how they spent the hours. Looking back now, it seemed to have passed in no more than the blink of an eye. How much faster would the years ahead pass, she wondered, years filled with nothing but watching Callie grow up. Had John so filled her life that there was nothing of her that he did not take with him?

She wept, deep hacking sobs manifested by huge tears, as the vision of their plans for life after John's retirement returned to taunt her, reminding her of how little she had to look forward to now. When John had twenty-five years in the force, he had promised, they'd buy a house in the country where they'd live out their days . . . maybe an old farm someplace, where John could have his own nursery, stocked with plants he'd grow in his own greenhouse, just like Ms. Evelyn. Athen would paint in the garden, wonderful watercolor reflections of his gardens. She would keep the books for John's business and entertain Callie's children, when they came to spend their summers.

Funny how she had never counted on this. A police officer's wife should know what can happen. Maybe we all just think it will happen to somebody else, that maybe we'll be called upon to be consoler, but surely never the consoled . . .

She rose and poured a glass of water, the silence of the house closing in on her. Callie had two more weeks of school, then day camp for the summer, then school would begin and the new year would follow, then yet another and another.

She forced the image of an endless succession of empty days from her mind. Maybe next year . . . maybe next year what, she demanded of herself, suddenly angry. She slammed the glass on the counter, water splashing onto the tiled floor. Maybe next year what?

No big event will come out of the blue and make something happen to make this better, she chided herself, no vision will appear to point the way towards the rest of my life. This is the rest of my life. I will not move from this spot until I take the first step. And there will never be a better time than now.

With the first sense of determination she'd felt in months, she pulled the phone book from the shelf, scanning the pages until locating the number she sought. Stubbornly refusing to give a second thought to her actions, lest she talk herself out of it, she lifted the receiver and dialed.

"Good morning," she told the unfamiliar voice which answered, "this is Athena Moran. I'd like to speak with Mayor Rossi . . ."

6

Athen's transition from her self-imposed hibernation to the demands of her new status as a working mother had been much smoother than she had dared hope. Callie, rather than berate her mother for abandoning her as Athen had feared, had barely raised her eyes from her newest Babysitter's Club book to pronounce the news as "cool." Meg, Johnny's sister, had been delighted—relieved, actually—at Athen's call and had immediately telephoned her mother in Florida to announce that Athen appeared to be joining the living again.

Her first-day jitters had been unwarranted, she later reflected. The entire staff at city hall seemed to be comprised of old friends of her father's, old friends from high school, the parents of old friends. Everyone had greeted her with the warmest of welcomes. If anyone had been disappointed to have been passed over for the job on Athen's behalf, no such displeasure was displayed. The butterflies in her stomach that had awakened her at three A.M. and had refused to permit her to return to sleep were all but forgotten by the end of the day.

Rossi himself had been all business, succinctly explaining what he expected of his new right hand.

"Read the paper," he instructed.

"Read the paper," she had repeated, an accurate though somewhat confused echo. Read the paper?

"The newspaper. *The Woodside Herald.* Tell you just about everything you'll need to know for the day. Who's bickering with who. What cars are out of commission because some bozo ran his city wheels into a fence. Which group of activists or malcontents will most likely be knocking on my door that day." He leaned back in his huge black leather chair and lit a cigar. "It'll all be right there, the whole day spread out in front of you. The most important thing you'll do for me is read the paper and circle the articles I need to read. Leave it on my desk. I get in at nine sharp, come hell or high water. I never schedule a meeting before ten-thirty and until that hour I only make phone calls, I never take them. Anyone calls before ten-thirty, you take a message and bring it in to me. You don't discuss anything—not who calls or who walks through that door— with anyone. Not anyone—except me. And you will tell me everything you hear and everything you see. Period."

She stared blankly at him from across the desk.

"Any questions?" He tapped the ash from the end of the cigar.

"Ah . . ." She smoothed the skirt of her gray linen suit, selected by Callie the previous weekend ("You have to buy it, Mommy, it matches your eyes."), struggling to find some response. Nothing intelligent came to mind.

"You'll start at eight-thirty. Gives you enough time to scan the paper and get my coffee ready. I take it black. The cups are on the middle shelf of the armoire behind you. I expect the coffee and the paper on my desk at nine. I have meetings with council everyday at three P.M. Starting today you will sit in on the meetings to listen and observe. You will not speak or voice an opinion unless I ask for one. You will take notes that you will type up and give to me. No copies. There's one of those newfangled word processors out there, Edie will show you how to use it. Edie can also type any letters you don't have time to do, God knows she only has about an hour and a half's worth of her own work to do on any given day. You will keep my personal files locked. I have the only key. Ask for it when you need it and return it as soon as you're done. It's not that I don't trust you, Athen." He softened slightly. "If I didn't trust you, you wouldn't be sitting in that chair, God knows. I'm more afraid someone would lift a key from your desk, maybe even have a copy made, who knows? Confidential stuff, a lot of what goes on inside this room. Can't take too many chances, you know."

The buzz of the intercom rudely intruded.

"What is it, Edie?" He lifted the receiver. "Okay, sure. Put him on. Jimmy. What's going on? . . . Yes, of course I did . . ."

Athen used the interruption to make as unobtrusive a survey of the room as possible. If she hadn't known better, she'd have sworn she was in the paneled library of the manor house of an English lord. The carpet was a huge red, black and cream oriental, the paintings were landscapes. Crimson drapes narrowly striped in black—custom-made, she was certain—hung from four large windows, effectively blocking out any view of the city beyond the room. The desk had a mahogany top large enough to play billiards on, and the left corner of the room just inside the door featured black leather furniture, sofa, loveseat, and two deep chairs centered with a mahogany coffee table. She twisted slightly in her seat to further inspect the vast armoire that dominated the wall behind her. It too was mahogany, a good nine feet tall and nearly as wide. It was obvious that no expense had been spared in His Honor's honor.

"Okay, then, sweetheart, you all straight?" He turned his attention to her as he hung up the phone, then without waiting for an answer, nodded. "Good. Let's get started."

He raised himself from the chair and walked around the desk, offering his hand to assist her from her seat. He guided her to the door.

"Edie here will give you a hand with things." He nodded towards a little silver-haired mouse of a woman who appeared to have been waiting all morning for nothing other than the opening of Rossi's door. "Show Athen where the coffeepot is, the ladies room, introduce her to whomever she doesn't already know." Then, to Athen, he added, "I have a meeting with the union people in twenty minutes. Should run through lunch. I'll be back in time for my three o'clock. I'll expect you to have the coffee ready . . ."

He punched the button for the elevator and was immediately rewarded with opening doors. He winked at Athen as he stepped into the elevator and was gone.

"Well," she said uncertainly, turning to Edie, trying hard not to focus on the purple, red, and black scarf which rode in an untidy heap around the neck of the older woman's lavender knit dress. "Well then."

He'd left her no work. No letters. No filing. No instructions. She looked at Edie expectantly, hoping she might make some suggestions. She did not.

"Would you give me a hand with this typewriter? Maybe help acquaint me with the machine . . . ?" Good place to begin, she told herself.

"No point in starting with that right now." Edie glanced at her watch. "It's almost eleven. I go to lunch at eleven-thirty. Be glad to help you when I get back . . . of course, by then you'll probably want lunch."

"No, no, that'll be fine," Athen assured her, "twelve-thirty will be fine."

"Well, it may not be right at twelve-thirty. I have a little shopping to do," she explained unapologetically. "But as soon as I get back . . ."

"That'll be fine." Athen smiled wanly as Edie returned to her desk on the other side of the hallway, just beyond the elevator. Whenever you get around to it, Edie, I'll be here. Right here, she sighed, reading the paper.

The Fourth of July holiday had interrupted her second full week of work. Athen had been surprised to find she'd actually looked forward to a weekday which did not begin with the insistent whine of the 6:30 A.M. alarm. Callie, however, not wanting to miss a minute of the festivities of the day, dragged her mother's reluctant body downstairs for breakfast at seven, reminding Athen that the early worm got the best viewing spot on the street.

"'I . . . love a parade,'" Callie sang gaily as she marched in time to the beat of the drums as the high school band passed before them.

This year, as every year, the folks in Woodside Heights were being treated to an Independence Day spectacle guaranteed to be "the best ever." A string band had been brought up from Philadelphia, bagpipers from Virginia, Revolutionary War–style drum and bugle corps from Connecticut, and of course, the Woodside Heights High School marching band. The parade proceeded for a full twenty-five minutes, the local children filling in at the end on bicycles patriotically decorated with red, white, and blue crepe paper.

Athen kept in step with the crowd as it followed the parade to the park where speeches would be offered by the city fathers, and all assembled would join in the pledge of allegiance and national anthem, after which the children's activities, races and a softball game, would be held throughout the afternoon. The long, hot day would end with a fireworks display over Woodside Park.

"Hey, Mom, watch my bike, okay?" Callie rolled the bike towards Athen, who barely caught it as it careened towards the ground. "This is my race."

Athen steered the bike towards the line forming along the

track and joined the other parents who gathered to watch their offspring in the footraces which were about to begin. Two dozen or so young girls, aged ten to twelve, lined up at the starting line. Athen stretched her neck to find Callie, whose recent birthday qualified her for the race, somewhere near the middle. Callie, always competitive, was in the act of performing warm-up exercises, as John had taught her to do.

The runners were called to the line and a balloon popped to start the race. Callie's churning legs carried her quickly to the finish line seconds before anyone else. She had won handily.

"Go, Callie," Athen had cried, applauding her effort.

"Your daughter, I take it," a deep voice from behind her commented.

"Yes," she replied, trying to catch Callie's eye in the crowd.

"She's a good runner. She has good form."

"Thank you, yes, she's quite an athlete." Athen turned around to acknowledge the compliment.

That his eyes exactly matched his shirt had been her first thought, both pale blue like an early January sky. She flushed scarlet when she realized those blue eyes were staring intently into her own.

"Well, I can't think of a better outlet for kids these days, things being what they are." He pulled off his maroon baseball cap, one hand trying to tame the unruly black curls which spilled in sweaty ringlets to droop across his forehead. "Boy, it's a hot one, isn't it? Must be close to ninety already."

"Yes." The red tinge had crept all the way to her earlobes.

The boys were now lining up for their race, and she pretended an interest she did not feel to excuse her from further conversation with the stranger. He had been standing too close, and she found his proximity inexplicably disconcerting. She moved slightly towards the track as a means of separating herself from him.

The boys' race was over in a flash, the winner jumping into the air with a hoot. From behind her came a loud whistle. She wondered if it had come from him, but did not turn around. Maybe she'd put enough distance between them, maybe he was gone . . .

"One more race and we can move out of this hot sun." He had not gone anywhere. She had not moved far enough.

She nodded without comment as the top three finishers from the girls' and boys' races lined up for the final competition.

"I'd be willing to bet your daughter will give them all a run for their money," he noted, leaning broad shoulders forward a bit and smiling at her.

Again she offered no response. She found herself hoping the race would be over quickly so that she could leave. He was making her uncomfortable and she didn't know why.

"Want me to hold onto that bike so your hands are free?" he offered.

"No, thank you, I'm fine," she mumbled, trying to ignore the fact that he now stood close enough for her to smell the faintest hint of aftershave. Close enough to notice the tan on his long, muscular legs below his white shorts when she had lowered her eyes towards the ground in an effort to divert her gaze from his handsome face.

The balloon popped loudly and the runners passed by in a dusty pack. Callie came in second to the boy who had won the previous race.

Callie walked slowly in a direct line to her mother, her hands on her hips, her expression sheer disappointment.

"You did really well, sweetie." Athen reached out to offer consolation.

"Not well enough," grumbled Callie.

"Hey, Callie, great race." The boy who had beaten her sought her out, but when he approached, Callie bent down in a pretense of retying her sneaker and barely acknowledged him. He backed away into the crowd.

"Come on, Callie, we'll get a cold drink and then maybe some lunch." Athen patted her on the shoulder, glancing behind her once as they walked away. The stranger had disappeared.

As they wheeled the bike across the field, Athen found

herself unconsciously sorting through the throng of people filling the park. She was not, she emphatically denied at the suggestion of a small voice inside her, looking for a last glimpse of a maroon baseball cap which topped a shock of black curls. . . .

She thought of him, the stranger, the next morning as she was going through her closet, looking for something to wear to work. She had pulled a blue knit dress from its hanger and over her head. As she closed the buttons down the front, she was reminded of a blue shirt which had perfectly matched blue eyes which perfectly matched her dress. She had slammed the closet door shut with a loud bang, hoping to scare the image away.

She had no time nor any inclination to dwell on strange men, she sternly reminded herself. She'd been widowed but seven months. She had a child to raise and a job to do. She was a single mother with responsibilities. She banished the intruder and turned her attention to the task of getting Callie to the camp bus on time and getting herself into the office.

All in all, she thought as she brushed her hair, working wasn't so bad. Her job gave her a reason to get up in the morning and get dressed in something other than shorts and a T-shirt. It gave her a purpose she had only vaguely suspected she had lacked.

And the work itself wasn't much of a challenge, particularly for a woman whose last working experience had been teaching sixth grade in an inner city school. She did, in fact, read the paper first thing every morning (after starting the coffee, of course), circling those items which would interest Rossi in red ink. By the end of the second week she'd become proficient at determining which items (other than the obvious "Trash Truck Injures Five") contained information her boss would need to begin his day.

The word processor was easy enough, with Edie a short stretch down the hall and the manual in the top drawer. Filing took less than ten minutes each day, since Rossi preferred to communicate many of his thoughts by telephone, rarely following up in letter form. Most of Athen's typing consisted of memorandums to the staff or the notes she took at the daily conferences with the council members. Using the morning hours when Rossi was behind closed doors to practice typing, she quickly graduated from two-fingered hunt and peck to a respectable speed and level of accuracy.

The three o'clock meeting had become the highlight of her day. The routine never changed nor was anyone ever late. The four members of council and the city solicitor would file in and take their seats, always the same seats. Rossi sat on the black leather chair facing the room. Jim Wolmar, the president of council, took the chair to Rossi's left. Angelo Giamboni shared the long sofa with George Konstantos, who had been appointed by Rossi to fill the vacancy on council following Ari's stroke three years earlier, and Riley Fallon, the lone African-American on council. Harlan Justis, the solicitor, sat facing Wolmar and Rossi from the loveseat. The seating arrangement never varied, Athen discovered, nor did the level of participation.

All discussions seemed to consist of a dialogue between Rossi and Wolmar. The occasional request for a legal opinion would elicit a brief and mostly vague response from Justis. Giamboni, a first cousin of Rossi's deceased wife, seemed never to speak, but nodded in unconscious agreement every time Dan opened his mouth. Konstantos, well into his seventies, appeared to sleep through most of the meetings. Fallon would, on occasion, make an attempt to offer a carefully worded opinion or present another point of view when an issue might be particularly thorny, but since no one ever seemed to respond or even to listen, it didn't seem to matter. Except, Athen suspected, maybe to Fallon, who could at least go back to his district and say he had made an attempt to sway council to a decision more favorable to their interests.

It had not taken Athen long to discover two important facts about the city's governing body. One was that the interests of the minorities—the Greeks, the African-Americans, the Hispanics—were of no consequence as far as council was concerned. The second was that council met only for the sake of appearance, because the only power in the city rested solely in Dan Rossi's hands. And, she rationalized, it could be worse.

Didn't Dante Rossi possess an unequaled devotion to the city, to its citizens? Hadn't he almost wept to her in private when the city's second largest employer, a packaging plant, had closed its doors, putting almost eighty people out of work, not two weeks after she'd become his assistant? Wasn't he outraged at the rise in crime, the rise in drug trafficking, the rise in poverty? Wasn't he taking a firm stand against the homeless who, more and more, seemed to haunt the streets of Woodside Heights?

And hadn't he taken Athen under his wing, explaining ever so patiently the inner workings of the city government, the nuances of political parlance? Wasn't he proud of her when he no longer had to explain the significance of the issues and their effects on the political powers?

"Ah, you're a natural for public service, Athen." He'd beam. Or, "The apple certainly didn't fall far from the tree, Athena. Ari'd sure be proud of his little girl."

Dan made it clear that he depended on her, which came as a surprise to her since she was the novice and he was the pro. He would frequently ask her opinon on matters relevant to the running of the city, though more often than not he would manage to change that opinion by his careful explanation of how her perception was ill-formed due to lack of all the facts. Once he explained things to her she could see clearly that he was right and she had, in fact, been misled by the media or his detractors or some other faction that hadn't been privy to what was really going on. More and more as the weeks progressed he would spend increasing amounts of time with her, rehashing meetings and who said what and what had they really meant until she had begun to see him as the caring and devoted servant of the taxpayers which he himself had professed to be. He was her father figure, her mentor, her best friend. What more could anyone ask for in a boss?

She would have given anything to have had a response

from her father on those nights when she would stop to visit.

"Pateras," she would tell him, "it's an exciting thing to be involved in the working of a city, but, of course, you know that. I only wished I'd learned more from you. Rossi says you had a better understanding of how the city runs, of how things get done, than anyone he'd ever known. That you'd be the next mayor if you hadn't . . . if you hadn't become ill. That you would know how to deal with the problems the city is having. He's teaching me, Papa, he's teaching me so much . . ."

Had she been less intent upon her sorrow that her father could not appreciate his daughter's political awakening, she might have noticed the dark cloud which passed over Ari's unblinking eyes as she continued to sing the praises of one Dante Rossi.

8

"Callie," Athen called from the back door, "are you almost ready?"

"Almost ready? I've been ready all week." Callie raced to the driveway, tossed a shovel into the backseat, and plopped herself into the front seat of the car. "I thought Saturday morning would never come."

Guess she's ready, Athen mused as she got into the driver's side.

"You remember how to get there?" asked Callie.

"Sort of. You can let me know if I make any wrong turns." Athen smiled.

No wrong turns and twenty minutes later Athen pulled onto the small grassy spot used by the patrons of Ms. Evelyn's nursery as a parking lot. Ms. Evelyn's was less of a garden center and more of a true nursery than was commonly found in most suburban areas. There was no real storefront, unless you counted the small cash register inside the door of the slightly dilapidated greenhouse. There were no rows of shiny brass flowerpots, no manicured displays of hothouse plants, no fancy garden furniture.

Ms. Evelyn grew perennials in the fields surrounding her tidy bungalow up on the hill, wherein resided the descendants of the original members of the city's African-American community, those whose forebearers made the harrowing trip along the Underground Railroad and never went beyond the welcome offered by the local Quaker abolitionists. Ms. Evelyn herself planted the seeds in her greenhouse, tended the seedlings, and set them out into the fields with the help of her two daughters, now grown, and her sixteen-year-old grandson Lamar. She grew for the sheer love of growing things, for the delight in the eyes of her customers when they found that species unheard of by the high school kids or retirees who worked for the big chain nurseries. Ms. Evelyn loved her plants and she loved her customers who appreciated them. She had adored John Moran.

"Lord, Callie, I'd given up on you this year. Goodness, child, let me look at you . . . Haven't seen you since the day they laid your daddy to rest, God bless him . . ." Welcoming Callie as she reached the top of the hill, Ms. Evelyn, spry and ageless in denim overalls, wiped a teary eye on the sleeve of her white shirt. "And you there, Athen," she greeted Athen with a warm smile, "thought maybe you'd gone to one of those fancy places this year . . ."

"Never!" Callie protested. "Daddy always said 'nobody had better plants than Ms. Evelyn.'"

"And your daddy knew his flowers, that's for sure." She smiled. "You planning on keeping that garden going, Callie?"

"I want to, but, see, we lost a lot of Dad's perennials." Callie told Ms. Evelyn about the tree falling and the resulting empty spaces in the garden.

"Well, now, it's August, Callie, you know my field's all but picked clean by the Fourth of July," she chided, then added gently, "but I do have a few things out back, in my private garden, that I'd be happy to share with you. You run on back and take a look. Did you remember to bring your shovel? Good. There's some peach-colored foxglove that I know you'll like, honey, and some of that dark pink old-fashioned geranium that your daddy was so fond of. You remember the name for that?"

"Crane's bill," recited Callie proudly as she armed herself with her shovel and started merrily up the hill, "sanguineum."

"Aren't you something, Callie Moran." Ms. Evelyn's eyes danced as she called after her. "And make sure to take some delphinium—there's blue, white, and some rose-colored too that did real well this year . . ."

"Ms. Evelyn, we don't want to dig up your garden," Athen protested, "we'll just come by in the spring and . . ."

"Nonsense, honey. It'll give me great pleasure to share with you . . . help you rebuild John's garden. Now you go along with Callie, I see she's got her shovel, did you only bring the one?" When Athen shook her head—having forgotten that the routine at Ms. Evelyn's was strictly dig your own—she was directed to help herself from a box filled with all manner of foreign-looking implements just to the right of the greenhouse door. Athen selected a short-handled shovel-type of thing with a long narrow blade, the only thing in the box which looked even vaguely familiar.

"Now be sure not to miss the rose achillea, and my goodness, there must be a dozen varieties of aquilegia . . . oh, and liatris . . ." Ms. Evelyn called after Athen as she trudged up the hill in the direction Callie had previously scampered.

"Callie, those look half-dead." She observed the stash of brown-stemmed, dried clusters Callie had set aside.

"They're perennials, Mom," Callie explained without looking up from her efforts.

"They're the ones that die back after they bloom and come back again next year?" Athen tried to recall the terms bandied about by John and Callie as they poured over seed catalogs. Perennials. Biennials. Annuals. Half-hardy something or others.

"Very good, Mom." Callie grinned as she dislodged a clump of something from the ground and carried it to a clear spot.

"What should I do?" The parent had the vague feeling she had just become the child.

"Dig up some of that gypsophila." Callie motioned with her head to an area to Athen's right.

"Ah . . . which one is that?"

"Baby's breath, Mom. The white stuff like you get in bouquets from the florist?" Callie was clearly relishing her position of superiority. "Mom, don't you know anything?"

"Apparently not," she admitted sheepishly.

She was still struggling with the first plant, silently cursing her lack of technique in dealing with the dried, hard earth when Callie ran off to the greenhouse in search of some flats on which to transport their new garden.

"Damn." Athen inspected splintered fingernails as she brushed dirt from her hands onto her jeans, which were making her legs feel like encased sausages as the temperature rose along with the humidity.

"You know, you're making this a lot harder than it needs to be." An amused voice seemed to float from the edge of the garden.

She looked up in annoyance. The source of the voice leaned casually against the trunk of a tree. Through the sun's glare she could distinguish only white shorts, a white shirt and white tennis shoes. She held her hand over her eyes to block the blinding intensity of the sun's harsh light.

"How long have you been standing there?" Even without the baseball cap, and with the dark glasses which covered a good portion of his face, Athen would have known him anywhere.

"Long enough to know this is not something you do very often. If at all."

"How can you tell?"

"No gloves. Real gardeners wear gloves." He walked towards her through the rows of plants. "And hats if they're out in the hot sun. Or at the very least, they tie up their hair."

She became suddenly conscious that her own hair, hanging straight down her back, weighed about seven tons and was white-hot.

"Here, let me help." He picked up Callie's discarded shovel. "What would you like me to dig up for you?"

"That's not really necessary, I can . . ."

"Don't be silly." He smiled and a buzz seemed to go off somewhere in her head. "You look all digged out for today. What's your pleasure?"

"Ah . . ." She sought to remember the names Callie and Ms. Evelyn had discussed, names which had meant absolutely nothing to her. Coreopsis. Centurea. Potentilla. Sidalcea. Who knew what the hell else. "Ah . . . maybe some, ah, aquilegia . . . ?"

Please God, let him know what it looks like.

"Sure. That's one of my favorites, too. Always makes me think of the house I grew up in. My mother always had tons of columbine along a walk in the backyard . . ."

Columbine?

". . . Now did you want the caerulea, the canadensis, the red-star . . . ? She certainly has a variety here . . ." He had bent to inspect the leafy fronds as she buried her face in her hands and fought the urge to scream.

"Ah . . . the red-star would be fine." Never order anything you can't pronounce, she reminded herself.

"I always liked the caerulea, myself. Did you know that it's the state flower of Colorado?" He looked back at her as he began to dig.

She tried to appear oblivious to his impressive form, as if strange men always appeared out of nowhere to do things for her like dig up plants she'd never heard of, flowers she couldn't identify on a dare.

"Mom, Ms. Evelyn sent you a Pepsi—it's diet, like you like— Who's he?" Callie handed Athen the cold can and eyed the stranger suspiciously.

"Just someone who likes to dig." She tilted the can back and swallowed gratefully, then pulled her hair up from her back and placed the frigid aluminum against her neck. It felt wonderful.

Callie began to pile the plants she'd dug onto heavy plastic flats.

"Hey, it's the runner," he said as he plunked a large clump of dirt and dried leaves onto a flat. "That was a good race you ran a few weeks back."

"Not good enough to beat that geeky little butt-head Timmy Forbes," Callie replied.

The stranger laughed heartily.

"Oh, Callie, that's an awful expression." Athen cringed.

"Well, he is." She picked up one of the flats and headed towards the car, calling over her shoulder to her mother, "I'm ready to go whenever you are."

Athen stood up and brushed herself off. Not that it helped. Her jeans needed more than a brushing, she noted with some embarrassment. The knees were caked with dirt and she saw lines of grime on her arms where the sweat had streaked downwards. She had never been this dirty in her life.

"Let me get that for you." He leaned over and effortlessly picked up two flats and smiled. He had deep dimples on each side of his mouth. She wished she hadn't noticed. "Lead the way."

They loaded the flats into the back of the car and she sought out Ms. Evelyn in the greenhouse to negotiate payment for the plants while he went back up the hill to help Callie with her remaining plants. Athen noticed then for the first time a young boy who met Callie as she started back towards the car. He had stopped to talk, but Callie had blown right past him as if she hadn't seen him. The man in the white shorts placed another flat into the trunk of her car. Athen watched from the window as he looked around, then shrugged, and after calling to the boy, got into a red car and drove off.

"Who was your friend?" Athen casually inquired of Callie on the way home.

"What friend?"

"The boy who was speaking to you at Ms. Evelyn's."

"Oh. You mean Timmy Forbes." Callie scowled. "He goes to my camp."

"Timmy Forbes?" Athen recalled Callie's previous description of the boy, and her face went white. "That man, the one who was helping me dig, was he . . ."

"Mr. Forbes." Callie nodded. "I heard Timmy call him 'Dad' when they were leaving."

Athen grimaced. The handsome stranger was the geeky little butt-head's father.

9

It was an obviously depressed Dan Rossi who stepped off the elevator on a sultry Monday morning in late August.

"Can I get you something, Dan?" a concerned Athen had asked. "Some coffee? Maybe some iced tea . . . some aspirin?"

"Aspirin and cold drinks won't help, honey," he said, shaking his head.

"Is there anything I can do, anything I can help you with?" She'd never seen him so down. Her heart went out to him.

"Well, now, I appreciate that, Athena, I truly do. But it's something I have to do myself." He made a gallant effort to smile.

She tiptoed out of the office, wondering at the cause of his troubles. She all but knocked over Edie, who'd obviously been lurking outside the door.

"Find out what's ailing him?" Edie nodded towards the door. Athen merely shook her head.

"If you ask me, it's that damned city charter," Edie volunteered.

Ignoring her, Athen sat down at her desk and looked for a copy of the memo she'd typed yesterday, the one Rossi had sent to Wolmar. Maybe there'd be a clue if she read it over again. Maybe Edie the chatterbox would think she was busy and go away. Maybe pigs could fly.

"Yup, that's my guess. It's that damned charter, all right," Edie repeated, oblivious to Athen's efforts to look busy. "You know that part that says you can only serve four consecutive terms? A mistake, if you ask me, putting something like that in there. Now poor Dan has to give up the office—and a finer man never sat in that chair, if you ask me. Yup, everyone's waiting for Dan to name his successor, and soon, too. The Labor Day rally is next week already . . ."

"So?"

"So that's when he has to announce who will run. Not that an election means anything in this city. Don't get me wrong," Edie hastened to add, "I'm a faithful member of the party. Always have been, always will be. And I'm loyal to Dan—God knows I'll be just as loyal to whoever it is that Dan picks—but Dan is my number-one man, don't you know. Just seems to me to be a waste of money, though, going to the expense of a campaign when everyone knows who will win. Once we know who's running, of course."

The elevator doors slid open noiselessly.

"Oh, my, would you look at Himself," Edie whispered as Jim Wolmar strode towards them, a jovial smile to greet them both.

"Good morning, ladies," he nodded cheerfully, smoothing his tie and the cuffs of his handsome gray Italian silk suit jacket. "Dan's expecting me, Athen. I'll just go right in . . ."

Something about Jim had bothered Athen since day one. Maybe it was the fact that he always wore the same self-satisfied expression. Maybe it was the overly solicitous manner in which he always agreed with Dan—nodding vigorously, proclaiming "Absolutely, Dan. Without question . . ."—as if Dan's words had been Jim's very thoughts. Maybe it was the way he looked. Tall and trim with a full thick head of perfectly groomed silver hair, he would be handsome if he lost that lifeless plastic gaze. He always reminded Athen of an older version of Barbie's friend Ken.

Everyone knew Wolmar was Rossi's protégé, that Dan had been priming him to take over the big chair someday. Apparently Jim believed that day was now near. Contrasting Dan's mood to Jim's lively step, only one of them was happy about it.

Jim was still wearing the same sappy smile when he emerged from Dan's office ten minutes later. The smile seemed to slide to one side of his face somewhat when he stepped towards the opening door of the elevator as Harlan Justis was stepping out. The two men greeted each other warily, Wolmar peeking through the closing doors as the solicitor nodded to Athen and entered the confines of Rossi's office.

Harlan Justis looked like the solicitor of a small city. Well-spoken, well-dressed, and well-manicured, he was also absolutely certain that he, not Wolmar, would be Rossi's choice for the big chair this time around.

He, too, stayed behind closed doors for about ten minutes before emerging with a hopeful look about him. Until Jack Sheldon, the front-runner from the third ward, stepped out of the elevator . . .

And so it went till noon, resuming again at two. Prospective candidates in, prospective candidates out. The usual council meeting was subdued, lasting less than a half hour before Rossi stood to indicate the session was concluded— announcing as an apparent afterthought that he'd come to no final decision on "that other matter." Wolmar and Justis both seemed to be inclined to linger, just in case, Athen surmised, Rossi might have words of encouragement for either of them. When it was apparent he had nothing further to say to anyone, the group disbanded.

Athen was in the process of gathering up the used coffee cups when Dan closed the office door.

"Can you sit and talk with me for a few, Athen?" he asked, slumping into his chair behind the big desk.

"Sure," she replied, sitting as he motioned for her to do so.

"I've a terrible dilemma, Athen. A terrible decision to make." He shook his head sadly.

"The election . . . ?" she offered quietly.

"How insightful of you. Yes, my dear, the election." He nodded. "I have to choose the next mayor of this good city, and my heart's burning over it. There just is no clear choice, you follow me? Jim, he's a good man, but he has no real feel for the people. Harlan's years away from being the man he needs to be to lead this city on to the greater things I can see happening here. Ah, and the worst of it, Athen, is that in my heart, I know I haven't finished the job. There's so much more I'd wanted to do for the good people of Woodside Heights . . ." He turned his head from her, as if shielding her from his display of emotion. "And the saddest part is that I know all the good things I'd planned will go undone . . ."

"Well, surely your successor . . . Jim, Harlan, whoever . . . will follow your agenda . . ."

"Ah, Athen, you're so naive." He smiled gently, kindly, as a father would to his foolish child. "They all have their own priorities, my dear. No, I'm afraid that Dan Rossi's plans for a better Woodside Heights will leave this office with him."

"But, Dan," she protested, "you'll still be head of the party, you'll still be influential in how things are done . . ."

He shrugged, cavalierly waving his right hand. "There will be other appointees to council, Athen. Whoever is elected will force a retirement here, challenge a position there . . . there is not one of them I would trust with complete loyalty, it breaks my heart to say it aloud, but there it is. There's not a man among them who won't use this office for his own gain, Athen. Not a one who won't put his own interests ahead of those of this city."

"Maybe you should look around a little more, Dan, maybe there's someone else you hadn't considered . . ."

"Ah, now there's an idea." He smiled quickly, almost, she thought, as if the idea had been his own and perhaps not a new one. "Perhaps someone who's outside the realm of the obvious . . . you may have hit upon something, Athen, you may indeed have given me something to ponder . . ."

"There are a lot of bright lights in city hall." She glanced at her watch and stood, preparing to leave. There would be open house at Callie's school tonight, and she didn't want to be late. "There's Ted Raspanti in the finance office . . . Julian Taylor in the solicitor's office . . . Jeff Keegan, Harold Greenspan . . ."

"Yes, yes." He nodded. "But who knows where their loyalties lie? I've kept you too long, my dear, run on home to Callie now. I'll see you in the morning. And thank you for listening to an old man whose days in public office are running out."

Poor Dan, she thought as she drove through the late rush hour traffic towards her home. He's so dedicated to this city that he's making himself sick over whose hands to leave it in. She shook her head at the injustice of it all. Here's a man who's dedicated himself to the people of this city, being forced out of office because of some fool clause in the city charter. His unhappy plight filled her with sadness, not just for Dan, but for the citizens who would never see the likes of him in office again.

She had just enough time to throw together a quick supper and eat, though not enough time to change her clothes, before dragging Callie off to the open house which preceeded the first week of school at Woods Academy.

"I haven't had dessert," Callie grumbled.

"They always have a dessert reception after the little speeches and you know it," Athen chided her. "Now smile and act like you're glad to be here."

"I'm not glad to be here." Callie dragged behind her mother as they entered the large gray stone administration building of the private school Callie had attended for the past three years. Her tuition had been paid for in part by John's overtime, the balance from cash gifts from John's family—his sister Meg in particular, who had felt that nothing was too good for her only niece. "The only good thing about this place is the athletic program," Callie whined uncharacteristically.

"Soccer tryouts are next week," Athen reminded her as she preceded a still-glum Callie into vacant seats towards the rear of the small auditorium.

"Yeah, but the public school kids get an extra week of summer vacation," Callie whispered none too discreetly. The boy seated in front of her turned around and recognizing her, smiled.

"Oh, brother," she grumbled and rolled her eyes, slumping into her seat.

Oh, brother, indeed. Athen blushed uncontrollably as the father of that geeky little butt-head Timmy Forbes turned slightly in his seat and flashed a million-dollar smile over his shoulder.

She tried to ignore his presence, tried to force herself to

listen to every word spoken by Mr. Landers, the new headmaster, as he outlined his programs for the coming year and his hopes for an even better Woods Academy under his leadership.

". . . and I bring with me a firm commitment to the arts . . ."

Where's the boy's mother, she wondered. She never seems to be around. Seems like a nice enough kid, Callie's assessment of him aside. Seems to like Callie . . . I'll have to ask her just what characterizes a geeky . . .

"Mom, can we leave now?" Callie squirmed next to her.

"No."

". . . and to continue the level of excellence in the classrooms . . ." The headmaster droned on and Athen's mind continued to wander . . .

It really was nice of him to help me at Ms. Evelyn's, digging up all those plants in the hot sun. A mental image of long, strong tanned legs drifted past her mind's eye. She was staring unconsciously at the broad shoulders directly in front of her. She could not help but notice the casual elegance of his linen suit, the way his thick black hair curled over the collar in little apostrophes. The man is certainly built, I'll give him that. And as handsome a man as I've ever seen, gorgeous eyes and the warmest smile, she mused . . .

Criminy, listen to me, John not dead but seven months. Suddenly filled with a sense of guilt, she forcibly drummed all thoughts of the intriguing Mr. Forbes from her brain and contritely tuned back in to Mr. Landers, resolutely determined to avoid any further contact with this man who seemed to be everywhere.

". . . and I conclude by inviting each of you to join me for some refreshments in the reception room where I can meet every one of you personally." Grateful applause greeted the conclusion of the speech.

"Can we eat now?" Callie stood, poised to make a break for the door.

Out of the corner of one eye Athen could see that Mr. Forbes was turning as if to speak to her.

"Yes, go." She nudged Callie in the back and followed her

daughter out into the aisle. They melted into the crowd which slowly flowed down the hall into the reception area.

She made a point of always being engaged in conversation, of looking beyond him when she'd turn and he appeared to be making an attempt to catch her eye. She ignored him as completely as possible, though not so completely that she failed to notice the number of mothers and female faculty members who had literally flocked around him. She turned her back on the scene and pretended to be interested in the conversation to her left.

She was congratulating herself on her successful efforts to remain faithful to John's memory when a voice whispered in her ear, "Are you deliberately avoiding me, or are you merely too nearsighted to have noticed that I've been trying to get your attention for the past fifteen minutes?"

"Oh, neither," she weakly explained, unexpectedly flustered by his sudden appearance. "I've just been catching up with some people I've not seen in a while. And it would seem that you've had plenty of attention to contend with." She nodded in the direction of the gaggle he'd left stranded near the dessert table, all but biting her tongue the second the words had slipped out.

"Ah, yes, the fifth grade mothers have taken Timmy and me under their wings, being the new boys in town." His eyes twinkled as he added, "You remember my son, Timmy. I think he was once described as a geeky . . ."

"Please," she begged, "don't say it."

His laugh was infectious, and in spite of her discomfort, she laughed along with him.

"I'm so sorry for that," she told him. "What an awful thing for Callie to have said. I can't imagine why she'd say that about him."

"He beat her in the race." He shrugged, still smiling, dimples in full attendance. "And she's obviously a competitive little girl who doesn't like to be beaten."

"Well, I apologize for her lack of manners," she told him sincerely, "and for mine. I never even thanked you for giving me a hand with those plants . . ."

He waved her apology aside as unnecessary. "And I

apologize for not having introduced myself properly. I'm Quentin Forbes." He offered her his hand and she took it.

"Athena Moran." She tried to gracefully disconnect from the handshake but he wouldn't let go.

"May I get you something from the dessert table, Mrs. Moran?" he asked, eyes still twinkling as she gently tried to pull her hand from his.

"No, no thank you." She wondered if she should just ask him to let go . . .

"And pardon me for asking, but is there a Mr. Moran?" he asked playfully.

"Yes, of course," she fairly snapped and he let her fingers slide free.

After an embarrassed silence, she added flatly, "My husband died in January."

"I'm so sorry." He obviously hadn't known, and was obviously chagrined. "Please forgive me for being such an oaf . . . I had no idea . . ."

"Being new to town, you'd have no way of knowing."

"Mom, can we please go now?" Having launched a successful raid on the dessert table, Callie was impatient to leave.

"I guess it's time I located Timmy and headed for home, too." He smiled at Athen gently. "It was a pleasure to see you again. Perhaps we'll bump into each other here or there again some time."

Athen nodded. Undoubtedly they would.

"And maybe you, young lady," he whispered to Callie, "will go a little easier on Timmy."

"Maybe not." Callie smiled sweetly, and he laughed good-naturedly as he strode off in search of his son.

It was the right thing to do, keeping Callie in Woods Academy, Athen told herself as she turned out the light and shifted around until she was comfortable. Academically, it's one of the best private schools in the state. That new science lab is amazing, better than a lot of college labs, I'd bet. And their athletic program is tops . . . maybe she'll be able to get a scholarship in basketball or track for the high school program.

I never asked him about his wife, about Timmy's mother, the thought broke through. *I wonder where she is. Not dead or he would have said so when I told him about John. He'd have said, I know how you feel. I lost my wife . . . but he didn't say that. I wonder what he's doing in Woodside Heights . . . what would bring him here from . . . wherever it is he's come.*

Annoyed that he'd invaded her thoughts yet again, she turned over and sought distraction from other sources. Callie had mentioned she'd like to try out for the theater group at school. Meg would be coming for a visit soon, she'd called last night. Athen drifted off to sleep thinking of how good it would be to have a whole week with Meg— maybe Dan would give her a few days off . . .

She woke sometime later from a dream which had left her heart pounding. In the dream she'd been speaking to John in the yard. He'd been asking her about the new plants in the garden, not angry, just quizzical. His face seemed to fade into Quentin's face, then John's, then Quentin's, then John's. It had jolted her awake and left her feeling sick to her stomach. She got out of bed quietly and stepped over Hannah, following the familiar path down the hall to the unfinished guest room.

I never loved anyone but you, John, she professed to the emptiness within the four walls. She stood in the darkness, more confused and alone than she had felt since the day he had been laid to rest. *I don't know why he's in my head, but I never loved anyone but you . . .*

10

It was a seemingly rejuvenated Dan Rossi who flew past Athen's desk at 8:45 the next morning. She'd been engrossed in the paper and hadn't heard the elevator, had failed to detect his step.

"Dan!" Startled to see him, not only fifteen minutes early

but in so obvious a good mood, she all but knocked over her coffee.

"Athen, get my coffee and come into my office." He grinned, then added, "You can forget the paper for now. We have other things to discuss . . ."

She followed him into his office, put his cup on the coaster and sat herself in a chair facing him, mystified. This morning's Dan was a sharp contrast to the man she had seen late yesterday afternoon.

"You're awfully chipper this morning," she ventured.

"And with good reason, my dear." His large arms leaned across the desk, his hands toying with the handle of his cup. "Athen, I have found the solution to my dilemma. Took me all night, not a bit of sleep, mind you, but the problem has been resolved. And I have you to thank . . ."

"Me?"

"Yes, my dear. You hit the nail right on the head. Look beyond the obvious, you said. Look for someone who can be trusted to lead this city without regard for their own personal gain . . . now, that right there eliminates ninety percent of the obvious choices . . . Look, you said, for someone who is loyal to you, Dan Rossi, someone who will carry on your agenda to ensure the taxpayers of Woodside Heights get the best representation for their money . . . figuratively speaking, of course . . . pass the mantle to someone whose motives are pure, who has a true and deep commitment to this city and its future . . ."

"I said that?" Athen's eyebrows raised.

"In so many words." He nodded. "That was what you meant, in any case. And so I lay awake all night, pondering and praying. And at precisely five forty-five A.M.—I noted the time exactly—it came to me, clear as crystal. There is only one person in whose hands I can safely leave this city." Dan was on a roll. "Do you know who that person is, Athen?"

She shook her head, waiting for his announcement.

"That person, Athen . . ." He paused to add yet another touch of drama to the moment. ". . . is you."

"Me?" she squeaked. "You can't be serious . . ."

"Serious as a heart attack," he assured her.

"Dan, this is crazy. I don't . . ."

"I know what you're going to say." He held up a pudgy hand as if to ward off her protests. "You're going to say you have no experience, to which I'll say poppycock. You've had more experience in seeing how this office is run over the past three months than anyone, being as close to the scene as you have been . . ."

"Dan, I—I couldn't," she sputtered, horrified at the very thought. "I don't want to . . ."

"Of course you could, haven't I told you a hundred times what a natural you are? And of course you want to . . . you just don't know it yet," he assured her.

"Dan." She shook her head slowly in consternation. "People would be crazy to vote for me. Who would vote for me?"

"Everyone will vote for you, my dear, and be pleased to do so." He nodded confidently.

"I have no credentials, I have no record, why would anyone want me for mayor?" She stood up and crossed her arms over her chest, hoping the protective move would keep her heart from falling out, its pounding was so intense. She started to pace anxiously.

"Very simple, Athen." He chuckled. "They will vote for you because I will nominate you. I am and will remain the head of the party. You will have my full and total support."

"I can't afford a political campaign, Dan. It costs a lot of money to run for office." She tried a new tactic.

"Not to worry." He leaned back and lit a cigar. "The party has the means to cover all the expenses. And since mayoral races in this city are pretty much uncontested, the expenses will be relatively low."

"I won't know what to do," she told him, her head swimming with a thousand jumbled thoughts.

"I will be behind you every minute, Athen, I promise you. You will never go into a meeting or a negotiation for which I have not personally prepared you." His eyes narrowed and he leaned across the desk, his gaze intent. "You will not be thrown to the wolves, my dear."

"Dan . . ." Her senses were beginning to return to her

slowly. "I appreciate your confidence in me, I really do. But there's no way I can do something like this . . ."

"Don't give me an answer now, my dear, I realize this is unexpected and will require a great deal of thought on your part." He smiled gently, once again the kind father. "Take the rest of the day off and think about it, about the advantages . . . the salary for mayor is close to sixty thousand dollars . . . and then there's the matter of the pension . . ."

"The pension?"

"Why, yes," he told her casually, "once you've served as mayor you are entitled to a yearly pension equal to one-third of your salary and full medical benefits for the rest of your life. I imagine, with Callie in private school and college just a few years down the road, an extra twenty thousand dollars a year would come in pretty handy . . ."

"Twenty thousand dollars a year?" She gasped.

"For the rest of your life." He nodded.

"That's outrageous!" She was dumbfounded. Twenty thousand dollars a year for having served two years?

"It's in the city charter, Athen." He smiled. "It's the city's way of showing appreciation for our service . . ."

"But the others, Harlan, Jim . . ." She reminded him of those who fully expected to get the nod and who would not be pleased with his choice.

"You just let me worry about them." He waved as if to dismiss them. "I will explain it all to them in terms they can understand. They'll accept my decision, I assure you."

"Dan, I really don't think I want to do this," she told him. "I don't think I'd be a very good mayor . . ."

"Athen, do you trust me?"

"Certainly I trust you, but . . ."

"Then trust me in this. I know exactly what I'm doing." His gaze was confident as he studied her face. "Look, Athen, it's only two years out of your life. At the end of those two years you can do whatever you want."

"And then what happens?" She asked the question he seemed to be waiting for.

He hesitated momentarily, as if debating between a choice of responses, then smiled that gentle smile and shrugged. "Who knows what can happen in two years? Perhaps Harlan will have matured enough at that point, perhaps someone else might be a better choice . . . but that's a decision for another day, my dear. Today's decision is in your hands. Take the day off, Athen, give it very serious consideration. Take tomorrow if you need it. But come back before Friday morning and tell me you'll accept."

"What happens on Friday?" she asked as she rose from her chair.

"On Friday I will have to tell council of my choice. You know that the candidate is always introduced formally at the Labor Day rally. That's next Monday, honey. We're running out of time."

Monday. Less than a week away . . .

"Go now." He stood up and escorted her to the door. "Think of the years of service your father gave this city, of how proud he'd be that you have followed in his footsteps. Think of the great sacrifice John made on behalf of the good people of Woodside Heights. Think of what your pension would mean in terms of the education you could offer Callie . . . I know you'll make the right decision, Athen . . . And remember, I'll be behind you every step of the way."

She cleared off her desk as in a daze, gathered her purse and started towards the elevator.

"You don't look so good, Athen." Edie peered over the top of her glasses as Athen pushed the down button and waited for the car. "You feeling all right?"

Athen shook her head and walked through the doors the second they opened.

11

"So, what do you think, John?" she asked the empty room after having sat in the middle of the floor and talked, seemingly to the air, nonstop for the past twenty minutes. What Rossi said. What she said. What should she do?

Something about Dan's proposal—something unspoken —nagged at her. Something she could not quite put her finger on lurked in the back of her mind. She stood and walked to the window and looked out across the yard, naked without the magnolia and barren without the masses of blooms which had, every year, peppered the landscape with rich variations of color. She sighed. She paced. She could not clear her head.

If John were here, she knew, he would tell her to get on her bike and go for a long ride and think it through. And he'd be absolutely right. It was just what she needed. Unfortunately, she reminded herself, the last time she'd seen her bike, it had been in pieces, flying through the air towards the Dumpster. She tapped her foot thoughtfully. She could buy another. Maybe one of those super new Raleigh fourteen speeds she'd seen last summer.

She glanced at her watch. She had part of the morning and most of the afternoon ahead of her, plenty of time to run out to the bike shop in the new shopping center on the outskirts of town and still have time to try it out. She changed into shorts, T-shirt and sneakers, then brushed her hair out, tying it into a loose ponytail with a white ribbon. She paused briefly in the kitchen. If she found the bike she wanted, she could ride out to see her father. Grabbing a half-full package of two-day-old rolls—she'd stop and feed the ducks after visiting with Ari—she headed for the car. She'd tell Ari everything and maybe, if she laid all her thoughts out in a rational manner, the right decision would come to her.

"Damn that woman!" Athen exploded at the sight of Diana's red car in the parking lot. Diana must be spending her lunch hours out here now. Damn her.

She wheeled slowly around the parking lot, making huge circles on her new bike. It had been exactly what she wanted. More pleased than she had expected to be, she had bought it, fastened it to the bike rack on her car, and driven home from the mall. Then tossing the stale rolls into the small vinyl bag behind the seat, she had ridden slowly down the driveway, getting the feel of the new tires. She had stopped once to adjust the seat before heading out towards Woodside Manor. The ride had been just what she needed, sweeping aside the cobwebs and filling her with a sense of exhilaration she had not felt in months. For a few moments, she had sensed a piece of her old self returning. She wondered if her father would notice. She would have to wait to find out.

Athen sighed and pedaled over towards the pond, stopping her bike under the tall trees and standing it at the edge of the parking lot. She unhooked the black seat bag and took out the package of bread. The ducks were all clustered on the opposite shore, and so she took the footbridge to the park side of the pond.

The birds flocked to her as she approached. Long since accustomed to the treats offered by human hands, they clustered around her, their quacks a chaotic chorus on this quiet, hot afternoon. She dribbled the last crumbs into the open beak of a brown duck at her feet and shoved the empty plastic bag into her pocket. Diana's lunch hour must be over by now, she thought . . .

"Here, give them some of this." The voice startled her and she jumped.

"Sorry if I scared you." Quentin Forbes held out an open bag of popcorn. "I thought you'd have heard me coming down the incline . . ."

"I guess my mind was wandering," was the best she could manage. She had been right. He was everywhere.

"Fickle little buggers, aren't they?" He grinned. "One minute they're at your feet, the next minute they're quacking their tune for someone else. Here, hold out your hands . . ."

He poured popcorn into her outreached hands. A crowd of quackers followed the transfer of food from one to the other. Soon they were both surrounded, tossing the small white kernels to this one or that until both the bag and her hands were empty.

"That's all for today, folks. See you tomorrow, same time, same place. Same menu." He rolled the paper bag into a ball and tossed it easily and accurately into the trash can twenty feet from where they stood.

The ducks ambled back towards the water's edge.

"Same time, same place?" she asked to make conversation. "Is this part of your daily routine?"

"Religiously." He nodded solemnly. "My feathered friends have come to depend on the popcorn man. Hate to disappoint them."

She began to walk slowly up the incline.

"Hey, Athen," he called. It had been the first time he'd called her by name.

She half-turned towards him.

"Have you had lunch?"

Mesmerized by blue eyes, she dumbly shook her head no.

"Join me in the park for a hot dog? Maybe a Popsicle for dessert?" he offered casually.

She glanced over at the parking lot on the other side of the pond. Diana's car had not moved.

"Well, I guess I've some time to kill . . ." she said half under her breath.

"There's a gracious acceptance to a gracious offer," he noted dryly as he joined her at the top of the incline.

"Oh, what I meant was, I want to visit my father." She blushed when she realized how rude she had sounded. What was it about this man that caused her to blush every time they had words? "He's at Woodside Manor . . ."

"Is he ill?" he asked with some concern.

"Stroke . . . three years ago," she explained.

He looked at his watch. "So you're . . . what, killing time till he's finished his lunch?"

"Not exactly." She hesitated. How much explanation to offer? "He has another visitor right now."

"Oh? Your mother? Sister?" he persisted.

"My mother died when I was five. I have no sisters, no brothers. My father's visitor is a . . . friend. Of his, not mine." The stiff retort shot from her lips before she could stop it.

"Okay, okay." He held up both hands in surrender. "Next time just tell me it's none of my business. What do you like on your hot dog?"

He led her to a park bench which was heavily shaded and plunked the paper plate holding her hot dog—mustard

62

only, fries on the side—and a can of Diet Pepsi in front of her. She watched wide-eyed as he assaulted the first of his two hot dogs. Chili, mustard, relish, sauerkraut all glopped from the bun in clumps.

"How can you eat that?" she asked, her appetite diminishing with every bite he took.

"Only way to kill the taste of the hot dog." He grinned, wiping mustard from his bottom lip. "Want a bite?"

"No, thanks." She grimaced.

"It's great, really. I have two a day, every day."

"What kind of work do you do that gives you the freedom to lunch every day in the park, feed the ducks, socialize with whomever you run into?" she asked. "Or is that too personal?"

"Cut that out, will you?" he said quietly. "We can be friends, Athen . . ."

"That would be nice," she said somewhat wistfully, turning her eyes from his and playing with a french fry.

"You say that as if you don't have any friends," he noted, "and I would find that very hard to believe."

"I don't have many," she admitted. "I know a lot of people, but it seems that everyone I've been close to is out of reach . . ."

He looked at her quizzically.

"My husband was a police officer. He was killed last January on the job. We used to socialize a lot with some of his buddies and their wives, but after he died, I don't know, it was like I was a pariah or something. My old friends started acting like I was a black cat . . ."

"Like a bad-luck charm?"

"Something like that. My father's stroke left him unable to speak, so it's all one-sided conversations when I visit. I miss his counsel, if you know what I mean."

"I do know." He nodded thoughtfully. "My dad died eighteen months ago. We were great friends. I still miss him. No girlfriends to talk to?"

"My only really close friend is John's sister. She lives out west now. We talk on the phone and she gets back here a few times each year—but it's not the same as her being here in town."

"You've weathered a lot of storms for such a tiny ship, haven't you?" he observed gently.

"Well, don't think I'm a better person for it," she told him.

"I think you have the right to an occasional bad day, all you've had to deal with over the past few years . . ."

"You don't understand," she told him, "I've barely been able to function at times."

"That's understandable." He took a big swig from his soda can. "It can be hard to keep going, sometimes. Everyone takes a tumble at one time or another, Athen."

He met her eyes, as if about to say something more, but did not.

"So, what about you?" She sought to divert the subject from herself. "What brings you to the park every day?"

"I spend a few hours in the library." He motioned with his head towards the red brick building at the other side of the field. "Doing a little research for a book I've been working at on and off for the past few years, checking into some local connections with the Underground Railroad . . ."

"Ah, Ms. Evelyn." She nodded.

"She's a prime source," he agreed. "Did you know that years ago, she wrote down the stories she heard as a child from the old folks up on the hill? She interviewed her grandmother—she lived to be a little over a hundred—who had made her way north with her mother and an older brother. It's all there, in the old woman's own words. Ms. Evelyn wrote down every word just as she'd heard it. A few years back she typed it all up and gave a copy to the library. It's wonderful material . . ."

"You came here just to do research?" she prodded him on.

"Not exactly. I sort of stumbled onto that when I got out here."

"From . . . ?"

"Kansas City. That's where my family is from, originally. Grew up there. Only left to go to college, but I went back after graduation. Worked there. Married there . . ."

"Where's your wife . . . ?" she heard herself ask.

"Well, I guess right now she's in central Europe some-place."

"Don't you know where she is?" So, she thought with some unexplainable disappointment, there is a Mrs. Quentin Forbes . . .

"Cynthia works for *American Perspective . . ."*

"The magazine?" Athen was unavoidably impressed. *American Perspective* was big time.

He nodded. "She's a photographer. A very good one, I might add. Maybe too good. Three years ago they offered her the European desk and she took it . . ."

"And you and Timmy couldn't go?"

"Go where? She lives out of hotels. She goes where the news is. Follows the big events . . ." There was more than a trace of bitterness in his explanation.

"Doesn't she miss Timmy?"

"If she does, she's doing a fine job of hiding it. She's only been back once, Athen. To sign the divorce papers. How do you think that makes my son feel?" He crushed the empty soda can with his left hand. Athen had the feeling he'd wished it had been his ex-wife's neck.

"I'm sorry." She could think of nothing more appropriate to say.

"So was I." He tossed the can towards the trash bin and missed.

She leaned back and peered through the trees. The red car was nowhere to be seen.

"I guess I should get going, see my father before it gets too late . . ." The conversation had taken a bleak turn. Witness-ing his pain had disturbed her.

"I'll walk you to the bridge . . ."

He cleaned up the trash and her empty soda can and tossed them into the garbage.

"Why'd you come to Woodside Heights?" she asked.

"My mother remarried about six months ago . . . Her husband lives just outside of town. I thought it was time Timmy got to know her . . ."

"What about work?"

"Well, as of next week, I'll be working for my stepfather."

"Doing what?"

"Don't know exactly yet. There are several options open . . ." he said vaguely. "What about you? Do you work?"

"I work for the city," was all she said.

"And in your spare time, you're a seasoned gardener," he concluded.

"Oh . . . well . . ." She wondered how to admit she didn't know a hollyhock from a ham hock without making herself look incredibly stupid.

He laughed, and the light mood returned as quickly as it had fled earlier.

"It's okay, Athen," he whispered, "your secret is safe with me."

"You knew all along . . ." she exclaimed, and laughed with him in spite of her charade having been so thinly veiled. "How did you know? I thought I'd done a pretty good job covering up my ignorance . . ."

"Well, let's start with the fact that you were using a six-inch trowel designed for transplanting little seedlings to dig up a plant three feet wide." His eyes were merry again, making her smile unconsciously when they met hers. "And these"— he reached for her hands —"are not the hands of a gardener. No callouses. No chipped nails, other, I suspect, than the ones you got fighting with the gypsophila out at Ms. Evelyn's."

He held her hands for the briefest moment before letting them drop and shoving his own hands into the pockets of his shorts. They walked the rest of the way to the pond in silence.

At their approach to the bridge, the ducks sang out and hurried up the ridge, begging hopefully.

"Nothing this time, pals." He displayed empty hands.

"This has been nice, Quentin, thank you. It was just exactly what I needed today."

"Then I'm glad we ran into each other." He smiled. "Happy to have been in the right place at the right time." He paused, then gently touched her elbow. "Listen, Athen, maybe I could call you sometime, maybe have dinner . . . ?"

"Quentin . . . I don't know . . . if . . ." The words "I'm ready" yet stuck in her throat.

"I understand." He nodded slowly. "But we could be friends. I would like to think of myself as your friend."

"That would be good. Thank you." She started across the bridge, then turned back and asked, "Quentin, if someone you cared about wanted you to do something you weren't sure you wanted to do, what would you do?"

He thought for a long minute.

"I guess I'd ask myself two questions," he replied. "What's in it for me? And what's in it for them?"

He waved and turned his back, taking the field with long strides.

What's in it for me . . . and what's in it for Rossi? She wished she knew.

12

The news had hit the city like a bombshell. Dan Rossi's choice for the mayor's seat was . . . Athena Moran? Disbelief spread throughout city hall all day Friday. The evening newscasters from both the local and the cable stations had each called no fewer than three irrefutable sources to confirm the unlikely story.

Rossi himself had seemed to relish the frenzy. She'd stood by his desk—soon to be her desk—almost numbly as he made the formal announcement to council, a moment which appeared to give him particular pleasure, Athen had thought at the time. The coldly cordial good wishes expressed by the two most stung by Rossi's choice had chilled her. Dan's assurances that both Jim and Harlan would come around did little to dispel the feeling that all might not go exactly as Rossi had promised. It would be but the first time she'd question the wisdom of her decision.

She had spent the remainder of Wednesday afternoon with her father, talking things out. Try though she might, she could not imagine what his response would have been. She almost regretted having put such distance between herself and Diana. Knowing instinctively that Diana would be a good source of sound advice, Athen wished she had the courage to call her. In the end, the decision had been based on the rationale that, for better or for worse, she was taking a positive step on her own behalf, a step forward into her own future. Besides, it would be an opportunity to do something of value for someone other than herself. She had lived her entire life in Woodside Heights. She had taught its children, the parents and grandparents of whom had voted her father into office and had stood by her side when John had fallen. Perhaps, in her capacity as mayor, she could do something of lasting benefit—with Dan's help, of course.

Rossi had kept Athen pretty much out of sight and mute up until the night of the rally, when he would introduce her and she would meet the party officially. Requests for interviews from the media had been declined by Rossi himself until after Monday.

Athen had splurged on a new dress for the occasion, Callie reminding her that she had nothing suitably formal and yet professional enough.

"It's the nineties, Mom." Callie had scowled at every dress Athen withdrew from her closet for consideration. "Women are into power dressing. I saw it on 'Oprah.'"

Athen merely rolled her eyes as her offspring dragged her to the dress shop for something more appropriate.

Callie herself had been content to wear a dress Meg had sent her last spring, a light green dotted Swiss with a light sprinkling of floral embroidery across the bodice and a sash that tied in the back.

"I thought you hated that dress," Athen noted, grateful to her core she'd not had to bribe Callie out of her favorite cutoffs and new soccer cleats for the event.

"Mom." Callie grinned. "I'm going to be First Kid. It's okay if I look like a geek for one night."

Athen had barely gotten herself into her own new dress— a linen sheath in a deep shade of red, not too tight, not too short—before Rossi's driver rang the doorbell. She called to

Callie to go on out and tell Mr. Rossi she'd be down in a second.

Last-minute doubts plagued her and she fumbled with her necklace. The garnet and gold piece her mother had worn on her wedding day was perfect with the dress. She wondered at the wisdom of her decision not to cut her hair or, at the very least, to have piled it on top of her head instead of leaving it to hang straight down her back in a thick black waterfall.

"It's too late now," she muttered to herself as she fastened the garnet earrings on and stepped back to take a last look at herself.

"You look fine," she announced to the image in the mirror. "You look . . . pretty."

"Mom," Callie shouted up the steps, "Mr. Rossi said we have to leave now."

The butterflies in her stomach had transformed themselves into something more sinister and were now in the process of gnawing away painfully at her insides as she ran down the steps. From the moment she'd made her decision she'd had no time for second thoughts. God, she prayed fervently as she closed the front door behind her, I hope I'm doing the right thing.

The biannual rally was traditionally hosted by the party at the home of one of the more well-to-do contributors. This year's honor went to Hughes Chapman, who, with his new wife in tow, would greet the movers and shakers on the spacious grounds of their sprawling home just beyond the city limits. Rossi's driver carefully made the sharp turn into the Chapmans' drive and ceremoniously opened the back door to assist his passengers as they exited.

Athen caught her breath at the sight of the red brick Georgian mansion and the graceful lawns which spread out in every direction.

"What does Mr. Chapman do?" she whispered to Dan.

"He owns *The Woodside Herald,* among other things. A bit of an entrepreneur, fingers in many pots. Doesn't get much involved in politics except through his wallet." Dan shook out the arms of his dinner jacket so that the sleeves hung just so. "Only reason I tolerate that damned rag and its liberal reporters—heard he pretty much turned it over to his daughter last year—is because he owns it . . . Hughes, great to see you again . . ."

"Dan, welcome," their host said, offering a warm greeting.

At first glance, Hughes Chapman called to mind jolly old St. Nick—without the beard: jovial and round with twinkling eyes. He grabbed both of Athen's hands in his and chuckled. "So this is Athena Moran. We've heard quite a bit about you over the past week or so. Lydia," he said to the elegantly dressed woman to his left. "Lydia, dear, say hello to Dan Rossi and Athena Moran . . ."

Lydia Chapman's greeting was, Athen felt, oddly cool under the circumstances. Maybe she disapproved of women in politics . . . of working mothers in general.

"It's a pleasure to meet you, Mrs. Chapman." She tried to smile even as she felt the close scrutiny of the very sophisticated Mrs. Chapman.

"The pleasure is mine, Mrs. Moran." She smiled cordially, yet there was no real warmth in the gaze of her blue eyes. She turned to the young woman who stood next to her and said, "Brenda, meet Athen Moran. Brenda is my stepdaughter . . ."

Brenda's eyebrows raised slightly as she inspected Athen more carefully than the occasion would seem to have warranted.

"So you're Athen Moran," she said in a low voice, nodding slightly. She was no more than thirty, long golden blond hair piled atop her head, errant wisps floating around her face and hairline. She wore an ankle-length white silk dress which made absolutely no attempt to hide any of the many curves of her body.

Moved forward by the incoming partygoers, Dan caught Athen by the elbow and, following the crowd, steered her and Callie towards the tent which dominated the vast lawn to the left of the house. Athen turned back once, feeling Brenda Chapman's eyes burning between her shoulder blades. What, she wondered, is that all about? She managed one last peek at Mrs. Chapman. Something is familiar about her, she thought, though I know we've never met before . . .

"Boy," Callie exclaimed, "you could have one heck of a track here . . . you could do a quarter-mile with no problem."

Hundreds of people swarmed inside the tents, happy, friendly bees in an oversized hive. A podium of sorts had been built at the far end for the occasion. It loomed before Athen's eyes like Mt. Everest.

Oh, God, she thought as her head began to swim, there is no way I can get up there in front of all these people. The small shred of self-confidence she had recently rediscovered was suddenly nowhere to be found.

"Dan . . ." Panicked, she clutched at his sleeve. "I changed my mind. I can't do this."

"Athen, my dear." He chuckled kindly and patted her arm. "You have stage fright, that's all. You'll be fine."

"You don't understand." Her voice was a wild whisper. "It's not just stage fright. I'm scared to death. I won't remember what to say . . ."

"Now, Athen, you just read the speech I gave you in the car and you'll do fine."

He motioned to Harlan to get the show on the road.

Dan wants to get this over with. He thinks I'm about to bolt, she noted grimly. And he's right . . .

"Athen, I want you to stand right here . . . come on, Callie, you stay with your mother and keep her calm, that's a good girl . . ." Dan escorted them to a position in the front right section of the happy crowd.

Thunderous applause greeted Rossi as he approached the microphone atop the podium.

"Friends . . ." he said, and a wave of cheers washed over him, the crowd assuring him that they were, indeed, his friends. ". . . thank you, thank you, I appreciate that . . . thank you . . ."

When the crowd subdued slightly, he began again. "Friends, eight years ago I stood here and accepted your nomination for mayor. It has been the greatest honor of my life to have served you. Nothing I've ever done has given me greater satisfaction than holding this esteemed office. I thank each and every one of you for the support you've given me over the years . . ." More applause. "Tonight we meet to officially nominate my successor, the person who, as mayor, will lead this city through the nineties. Now, some might say that choosing your own successor is a little like choosing your own executioner," he quipped and the crowd laughed. "But not so. There were many fine possibilities offered by the party, many good and willing servants to choose from. Our city faces serious challenges over the next few years, my friends. We've lost countless jobs as the factories have closed and businesses have moved elsewhere. Our streets are lined with the homeless and the north side of town has been described as a battle-zone. I searched my heart long and hard, good friends, for the answer to the question, 'In whose hands would this city be most secure?' Well, in seeking the answer, I knew we had to find a fresh approach to government. I recognized that the old ways will not resolve the new problems. And I knew, too, that the person I sought needed to be someone of unblemished character, someone whose life was nurtured with the very essence of public service. Yes, it was my responsibility to bring before you the best man . . ."

The silence was overwhelming. Rossi held every member of the audience firmly in his hands. Heads nodded in agreement as he spoke. If Justis or Wolmar had hoped for a miraculous mandate from the floor on their behalf, all such hope was gone. This crowd would, as Diana Bennett had once noted, vote for Lassie, had Rossi implored them to do so.

". . . the man most worthy to represent you fine people in city hall, the best man to continue the job I began eight years ago." He paused thoughtfully, then slowly unveiled his best politician's smile. "Only this time, ladies and gentlemen, the best man for the job . . . is a woman. Good friends, I give you Athena Moran."

He motioned joyfully to her, his signal for her to join him at the podium. She could not move . . . not her legs, not her mouth, not one muscle in her body would respond to the commands he was giving her. Finally, still smiling broadly, he stepped down and held out his arm to her.

"Dan, I can't . . ." Her terrified whisper was totally ignored as if he had not heard her. He grabbed her arm and placed it through his and all but dragged her through the beaming crowd which was now loudly applauding her appearance on the stage beside him.

He let the cheering of the crowd feed upon itself, knowing it would incite them to a level of acceptance of anything he had yet to say. At the appropriate moment, he motioned for their attention. When the din beneath the tent began to diminish slightly, he again began to speak.

"Thirty years ago, I entered public life as leader of the second ward," he told them solemnly, "a position I am not ashamed to say I battled city hall to achieve. At the same time, our fellow citizens in the fourth ward led a battle of their own. Our growing number of stalwart Greek residents fought to be heard. They selected as their spokesman a man named Ari Stavros. A man who had brought his bride to this country just ten years earlier, seeking work on the new bridges going up between here and New York, seeking a better life for his beloved and the family they hoped to raise here. Sadly, his dream was shattered in the worst possible way. Many of us were there with him, sharing his grief the day his beautiful wife, Melina, lost the battle she fought so bravely for so long."

Athen wanted to run, to hide. Her throat constricted as she fought back tears. She wished Dan had told her he was going to do this.

"But personal tragedy did not deter this fine man from giving his all to the community. As the years passed, we watched Ari grow in wisdom and in leadership. We applauded his rise to city council, for we knew he was a man of honor who would serve his people with the utmost devotion. And we watched his little girl grow up in Woodside Heights . . ."

Oh, Dan, enough, she moaned inwardly.

". . . and marry one of our own. Sadly, we watched as the devastation of Ari's first stroke took his voice from council.

Then, less than three years later, we watched as yet another cruel blow of fate struck this good family."

For the love of God, Rossi. She fought the urge to grab the microphone from him and hit him over the head with it.

"Was there a sadder day in Woodside Heights than the day young John Moran was shot down on the street, sacrificing himself for each and every one of us?" He wiped his eyes with his handkerchief, as many of the onlookers had been doing for the past five minutes.

Callie squirmed uncomfortably and finally buried her face in Athen's chest. My poor baby, I'm so sorry, Athen told her wordlessly as she stroked the child's back. I had no idea he'd do this, baby, I'm so sorry. She kicked Rossi's ankle sharply in anger, telling him to shut up, hoping he got the message.

"Athen Moran is a woman whose roots are firmly buried in the soil of this city." He raised a clenched fist in the air and Athen flinched, exhaling through her teeth. "A woman who understands sacrifice for the common good, understands what it takes to be a dedicated public servant, and she has graciously agreed to offer her service to you. Please lend your support to her as you once did to her father . . . to her husband . . . to me. Please welcome Athena Moran . . ."

The crowd exploded, nearly lifting the top off the tent as Rossi drew her up to the microphone. Her legs were on the verge of giving out, melting like ice in the ninety-degree heat inside the tent, her knees knocking together like crazed bongos.

"Smile pretty," he shouted into her ear and she tried to force her mouth into some shape that might pass for one. She held onto Callie, gripping the child's hands in hers until Callie yelled, "Mom, you're breaking my fingers!"

"Where's your speech, Athen?" Dan asked through his teeth. "The one I gave you . . . ?"

She fumbled in her purse.

"This is your debut, honey, don't blow it." He was still grinning, continuing to wave to the crowd as he stepped back and pushed her to the center of the podium. Adjusting the microphone to her shorter height, he jabbed her in the back and said, "Go."

She cleared her voice as she unfolded the speech Dan had written for her, praying she could do more than squeak unintelligibly as she had in last night's dream. The prepared speech was long and as she scanned it she saw references to her father and to John. Out of the corner of her eye she saw her daughter waiting anxiously for her to begin. Athen folded Dan's speech up and hid it in the palm of her hand. She could not subject Callie to any more of the painful reminders of the past, not for Dan, not for anyone. She leaned towards the microphone and prayed she would not make a fool out of herself.

"I would like to thank Dan Rossi for this opportunity to address you, not only as a citizen of Woodside Heights, but as a hopeful candidate for office. I know that my experience is thin"—it was Rossi's turn to kick her—"but I assure you my convictions run deep. I love this city and I promise you that if I am fortunate enough to have your support, I will continue the fine work begun under Dan's leadership. If I am elected, I will do my best to make you all proud of me . . ."

Out of the corner of one eye she could see a white shadow. Brenda Chapman had moved closer to the podium. It was not the woman's stare which had momentarily rendered Athen unable to speak, but the stance of the man who accompanied her. Quentin Forbes stood with his arms folded over his chest, his face tight, his eyes locking into Athen's, clearly mocking her from across the room. There was no smile of recognition, no sign they had only so recently decided to be friends. Dumbstruck, Athen forgot her speech. Rossi's second kick at the back of her ankle reminded her.

". . . and I . . . I guess that, umm, other than to, umm, thank my daughter for accompanying me, and, umm, thanking Dan for his support, I . . . I've not much else to say . . ." She backed away from the podium to enthused cheers of encouragement, looking for Quentin in the crowd. She saw only a glimpse of his back as Brenda looped a bare arm through his and led him towards the bar at the back of the tent.

Why is he acting like that? she wondered. Why would he look at me as if I was a stranger, a stranger to whom he wouldn't give the time of day?

". . . and so I ask you to support my nomination of Athena Moran for mayor of this fine city," she heard Rossi say from somewhere in the background of her mind, "all in favor . . ."

The ayes were like thunder, the nayes nonexistent. And so her nomination for mayor was official.

She shook hands with and accepted kisses on the cheek from what had seemed to be hundreds of well-wishers as she attempted to make her way towards the bar.

"Well, congratulations, Athen." Diana Bennett stood before her. "I must say this all came as a big surprise . . . a very big surprise, under the circumstances. I wish you well, of course."

"What do you mean, under the circumstances?"

"Suffice it to say that I wish you had talked to me before you let Dan talk you into this." Diana's gaze was level and cool.

"What are you talking about?" Athen felt a creeping rush of fear, like a child who'd been caught cheating on a test.

"Mom, there's a stable down there, I can see it." Callie tugged at her sleeve. "Can I go down and see if there are horses?"

"They have lovely horses, Callie, would you like me to show you?" Diana offered as she broke eye contact with Athen.

"Can I, Mom?" Callie pleaded.

"Of course." Athen nodded, chilled by Diana's ominous remark.

"Call me sometime, Athen," Diana said as she walked off with Callie. "We'll have a chat."

Everyone is acting so odd tonight. Diana, Quentin, even Quentin's . . . his what, date? Judging from the degree of familiarity that had seemed to pass between them, she'd bet that Brenda was no casual date. Was that it? Did Brenda see her as a potential rival? And Quentin . . . was he annoyed at seeing her here, in his girlfriend's own house—an obviously very wealthy girlfriend who has an obviously very wealthy father—after he had expressed what had appeared to be a very genuine interest in Athen?

She could not keep up with the conversations around her, and at the first opportunity fled for the house and the ladies' room where she could think more clearly. She entered the back door and followed the signs that led to a long hall.

He was leaning against an open doorway.

"Well, well, if it isn't the next mayor of Woodside Heights." Judging by his speech, the drink he held was not his first.

"Hello, Quentin," she said cautiously.

"Nice little speech Mr. Rossi gave for you. Did you write it yourself?" He emptied the glass. "Nice touch, dragging out your family tree, Athen, or should I say Your Honor? Now there's a joke—"

"What the hell is wrong with you?" Her hands shot to her hips in a display of anger she was just beginning to feel.

"What's wrong with *me*? What's wrong with *you* is the question . . ."

"What are you talking about? You've acted like I have some disease since the minute I saw you tonight, Quentin . . ."

"You do have a disease, all right. It's called political ambition. Manifested by letting a pimp like Rossi lead you out in front of the gathered faithful to step over the bodies of your father and your husband to get you where you want to be."

"That's preposterous . . ."

"Are you denying that Rossi handpicked you for the job . . . what was the line, the best man for the job turned out to be a woman? Very catchy, Athen. Did you give him that line or was that his own?"

"You've been here, what, three months? What the hell do you know about Dan Rossi?"

"I know plenty, Mrs. Soon-To-Be-Mayor. I know he's as crooked as a poorly hung picture and he's a political pimp.

And if you're smart enough to be mayor, I guess you're smart enough to figure out what that makes you."

"Acriste," she sputtered in Greek, questioning his worth as a human being. "How dare you . . ."

"Oh, yeah, go into your little righteous and innocent act. Boy, did I buy into that one. Poor little lonely Athen, struggling so hard to raise her little girl . . . you really had me fooled. Well, you know the expression, 'Fool me once, shame on you. Fool me twice . . .'"

"Stop it! Leave me alone," she demanded, attempting to brush past him. He grabbed her by the arm.

"Leave you alone? Not a chance." He laughed and put his glass down on the hall table, reaching into his coat pocket to retrieve a business card which he snapped onto the table.

Quentin Forbes. *The Woodside Herald.*

"I don't get it," she said coldly.

"Then I'll explain it to you." His eyes were no longer the warm and gentle blue they'd been on past meetings, but chips of ice which lacked expression. "I am, as of last Thursday, the reporter on the city hall beat. I will be in your face every time you turn around. I will be in the front row at every press conference, and I will be the first person outside your door every time there's a crisis or even the hint of one. And every time you screw up the entire city will know about it by the next morning."

"Why?" she whispered, shaken by his outburst.

"Because there's nothing lower than a man who looks people in the eye and convinces them that he's killing himself on their behalf at the same time he's robbing them blind. Unless it's someone who sells herself to help him to do it."

"Quentin, you don't understand . . ." Why was it so very important to her that he understand . . . ?

"I understand all too well, Athen. And I also understand that you are not the woman I thought you were," he muttered and turned his back to walk away as the ladies' room door opened. Brenda Chapman flowed into the hallway.

"Have you met Brenda?" He gestured to the blond goddess who approached them. "Brenda's the new city editor. Yes, I know she's young, but her daddy does own the paper. There are worse ways to get a job . . ."

He took the arm of a mildly amused Brenda and led her back to the rally, leaving Athen stunned and confused, alone in the great hall.

13

As Dan had predicted, the election went off without a hitch. What little opposition may have existed became lost in the votes of confidence for Rossi's new protégée. Dan had campaigned vigorously on her behalf, so much so that Athen had rarely had to make one of the dreaded speeches herself.

Accustomed to arriving at city hall at eight-thirty, she had continued to do so. At Dan's suggestion, she had moved Edie up the hall to sit at her old desk and serve as her new assistant. Athen had agreed for Dan's sake, although Edie drove her crazy. She talked too much—to Athen or whoever was closest. Athen was afraid to speak openly in front of her, fearing that Edie's idea of a closely guarded secret was only telling the first fifteen people she ran into.

Her first call of the day came every morning at nine. From Dan. They'd discuss her agenda, and he was ever so helpful in guiding her through her meetings. As he had suggested, at her first council meeting she had thanked them all for their support and assured them that nothing would change. Since Dan had already spoken with both Harlan and Jim that day, most of the discussion appeared to transpire between the two of them.

As a matter of fact, each day's meeting seemed to follow the same agenda, Jim or Harlan occasionally asking her, "Isn't that what you understood Dan to have said, Athen?" And she'd nod in agreement or correct them and they'd continue on around her. Soon she felt about as useless as Angelo Giamboni—who after the first month or so cut his attendance to two or three meetings a week—or George

Konstantos, who after greeting Athen affectionately and inquiring after Ari—in Greek—had continued his practice of sleeping through each meeting, apparently unconcerned over who was speaking, what they were saying, or even who was mayor. Fallon seemed to be the only member of the group who recognized her new position. She chose to take her own notes, having little else to do.

True to his word, Quentin Forbes faced off with her at every week's press conference, sitting right in the middle of the front row where she could not avoid seeing him. Even if she refused to meet his eyes she would have to address his questions. She began to dread these open confrontations, when she would step up to the microphone, primed by Dan to discuss the progress on the new budget or the progress of the negotiations with the trash collectors, and he'd throw her a curve.

"Mrs. Moran," he'd say, demanding her attention. "What is your position on the new shelter for the homeless which has been proposed by the Council of Churches?"

"I . . . ah . . . I haven't had time to, ah, study that proposal," she'd stumble, unprepared by Dan to discuss anything other than what he'd placed on her agenda for that day. Whenever she suggested to Dan that she discuss something other than what he'd given her, he'd say, "Wait till you get your feet wet, honey," or, "Let's just deal with one thing at a time. Right now, this is the priority. There's time enough to get into these other things, after you learn to handle the reins."

"Has Mr. Rossi had time to study it?" He would look down at his notes, knowing she'd be red with rage as she forced control into her response.

"Mr. Rossi no longer holds public office, Mr. Forbes," she would reply as calmly as clenched jaws would permit. The man was driving her crazy.

"Then may I assume that you will in fact read the proposal yourself?" he would ask, his eyes challenging her.

"You may, Mr. Forbes." She would abruptly break eye contact—just who the hell did Quentin Forbes think he was?—and look about the room for further questions.

And so it went, week after week, sparring back and forth,

she alternately cursing the day she met him and the day she was sworn in as mayor.

He had not exaggerated. He was making her every move news of the worst sort, slanting his stories to put her in the worst possible light. "Mayor ignores pleas from city churches for homeless refuge" the headlines would shout, followed by a story that projected her as a modern-day Marie Antoinette. "Mayor signs new pact with FOP on first day of negotiations" preceeded the article which went into detail on her late husband's police service and made a point of highlighting the clause that increased the pension for retired officers by six percent when the firemen only got four—failing to note, of course, that during the last session of bargaining the firemen had gotten three and the police but one percent. She could not attend a meeting without him being exactly where he'd promised he'd be—in her face.

She had opted to take a week off at Christmas. Meg would be home for the first time since last spring, her plans for a visit in the fall having been aborted due to her work schedule. Athen looked forward to her time off anxiously, knowing for that one week she could be herself, enjoy Meg's company, and not have to look into Quentin Forbes's mocking eyes. At the same time, she dreaded the holiday, their first without John. It would be hard for Callie this year, she knew, and she wanted to be there when her daughter needed her.

"Anyone here got a tree they need help decorating?" Meg had blown in through the front door. The plane had been delayed due to bad weather in Chicago, and she'd phoned earlier in the day to tell Athen she'd take a cab from the airport whenever she had the good fortune to arrive.

"Aunt Meg!" Callie whooped and flew down the steps, tripping over Meg's luggage and all but knocking the small woman over.

"Whoa, look at this girl! You're near as tall as me, Callie." Meg stepped back to take a good look at her niece.

"That's not so tall." Callie grinned.

"Oh, a jokester, eh? Where's the mama-san? There she is . . ."

Athen embraced her sister-in-law, feeling, as she always did, like an Amazon hugging a pygmy. Meg, barely five-two, made up for her lack of size with her boundless energy.

"Your Honor." Meg feigned a curtsy and Athen laughed.

"God, it's good to see you . . . you look great. I love the new hair . . ." Athen held Meg at arm's length, inspecting the short permed curls which fell around Meg's face, replacing the miles of honey blond hair she'd sported all her life. "It's wonderful, Meg, you look ten years younger . . ."

"Music to my ears . . . oh, honey, where'd you get that tree?" Meg stood, hands on her hips, surveying the scrawny little number Athen had dragged home over the weekend.

"I told you it was too small." Callie turned to her mother with an accusatory air. "I told you it was a poor excuse for a tree. Daddy always brought home perfect trees . . ."

Athen exchanged a chagrined look with Meg, then attempted to put her arms around Callie. "It was as perfect as I could find five days before Christmas. And it was the biggest one I could fit on top of my little car. I'm sorry if it falls short of your expectations, Callie, but . . ."

"Daddy would never have brought home a tree like that," she insisted, tears welling up as she shook her mother off.

"It'll be grand when we get the lights and all the decorations on," Meg assured her, draping her coat over the back of the sofa. "You'll see. It will be beautiful."

"Fat chance," grumbled Callie, "and besides, Daddy always put the lights on . . ."

"And who do you think taught your father to do so masterful a job, hmm? None other than his little sister, that's who. We can take care of this sucker in no time flat. Athen, the lights, please . . ."

Athen produced the lights and ornaments as Meg sorted through the boxes, checking each strand to make sure all the bulbs worked. Soon the little tree had been transformed and they stood back to admire their handiwork.

"Oh, the angel!" Athen poked around to find the box and drew out the angel she'd bought for their first tree. "Callie, it's your job . . ."

"I can't do it this year." Her bottom lip trembled. "There's no one to lift me to the top . . ."

"Look, Callie, the tree's not so tall. I'll bet a chair would do the trick . . ." Athen dragged in a chair from the dining room. It elevated Callie just enough to reach the top of the tree and gently place the angel on the uppermost branch.

"Wonderful!" Meg clapped her hands.

"See, it's not so bad." Athen nodded towards the tree.

"It's not the same, though." Callie fought bravely to blink back tears.

"No, sweetheart, it's not the same," agreed Athen slowly, her heart breaking along with her child's.

"I think I'll go to bed now," Callie told them quietly. "Goodnight, Aunt Meg. I'm glad you're here. Goodnight, Mom." She kissed them both and headed up the steps stiffly.

"Oh, Athen . . ." Meg shook her head sadly.

"It's very hard on her, Meg. She and John were so close, they did so much together. I was afraid she'd have a hard time . . ."

"And you?" Meg asked.

"It's a little easier for me, I guess being an adult . . . but it's not easy . . ." She glanced at the tree. "I can tell you a story about every item on that tree. Those pinecones . . . John and Callie gathered them in the park and brought them home and sprayed them gold. Callie was five that year. The plaster angels . . . we made them three years ago in little plastic molds John found in the toy store. The papier-mâché bells . . . John made them for Callie her first Christmas . . ."

"Stop," begged Meg, and before either of them knew what was happening, they were seated on the floor, leaning against each other, crying their eyes out.

"Oh, God, I hope Callie didn't hear us," Meg sniffed when the storm of tears had begun to subside.

"I should go check on her." Athen stood up.

"Get a tissue and dry your face before you go upstairs," Meg cautioned, "you look ghastly."

"*I* look ghastly!" Athen laughed shakily. "You should see your face, mascara down to your lower lip . . ."

"I must look like a raccoon . . ." Meg helped herself to a tissue and rubbed at the space below her eyes. "Better?"

"Much," Athen replied as she went up the steps to her daughter's darkened room.

Meg had tea made and it had cooled somewhat by the time Athen had joined her in the living room.

"Is she okay?" she asked Athen.

"She's better, but she's hurting," Athen told her. "I think she feels guilty about celebrating Christmas without her dad . . . like she's betraying him or something . . ."

"I would guess that's normal," noted Meg. "I guess it's hard for a child to grasp a concept like 'life goes on.' The last thing in the world John would have wanted for any of us would have been for our lives to stop when his did. You both have a lot of miles to go, you know, and he would have wanted you both to enjoy every inch of the way."

Athen nodded thoughtfully. *Izoie synehizete,* her father would say. Life goes on . . .

"So tell me how it feels to be the duly elected mayor of Woodside Heights . . . what a kick." Meg slid her shoes off, pulling the heels of her feet onto the sofa, settling in for a long chat.

They sat and talked till well past two, switching from tea to a glass of wine to toast Athen's new position and Meg's homecoming.

"So all in all, it's been pretty smooth sailing," Athen told her as she emptied her glass. "Everyone's been pretty nice to me, Dan gives me advice whenever I need it, which is every day. The only real problems I have are from council and this one damned reporter for the *Herald* whose crusade in life is to make me as miserable as possible . . ."

"Oh?" Meg poured a second glass of wine for herself, offering a refill to Athen, who declined.

"Council generally ignores me and the reporter won't leave me alone . . ." She pulled her feet up under her.

"What do you mean, council ignores you?" Meg asked curiously. "How can they ignore you—you're the mayor . . ."

"Well, there's only one member of council who's very . . . active, I guess is the best word . . . he and the solicitor both talk to Dan every day, so I guess by the time we meet in the afternoon, there's not a whole lot left to talk about . . ." She realized as she spoke how ineffectual it made her sound.

"Wait a minute." Meg flicked her cigarette into the ashtray, "I thought you replaced Dan as mayor . . ."

Athen nodded.

"Then why is he still calling the shots?"

"Well . . ." Athen sought an explanation which would make her look less stupid than she felt at that minute.

"So you just let him tell you what to do?" Meg's eyebrows raised slightly.

"Most of the time," Athen admitted, then nodded slowly, adding, "I guess all of the time . . ."

"Why do you do that? Why do you let him tell you what to do?" Meg pressed.

"Well, I guess because he knows more than I do about what's going on . . ."

"Then what are you doing to educate yourself?"

"I haven't really had much time to get into things as much as I'd like to . . ." Athen squirmed uncomfortably under Meg's glare. "I've only been in office for two months. Not even two months . . ."

"Well, what do you do when you don't agree with him?"

"Well . . . I pretty much always agree with him . . ."

"Because he tells you he's right?" Meg stared at Athen in disbelief.

"Pretty much . . ."

"Don't you have your own agenda, things you think are important?"

"Of course I do," Athen said, defending herself staunchly, "and I'll get to it . . . I mean I plan to, but things seem to keep popping up that need to be tended to . . ."

"Things Dan tells you to tend to, no doubt."

"Look, Meg, you're not born knowing how to run a city. Dan has years of experience, I have none. I don't think it's so odd that he gives me advice."

"Just let me get this straight." Meg tapped her fingers on the arm of the chair. "Dan asks you to run for mayor, gets you elected, and then tells you what to do."

Athen did not respond.

"Athen," Meg said quietly, "if Dan still wanted to be mayor, why didn't he just run again? Why did he even go to the trouble of running someone else?"

"Because he'd already served four consecutive terms." The true meaning of the words became clear as glass as she spoke them aloud. "And that's all the charter allows."

"So after your term he can run again . . ." Meg spoke the obvious.

"I guess so." Athen had never felt so small, so stupid in her life.

They sat in silence for a very long minute.

"No wonder the press beats up on you." Meg shook her head.

"Meg, I don't think it's as bad as you make it sound." Athen struggled to defend Dan as well as herself. "Dan really knows this city, he loves it like nothing else in this world. He knows what's best . . ."

"In whose opinion?" Meg challenged her.

"I—I guess in everyone's opinion," Athen told her. "He was a great mayor, Meg, he's done more for this city . . ."

"Like what? Name three major things he's accomplished over the past eight years and I'll get off your back and never bring it up again." Meg crossed her arms over her chest and waited.

"Well . . ." Athen thought hard.

"Has he brought new businesses into the city? More jobs?" Meg asked.

Athen thought of the layoffs announced just two weeks ago at the paper plant, only one of several factories to suffer severe setbacks over the past two years.

"Has he been able to make a dent in the drug problem? Hired new law enforcement officers, encouraged a town watch in the inner-city neighborhoods?"

Athen recalled a conversation she'd had with one of John's classmates from the police academy back around Thanksgiving. He was thinking of quitting the force. Their weapons were outdated, not enough men on the streets, indifference at the top to the problems facing the rank and file. He'd expressed the hope that Athen would take a more aggressive approach . . .

"Has he formulated a plan to rejuvenate the business district? Improve public housing?" Meg's finely honed ability to see clearly to the heart of things, developed through years first as an investigative reporter and later a news anchor, quickly sought facts and discarded sentimentality.

Athen thought of the recent HUD report which had declared Woodside Heights's public housing "grossly inadequate" . . . of the boarded-up, abandoned buildings in the northern section of the city . . .

"Seems to me all Mr. Rossi has done in eight years is to find a way to legally serve eight more," Meg noted bluntly.

What was it Quentin had said to her that day in the park? What's in it for me . . . what's in it for him? I guess that's been obvious to everyone but me, she thought dumbly, suddenly sick to her stomach. Dan had needed someone to hold his place in line, and she'd naively agreed to do it for him.

14

"So bring me up to date on your life." Athen poured coffee for Meg at breakfast the next morning, trying to ignore the fact that she still felt the sting of Meg's comments from the night before. Meg's ability to cut so cleanly to the heart of the situation left Athen with the unavoidable knowledge that she had some serious questions to ask herself between now and the time her Christmas holiday concluded. "I take it things did not work out with Grady?"

"That son of a bitch," she all but snarled. "Remember I told you I thought he was seeing someone else? Well, guess who? Jenny Scott!"

"Your next-door neighbor?"

"The same. Of course, we're not neighbors anymore. They moved into a neat little town house on the other side of Tulsa . . . can you believe it?" She put her head back and fairly screamed, "I hate men!"

"Until the next one comes along." Athen laughed.

"That goes without saying." Meg grinned.

"Where are you off to?" Athen asked Callie, who was pulling on her jacket and hat.

"To Nina's," she told her with a grin. "We're working on a project at her house."

"School project?" Meg poured cream into her cup.

"Nope. Something special. A surprise." Callie kissed them both and headed for the back door. "See ya."

"Must be a last-minute Christmas present." Athen winked at Meg. "Callie's into arts and crafts this year."

"Speaking of last-minute things, I've a few items to pick up myself," Meg noted. "Could you drive me into town?"

"Well, I've got some baking to do, and I haven't finished wrapping Callie's presents." Athen frowned. "Why don't you just take the car and run your errands?"

"Good idea." Meg drained her cup. "Listen, Athen, not that I really mind sharing a room with a ten year old for a week—God knows I love Callie like she was my own—but don't you think it's time to finish that guest room? I mean, the chances of my beloved brother coming back to hang those last few rolls of paper are slim to none."

"I know." Athen sighed. "I think about it from time to time, but then I forget about it . . ."

"Ignore it is more like it," Meg pointed out accurately. "And if you don't mind my saying so, the hall bath—and the hall, for that matter—are ready to be done over. And maybe it's time to get the bunny paper off Callie's walls."

"I wouldn't know where to start." Athen clenched her jaw and cleaned off the table.

"Start here." Meg tossed her the phone book as she pulled on her jacket. "The Yellow Pages. Under Paint and Paper . . ."

Damn Meg, anyway, Athen thought angrily as she measured flour into a bowl for the first batch of cookies. She always has a way of making everyone else feel like an idiot. You're nothing more than a figurehead mayor, Athen. How could you be so stupid, Athen? Your daughter isn't a two year old anymore, Athen . . .

She vented her anger on the cookie dough, and it took four batches until the bitter feeling inside her subsided. Meg is my best friend, she reminded herself. She only says things to help. Meg has always been able to see clear through to the core of things better than anyone I ever knew. Except where her love life is concerned.

When Meg had failed to return by two, Athen began to wonder just how many stops her sister-in-law had to make. At four-thirty, she left a note on the table, telling Meg she'd be back by five and arranged a plate of cookies for her elderly neighbor. When she had delivered her plate of goodies to the grateful Mrs. Sands and walked back across the street, her car was safely in the driveway.

"Where's Meg?" she asked Callie, who was gleefully raiding the cookie jar, her secret present completed and hidden somewhere in her room, Athen surmised.

"She's in the shower," a cookie-crammed mouth told her. "She has a date."

"She has a what?" Athen hung her coat up in the hall closet and stuck her head back into the kitchen.

"A date. With a man." Callie grinned. "Someone she went to college with or something. She's real excited, Mom."

Athen started dinner, splashing a jar of spaghetti sauce into a pan and splattering the front of her shirt, wondering who Meg's mystery man was. When the hum of the hair dryer ceased, she went upstairs to find out.

Meg was in a frenzy, struggling into a short black velvet dress and cursing at the zipper.

"Here, I'll do it." Athen laughed and lent a hand.

"I hope you don't mind, Athen." Meg leaned over the dresser and attempted to apply her eye makeup with shaky hands. ". . . I mean, with me just getting here last night and everything. But I have waited fourteen years for this date and I'd walk through Tulsa naked before I'd have missed this opportunity . . ."

"Whoa . . ." Athen sat down on the bed and laughed. "Tell me, tell me . . ."

"Well, when I was in college, there was one guy who was so phenomenal . . . everyone was in love with him . . . he dated a girl on my floor senior year and we all used to hang out the window when he'd come to pick her up just so we could watch him walk . . ." Meg groaned as a poorly aimed brush slid eyeshadow onto her face. "Anyway, who do I see when I walk into Shrader's card shop this afternoon but Buddy . . . tall, dark, and incredibly handsome Buddy— the years have been good to this man, Athen—and I couldn't help myself, I had to go over and talk to him, see if it was really him, you know? So we started talking, and he suggested we take a stroll through town to see the Christmas displays, and we ended up having coffee over at Lorenzo's . . . I didn't even know that place was still there . . . and the next thing I knew he was asking me if I'd like to go to a cocktail and dinner party his mother is having tonight . . . well, he didn't have to ask me twice . . ."

Meg flounced her hair, nervously glancing at the clock on Callie's desk. "Oh, God, Athen, he'll be here in five minutes . . . what do you think? How do I look?"

"Gorgeous. He'll fall at your feet . . ." Athen assured her.

"That's close enough for starters . . . thank God I had the sense to pack my lucky dress . . ." She grinned. "This little number has never let me down . . . oh, shit, where're my shoes . . . oh, God, that's the doorbell . . ."

"Calm down, Meg, I'll get it." She headed for the landing.

". . . talk about miracles of fate." Meg kept up a nervous patter as Athen took the steps two at a time. "Him coming here from Kansas City, me coming home from Tulsa . . ."

Athen all but froze in midair.

"What does he do?" Her legs started to shake.

"Well, he's writing a book on the Underground Railroad, the local connections and that sort of thing, but he's working for his stepfather, too . . . Athen, will you please get that door?"

Cement feet carried her to the front door. Wooden hands opened it. An obviously startled Quentin Forbes stood on the top step.

"I—I think I have the wrong house . . ." he stuttered. "I was looking for number two thirty-five . . ."

"You found it. Please come in so I can close the door . . . 'Buddy.'" She motioned stiffly for him to enter.

He stepped inside but only enough to push the door over behind him.

"Meg . . . ?" he cleared his throat awkwardly.

"My sister-in-law . . ."

"Meg . . . ?" He looked at her blankly.

". . . Moran . . ." she finished for him.

"Oh . . . I hadn't remembered her last name . . . Your husband's . . ."

"Sister . . ."

"I see." He was obviously unaccustomed to such discomfort. She found herself enjoying it.

"Buddy, hi." Meg sauntered down the steps in her short black dress, looking casually gorgeous, and it was then that Athen realized how frumpy she herself looked . . . white sweatshirt liberally doused with spaghetti sauce, shoeless feet in white wool socks, faded jeans, hair a rumble, half hanging from a knot at the back of her neck . . .

"Athen, I guess you've met . . ." Meg began to formally introduce them.

"'Buddy' . . ." She nodded. "Yes, we've met . . ."

"Well," he said, looking not at Meg, but at Athen. "I guess we should . . ."

"Yes," she told him, "I guess you should . . ."

Meg looked at her, questioning, her eyes narrowing slightly, not for a second unaware of the strange undercurrent running between the man of her dreams and her sister-in-law.

"Have a good time." Athen fairly pushed them out onto the front steps. Closing the door quietly behind them, she wondered why she had a sudden urge to bang her forehead against its dark oak panels . . .

Athen was still wide awake when she heard the car doors slam. Callie, having taken her to task for being such a grump, convinced Athen to take her foul mood to bed before ten.

She heard them in the hallway for a few minutes, their laughter floating up the stairwell to her room. For some unexplainable reason, she closed her eyes and pulled the covers up when she heard Meg tiptoe into her room.

"Don't you even pretend to be sleeping, Athen, I know you're not." Meg poked her.

"How was the party?" Athen dropped the childish ruse and sat up somewhat.

"It would have been a hell of a lot more fun—not to mention less awkward—if you had told me you'd had something going with my date." Meg was ready to explode.

"What?" Athen sat all the way up.

"You could have told me that you and Buddy were more than casual acquaintances . . ."

"Now you wait just a minute, Meg." Athen began to steam at the implication. "How was I supposed to know that your old college chum 'Buddy" was the same man who has been making my life a living hell for the past three months? And for the record, there is nothing between 'Buddy' and me except animosity and hostility."

"Athen, I have known enough men in my life to recognize when a man is dead on his face over someone . . ."

"You are out of your mind . . ."

". . . all he wanted to talk about the entire night was you . . ."

"I can't imagine why . . ."

". . . and there was enough electricity in that little vestibule when I walked downstairs tonight to have lit half the Christmas lights in Woodside Heights . . ."

"Meg, you have the most incredible imagination of anyone I have ever met." Athen shook her head. "Look, you don't know what this man has done to me. He goes out of his way to publicly humiliate me every chance he gets. He thinks I'm a political slut, he . . ."

". . . is fascinated by you." Meg kicked high heels across the room and made a spot for herself on the bed. "I'm telling you, all night long, one question after another . . ."

"Like what?" Athen eyed her suspiciously.

"Like everything . . . everything from how long you and

John had been married to what kind of a deal you made with that 'scumbag Rossi' . . ."

"What?" Athen all but screamed.

"Those were his exact words . . ." Meg nodded.

"There was no 'deal,' Meg. I did this because . . . because . . ." Athen was suddenly at a loss. "Because at the time I thought it was the right thing for me to do. Because I thought I could do something good . . ."

"That's what I told him. I told him you were absolutely incapable of anything that even hinted at being underhanded. Athen, do you still think this was a good move . . . ?" Meg pressed.

"I do, and no vague little innuendoes coming from someone who, up until six months ago, had never set foot in Woodside Heights, is going to change my mind," she steamed.

"Apparently he feels Rossi is long on rhetoric and short on accomplishment," Meg told her. "I think he thinks Rossi is into something shady . . ."

"I don't want to hear a word that man had to say," Athen said pointedly, "and I don't want to hear his name—either of them—again."

"Okay, Athen." Meg sighed. "But I'm really surprised to find you have such a closed mind. Buddy has no motivation to go witch-hunting . . . what possible reason could he have for going after Rossi if there's nothing there?"

"Because he—he hates me," Athen sputtered. "I don't know why but he does. And because he's a reporter—reporters are always suspicious of anyone in politics. It's a prerequisite for the job. And because he's trying to impress Brenda Chapman . . ."

"His stepsister . . . she's really one bright young woman. . . ," Meg began.

"His stepsister?" Athen said. "Then Lydia Chapman . . ."

". . . is his mother." Meg nodded. "She mentioned she'd met you."

"She and her husband hosted the rally the night Rossi nominated me." Athen's face flushed at the memory of the cool reception she'd received from Mrs. Chapman, the amused glances from Brenda, Quentin's insults . . . "Quentin Forbes is a . . . a geeky little butt-head."

Meg hooted. "He's hardly that, 'Thena. I think he's really concerned that . . ."

"I could care less what he's concerned about." Athen pushed Meg off the bed with her foot. "I am going to sleep now. And tomorrow when I wake up, I will hopefully have forgiven you for consorting with the enemy and for bringing that man into my home . . ."

"Okay, okay." Meg found her shoes. "But I would think you'd want to know if there was something going on in which you could eventually be implicated . . ."

"There is nothing going on. Nothing. Do you really think I'd brush this off if there was the slightest possibility there was any truth to it? My God, Meg, you've known me for thirty years . . . even if I didn't care about myself, I'd have Callie to consider. And Dan Rossi has been a close friend of my father's for years—I've known him since I was a child. No, Meg, Mr. Forbes is blowing smoke in your face. I am not the least bit concerned over his gossip, and neither should you be. Now go to bed, please . . ."

"I'm going." Meg turned for the door. "But, Athen . . ."

"Enough, Meg." Athen buried her face in her pillow, and for the next several hours, fitfully battled the mean demons Meg had brought home with her.

15

The holiday had passed without further reminder of the shadow that Quentin Forbes had cast over her. Athen had pondered his insinuations as she, Meg, and Callie were on their way to see her father on Christmas morning. It annoyed her that, even on this day, Quentin Forbes managed to be under her skin.

Unconsciously she scanned the parking lot for a little red car, gratefully noting it was nowhere in sight.

"Come on, you two," she commanded her passengers, who were merrily singing carols. Callie had insisted on bringing the portable cassette player and tapes to fill her grandfather's small room with the sounds of the holidays. "Help me, Callie. Meg, you grab that bag . . ."

Athen and Callie struggled with an enormous poinsettia. Ari had always filled their house with them at Christmas—always the red, never the white—and each year on the holiday she would bring the biggest one she could find to add a touch of cheer to his room.

She had thought he almost smiled at the sight of them, his eyes giving welcome his voice could not extend, his gaze lingering upon his beloved Callie. Opening a cardboard box, Athen removed the brass candelabra, shaped like a fishing boat, which Ari had brought from Greece. She placed the candles in their places and lit them, one by one. Her father stared at their lights, recalling, she was certain, the many Christmases the small boat had seen over the years.

Next Athen delivered gifts to the nurses' station, seeking out the ever-faithful Lilly for a special cash gift for all the extra care she showered on Ari.

"Why, thank you, Ms. Moran. Thank you for thinking of me." Lilly beamed, and as Athen started back to her room, Lilly added, "Just missed Ms. Bennett . . . said she wanted to catch the last Mass over there at the Catholic church but said she'd be back . . ."

Athen stopped in her tracks.

"She's been here already?"

"Oh, yes. Break of dawn, she was here. Brought a special breakfast to share with Mr. Stavros . . ."

"Is she here every day?" Athen heard herself ask.

"Oh, yes ma'am. Most days twice a day. She sure is devoted to that man, Ms. Moran . . ."

"Yes." Athen nodded thoughtfully. "It would appear she is . . ."

Athen walked slowly back to Ari's room, suddenly grateful to her soul that her father had found someone whose devotion and love was so complete that it could survive such tragedy. In the depths of her own sorrow, she had forgotten that such boundless love did indeed exist. She could almost envy Diana, she thought, as she joined the others who were now singing "Away in a Manger" in Ari's room.

Two days later, Meg and Athen were seated in the living room, enjoying the blaze of a dancing fire in the fireplace, listening to the "Messiah," and in general enjoying the first bit of lounging Athen had allowed herself in months.

"Athen."

She had heard Meg, but only barely, having leaned her head back and closed her eyes.

"Athen," Meg persisted, "I want to talk . . ."

"Don't do it, Meg," Athen said without even opening her eyes, "don't even mention his name . . ."

"I don't want to talk about him," she said, knowing full well who Athen referred to. "I want to talk about you."

"What about me?" Athen yawned.

"About your life . . ."

"What is wrong with my life?"

"Well . . ." She hesitated, seeking the right words. "Don't you think it's time to get John's toothbrush out of the bathroom?"

Silence.

"Athen, you can't spend the rest of your life grieving over John."

"Meg, please . . ."

"No, Athen, I mean it. You're young, you're bright—though your career path has led me to question that somewhat lately but we'll let that ride for now—and you're beautiful and sweet . . . you can't wrap yourself in the past, build a shrine to a dead man . . ."

"What the hell is that supposed to mean?" Athen's head shot up.

"Look at this house, Athen. You haven't touched a thing of John's since the day he died. I'll bet his clothes are still in the closet . . ."

Meg waited, and Athen nodded.

"How long are they going to hang there?"

"Meg, this is none of your business. You are overstepping the line . . ." The afternoon's peace evaporated.

"What line? We're family, Athen, and as far as I can see there's no one else around to tell you what you need to hear."

"You don't know what it's been like . . ."

"Don't I? Johnny was my brother, my best friend in this world—next to you. He was always there for me, Athen, for as long as I can remember. I could scream with rage every time I think about his dying . . . I think about him every day." Meg's voice was controlled and calm. "But my life didn't end with his, and neither should yours."

"That's not quite fair, Meg," Athen told her. "I've come a long way in the past six months."

"Athen, you have no social life . . . you go from work to Callie's school and home and back to work again . . . you don't even paint anymore. And how long has it been since you tutored? I'll bet you haven't even had that new bike out more than five times since you bought it."

"Meg, I'm a working mother . . . a single working mother. And with all the meetings I attend, I haven't time for anything else."

"Stop hiding behind your job! Don't you realize that for the past year, you've done nothing but hide? You've hidden inside this house, hidden inside your sorrow, hidden from yourself. Now you're hiding behind Dan Rossi and you can't keep doing that."

Meg held her breath, waiting for Athen to explode.

"Look, Athen, I love you dearly. You're more than a sister, more than a friend. You can't spend the rest of your life with nothing more to look forward to than a trip to the cemetery to put flowers on Johnny's grave." Meg swallowed hard.

Still Athen did not respond.

"Look, there's a brand-new year starting next week . . . I know it's hard, but 'thena, John's not coming back . . ." she said as gently as she could.

"I know." Athen bit her lip. "I don't even know where to begin . . ."

"Begin by getting this house spruced up. Move the furniture around. Give John's clothes away . . . call the Salvation Army. I'll help you. You can go into the new year on all fresh ground."

"Okay." Athen nodded. "You're right. And next week I'll . . ."

"Forget next week," Meg told her. "Tomorrow. We'll start on John's things tomorrow . . ."

16

Upon first seeing her father's clothes removed from the dresser and packed into paper bags, Callie had burst into tears. When Athen explained to her that they would be given to people who really needed them, she brightened.

"Oh, you mean like the homeless guys who hang around Schyler Avenue?" she had asked. "Cool. Dad would have liked his warm things to keep someone else warm . . ."

"When were you down on Schyler Avenue?" Athen frowned, folding shirts and placing them into a bag.

"Last week when Julie's mom took us to the movies, we had to detour around Third Street. They were all hanging out around the big church on the corner." She picked through a pile of sweatshirts. "Can I keep some of these?"

"You may keep all of them if you want." Athen smiled.

"Well, I think I'll just keep a few. I have warm shirts of my own." She thumbed through the pile, selecting several that had been particular favorites of John's. "Maybe I should go through my stuff, too, Mom. There were a lot of little kids with their moms outside that church . . . it made me feel real sad. Maybe you could clean out your own closet and we could send lots of stuff down. Ms. Evelyn said—"

"Where'd you see Ms. Evelyn?" Athen stuck a stack of brand-new wool socks into the bag.

"She was outside the church. I ran over to see her but Julie's mom made me come right back."

"What was Ms. Evelyn doing there?" White undershirts, still in their wrappings from last Christmas, followed the socks.

"She does volunteer work there. She cooks at dinnertime. She said the situation is getting out of hand."

"What is getting out of hand?" Meg asked as she carried an empty box into the room. "What do you think, 'thena? Shoes, belts, in here?"

Athen nodded.

"Ms. Evelyn says there's too many people out of work and more mouths to feed at the church than she can deal with," Callie reported as she gathered up the shirts she had selected. "I'm going to clean out my dresser. Then we'll have lots of things to take down to Ms. Evelyn."

"Better watch out, Athen." Meg winked. "You just might have a budding social activist on your hands."

"There are worse things she could do," Athen noted. "And quite frankly, I've been concerned about the situation myself. Here, give me a hand with these suits . . ."

Callie came back in for some plastic bags, then dragged them, filled, to the bottom of the steps.

"I'm going over to Julie's, Mom," she called up the stairwell. "She's going to clean out her closets too."

"Well, while you finish up that last shelf there," Meg said as she motioned to the closet, "I'll go down and make us some lunch. We should be about ready to take this stuff to wherever it is you want it to go."

Athen was sitting cross-legged on the floor, her back against the bed, when Meg came in twenty minutes later.

"Hey, are you deaf? I've been calling you . . ." Meg paused in the doorway. "Honey, are you all right?"

Athen looked up at her with a white, tear-stained face, her bottom lip quivering. The pale gray sheet of paper in her hand all but rustled, her hands were shaking so.

"What is it?" Meg knelt down and gently placed her hand on her shoulder.

Without a word, Athen passed the letter in her hand to a puzzled Meg, who scanned it quickly.

"Oh," she exclaimed with only mild interest, "where'd you find this?"

"At the back of the closet shelf." Athen stretched her arm towards the tissue box. "There's a whole box of them."

"Athen, for heaven's sake, don't tell me this is bothering you . . . a letter from an old girlfriend written fifteen years ago . . . ?"

Athen nodded.

"Why?"

"Do you realize John saved every letter she ever wrote to him? I had no idea they were there." Athen blew her nose.

"So what?"

"So don't you know what that means?"

"It means it was a time in his life that was important to him."

"It means more than that," Athen sniffed. "It means he probably never stopped loving her."

"Don't be ridiculous."

"How could he have? I mean, Dallas MacGregor is every man's fantasy. How could I have thought I could step into her place in John's life?"

"You didn't," Meg said bluntly, "nor should you have expected to."

"Thank you oh, so very much."

"'Thena, you had your own place in John's life. The fact that he had loved someone else . . ."

"Not just someone else, Meg. *Dallas MacGregor.* How would you feel, marrying a man who had been in love with a woman like that, a movie star, for God's sake . . ."

"I'd feel damn flattered." Meg crossed her arms. "And it's not as if you hadn't known about it. Why, all of a sudden, is it bothering you?"

"I guess because I hadn't realized he'd cared enough to save all these," Athen whispered.

"Look, John and Dallas were together all through college. He always knew where she was headed, that after graduation she'd take off for California. I don't think he ever understood it, that single-minded drive she had. But all she ever wanted was to be a real movie star, and she wasn't about to let a little thing like love stand in her way. Two days after she graduated from Douglass, it was *adios,* John, *buenos dias,* L.A."

Athen recalled how John had withdrawn that summer, how subdued he had seemed when she would visit the usually bustling Moran house. He had asked her out for the first time the following Christmas, taking her to a party at his old fraternity house at Rutgers. A huge photograph hanging over the bar in a downstairs room had stopped John cold as he had entered the room. "Bound for glory" exclaimed a sign above the photo of Dallas—Dallas of the platinum hair and the perfect face, eyes to die for, not blue, not gray, not lavender . . .

"Athen." Meg drew her attention from the long forgotten image. "What difference does any of this make? John loved you, he married you . . ."

"On the rebound apparently . . ." She glumly reached for another tissue.

"Now why would you say that?" Meg lowered herself to the floor beside Athen. "Athen, we humans are amazingly fortunate. We have the ability to fall in love, to fall out of love, to fall in love again. And again. And even again . . ."

"I never fell out of love with John—and apparently he never stopped loving Dallas."

"Why would you say that?" argued Meg. "Just because she's gorgeous and famous, you think my brother carried a torch for her the rest of his life?"

Athen shook her head, unable to share the memory which flashed suddenly, painfully before her eyes . . . the look on John's face when he came home one night to find Athen waiting up for him, deeply engrossed in "Lucinda's Pride" on the VCR, the movie for which Dallas had received an Academy Award nomination. He had retreated suddenly from the room, and Athen had known at once where he had gone all those times he would almost seem to disappear before her eyes, his face taking on a faraway look as he mentally vanished to some secret room inside himself, a room she'd never been invited to enter . . .

"Don't make more out of this than what it is," grumbled

Meg. "Good grief, I have been in and out of love with so many men in my lifetime . . . at least, I believed I was in love with each one of them at the time . . . then again, sometimes I wonder if I ever loved any of them." She smiled wryly. "Not that I'm sure any of it matters . . . but that's another story entirely. The bottom line here is that John loved you enough to marry you, produce the world's most remarkable child, and live, as I recall, a pretty damned happy life with you."

"Yes, we were happy . . ."

"Then what is the big freaking deal?" Meg shouted to the ceiling.

"Well, somehow I always thought that John and I were, you know, meant to be together, that somehow we were . . ." She groped for words.

"No, don't tell me." Meg held up one hand, palm out in Athen's direction. "Written in the stars? Destined for each other?" Meg groaned in disbelief and frustration. "Athen, you are the last living soul on the face of this earth—over the age of maybe three—who still believes in fairy tales . . . I'll bet you even clap your hands when Tinkerbell's light starts to go out . . ."

Athen burst into tears.

"Oh, God, Athen, I'm sorry." Meg's voice softened as she attempted to comfort the weeping heap that was her sister-in-law. "Look, I think you're just overly sensitive right now, what with all John's things being packed up. This can't be easy for you."

"Maybe you're right." Athen took the tissue Meg held out to her, then motioned for Meg to pass the box over. "But Meg, you know, I always believed I'd grow up and find the absolute love of my life and live happily ever after . . ."

"Well, your life's far from being over, honey. You've a long, long way to go." Meg rubbed Athen's back between her shoulder blades to comfort her. "And who knows, maybe the absolute love of your life is out there somewhere, looking for you . . ."

17

"Buddy said to tell you to watch your back," Meg had whispered in Athen's ear as she fled through the gate to her waiting plane.

"If you ask me, the only person I need to guard my back against is 'Buddy,'" she'd muttered.

Athen had been saddened at Meg's departure. Meg was, Athen had reflected on her drive back from the airport, one of those people who always seemed to be able to put things in perspective. While not necessarily a soothing personality, she did have the ability to shake things up. She had certainly done that, Athen thought with a smile as she pulled into her driveway.

She and Meg had agreed to make a list of their New Year's resolutions and read them to each other on New Year's Eve. At the top of her own list Athen had written, "Be more assertive in my job." If she accomplished nothing else this year, she promised herself, she would do that much.

She vowed to speak up at meetings, express her own opinions and even present some ideas of her own. It was time, she told herself, to cut the umbilical cord which tied her to Dan, and to assert herself. It had been easier, she acknowledged, to follow as she had been led, but starting immediately, she would personally read everything—every memo, every proposal, every newspaper article—that came across her desk. She would not wait for Dan to tell her what was important and what to toss out. She was smart enough to figure that out on her own. She would have to educate herself, and quickly. She would start with something elementary.

"Guess all that stuff's like Greek to you, huh, Athen," Edie had commented, placing a cup of coffee before Athen as she poured over the proposed budget the following morning.

"If it was Greek it would make more sense," Athen said, peering over the top of her glasses.

At the three o'clock meeting she had tried her hand at being more of a presence.

"Jim, I was looking over the budget proposal"—she'd taken a deep breath and forced herself to speak before he could begin his one-on-one with Harlan Justis—"and I was wondering why the transportation numbers are so high. How many cars does the city own, anyway?"

Justis and Wolmar exchanged a surprised look.

"Well, the city has a lot of cars, Athen." Wolmar cleared his throat, speaking as if to a six year old. "We have police cars and cars for the code inspectors and of course all the department heads—and members of council—have city cars. Why do you ask?"

"It just seems like we have a lot of money in the budget for vehicles," she said. "Does anyone have a list of who exactly has these cars?"

"Well, now, I suppose someone in finance—or is it personnel, now, Harlan . . . ?"

"I think it's personnel . . . could be finance . . ." Harlan nodded, smoothing his handsome silk tie, visibly admiring its rich green and maroon paisley, which was obviously of greater consequence to him than her inquiries.

"In any event, someone has a list, I'm sure you could get one if you really think you need to." Harlan forced a patience he obviously did not feel, then turned to Jim as he clearly dismissed her. "So now Jim, how do you think we should handle the residents of Fourth Street? They're on the rampage again about wanting more officers assigned to that three-block stretch where the drug traffic has increased . . ."

"I already talked to Dan." Jim leaned back in his chair. "He said just let 'em all shoot it out . . ."

Stung by their curt rebuff of her effort to participate, Athen got up from her seat and walked to her desk. Beyond the handsomely decorated room she could see the area of the city known as the Devil's Passage, an area two blocks north of city hall, between Fourth Street and the overpass from the superhighway beyond the city limits. Even from this distance she could see the ugly boarded-up houses, the vacant lots, the abandoned warehouses. She recalled how the neighborhood had once looked, and wondered how it had all happened so quickly . . .

"Why?" she heard herself say aloud.

"Why what?" Harlan looked up from his briefcase, from which he had withdrawn some documents which were being scrutinized by Wolmar.

"Why 'just let 'em shoot it out'? Why not send more police officers in if that's where they're needed?"

Riley Fallon, the lone black on council, raised his eyebrows and turned to take a long, slow look at her.

"Now, Athen." Harlan took on that expression of having been interrupted by an ill-mannered child. "You of all people should understand the risks to a police officer in an area like that . . ."

"What about the risks to the residents?" she asked.

"Well, now, I would think if anyone was that concerned about their safety, they'd move," he said sarcastically, and she nodded slowly, fully understanding the not-so-subtle reminder that she was expected to be seen and not heard.

But at the Wednesday morning press conference, when Quentin Forbes questioned the lack of response from the city to the growing concerns of those residents who had complained yet again to the press about the increasing number of incidents involving handguns in the area south of city hall, Athen had a surprise for him.

"I'm glad you brought that up, Mr. Forbes." She forced herself to smile, not at him exactly, but at the space slightly above his head. "I spoke very recently with Councilman Fallon who has agreed to look into the formation of a town watch with the residents. He will also meet with Chief Henderson in the very near future to arrange a neighborhood meeting to discuss the situation. Councilman Fallon, perhaps you'd like to take the microphone and answer any further questions on this issue . . . ?"

She could feel Quentin's eyes on her as she packed up her notes. It gave her great satisfaction to know that just this once he had not caught her off guard. She felt the tiniest surge of triumph, knowing that for the first time, she would leave a public meeting with her head up.

She felt terrific, all but dancing back to her office from the big meeting room at the end of the hall.

"Oh, Athen, Dan Rossi's on line one . . ." Edie told her as she walked by.

"Hi, Dan . . ." was all she'd had time to say.

"Rule number one," he said softly, "you never discuss anything—anything—at a public meeting without discussing it first with me. Rule number two, you do not discuss anything with any member of council without discussing it first with me. Rule number three, you do not make announcements without first discussing them with me. Rule number four . . ."

"Dan," she began, but he cut her off again.

"Rule number four, you do not commit the police department or any other department of the city to any project which you have not discussed with me. Do you understand, Athen?"

"No, Dan . . ." She paused. "I don't understand. I don't understand what's so harmful about agreeing to meet with a group of residents who are tired of being shot at every time they open their front door."

"Athen, honey, I just don't like surprises." His tone was tightly controlled, each word pronounced slowly and carefully. "And what's all this I've been hearing, anyway. Budget figures, city cars, how many and who's got one . . ."

"Dan, I need to be more involved in what's going on around here, I want to know what's going on," she told him. "I am the mayor of this city . . ."

"Sweetheart, you are doing fine," he verbally patted her on the head.

"Well, I don't feel like I'm doing anything worthwhile. I want to be more involved, I want to feel like I'm doing something around here besides reading the paper and talking to you on the phone." She closed her eyes, trying to imagine the look on his face.

"All right, honey." He chuckled good-naturedly. "You just tell me first, okay? So that I don't have to hear it from someone else, or wait to read it in the paper. Just let me know what it is you want to do, and we'll talk about it, maybe I can give you some ideas or point you in the right direction . . ."

How had he known so fast? she thought as she hung up the phone. Who had called him?

Harlan Justis had left the meeting the second it had begun to break up. He must have flown down to the second floor to his office to report to Dan that little Athen had made some unscheduled remarks . . .

She sat down at her desk and sighed, dejected and still smarting somewhat from the dressing down she'd gotten from Dan. It was worth it, enduring his patronizing manner, she thought as a slow smile creased her lips, just to have seen the look on Quentin Forbes's face . . .

18

It had taken her a week to get the information she'd wanted to back up the transportation numbers on the budget.

"Mrs. Moran?" A young woman peeked around the corner into her office. "Sorry to disturb you, but your secretary's not at her desk . . ."

"She's at lunch." Athen looked up from her desk. Edie was always at lunch. Or a coffee break. Or the ladies' room . . .

"They said . . . Mrs. Fulton in personnel, that is . . . said you wanted to see the file on the city cars . . ."

"Yes, I did." Athen motioned her in. "Thank you, ahh . . ."

"Veronica. Veronica Spicata . . ."

Athen's eyebrows raised slightly in amusement as the young woman placed the file on her desk. Veronica's inky black hair was pulled into a sort of twist at the back of her head and lacquered into submission, reaching skyward in the front, teased into a frothy mist which seemed to account for half of her diminutive stature. Long silver earrings dangled half-moons, tinkling like temple bells, almost to her shoulders. A small army of silver stars marched up each multiple-pierced earlobe and a half-dozen silver chains circled her neck to fall into the space between her collar bone and the top of her low-cut yellow knit shirt. Tiny feet in black patent-leather high heels, shapely legs encased in black stockings, a short black leather skirt—more leg than leather—wrapped around the killer curves of Veronica's hips. Athen's eyes returned to the hair. She hadn't seen anything like it since Annie Keller back in high school . . .

"Thank you, Veronica." Athen smiled and opened the file. Veronica continued to stand before her desk, snapping a wad of gum the size of Athen's fist, prompting Athen to inquire, "Was there something else?"

"I, ah, I'm supposed to wait." She shifted her weight somewhat uncomfortably, swaying slightly on the razor thin high heels.

"Wait for what?"

"For the file." She nodded towards Athen's desk, her silver earrings jingling a tune in time with the movements of her head.

"But I could be reading this for the next two hours," Athen told her.

"I know, but that's what I was told to do."

"Well, why don't we just make a copy?"

"I'm not allowed to do that, Mrs. Moran."

"What is this, some top secret document?" Athen exploded. "Look, you walk outside that door and you copy this file. And you bring the whole thing back in to me, okay?"

Veronica hesitated, obviously torn.

"Are you going to tell me you don't know how to use that new machine?"

"No, Mrs. Moran. It's just that if I get caught copying the file . . ."

"Don't worry, I won't let Mrs. Fulton fire you for insubordination." Athen shook her head in disbelief. "Besides, everyone on this floor takes two-hour lunches—you have a good twenty-five minutes before anyone else arrives on the scene."

Veronica was back in less than five minutes with the file and copy in tow.

"Sit down, Veronica." Athen smiled. "Let's see what's in this file that Mrs. Fulton doesn't want me to look at too closely . . ."

Athen opened the file and scanned the first few pages in silence. She lingered momentarily over the fourth sheet and turned it around, then slid it across the desk in Veronica's direction.

"Veronica, you'll have to help me a bit. Are all these people department heads? Look here, under code enforcement, there are nine names . . . How many people are in that department, do you know?"

"Nine," she replied readily, her gum snapping like popguns at an amusement park.

"All nine people have city cars?"

Veronica's lacquered head nodded emphatically, not a hair moving independently of any other.

"And the parks department . . . I can see why they'd have six trucks . . . but seven city cars . . . how many . . ."

"Seven employees," Veronica told her.

"Seven cars and six trucks for seven people?" she asked incredulously. "Does everyone who works for this city have a city car?"

"I don't," Veronica volunteered.

"Well, how'd they miss you?" Athen mumbled, scanning the list for personnel. "Four cars for personnel?"

"Mrs. Fulton, her assistant, and her personal secretary." Veronica's gum snapped again.

"That's three, Veronica, the list says four. See." Athen turned the paper around to show her. "Here's the list of vehicle numbers . . . maybe this is an old list . . . ?"

"No, ma'am, I typed that list three weeks ago."

"Then who has the other car?"

"Come on, Mrs. Moran, you know . . ." Veronica rolled her eyes skyward.

"If I knew, I wouldn't ask."

"It's Mary Jo's car . . ." Veronica said as if reminding Athen of something she already knew.

"Who is Mary Jo?"

"You know . . . Mary Jo Dolan." The name was all but whispered.

"Who is Mary Jo Dolan?" Athen hadn't a clue.

"Mrs. Moran." Veronica leaned forward, pained at having to speak the obvious. ". . . Mr. Rossi's . . . friend . . ."

"Mr. Rossi's 'friend'?

Athen cleared her throat. "And just what is Miss Dolan's position with the city?"

"Who could know?" Veronica held up her hands, and grinned mischievously. "Except for Mr. Rossi . . ."

"Where does she sit?" Athen toyed with her glasses.

"Anyplace she wants," the young woman quipped.

"Veronica, if she has a city car, she must work for the city." Athen was totally out of patience with this exasperating game. "So tell me who she works for, what she does . . ."

"Wow." Veronica's kohl-lined eyes widened slowly. "You really don't know, do you?"

"Perhaps you should enlighten me." Athen probed for information she instinctively knew she wouldn't like hearing.

"Well, the story is that she supposedly works in the personnel office, but she's on some kind of leave," Veronica said, leaning closer to Athen's desk to confide in a low voice.

"What kind of leave?"

"Officially, it's written up as some kind of medical leave."

"She's ill, then? She's on a medical disability because she's sick?" Of course, Athen sighed inwardly with relief, she had known there had to be a logical explanation.

"Well, I don't know how sick she is, I mean, I see her around town all the time . . ." The implication was left hanging between them.

"But the city's not paying her, right?" Athen paused expectantly.

"She gets paid every other week, just like everyone else." She shrugged, adding, "Mrs. Moran, I'd get killed if anyone knew I was telling you this . . . I only know because I overheard Mrs. Fulton on the phone to . . ."

"To . . . ?" Athen pressed her to continue.

"To Mr. Rossi."

"When? Last summer? Last fall? Before the election?" she prompted.

"No. About a week before Christmas."

Athen gestured for her to spill it all.

"Mrs. Fulton was in her office on the speakerphone with Mr. Rossi. The door was open . . . everyone was at lunch. I came back early and I guess she didn't hear me come in," Veronica whispered. "I heard Mr. Rossi tell Mrs. Fulton to carry Mary Jo—continue to pay her full salary—and to keep the car in the department for Mary Jo's use until he told her otherwise."

"There must be reports from her doctor in her personnel file . . ." Trying to sort fact from ugly supposition, Athen glanced at Veronica for confirmation.

"There's nothing in the file, Mrs. Moran."

"Well, somebody must be authorizing her checks . . . somebody has to sign them . . ." Athen thought aloud.

"Mr. Wolmar signs all the checks," Veronica told her pointedly.

"How long has this woman been on sick leave?"

"Well, since right after I started, about four years ago . . ."

Four years!

Athen was stunned. Four years at full salary, with a city car . . . with no medical reports to justify her infirmity?

"Mrs. Moran, Mary Jo is Mr. Rossi's . . . um, his, ah . . ." Veronica struggled to find the least offensive path to the obvious.

"I think I can guess what she is," Athen said more curtly than she'd intended. The full import of the unsavory news had made her almost nauseated. With shaking hands she unceremoniously dumped the copy of the automobile file into her bottom drawer. "Thank you, Veronica. You can go back to your office now."

"But Mrs. Moran, you won't tell anyone that I told you . . . ?"

"Of course not," Athen assured her. "It'll be our secret."

"Thanks, Mrs. Moran." Veronica sighed with genuine

relief. "I really need this job. At least till Sal—that's my husband—Salvatore Spicata—don't you just love alliterative names?—finishes college." The sound of tiny bells followed her as she headed towards the door, the original file tucked under her arm.

"Veronica," Athen called to her, "how old is Mary Jo?"

"I think she's three years younger than me . . . so she'd be about twenty-one."

Athen nodded her thanks and motioned for Veronica to close the door.

She walked to the big window, drew open the curtains, and stared at the world outside. Somewhere out there a young woman is being paid by the city for work she doesn't do, driving a city-owned car that the city is insuring. She has been collecting a paycheck and driving this car since she was seventeen. And she was Dan Rossi's mistress. Athen's stomach turned at the thought.

What to do with the worms, she wondered, now that the can had been opened?

19

"Athen," Edie spoke to her through the intercom, "Hal Brader from Channel Eight is on line three."

"Tell him I'm in a meeting," she grumbled, "then get Dan on the phone."

She'd started the day in a state of agitation, the spring rain having continued for four days without ceasing. March had, indeed, come in like a lion, the temperatures just above freezing and the wind coming down from the north in cold blusters. I could just as well be in England, she muttered to herself, but then, at least I'd probably be having a better time.

"How are you, Athen?" Dan was obviously in a better frame of mind than she was.

"Peevish and annoyed," she told him. "Every reporter in the city is on my case over this thing with the United Council of Churches. Dan, why can't we just let these people stay in those houses up on Fourth Street? I don't see any harm in turning those buildings over for a good cause. The city isn't using them, and since the UCC is offering to do the renovations at no cost to the city, I just don't understand . . ."

"You don't have to understand," he snapped abruptly, "you just stay out of it, do you hear me? No comments to the press. No meetings with these self-appointed do-gooders, hear me? Athen, do you hear me?" he demanded impatiently.

"Yes, of course I hear you." She bit her lip, taken aback by his outburst. "But I can't continue to avoid this issue and to dodge the reporters . . ."

"Yes, Athen, you can. And you will. Do you understand?"

"No. No, I do not. There are people in my face every time I open my office door, Dan. They want answers. Why is the city refusing to talk to these people? Why am I taking so long to review a sixty-page proposal? And I have no rational answer, Dan. I have no explanation for it. The newspapers are crucifying me." She squeezed her eyes closed as tightly as she could, knowing she was pushing her luck by her persistence.

She could still see Quentin Forbes's icy blue eyes as he had challenged her two days ago, demanding to know just when Her Honor would complete her review of the Council of Churches's request that the city turn over three old twin houses—confiscated by the city three years ago for nonpayment of taxes—for use as shelters for the homeless who, in ever-increasing numbers, lined the streets of Woodside Heights.

"Let them," he told her coldly. "Let them do whatever they want. But you are to continue to ignore it. You are not to get involved in this issue."

"What do you suggest I say?" She fought to maintain her temper.

"You say that the citizens of Woodside Heights are

already overburdened with taxes. You say that the hard-working citizens are having a tough enough time supporting themselves without having to support a bunch of free-loaders."

"Dan," she all but cried in frustration, "these aren't freeloaders. And not too long ago, most of these people were hardworking taxpayers themselves—people who lost their jobs when the mills cut back or closed down. I can't insult them by saying . . ."

"Then you say 'no comment,'" he growled into the phone, "but you do not meet with them and you do not get involved. Period."

"But Dan, I want to meet with them. I want to help them to . . ."

It had taken her a long moment to realize he had hung up on her. She quietly replaced the receiver and sat down at her desk, turning a pen over and over in her hands, her cheeks burning, trying to put it all in perspective, trying to understand. Dan had never yelled at her like that, had never been so brusque with her. He had completely disregarded her feelings and her concerns, had made it clear that she was forbidden to address the issue. His last words had stung deeply. It was none of her business. She was the elected mayor but the most vital concerns of the people who had elected her were none of her business . . .

In spite of her efforts, she felt the tears well in her eyes. Shattered and shamefaced, she sat motionless at her desk. She had allowed herself to get caught in this situation, and she was beginning to hate it. She was stuck here for another eighteen months, trapped in this office. Her palms began to sweat and the room grew smaller around her. She went to the window and opened it, letting the cold rain blow in upon her. When she'd had enough, she closed the window and brushed both rain and tears from her face.

She was reaching for a tissue when reason began to return to her. Why, she wondered, are those three houses so important to Dan that he would risk making her an object of scorn, not just to the press, but to the growing number of citizens who appeared to be supporting the idea of a shelter?

The city had no use for the properties. Two blocks from city hall . . . a block from a series of abandoned warehouses . . . of what possible value could they be to Rossi?

It *is* my business, she thought, clenching her fists as anger grew hotly inside her chest. And he had no cause to speak to me like that, as if I have no right to an opinion of my own, no right to question his orders . . .

His orders. Of course she had no right to questions his orders. He had made that perfectly clear in the beginning, although she hadn't realized it at the time. He would tell her what to do and she would do it. Everyone—except for her—had seemed to recognize her position for what it was. Until now.

She had forgotten the rules and Dan had put her back in her place. Whether or not she would stay there was another matter entirely.

"That was Mr. Lowry on the phone, Callie." Athen poked her head into the living room. "Softball practice has been called off again tonight because of the rain."

Callie nodded without response.

"Callie?" Athen poked her head in a little farther. "What are you watching?"

Athen came into the room and stood behind the chair where her daughter sat, riveted, to the television screen.

"Oh . . ." whispered Athen.

"Is that all you can say?" Callie demanded angrily. "People are standing out in the freezing rain because you won't unlock the door so they can go inside that house to get warm and dry and all you can say is 'oh'?"

"Callie, it's not that simple . . ."

"It *is* that simple." Callie spun around in her seat, eyes crackling with accusation. "The city owns that house—it said so on the news—and you are the mayor of the city. You can open that house up, Mom. You know it and I know it. I just don't know why you won't do it." Callie got up and rushed from the room, yelling over her shoulder, "Sometimes I wish you weren't my mother."

Stung to her very core, Athen lowered herself into the

chair Callie had vacated. She had never felt so small, so humiliated, as she did at that moment. Nothing the press had said about her, none of Quentin's jabs had dug as deeply into her soul as her daughter's angry words. A huge knot threatened to push her heart from her chest.

It's not worth it, she cried to herself. Nothing is worth enduring that look of repulsion in Callie's eyes. Nothing.

She rose to turn off the TV, bending slightly to push the power button off. The scene on the screen held her motionless. The Council of Churches had organized a sit-in, and for the past four days the news had been filled with the stories of the individuals who had kept the vigil in spite of the storm. She sat back down and studied the faces, old and young, men and women, black and white and hispanic.

"Yes, ma'am." An elderly gentleman was responding to the question posed by the reporter, a young woman wrapped in a heavy parka. "We will stay here until the city agrees to talk with us. That's all we're asking for. We just want them to listen . . ."

I hear you, Athen silently replied to the nameless, weathered face on the screen. I hear you . . .

20

I have to tell him, she repeated over and over to herself as she drove into her office the next day. I cannot stand the way Callie looks at me, as if I have betrayed her. And in a way I have. I've always taught her to do right, and here I am, going against everything I know is right and I can't even give her a reason why. It has to stop. We have to talk, Dan and I. And he will have to listen. He has to let me follow my conscience.

She stepped into the elevator, grateful that no reporters awaited her at this earlier than usual hour. Callie's anger had gnawed at her all night, giving her no rest. Her daughter's recriminations had given way to the nagging of her conscience, and her inner voice had refused to let her sleep until she had concluded that she would have to take the initiative. First thing in the morning she would call Dan and tell him. There was no other way. What was the worst he could do, force her out of office? Judging from Dan's reaction earlier in the week, he might be just as happy to have someone else—Wolmar? Justis?—step in for her. She wondered just how good her chances were that he'd back down. Slim to none, she suspected.

The doors slid open and she fished in her pockets for the key to her office. Raising her eyes as she crossed the lobby, she noticed a slight figure wrapped in a red raincoat just outside the door to her office.

"Ms. Evelyn?" she asked.

"Yes, Athen." The woman turned towards her.

"What are you doing here?" Athen shook the water from her raincoat as she removed it.

"I wanted to speak with you, if you have a moment to spare." The woman looked at her with weary eyes.

"Come in." Athen unlocked the office door and gestured for Ms. Evelyn to follow. She hung her coat up and motioned for the woman to hand over her own. "Why, you're wet clear through!" she exclaimed.

"Well, yes, I suppose I am." Ms. Evelyn appeared neither concerned nor surprised as she looked down on her soaking trousers.

"Here, put this on." Athen handed her a sweater which she kept in the office. "Let me get you some coffee. Sit down, please." She gestured towards the sofa. "I'll just be a minute."

Placing the mug of steaming coffee on the table in front of her unexpected visitor, Athen asked, "What brings you down here so early, on such a dreary morning?"

"Well, it's the people . . ."

Ah, yes, Athen nodded slowly. Somehow she had known this had been the woman's mission.

". . . there's just so many of them. Good, hardworking people, Athen, just like you and me, on the streets for the first time in their lives. People who had held jobs from the time they were eighteen, losing those jobs, their homes, through no fault of their own." Ms. Evelyn's voice was soft, devoid of anger or accusation. Just the facts. "Jobs moving out of town, banks foreclosing on mortgages, people with no place to go till they can get back on their feet again. It would break your heart as surely as it breaks mine. I'm asking for twenty minutes of your time, Athen, to come down and see for yourself . . ."

The lump in Athen's throat was enormous. She wanted to tell Ms. Evelyn everything: that she wanted to help, but had been forbidden to intervene. The words stuck in her throat.

"All we're asking for is a place for folks to stay while they figure out where to go from here," Ms. Evelyn continued, her voice hypnotically gentle, "a place where they can get out of the cold and have a warm shower, sleep in a warm bed. The churches'll take care of the cost, we've raised the money . . . we've had beds donated, food donated all winter long. But we need a place to shelter these souls. And I knew if I explained it to you, you'd do what's right . . ."

Ms. Evelyn took a long, slow sip from the mug, wrapping her fingers around it to warm them.

". . . I knew you'd hear me out, Athen. Now, some folks say I'm wasting my time, that you are just a cog in the wheel, but I know you. I know what stuff you're made of. If you just saw for yourself . . . well, I know you are too good to let this go on . . ."

The simple words, their sheer sincerity, humbled Athen, who sat in a humiliated silence, knowing that whole families had suffered—continued to suffer—because of her inability to defy the command of the man who pulled her strings.

She glanced around the well-appointed room. The Office of the Mayor of Woodside Heights. Did this office grant no power? Perhaps it was time to find out . . .

Wordlessly she rose and put on her coat, mindlessly wrapping the gray woolen scarf around her neck. She handed Ms. Evelyn the still soggy overcoat.

"Come on." She met the woman's eyes without shame for the first time since she'd arrived. "The rain appears to have stopped. Let's take a walk . . ."

21

Despite having seen the news coverage, Athen had not expected the crowd to be quite so large. The wet huddled mass of men, women, and small children extended from the corner of Fourth and Sycamore all the way up the sidewalk past the third of the big twin houses which were at the apex of the dispute. Word of her arrival spread quickly, so that by the time she had gone less than twenty feet a path opened before her. The anonymous faces from the news reports were suddenly flesh and blood. Patiently expectant eyes followed her as she passed by, but no one ventured to speak to her. They were all, she knew, carefully watching to see what she would do.

Those huddled closest to the front of the first house parted ranks silently to permit her access to the building. Police guards stood on the porch, arms folded impassively across their chests.

"Hello, Harry. Jack. Stan." Smiling as she climbed the steps, she assumed an air of confidence she did not feel.

"'Morning, Athen." The officer blocking the door returned her greeting pleasantly. The two younger men shuffled uncomfortably, unsure as to what, if any, action they should be prepared to take.

"I'd like to go inside, Harry," she told him without breaking stride as she crossed the porch.

"Athen, Chief said no one's to go in," he said apologetically.

"Harry, I'm the mayor," she whispered a reminder. "Chief Tate works for me."

He mentally debated for a very long moment, then asked, "Do you have the key?"

The key. Of course she had no key.

"I can probably get it open for you." He grinned noncha-

119

lantly, assuring her that a locked door was no obstacle to the former center of the Woodside Heights football team.

She hesitated, her zeal slowed by the unexpected dilemma that faced her. Breaking in to the building had certain implications, she knew. But who would have the key? She tapped a foot in agitation. She couldn't very well call city hall and inquire as to its keeper. And besides, she knew Rossi would know within minutes, and then she'd never get inside . . .

"Go ahead, see if you can force it open," she told him determinedly, "break it down if you have to."

"No problem." He put a shoulder into the door and pushed. And pushed. The door didn't so much as creak.

"Stand back there, Athen . . ." He put his left shoulder down, got a running start and slammed into the solid door. The lock gave easily, sending the officer flying into the front hallway.

Cheers and applause erupted from the watchful crowd. The mood of the crowd had turned from skepticism to hope in a heartbeat.

"Harry . . . are you all right?" Athen peered anxiously after him through the doorway.

"Piece of cake." He grinned, picking himself up off the dusty floor where he'd landed.

"I owe you one." She patted his arm as she stepped into the hallway.

He smiled broadly, his square frame filling the doorway as he returned to his post. "You weren't planning on having this whole crowd come in now, were you?"

She hadn't really planned on anything, she realized. "Just Ms. Evelyn . . ."

"I'll get her," he told her.

Entering the hallway tentatively, Ms. Evelyn's eyes glistened with anticipation as she looked about. Although the house had no electricity, heat, or water, the windows were boarded up on the first floor and years of dust and grime covered everything, Ms. Evelyn bore the look of one gazing upon the interior of a palace for the first time.

"Well, now," she said with restrained satisfaction, "this would do just fine."

"It's a bit musty," Athen noted, following the wide hallway straight ahead into what was probably the dining room.

"A few bright sunny days with the windows open will cure that," Ms. Evelyn assured her.

The two women walked silently through the rest of the house, room to room. The dampness was everywhere and the house had a cold claustrophobic atmosphere. Ms. Evelyn appeared not to notice.

And yet, it occurred to Athen, the house was actually in pretty good condition. Aside from needing paint, some plaster patching, some minor repairs to the windows and a good cleaning, she saw no major damage, no evidence of broken pipes or rotting floorboards as she'd anticipated. Why would anyone abandon such a house, permitting the city to confiscate it?

Athen pushed aside a window shade in one of the second-floor bedrooms. She could barely see city hall through the fog which was rolling in at a rapid pace. From above she heard the first rumble of thunder as yet another storm front approached.

"Are all of the houses the same?" she asked.

"Identical." Ms. Evelyn nodded.

"What will you do for heat?" Athen pulled on the bottom of the shade and let go, sending the vinyl flapping rudely towards the top of the window. "And repairs?"

"We have an army of volunteers. And we can apply for grants . . . from the state, from private foundations . . . and all the churches have funds set up . . ."

"You'll have to get all the properties up to code standards before the city will permit anyone to move in . . ." Athen thought aloud, certain the code enforcement officer would be told to do what had to be done to prevent the buildings from passing inspection. The growing, twisted knot in her stomach reminded her that the real battle had not yet begun.

"You leave all that to me, Athen. You lease these houses to the UCC and you will be amazed at what we can do in His name." The words were spoken softly, with certainty.

I hope He knows a way around Dan Rossi, Athen thought

as she headed down the stairwell and through the still open front door. The crowd hushed as she stepped outside. They were waiting, she knew, for some pronouncement from her, but she had no coherent thoughts to share. She thanked Harry for his part in getting her into the house, all the while wondering how she could get back out without having to say something.

Trusting faces watched her eagerly, hopeful eyes followed her as she reached the top step. Words formed and reformed within her mind, yet no sound passed her lips. The tableau before her remained frozen, expectant.

"Mrs. Moran, does your presence here this morning signal a change in the city's position regarding these properties? Have you and the Council of Churches come to an agreement?" A deep voice she knew all too well broke the anticipatory silence.

Quentin stood no more than six feet from her. She tried not to look at him, wanting to avoid the taunt that only she would detect in his eyes. He was too close to her to be ignored, and she was forced to face him there before the crowd. She wanted to respond intelligently, confidently, was unexplainably driven to impress upon him that this was not the old Athena Moran who stood before him . . . and that she wanted him to be the first to know.

Before she could open her mouth, the lights from a TV camera on her right nearly blinded her as a reporter in a heavy parka thrust a microphone into her face and asked, "Mrs. Moran, these people have been camped here for the past four days waiting for a word from city hall. Why today? What brought you here today after almost a week of silence?"

"A friend asked me to come," she said as she decended the steps. Massive clouds, gunmetal gray and almost low enough to touch, sped overhead, rumbling ominously. She'd barely make it back to city hall before the deluge began.

"Are you considering negotiating a lease with the UCC for all three buildings?" The reporter followed her down the steps. "If so, when might the buildings be available?"

"I don't know," she replied as the first fat drops of rain

began to splash on the sidewalk in front of her. "I wanted to see for myself before making a final decision . . ."

"Will what you've seen here today influence your decision?" the reporter shouted above the thunder.

Athen nodded and took a step forward. It was only a matter of seconds before the downpour began for real.

"Can you comment on the suitability of these buildings for use as a shelter as proposed by the Council of Churches?" The reporter made it clear that storm or no storm, she had not quite finished with the good mayor.

"I think the homes are highly suitable . . . easily adaptable . . ." Athen was all but yelling at the top of her voice as the thunder crashed.

"Will you be recommending to city council that these buildings be made available for that purpose?" the camera crew was preparing to shut down as the final question was asked.

"Yes," Athen replied, pulling her already saturated collar around her neck and heading into the storm to return to her office.

"But will you have enough votes to get it passed?" Quentin's note of sarcasm had stopped her in her tracks. She turned to meet his eyes, and having no response, she glumly shrugged her shoulders and turned away.

22

The sidewalk was already washing over with rain that sped downhill like a swollen stream. Fifty feet ahead, the intersection was cresting the curb, the storm sewers unable to hold yet another drop of water in the wake of the week's all but continuous deluge. Bent over by fierce wind, she tucked her chin in and hoped she'd be able to tell where the sidewalk ended and the street began. City hall, though only a few blocks away, was barely visible through the relentless wall of water.

She cursed her high heels and she cursed the storm. The wind lashed wildly at her, driving the rain under her raincoat to drench her legs. Her long hair, soaking as if she'd just emerged from the shower, wrapped around her face. Halfway to the corner, a car stopped next to her.

"Get in," Quentin shouted through the half-lowered window.

"I'd rather walk," she returned the shout without breaking stride. She reached the end of the sidewalk and took a deep breath as she prepared to step into the swirling water.

"Don't be an idiot." He pulled over to the wrong side of the street so that he was but a few feet from her. "The street is half-washed away up there. Athen, get in. Let me drive you back . . ."

She paused at the edge of the curb, unable to tell where the surface of the street lay. Looking up ahead, she could see that the next intersection was fully under water, a small pickup stuck smack in its center. The overburdened inlets spewed water of indiscernible depth.

Reluctantly she walked to the car. No need to rush, she told herself, I can't get any wetter . . .

"Thank you," she said stiffly, refusing to look at him.

"Well, it wouldn't do to have our good mayor washed away in a flash flood so soon after becoming a hero." He leaned over and turned on the heat, manually adjusting the warm air flow in her direction.

Athen hunched into the seat, grateful for the warmth, and stared out the window. The wipers slashed uselessly at the windshield. Quentin drove slowly, turning hard to the right in an attempt to avoid the lake which churned in the middle of the intersection. He made a quick right turn onto a side street.

"City hall was straight ahead," she told him flatly. "Where are you going?"

"The street is impassable," he said, calmly pointing out the obvious. "I thought a detour might be in order. Unless of course you'd rather backstroke down Fourth Street."

He slowed yet again, torrents of rain rushing wildly down both sides of the street. He took a left and headed up the hill on Ashbridge, but that street, too, was flooding. He turned up Hoffman Boulevard, seeking the highest elevation in the city. If anything, the rain now seemed to intensify.

"This is futile," he mumbled and pulled slowly into a small parking lot behind a convenience store and turned off the engine. He was not oblivious to her annoyance at being stuck with him in the confines of the small car. "I think we'll have to wait it out a bit. I'm sorry . . ."

He pulled the hood of his dark green parka back off his head, allowing dark, damp curls to tumble almost to his eyebrows. Small rivers of water ran down his forehead, and he brushed them away with the back of his hand.

Athen continued to stare out the window, choosing not to respond to his perfunctory apology. She had more on her mind than the storm. The knot in her stomach spread, sending burning fingers of fear and doubt to reach into her chest as she contemplated the commitment she'd made in spite of the explicit command to the contrary.

Quentin turned on the radio, searching for a station that offered more than static or rap music. He cocked an ear, listening closely as he sped up the dial, then backtracked to tune in something which had caught his fancy.

"So." He punctuated the one word with a drum roll of sorts on the dashboard.

"You don't have to make conversation," she told him curtly.

"Fine." Rebuffed, he turned up the volume on the radio.

She folded her hands on her lap and gazed straight ahead, wondering if perhaps she should have taken her chances with the tidal wave at the intersection.

He, too, stared out the front window, watching the buckets of water as they poured from the sky onto his car. The storm gave no indication that it would subside anytime in the very near future. They sat like total strangers sharing bus seats.

Finally, she couldn't stand it any longer. She had to ask. "Why are you so mean to me?"

She watched his reflection in the window but did not turn towards him.

"I'd hardly call rescuing you from a watery grave being mean," he noted dryly.

"You know what I'm talking about," she snapped. "Every week. Every opportunity. Grilling me. Harassing me . . ."

"Since when is it harassment for a reporter to ask an elected official for a statement on issues that directly relate to the city?" Cramped in the small seat, he shifted his weight slightly to turn towards her.

"When that reporter knows . . ."

"When that reporter knows that the elected official in question is duping the people of the city by permitting someone other than herself to make all the decisions—a someone whose motives are decidedly suspect—when that reporter knows that the elected official in question has no opinions of her own and allows herself to be moved around this city like the queen on a chessboard . . ."

"That is not true," she hissed from behind clenched teeth, cutting off the voice that seemed to boom inside the small car.

"Give me a break, Athen," he groaned. "You haven't publicly uttered two words that didn't have Rossi's fingerprints on them since Labor Day. Now I have to admit that was quite a convincing little show you put on this morning. I would have fallen for that act myself, if I didn't know that Rossi had carefully orchestrated . . ."

"You couldn't be farther from the truth," she spat from between clenched jaws.

"Come on, Athen, I know the game. You could at least be honest enough to admit that, for whatever devious little reason, Rossi told you to make nice with the UCC. Of course the fun part—from my standpoint, anyway—is figuring out what comes next. Maybe the strategy is for you to make a big show for the press and then have the buildings fail inspection. 'Well, now, folks, we did our best to help you out, but those old houses just aren't fit for habitation.' Is that the plan?"

Quentin's impressions of Dan at his politicking best were annoyingly accurate.

"You are so far off base . . ." She leaned her right elbow onto the narrow molding below the passenger side window, tilting her head as she ran her hand through her sopping wet hair. "Quentin, you have no idea . . ."

"Then why don't you clue me in?" He twisted in his seat so that he now faced her and leaned back against the car door. "If I'm wrong, you tell me what was the point of that little act this morning."

"It wasn't an act!" The force of her protest caused him to smile with amusement.

"Right." He grinned. "Your compassionate concern wasn't an act, your indignation at having been called on it isn't an act . . . while we're on the subject, though, I thought having the cop break the door down was a great move. Added a touch of drama, don't you think? Was that part of the script or were you ad-libbing . . ."

"God, but you're infuriating," she all but shouted in frustration.

She glanced frantically out the window, taking deep breaths to calm herself as she tried to gauge if the rain had let up enough to free her from the tiny imported prison which trapped her with the most annoying human being she'd ever known. The wind and water continued their savage slashing against the car.

"Well, I have to admit you've piqued my curiosity, Athen," he said, his smile still a taunt. "So if I'm off base, now's your big chance to set me straight."

"Rossi doesn't know," she said as much to the storm as to him. "At least he didn't. I'd be willing to bet he does by now . . ."

"Rossi didn't know what?" He rested an elbow on the steering wheel.

"Rossi didn't know I was going to Fourth Street."

"What do you take me for?" He laughed. "There's no way in hell you'd make a move like that without him directing you."

"Believe what you want." She shrugged, tired of his ridicule, tired of the effort it took to fight back.

Something in her face, in the way she squared her shoulders, choked off the caustic remark he was about to deliver, leaving it to die in his throat.

"And what would you have me believe?" he asked cautiously.

She knew she shouldn't trust him, past history had taught

her that. She could not explain even to herself why the words came out of her mouth. "He told me to ignore the issue. He told me to stay out of it completely."

He whistled one long, slow steady stream.

"What happens when you tug on Superman's cape?" he wondered aloud. "What do you suppose he'll do?"

"I don't know." She shrugged dispassionately. "Make me back down. Maybe make me resign."

"Don't do it. Don't do either." His fingers wound lightly around her left wrist.

"I may not have a choice."

"Of course you have a choice. Listen, stand your ground. If you quit, he'll just appoint another lackey—if you'll pardon the expression—and if you back down, the city will be the same as it was two hours ago. With no hope of things ever changing." The rude stranger with the icy stare had vanished. In his place sat the man she had met the previous summer, a man with warmth in his voice and in his eyes.

"You don't understand how things are." She could not bear the earnestness of his gaze, the warmth of his hand on her arm.

"I understand much more than you realize." He looked directly into her eyes, a small smile on his lips. "Though I'm not sure that I understand what caused you to do what you did this morning."

"I couldn't not do it." She sighed wearily, suddenly tired and chilled and wishing she was home. "I couldn't keep those people out on the street. And between my daughter, and Ms. Evelyn, and my own conscience . . ." She struggled to explain the forces that had compelled her.

"Now what?" he asked, studying her expression with new eyes. "What comes next?"

"I have no idea." She turned her head back towards the window to escape his intensity, and for a few long minutes the only sound came from the rain and wind outside the car.

"Why did you turn on me that night, at the rally?" she asked without turning towards him.

"Well, since we're trading truths, I guess I was angry," he admitted sheepishly.

"Angry? Why?" She watched his reflection in the windshield.

"I guess because I thought we were . . . starting to be friends . . . and I just couldn't reconcile the woman I thought I was beginning to know with the woman who was willing to be used as a mouthpiece for a man like Rossi." His jaw clenched slightly. "At the risk of sounding self-righteous, I could not comprehend why you would agree to such a sham."

"I didn't know it was a sham," she whispered.

"How could you not know?" he demanded. "What did he promise you?"

"Nothing."

"Oh, come on, Athen. You expect me to believe you did this for him out of the goodness of your heart?"

"No, Quentin, it wasn't like that . . . I needed to get my life moving, I needed something to do with myself . . . He offered me a job as his assistant . . . and everything else seemed to happen so quickly . . ." she struggled to explain.

"Well, that's one hell of a promotion, wouldn't you say, for a woman with no political experience, to go from assistant to top banana in, what, four months?" he scoffed. "It's obvious what he got from this little arrangement. What do *you* get out of it?"

"Something to give some direction to my life. A chance to do something good for the city. At least, I thought I could do something good." She knew it sounded lame. "And . . . he told me I'd be entitled to a pension when my term was completed. I knew I'd need the money for Callie's education."

"That's all?"

She nodded.

"Didn't it occur to you that you'd have to make some concessions?" Was the familiar note of ridicule creeping back into his tone?

"I didn't think of it like that . . . he told me he'd help me when I needed it, I didn't know it would be like—like this," Athen sputtered, confused, wondering why he seemed to view her as the villain rather than the victim.

"So you get a pension and he gets to keep control while he's waiting to get his office back." His sardonic ability to reduce the scenario to its most basic level was not unlike Meg's, and every bit as infuriating.

"You make it sound like some shady back room deal," Athen protested, hating the need to defend herself to him.

"What would you call it?"

"It just sort of . . . happened," she said weakly.

He scowled. "That's what a sixteen year old tells her mother when she finds out she's pregnant."

"I am so tired of this," she said wearily. "Is Rossi so bad?"

"Rossi epitomizes the worst in small-town politicians . . ." The handsome man with the heavenly blue eyes who, only minutes earlier, had seemed to understand the truth of the matter, began to fade rapidly before her eyes. In a blink, the master of the cutting remark emerged to take his place.

"That's not fair . . ."

". . . that he has permitted this city to be robbed of its livelihood, then holds it hostage when the people get tossed out onto the street . . ." Without doubt, the rude stranger had returned.

". . . *malaka* . . ." she muttered aloud in Greek to the waning storm.

"What's that mean?" he demanded.

"It means you're a jerk. Of sorts." She crossed her arms over her chest and stared straight ahead.

"Am I? Athen, there's a large minority population in this city that has been virtually ignored . . ." His voice rose angrily, filling the small space inside the car.

"Excuse me, there are two minority representatives on city council," she shot back, unaware that she, too, was now shouting.

"Oh, Christ, Athen, give me a break." He ran his fingers through his hair. "You mean Riley Fallon and George Konstantos? Fallon is so grateful to Rossi for putting him on council he'd publicly kiss Dan's butt and thank him for the opportunity to do so. And Konstantos is so senile he thinks Bush is still in the White House."

"You can be insufferable, you know that? I concede that Rossi has given me more direction than he should. But it's my own fault, Quentin. I let him do it. I went along with it and did nothing to find out for myself what was going on. It was easier for me to just drift along . . ."

"And now?"

"Now . . . I don't know what will happen now." She bit her lip, more fearful of Dan's ire than she wanted Quentin to know. "I really don't think Dan's as bad as you think he is."

"Well, then, maybe he'll have a change of heart and be really happy that you took the initiative this morning."

She didn't answer.

"Sure, I'll bet once you explain to old Dan that what you did today really was best for the good people of Woodside Heights, he'll thank you for opening his eyes. I'll bet you get a big pat on the back for doing the right thing," he jeered.

She wanted to slap that mocking half-smile from his face. The fact that he was right on target made his derision all the more intolerable.

"Well, I see the rain has slowed down, and since you still have to face the music over your little display of disobedience this morning, I guess I'd better get you back to your office." He shifted in his seat and turned the key in the ignition. "My guess is that Dan is trying to track you down right about now for a little heart to heart."

They shared no further conversation, the animosity slipping back around them both like a cloak. He drove slowly through the water-logged streets, and pulled into the parking lot behind city hall.

"I wish you luck, Athen. I truly do," he told her.

"Thanks for the ride." She could not look at him.

She started to open the door when she felt his hand on hers, his fingers cold.

"Athen . . ."

She turned to him, forcing herself to look into his eyes.

"I liked it better when we were friends," he said very softly.

"So did I."

She got out of the car and slammed the door.

23

Athen rode the elevator alone, pondering her situation. The smart thing to do would be to go back into the office and call Dan instead of waiting for him to call her. She'd explain to him about Ms. Evelyn coming here . . . how could she refuse such a small request of an old friend? Maybe Dan just hadn't had an opportunity to go through the houses with the idea of turning them into a shelter in mind. Maybe she could get him to walk through with her . . . maybe have Ms. Evelyn join them, and he'll see what a good idea it would be. Once he sees for himself, maybe he'll come around . . .

Buoyed by this shred of optimism, she stepped through the opening doors, surprised to find Edie at her desk during the lunch hour. The secretary gestured towards Athen's office, her expression curiously smug.

Puzzled, Athen opened the door, unbuttoning her still-soggy coat as she crossed the carpet.

Dan Rossi sat behind her desk, in her chair, reading her mail.

"Ah, there you are." He pushed back the chair slightly from the desk. "Just glancing over the agenda, so to speak. Old habits die hard, I guess. Do forgive me . . ."

He rose and helped her off with her coat. Her instincts told her this was not an act of chivalry on his part, but a means of reminding her whose office this really was. She leaned against the side of the desk, waiting, all of her confidence dissolving in the wake of the chill which went through her.

"Oh, please." He gestured gallantly to her chair. "Do sit."

She walked slowly behind the desk, easing herself into the seat, watching his face.

"So. Athen." He too now sat, directly across from her, his eyes smoldering, his voice completely controlled.

She willed herself not to look away.

"What a little newsmaker you turned out to be. You looked wonderful on TV, by the way. The noontime news really did right by you."

When she failed to respond, he tapped softly on the edge of the desk, and said in the calmest of tones, "Would you like to tell me what prompted your actions?"

She fought the feeling of being a child caught in a forbidden deed, but the sinkhole inside her grew. She began to sweat.

"I could not refuse to talk to Ms. Evelyn, Dan . . ."

"Speaking with Ms. Evelyn is one thing, showing up at the building—having a police officer break into the house with the TV cameras running for Christ's sake!—is something entirely different, Athen." His eyes narrowed, the hound cornering the fox. "Especially after I had expressly instructed you to stay out of that situation." He paused meaningfully. "I did, did I not, expressly tell you not to become involved in any way with this?"

"Yes." She found her voice, and wished it had not sounded so small, so timid.

"You've no idea of the trouble you've caused me, Athen. Now I will have to find a way to undo this mess you've made . . ."

"Dan, I don't understand—"

"You do not have to understand," he cut her off brusquely. "We'll just treat this as a little delay, that's all."

"Delay?" She was confused. "Delay of what?"

Pointedly ignoring her question, he leaned forward, his eyes boring into hers. "You seem to forget just why and how you got to sit at that big desk, young lady. Well, I'm here to remind you. You are here to do exactly what I tell you to do . . ."

She tried to stare him down, watching the storm within him rise.

". . . and what I am telling you to do is to call a press conference on Friday and announce that you are still studying the plan. Put off any further announcements until all the hoopla you've stirred up dies down. Then you will announce that the city has declined to release the properties . . ."

"I won't do that!"

". . . because they are not up to code . . ."

"Those buildings are in good condition . . . they need some updating but . . ."

". . . and are structurally unsound." He sat back, arms crossed over his large chest.

"I cannot do that. I can't reneg on this, Dan." Her words were a plea.

"You will do exactly what I tell you to do," he repeated softly.

"Dan, I'll look like an idiot . . . or worse," she protested.

"You play with fire, you get burned." He shrugged nonchalantly. "You had no business making any kind of commitment, particularly one that was in direct defiance of my instructions. You have been a terrible disappointment to me, Athen." He shook his head in feigned sorrow.

She thought of the look on Callie's face as she had watched the crowd huddled in the rain on the TV screen . . . of the look in Ms. Evelyn's eyes as she had walked through the vacant house that morning. Backing down now would be no less than an act of betrayal. Even Quentin's eyes had held a moment's admiration when he had realized what she had done. How could she discard the self-respect she'd so recently found?

"I won't," she whispered.

"Are you deliberately refusing to obey me? Answer me, Athen. We both need to know where we stand," he demanded.

"Yes." It had been easier than she'd thought.

"You know, of course, that I will go around you. I do not need you, Athen. You will need to bring this before council. Council will vote. It will be defeated four to zero. The whole city will see you for the idealistic fool we both know you to be. So you see, my dear . . ." He smiled benevolently. ". . . I hold all the cards."

Mary Jo Dolan. She wanted to throw the name in his face, but her mouth would not cooperate.

"You have, as they say, bitten off more than you can chew . . ." He rose slowly.

Go on, she told herself. Say it. You have nothing to lose.

". . . and you'll find it infinitely more bitter than you can begin to imagine, Athen."

He headed towards the door.

Ma-ry Jo Do-lan. It echoed inside her head like thunder. She sneezed.

"Oh, catching cold? Must have been that little walk in the rain," he said with amusement. "Do take care of yourself, Athen. We certainly wouldn't want anything to happen to you."

He walked through the door, closing it behind him quietly.

"Mary Jo Dolan," she whispered to the empty room just before she sneezed again.

24

"Can I get you anything else, Mom?" Callie sat on the side of the bed after depositing a cup of hot tea and honey on Athen's bedside table.

"No, thank you, sweetheart." Athen's voice was raspy and several octaves lower than normal. "This is fine. Though you know I don't like you to be around the stove . . ."

"I made it in the microwave like Aunt Meg does. Two minutes on high," Callie told her proudly, then asked anxiously, "Is it okay?"

"It's perfect . . . ahhh choo! . . . thanks." Athen reached for a tissue and dabbed at her already-red nose.

"Boy, you sound awful," Callie noted, "and you don't look too good, either. Your eyes are all kind of weepy and your face is blotchy . . ."

"I get the picture." Athen managed a smile.

"I'm going to go finish my homework, but if you need anything, just call me, okay?" Eager to be helpful, to be needed, Callie straightened the blankets for her mother. "And I'll bring your aspirin at ten before I go to bed. That's when you should take them again."

"You're an absolute gem, Callie," she told her beaming daughter. "I do not know what I'd ever do without you."

"I love you, Mom," Callie said from the doorway, "and I'm really, really proud of you. I didn't mean what I said the other night, about wishing you weren't my mother . . ."

"I know, sweetie." Athen smiled, knowing full well that, at the time, Callie had meant every word of it. And with good reason.

She sat up and sipped at her tea. Hannah plunked her huge canine head on the side of the mattress and whined pathetically, begging to be invited up.

"Oh, all right, Hannah." Athen caved in and patted the other side of the bed. "You can come up for a while."

Gleefully Hannah sprang onto the bed and over Athen, who had barely managed to avoid spilling hot tea on both of them.

"What a lump you are," she told the large wiggling mass of golden fur which had cuddled next to her and happily plunked a big head on her mistress's abdomen. "You don't care that I've gotten myself into the biggest mess of my life and haven't the faintest idea of what to do next, do you, girl?" Hannah's tail thumped on the mattress. "Or that I got caught in a terrible storm and am now as sick as a dog—if you'll pardon the expression." The tail thumped again.

Athen placed the cup on the table next to the bed, slid down the pillow a bit and closed her eyes, her left hand stroking the dog's head slowly.

"It's all so confusing, Hannah . . . I just don't know what to think anymore," she mumbled, fever and fatigue rendering her nearly unintelligible. "I thought Dan was my friend, but he wasn't. He was using me, and I trusted him so much I couldn't even see it when people told me to my face. And now he's washed his hands of me because I won't let him use me anymore. And Quentin . . . I can't figure that man out at all. First he's my friend, then he's my enemy . . . then for just a few minutes today, he almost made me believe that he . . . but then that look was in his eyes again . . . I hate it when he looks at me like that . . ." The dog moved her head to encourage her mistress to continue the massage but the hand had fallen still as Athen drifted into a blur of fevered sleep.

25

Over the next several days, Athen seemed to drift in and out of a heavy, dreamless sleep. She would awaken, drenched in sweat, no sense of time or place, long-forgotten voices ringing in her ears, before once again falling back into the dark void of unconsciousness.

At some point Dr. Brennan appeared, called in by an anxious Callie. Athen had little recollection of his visit, other than that she was to stay in bed—as if she could have moved if she'd wanted to—until the fever broke and the coughing subsided. He'd left an arsenal of medication, which she took when Callie woke her to administer it. Several days had passed before she could keep awake for more than an hour at a time, and several more before she was aware enough to realize how sick she'd been.

"Mom." Callie stuck her head into Athen's room. "Mrs. Kelly sent over some homemade soup. Do you want to try to eat some?"

"Sure." Athen tried to sit up slightly. "That was nice of Mrs. Kelly."

Callie came into the room and pulled the pillows up behind her mother's back and shoulders.

"What time is it?" a disoriented Athen asked.

"Around eleven."

"A.M. or P.M.?" Athen frowned.

Grinning, Callie pulled the shades up to let the sunlight pour into the room.

"Is it Saturday?" What, then, had happened to Friday . . . to Thursday . . . ?

"No, Mom." Callie laughed. "It's Tuesday."

"Tuesday!" she sank back against the pillows. "Then why aren't you in school?"

"And leave you here alone? Mom, you were really sick. You still are." Callie sat down on the edge of the bed.

"Callie, you can't stay out of school because I'm sick." Athen's protest was punctuated by a deep hacking cough.

"There wasn't anybody else to stay with you, and I was afraid to leave you," Callie told her matter-of-factly. "Honest, Mom, it was no big sacrifice."

"Tomorrow you'll go to school." Athen coughed again.

"We'll see how you are tomorrow. Right now, I think some of Mrs. Kelly's soup might be a good idea." Callie bounced off the end of the bed and down the steps.

Mrs. Kelly's chicken soup seemed to have restorative powers. Athen had another bowl at dinnertime, and had enough strength to sit up for an hour or two to read a book Meg had given her for Christmas, the first opportunity she'd had in months to open its cover.

She awoke at dawn to find that during the night, Callie had removed the book from her hands and turned off the light. She rose on wobbly legs and shuffled into the bathroom, where she faced herself in the mirror for the first time in almost six days.

"Ugh!" She wrinkled her nose and made a face at her reflection. "You are a mess. And just between you and me, you smell like a goat."

Vowing to take a shower later that day, she stumbled back to bed as her daughter appeared in the doorway.

"How are you today?" she asked, pleased to see her mother moving about, if only for a minute.

"I feel a lot better." Athen smiled. "So much better, I'm happy to say, that you may rejoin your classmates this morning."

"But, Mom," Callie protested, "what will you do for lunch? And you don't even know when you're supposed to take which pills . . ."

"Go get a piece of paper and write it down for me . . . make that two pieces of paper," Athen said, sitting on the edge of the bed, "so that I can write a note for you to take to school."

"Aw, Mom . . ." Feigning dejection, Callie went slinking off from the room with her head hanging dramatically, and they both laughed at her performance.

"You have done remarkably well . . ." Athen told her when Callie came back to force a reluctant Hannah down the steps and out for her morning spin around the backyard.

"Don't say 'for a child your age,' " pleaded Callie, as she attempted to coax the huge beast through the doorway.

"I would not insult you by saying that. No one could have taken better care of me. I thank you for all you have done, and I love you for being such a wonderful, resourceful kid. Come here so I can give you a hug." Athen held out her arms.

"Thanks, Mom." Callie hugged her back, then turned her nose up slightly. "No offense, Mom, but you need a shower . . ."

"None taken." Athen laughed. "I'd already come to that same conclusion. I will take one this morning."

"Maybe you should wait until I get home from school, in case you get weak and fall or something . . ."

"I'll be fine," Athen assured her daughter, "but I think you'd better get Hannah outside and then get ready for school . . . I can't drive you if you miss the bus . . ."

Hurricane Callie dressed, made breakfast for herself, and brought Athen a plate of toast with butter and marmalade, a cup of tea and an orange before blasting out the front door for a mad dash to the bus stop.

Infinitely more hungry that she'd realized, Athen attacked the breakfast Callie had prepared, downing both pieces of toast in record time. Finishing the orange, she wiped her hands on the napkin to remove the traces of juice which had run down her fingers, then placed the tray beside her on the bed. She leaned back and sighed deeply, tired from the exertion of eating.

Once, as a very small child, she'd had such a fever.

Confined to her bed for days thereafter, her mother had sat with her every moment. Melina's face had been before her as she had drifted off to sleep, and there again when she had awaken. Ceaseless in her devotion to her child, Melina had read to her, sung to her, told her stories of her days in Greece, when she had been young and there had been no radio, no television to distract her from the joys of being a child growing up in the hills. She told of having waded in a cold mountain stream, seeking its source as far into the hills as she could go, but never finding it. What she had been looking for, Melina had explained, was a spot in the hills where the water gushed forth, like a spring, sending her stream on its course down into the valleys. As a child, she had been convinced that it existed. She had dreamed of it, she had told Athen, from time to time over the years, but lately the vision of the spring had returned to her on a nightly basis. What could it mean, Melina had mused, a half-smile on her face, but that soon she might return to Greece and her beloved hills.

"Perhaps," she had told Athen as she had smoothed the blankets over her sick child, "when you are well and I am stronger, we will go. The three of us. You and Papa and me, and I will have your Papa carry me into the hills and I will show you the stream I played in when I was a girl, just as young as you are now. And I will show you where I kept my goat. Did I tell you I had a pet goat? No? Well, he was the finest companion, Athena, the finest friend . . . ah, I can still see him, white and black and gray, he was . . ."

Athen had clung to that story, repeating it nightly to herself for months after her mother had died. Not until she had become an adult had she realized the significance of her mother's nightly dreams of returning to her homeland. Melina had caught cold a few weeks later, and within six weeks, had, indeed, returned to her hills. In Athen's mind, Melina had become linked with the source of the stream, and in her memory, her mother often walked on strong unfettered legs in the cool water of the stream. For years the vision would return to give Athen peace whenever she would lose herself in the anguish of missing her mother.

Melina's death had sent Athen adrift on not a stream, but a torrent of loneliness. Athen was well into her teens before she had ceased crying for her mother every night.

Such loss never ceases to haunt, she reminded herself, and is no stranger to me. Mama, John . . . even Papa is lost to me in so many ways. And now Dan, too, is lost to me. Everyone I trusted and depended on is gone from my life.

Her thoughts returned to the previous week, and for the first time since she'd become ill, she remembered the terrible scene with Dan. It had been like being disowned by a beloved parent. A spasm of anguish surged inside her as she recalled the harshness of his words. No, she reminded herself, not one of those who had loved her had ever treated her with such disregard. A loving parent does not tell his child to close her mind.

Dan had simply washed his hands of her because she was no longer of use to him. It was a loss, but one she would—could—deal with. She grimaced, reminded that she would soon be disgraced before the entire community when it became apparent that she was powerless to deliver the buildings to the UCC. How would her father react, she wondered, when he found out that she had defied Dan, and in doing so, had incurred his wrath? If he could speak, how would he council her? Would he chastise her for her actions? Would it create a rift in his old friendship with Dan?

Sighing, she picked up the book she'd been reading the night before and tried to force herself to focus on the words, hoping to bury her angst in the pages of a good romance. After realizing she'd read the same paragraph at least four times, she stuck a piece of paper between the pages to mark her spot and slapped the covers closed. She sat up and wrapped her arms around her knees, knowing she had to face certain unfortunate but unavoidable issues. Could he force her to resign? Or would he, as he had threatened, simply render her impotent by instructing council to ignore her? She had no means by which to fight, and no stomach for further humiliation at Dan Rossi's hands. But what of Callie, her conscience nagged, and Ms. Evelyn, and the flock of people who'd waited for her in the rain on Fourth Street?

The ringing of the phone was a harsh intrusion. She managed to get into the hallway by the fourth ring and leaned back against the wall as she lifted the receiver.

"Mrs. Moran?" the vaguely familiar voice of a woman inquired tentatively.

"Yes . . ."

"This is Veronica. Veronica Spicata, from personnel . . ."

"Oh, Veronica, of course. How are you?" she asked, puzzled at the unexpected call.

"I'm fine." Veronica snapped her gum. "Listen, Mrs. Moran, it's none of my business, but are you really sick?"

"Of course I'm really sick," Athen replied, slightly offended. "I caught a really nasty cold last week . . ."

"Oh, good . . ." sighed Veronica, the relief apparent. "I'm so glad that it's true . . ."

"You're glad what's true?" Totally confused, Athen wondered where this call was leading.

"That you're really sick, and that's why you're not here," Veronica explained.

"Why else would I be home?" Athen slid down the wall to seat herself upon the floor.

"Well, I had heard that you were sick, then I heard that maybe you weren't sick, and then they started setting up for the press conference in the big council room just now . . ."

"Who is setting up a press conference?" Athen was suddenly all ears.

"That creep, Wolmar . . . It's going to be televised live at noon, I heard, so I just wondered," Veronica came right to the point, "if you'd been dumped. You sure set off a lot of people last week."

"Yes, I suppose I did." Athen avoided a direct response. "I did not know about the press conference, but I will certainly tune in. I'm as curious as you are to see what Mr. Wolmar has on his mind today."

"I sort of figured you didn't know." Veronica snapped her gum again. "But I thought maybe you should."

"I appreciate that," Athen told her sincerely, then added, "I should be back in another day or so."

"I'm glad to hear that, Mrs. Moran," replied Veronica, then abruptly said, "I, um, have to hang up now."

"Thank you for calling," Athen said to the dial tone.

She remained on the floor for a very long minute, then hung up the receiver and returned to the bedroom to look at the clock. 11:52. The press conference would start in eight minutes. She grabbed a pillow and walked unsteadily down the steps—Hannah, as ever, at her heels—to the living room where she turned on the TV. Having several minutes to spare, she went into the kitchen. The cupboard being essentially bare, she grabbed another orange and a handful of napkins. She had just plunked herself on the sofa and wrapped herself in a soft white afghan when the noontime news began.

". . . bringing you live coverage of the press conference that is scheduled to begin momentarily here at Woodside Heights City Hall. It appears that Councilman Jim Wolmar has called the conference, Mayor Moran being on an indefinite sick leave . . ." the pert little blond reporter noted.

Indefinite sick leave? Athen's jaw dropped.

". . . it looks like Councilman Wolmar is about to begin . . ."

"I'd like to thank you all for attending on such short notice," he greeted the throng of reporters who sat before him and smiled benevolently for the cameras. "I just thought that the city's business should continue as usual in spite of Mrs. Moran's absence . . ."

"What is the nature of Mayor Moran's absence, Mr. Wolmar?" an unidentifiable voice asked.

"I believe she has a cold, Miss Sharpless." He smiled at the TV reporter, his offhanded manner implying that a mere cold was a pretty shaky excuse for a week's absence. "But, of course, the business of the city goes on, and I just thought you'd appreciate an update on council's efforts to increase the size of the police department . . ."

Athen sat mesmerized by his performance. He was perfectly at ease in her role, she realized. He's relishing every minute, the scoundrel. She scanned the small sea of reporters who were taking their turns asking questions . . . how many new officers? Rookies, or will they be taking applications from veterans of other forces? How many of the new officers would be assigned to the downtown area, where crime was ever on the rise?

"Has Mayor Moran recommended the increase in the force?"

She leaned forward towards the screen. She knew that voice . . .

"Mrs. Moran was not present when the motion came before council, Mr. Forbes," Jim replied, adding, "and not knowing when we'd see her again, we thought it best to proceed without her."

"Mr. Wolmar, has council addressed Mayor Moran's recommendation relative to the UCC's request for the buildings on Fourth Street?" Quentin stood in the first row, a small notebook in his hand.

"Mr. Forbes, Mrs. Moran has made no formal recommendation to council on that issue." Wolmar's sly smile made her stomach turn. "Nor for that matter, on any other issue since she took office."

Ignoring the obvious insult to Athen, Quentin persisted.

"Councilman, Mayor Moran gave every indication that the city was willing to work in concert with the UCC . . ."

"Mrs. Moran has, regrettably, acted well beyond the scope of her authority. May I remind you, Mr. Forbes, only council is authorized to dispose of or transfer title of any city-owned property. And it will take a majority vote on council to approve any such motion, a majority, I feel confident in saying, Mrs. Moran will not have, even should she succeed in having the issue formally presented to council. And, as I'm sure you know, only a member of council may introduce an issue for discussion and vote. Since Mrs. Moran has no support on council, it is highly unlikely this matter will go any farther than it already has."

"Why unlikely? It would appear the plans for the shelter have been well-received throughout the community," Quentin pressed.

"It has no support on council, Mr. Forbes," Wolmar stated emphatically. He appeared to be done with the matter, but could not resist one final jab. "Mrs. Moran has, unfortunately, needlessly raised the hopes and expectations of the kind-hearted and well-intentioned, and she has done so publicly. It could be said that she has, as the expression goes, stepped in it. Yes, Mr. Rand, you had a question?"

Athen's face flushed scarlet with rage, her eyes stinging from the effort it took to blink back the tears of anger and humiliation. She pushed the anger back, forcing herself to continue to watch the screen.

"What is council's main objection to the UCC proposal?"

"I think that's a fair question, deserving of a straightforward answer, sir." Jim flashed his best campaign smile. "Council is, I should tell you, in the process of studying a highly intriguing option for that piece of property. Now, keep in mind that, taken as a whole, the city owns several blocks in that area. The proposal we're looking at would increase revenues to the city by adding to its tax base, not drain the city's already limited resources, as Mrs. Moran would do."

"Can you give us some further information . . . ?"

"I feel—that is, council feels—it would be premature to make any announcement at this time. But rest assured, ladies and gentlemen, as soon as there is something more concrete to disclose, you will all be fully advised."

"Who is behind this other option?"

"Excuse me, Mr. Forbes?" Wolmar visibly bristled, his brows forming one straight line across his forehead as he leaned forward on the podium, peering down imperiously at the source of the irritation.

"I said, who has proposed the option that you mentioned?" Quentin's eyes narrowed as he studied Wolmar's expression and awaited a response.

"Why, city council, Mr. Forbes."

"Who, specifically . . ." Quentin repeated, only to have Wolmar turn his back on the pretext of giving his attention to the next question.

By this time Athen was on the floor directly in front of the television, fists clenched as tightly as her jaws, cursing alternatively in Greek and English, as she watched Wolmar slide oh-so-smoothly into her domain. The conference was coming to a close, and for just a few seconds the camera lingered on the front row. Quentin Forbes was slowly returning his pen to his pocket, his eyes following Wolmar, his expression deadly. It was the first time she had seen him turn that icy gaze on anyone but herself. It gave her the morning's only pleasure to know that Wolmar was its recipient.

26

She had meant to take a shower, had meant to go back upstairs, but she got stuck on the sofa, busy licking the wounds Wolmar had inflicted upon her and wondering how she would show her face at city hall now that he had announced her folly to the entire city. She worried over which part the evening news would dwell on—would they run and rerun the part where Wolmar had reminded everyone that she, as mayor, had no authority to commit city-owned property, or the part about how she had been irresponsible to the fine folks who had been duped by her into believing that the long-awaited shelter might in fact become a reality.

And what of tomorrow's papers? She could barely wait to see Quentin's article. He'd have a field day with her, she was certain. Her cheeks flamed as though the fever had returned, and she began to feel extremely sorry for herself. She sat and cried her eyes out until she heard Callie come in through the back door.

"Mom, I'm . . . hey, great, you're downstairs. You must be feeling better. Did you watch TV?" She threw her books on the nearest chair. "Were you crying? Your eyes are all red."

"No, of course not," Athen lied, "it's just from the cold."

"I don't remember them being so red this morning," Callie said, frowning.

"They weren't open so long this morning," her mother insisted.

"If you say so." Callie shrugged and went into the kitchen for a snack. She returned with a glass of milk in one hand

and an apple in the other. "Since you're feeling better, do you think I could go over to Nina's for a while? I missed a lot in French the past few days and there's a big test tomorrow. Nina said we could study together and she could help me with the stuff I missed . . ."

"Certainly. Go." Athen nodded.

"Will you be okay?"

"I've been fine all day," insisted Athen, "almost good as new."

"Not till you've had a shower and changed that nightshirt," Callie reminded her with a grin. "I think you've had that old yellow nightshirt on since last week."

"No, I have not." Athen laughed.

"Okay, since the weekend, then. In any event, it's time for a change, Mom." Callie grabbed her bookbag and leaned over her mother to kiss her on the forehead. "I'm real glad you're feeling better. Did you take your medicine at three like you were supposed to?"

"Actually, I did not," a sheepish Athen admitted. "I'd left them upstairs . . ."

Callie ran up the steps and was back down in a flash with two white bottles of prescribed tablets in her hand. She deposited them on the table next to her mother, then went into the kitchen for a glass of water.

"Take them now," she instructed, and Athen obediently dumped one of each into the palm of her hand. "I'll be at Nina's if you need me . . . oh, and Mrs. Kelly said she'd drop off some more soup later . . ."

"Bless Mrs. Kelly for the kind soul she is." Athen leaned back once more, and listened as the back door opened, Hannah came back in from her excursion, and Callie slammed the door on her way out. Hannah frolicked into the living room and attempted to climb up onto the sofa with her mistress.

"No way, lumpasaurus." Thwarted, Hannah had to be content to lay on the floor alongside the sofa.

After staring mindlessly at the ceiling for a few minutes, Athen picked up the remote control and turned on the TV. Reruns. Talk shows. Ditzy commercials. She turned it off and thought about the shower she so badly needed. Now's as good a time as any, she told herself, and started up the stairs.

She'd gotten almost to the top step when she heard a knock on the door. Hannah flew into the hallway, barking wildly.

The knocking persisted. Oh, of course. Mrs. Kelly . . .

One hand on Hannah's collar and one hand on the doorknob, Athen pulled the door open. On the top step stood, not the expected elderly Mrs. Kelly holding a pot of soup, but the totally unexpected Mr. Forbes holding a large bouquet of multicolored flowers.

"I, ah, brought you some flowers." He smiled somewhat weakly.

She leaned back against the door, hoping its wooden panels could absorb the shock.

"Get well flowers," he continued, holding out the bouquet to her.

"Why?" Flowers from the man who had made crucifying her his life's work?

"May I come in?" he asked, ignoring her question.

"Well, actually, no, Quentin . . ." She was in no frame of mind to spar with him.

He stepped into the small hallway as if he'd not heard her. Wide-eyed, she backed away from him as if he was visibly poxed.

"These should probably go in water . . ." He made a concentrated effort to disguise his amusement as he eyed her disheveled appearance. She blushed scarlet as she recalled she was barely dressed and smelled like a barnyard.

"Thank you, Quentin . . ." She held her hands out to take the bouquet, hoping he would accept her thanks and then leave. She should have known better.

"Where would I find a vase?" The slightest smile played at the corners of his mouth as he glanced down at her bare feet, half a leg away from her bare knees. One foot instinctively slid atop the other.

"Quentin, that won't be necessary," she protested to his back as he walked past her, stopping to let Hannah sniff his hand. The dog wagged her tail approvingly.

"Really, Quentin, I can . . ."

"Nonsense. You've been sick. Go sit down. Here? In the kitchen?" He'd led himself into the next room, a large mound of yellow fur sashaying merrily behind him.

"Traitor," Athen grumbled as Hannah's wagging behind disappeared through the doorway.

"What?" he called to her from the kitchen. She heard the water running in the sink.

"Second cupboard from the back door." She threw up her hands and returned to the sofa, painfully aware that she looked like an unmade bed. At least she could hide under the afghan, but there was absolutely nothing she could do about the unkempt web of hair that hung over her shoulders and halfway down her back in thick dark clumps. She fought an urge to pull the blanket over her head.

"Where would you like them?" Quentin returned to the living room, the flowers harbored in a pale green vase.

"Anywhere . . . here, how 'bout on the table here?" she gestured and he placed the vase as she directed.

"So." He seemed a bit uncomfortable, standing as he was in the middle of the living room floor while she lounged like Cleopatra on the sofa. "Those are beautiful paintings. The flowers look almost real. Who was the artist?" He walked across the room for a closer look. "A.S.M. Did you paint these?"

"Yes, I . . ."

"They're wonderful. I had no idea that you painted."

"I don't. I mean, I used to, but I haven't in a long time."

"You should start again. These are lovely. The shading is exquisite, and the colors are . . ."

"Thank you, Quentin. Now if you don't mind . . ."

He snapped his fingers. "I almost forgot . . . I'll be right back . . ."

What was he up to now, she wondered, as she heard him leave the house, only to return in a flash with a brown paper bag.

"I thought it would be nice if we could visit over a cup of coffee." He opened the bag without looking at her. Pulling the small table to a spot located midway between them, he placed a cardboard cup in front of her and dumped small white containers of cream onto the table. "How do you like yours?"

"Light with half a sweetener . . ." She stared at him suspiciously as he prepared it to her preference, then opened the second cup and poured in some cream, all the while acting as nonchalant as you please.

"Okay, Quentin, what gives?" she asked pointedly.

"I just thought I'd stop by and see how you were." He flashed a double dose of dimples to disarm her.

"Since when has it mattered to you how I am?" She ignored his attempt to be irresistible, trying to figure out the motive which prompted this inexplicable visit. "And flowers? Don't you think that's a bit much?"

"Actually . . . well, it's the only way I could think of to apologize." He affected what he thought to be a penitent pose.

"Apologize?" Her eyebrows climbed halfway up her forehead. Had she heard correctly?

"I have been every bit as much of a . . . what was that Greek name you called me that day in the car?"

"Malaka?" Amused in spite of herself, she leaned back against the sofa.

"Yes. *Malaka.* A jerk. I have been a jerk," he told her with the utmost sincerity.

"Do tell." She tapped her fingers on the side of her coffee container, avoiding direct eye contact. He was not, she had to admit, without a certain charm.

"Athen, may I sit down?" he asked, and she gestured towards the chair across the room. He took the one nearest the sofa.

"Rossi's after you, Athen," he declared frankly.

"No?!" She feigned surprise. "Why, thank you, Quentin, for tipping me off."

"I mean it, Athen. He had Wolmar call a press conference this morning . . ." He leaned forward as if sharing a secret.

"I saw it," she told him, "someone called to tell me . . ."

"Who?" he asked.

"A friend in city hall." She sipped at her coffee, grateful

to Veronica that she need not be beholden to Quentin for the news.

"I didn't think you had any friends in city hall," he said bluntly, "not after that dog and pony show I witnessed this morning."

"So you thought you'd stop over here and be the first to get my reaction." She bit her bottom lip. At least now she knew why he was really here. "Wouldn't that add a nice touch to tomorrow's story . . . ?"

"No, Athen, I didn't come for a story." He put his cup down on the table.

"Then why are you here?" She crossed her arms in front of her chest, unable to resist adding a touch of cynicism.

"I wanted to tell you that I'm sorry." His gaze was steady, his voice hypnotically soft and completely sincere. "Because you told me the truth and I didn't believe you."

"Why would you believe me now?" Sipping from her cup, she attempted to resist the spell cast by his eyes.

"Rossi had Wolmar call that press conference for the express purpose of letting everyone know you are on Rossi's shit list," he told her solemnly.

"I know that." She jutted her chin out just a bit, refusing to hang her head in his presence.

"Why?" He swished his coffee round and round in the bottom of its container, but did not take his eyes from her face.

"What difference does it make?" she asked warily.

"Was it because of what you did last week?"

"It would appear so."

"I'm so sorry," he said gently.

"You're sorry he's trying to push me out?" She remained unconvinced of the purity of his motives, and could not resist playing as hard with him as he once had with her.

"I'm sorry because you don't deserve what they did to you today."

"But I deserved all the crap you've been throwing at me all these months," she snapped indignantly.

"That was different," he replied.

"Oh, of course. Your motives were strictly professional

. . . the journalist's right to know." She drew a sharp breath. "Whereas Wolmar blatantly intended to cut me off at the knees. Is that what you see as the difference?"

"Athen, I never intended to hurt you personally," he protested.

"Yes, you did, Quentin, every bit as much as Jim did. Only he's a hired gun . . ." She paused to cough, and he handed her the water glass which sat at the far end of the table. "At least I know why he's after me. I never understood why you were."

They stared each other down for a very long moment.

Finally, he said, "For a long time I really believed that you were part of it. Now I know better. And . . . well, I guess it bothered me that you were involved with Rossi."

"Why?" she demanded. "Why would you care?"

"Because it wasn't what I wanted you to be . . . I know I had no right to feel that way, but I wanted you to be the woman I thought you were when I first met you . . . if that makes any sense at all to you." He held his hands out in front of him as he sought to explain.

"What was it you thought me to be?" she asked.

"Sweet. Honest. Straightforward. Intelligent. Beautiful." He hesitated momentarily, embarrassed to have said more than he'd intended.

She stole a sideward glance at his face, seeking a sign of guile. She found none.

His chin leaned upon the fists of both hands, his elbows resting on his knees. "Can you forgive me for thinking you were a . . ."

". . . a political whore?" She squared her shoulders and completed the sentence for him.

He winced at the memory of having called her exactly that. "For all the things I thought you were since you took this job."

"Can you promise never to make a fool out of me again?" she asked pointedly.

"Athen, a reporter doesn't make the news. If you stand up at an open meeting and make statements that indicate you don't have the faintest idea of what's going on, how can I ignore it?" he said, challenging her sense of fair play.

For the first time it dawned on her that if he had made a fool out of her, it had been because her own actions had made it so easy for him to do so.

"That will not happen again," she vowed firmly.

"Then you have nothing to worry about as far as *The Woodside Herald* is concerned." He smiled gently. "I promise to be fair to you if you will be honest with me. And if you will forgive me for . . . well, for everything. Do we have a deal?"

She nodded, understanding that a truce of sorts had been called, though uncertain if she'd made a friend or made a pact with the devil.

"Well," he said to break the silence, "are you going to let Rossi push you out?"

"I don't want to make any statements . . ." She shook her head.

"No, no," he assured her, "strictly off the record. This is friend to friend now."

"I can't stop him if he wants me out, Quentin." She shrugged.

"You can refuse to go." Blue eyes studied her intently.

"To what end?"

"If nothing more, to be as big a pain in his butt as he is in everyone else's." He smiled wryly.

"I don't know that it's worth the humiliation . . ." Athen shook her head slowly.

"What happens if you resign?" he wondered aloud.

"You saw it this morning."

"Wolmar?" He frowned. "I guess that follows."

Quentin's eyes lingered on the photos Callie had placed on the mantel. Callie and John. John in his uniform. Athen holding a newborn Callie, John standing by proudly . . .

"What?" she asked, wondering what he was thinking.

"What? Oh, I don't know." He smiled. "I guess in a way, I'm disappointed."

"About what?"

"That you're giving up so easily. That you're giving in . . ."

"Why, because you won't have old Athena to kick around anymore?" She tried to make a halfhearted joke.

"Hey, a good reporter doesn't care who he kicks around," he quipped. "Actually, I guess I expected you to fight him."

"Fight a man I can't beat to keep a job I don't want? I don't see any logic in that." She dismissed the possibility with a wave of her hand.

"Would you want it if it was real?" His eyes narrowed.

"You mean if Rossi didn't hold this city in his iron grip and I could do things the way I wanted to?"

"Something like that." He had become thoughtful again. "It's an unlikely scenario."

The slamming of the back door announced Callie's arrival home.

"Mom . . . oh, Mr. Forbes. Hi." She stopped dead in the doorway, as surprised to see him as her mother had been.

"Callie, good to see you." He smiled his best smile.

Callie looked warily around the room. "Is Timmy . . ."

"Nah." Quentin's eyes danced. "The little geek is riding this afternoon at my mother's."

"Riding?" Callie asked.

"Horseback riding," Quentin explained. "My mother and stepfather have quite a stable. Say, maybe some afternoon you might like to . . ."

"I don't think so," Callie said pointedly, and Quentin laughed good-naturedly.

"Callie, you're being rude," her mother whispered.

"It's okay," Quentin assured her, "but the offer is always open, Callie."

"Thanks anyway, Mr. Forbes." Callie stood looking at them from the doorway.

Quentin took the hint.

"Well, I should be getting back to work." He rose from his seat. "Athen, I'm glad you're feeling better."

"I am, thanks." She debated whether or not to walk him to the door. She recalled suddenly how she was dressed, what she must look like, and decided to stay put.

"I can find my way out." He smiled, as if reading her mind.

"Thank you for the flowers." She found herself looking up at him, unable to look away. "And for the apology."

He appeared about to say something more, then glanced at Callie, standing like a sentinel at the entrance to the front hallway.

"Well," Quentin said, "I guess I'll be talking to you . . . bye, Callie . . ."

Callie closed the door behind him.

"Why was he here?" she demanded.

"He brought me flowers," Athen told her, trying to appear nonchalant.

"Why?"

"It's customary to bring flowers to friends when they're sick."

"Since when has Mr. Forbes been your friend?" Callie asked suspiciously.

Athen barely heard her, suddenly lost in thought.

"And what did he have to apologize to you for?" Callie pressed.

"For being wrong about something." Athen smiled to herself.

"What was he wrong about?"

"Me." He was wrong about me and he admitted it. And, will wonders never cease . . . the man brought me flowers . . .

"Sometimes grown-ups make no sense," Callie muttered as she went to answer the front door where Mrs. Kelly waited to make her soup delivery.

27

Athen had thought she'd try to make it into the office the next day, but at dawn found herself still too weak to get up and get dressed. She decided to take one more day off—it's not as if I have piles of work to do when I get back, she noted grimly. Chances are Edie's taking the mail home to Dan anyway . . .

Around noon she showered and dressed in jeans and a chambray shirt, ate a leisurely lunch, and decided to spend some time with her father.

The day was warm and clear, a perfect early April afternoon. She rolled the windows down and breathed in the sweetly scented breeze as she drove through the park. Pulling into the lot behind Woodside Manor, she searched for a spot under the trees. Walking towards the building, she could see Diana Bennett's red sports car up close to the front walk. She glanced at her watch. Diana's lunch hour would be almost over. She would wait, and leave her father alone with his beloved for the short time they had to spend together. She walked to the pond and sat down on the bench to kill some time.

A group of small children—a nursery school class, perhaps—was gathered on the opposite side of the pond. Laughing with delight, they tossed pieces of bread to the ducks, which swam ever closer to the shore. She thought of the day last summer, when she had stood right in that same spot, and Quentin had come from nowhere, a bag of popcorn to share with his feathered friends. She had liked him that day, had liked his easy smile and his affability.

She had thought about him a great deal since his visit the previous afternoon. Once she had been able to admit that it had been she who had set herself up to look like an idiot—and that Quentin, while perhaps the most persistent, had not been the only newsperson to recognize her blunders—she could no longer hold him responsible for a situation she had created. It's always easier to find someone else to blame, she acknowledged, than to admit that the blame lies within ourselves. Maybe I should be thanking him, she mused, since it was his harassment that prodded me into wanting to be more informed. And just look where that's gotten me, she ruefully reminded herself . . .

"Athen?" Diana had driven almost past the pond when she'd seen the young woman on the bench. Athen waved a friendly greeting.

Diana parked the car and walked to the pond on high navy leather heels which clicked on the asphalt. She wore a navy linen suit with a silk shirt the color of wheat, like her hair. As always, Diana looked like she'd stepped from the pages of a magazine.

"How are you?" Athen asked as Diana approached on the bench.

"How are *you* is the question," Diana removed her sunglasses.

"I'm better," Athen told her truthfully. "I think I'll be back tomorrow."

"I'm glad to hear it, and Ari will be greatly relieved," Diana told her. "He's really been quite concerned about you . . . your health, and of course, everything else that's going on . . ."

"How can you tell?" Athen asked.

"We communicate quite well, your father and I." Diana smiled. "I read the paper with him every evening. It's not difficult to tell when he's upset, when he's amused . . . it's all in his eyes."

"I'm glad I decided to come out today, then," Athen said half-aloud, "I wouldn't want him to worry about me."

"I think he's more concerned about what Rossi is doing," Diana told her. "Ari'd wring his neck if he could . . ."

"That's so sad, after all the years they were such close friends . . ." It was so depressing to think that she was the cause of her father's ill feelings towards his old companion.

"Who were such close friends?" Diana asked.

"My dad and Dan." Athen ground the heel of one sneakered foot into the stones at the base of the bench.

"Where did you ever get that idea?" Diana laughed scornfully.

"Why, Dad's known him forever. They served on council together . . . they campaigned for each other . . ." recited Athen.

"All true. But whoever told you that they were friends?"

"Why, Dan did. And I can remember Dan coming to the hospital the night my father had the stroke . . ."

"That S.O.B. just couldn't wait to see if it was really true," Diana growled.

"What do you mean?" a confused Athen asked.

"Athen, your father's stroke was the best thing that ever happened to Dan Rossi," Diana replied bitterly.

"I don't understand . . ."

"Ari worked with Dan for years, but they hated each other. Your father ranked Dan right up there with Mussolini and Vlad the Impaler."

"What?" Athen's eyes widened with shock. "Why?"

"Athen, Ari always knew Dan took kickbacks, but he could never prove it. But there's no question your father was on to something else right before he had the stroke," Diana related bluntly.

"I can't believe this . . ." Athen gasped.

"Oh, it's true enough. The last conversation I had with Ari on the day he had the first stroke was at about nine A.M. He was railing about something Dan had done, and said he was meeting with him later in the morning and that he would put a stop to it." Diana searched through her purse and pulled out a pack of cigarettes.

"Put a stop to what?"

"I haven't the faintest idea." Diana lit the cigarette with trembling hands. "I wish I did. I knew Ari was watching him—Dan knew it too—and whatever it was that set your father off that day must have happened early on."

"He didn't give you any clue?"

"He didn't have a chance." Diana exhaled sharply. "At one o'clock I got a call that he'd been rushed to the hospital."

"What did he say, that morning on the phone, do you remember?" Athen prodded.

"Of course. He said, 'I see he's gone too far this time.' Then he said he had arranged to meet with Dan and that he'd tell me about it over dinner." She flicked a long ash to the ground and watched a light breeze carry it to the edge of the pond.

"Why didn't you tell me this before? Before I got into this mess with Rossi?" Athen was horrified.

"I don't recall your having asked for my advice," Diana reminded her pointedly.

"And why would Dan even want me around, if he and my dad hated each other so?" pondered Athen as she sought to make sense of Diana's revelation.

"You have to be kidding?" Diana laughed. "My dear

Athen, you were the perfect choice. Widow of the city's own dead hero. Daughter of the city's most popular council member. And politically naive to boot . . . You weren't even aware that your own father wanted to bring Dan down. And who else could have held the line on the restless Greek vote?"

"I wish I'd known . . ." Athen closed her eyes, thinking of how her father must have felt, forced to watch in silence as his beloved daughter made camp with the enemy. "I'll bet it just about killed Dad to have me so close to Dan for the past six months . . ."

"It did, but he's kept an eye on you," Diana assured her. "We both have. And I have to tell you how proud he is that you finally defied Dan. I think Ari knew all along it was only a matter of time before you caught on to him."

"How does he know?"

"We watched the noontime news last week, we saw you with Ms. Evelyn. You should have seen your father's eyes, watching you." Diana smiled. "It was the best therapy he could possibly have . . ."

"How could Dad have known that Dan had told me . . ."

"Not to go? It was obvious. Dan has been sitting on those properties for three years now. If they weren't important to him somehow, he'd have given them to the UCC himself, if for no other reason than for the publicity."

"I wonder what it could be," Athen thought aloud.

"Whatever it is, Dan will profit mightily from it, you can be sure of that," Diana said. "Well, maybe in time you can flush him out."

"What do you mean, in time? I'm out of time," Athen stated flatly.

"Athen, you have over a year left on your term," reminded Diana.

Athen averted her gaze to the ducks who dove for treats pitched by the children across the pond.

"Has he threatened you?" Diana demanded.

"Not with bodily harm, if that's what you mean. But he has made it clear that I'll be nothing more than his whipping post till the primary."

"Tell me what you plan to do now." Leaning back against

the bench, Diana crossed first her arms, then her legs, a shoe slipping off to dangle from the toes of one foot.

"I don't see where I have any option but to go to Ms. Evelyn and tell her I can't help her . . ."

"You mean back down? Let Rossi toss you out like last week's papers?" Diana stood up, hands on her hips.

"I don't see where I have a choice . . ."

"That's just what he wants you to think. Don't let him do that to you, Athen," pleaded Diana.

"Diana, Wolmar's right. Only council can direct the title transfer. I acted stupidly . . ."

"Then put the issue on the back burner until you have enough votes in your pocket to win," Diana snapped.

"Are you crazy? I have no votes. Dan has all the votes." How could someone so politically astute be so blind to the obvious?

"Not necessarily," Diana replied with a level gaze.

"How do you figure?"

"It takes a majority to pass a motion. Four council votes, the mayor votes in the case of a tie, right?"

"There wouldn't be a tie, Diana." Athen fought to control the exasperation welling up within her.

"You concede too quickly," Diana insisted.

"Diana, I wouldn't have one vote . . ."

"Of course you would. Konstantos is first a Greek—his first loyalty is to Ari, and therefore to you," Diana pointed out.

"Even if that's true, that's one vote."

"Athen." Diana sat back down and looked at her point-blank. "It's time you learned to play the game."

"I don't know if I want to play the game."

"That's exactly what Dan is counting on. Turn up the heat and you'll run from the kitchen. Don't give him that satisfaction." Diana's index finger tapped Athen's arm.

"What would you do?" Athen leaned one elbow on the back of the bench and turned sideways to face the blond woman.

"I'd play from my strength," Diana told her, as if stating the obvious.

"I have no strength," laughed Athen ruefully.

"You have one definite ally in Konstantos. One potential one." Diana held up two fingers.

"Who . . . ?" puzzled Athen.

"Riley Fallon," Diana announced.

"How do you figure? Dan himself appointed Fallon to council after Bill Saunders died. I can't think of any power on this earth that could turn Riley against Dan."

"Then perhaps you'll have to appeal to an unearthly power." Diana grinned.

"You mean pray?"

"Athen, Riley Fallon is engaged to Georgia Davison," Diana told her with emphasis on the woman's last name.

"So?" Athen asked blankly.

"Georgia's father is the Reverend Davison. Of the AME Church of the Brethren." Diana paused meaningfully.

"Okay, I see the connection with the church, but I can't call Reverend Davison and say I need the vote of your future son-in-law if you want that shelter . . ."

"Of course not. You wouldn't be that obvious." Diana smiled. "You would go to Ms. Evelyn—who of course is a member of Reverend Davison's church—and you tell her how sorry you are that you will be unable to deliver those properties to the UCC. You tell her you simply don't have the votes, that you need at least one more and you just can't see how that will happen . . ."

"Assuming that I was interested in doing this, what good would that do?"

"Ms. Evelyn is a highly creative lady," Diana assured her, "and she's not likely to sit by idly while her vision of a shelter is in jeopardy. She'll think of something."

"You think she could?"

"There's no doubt in my mind . . . think it over, Athen, what have you got to lose?" Diana looked at her watch, "Good grief, I'm a half hour late. Go see Ari, Athen, but don't let him suspect for a minute you would let Rossi back you down. Give me a call, we'll talk more if you like . . ."

"Pateras," she said as she entered the cool room, and he followed her with anxious eyes which scanned her face and mirrored his deep concern for her.

"I'm sorry I haven't been to see you for a while, Papa, but I caught a devil of a cold wandering around Fourth Street in the rain last week. I'm much better today," she told him. "Papa, Dan is very angry with me for going there, and for saying I thought the shelter should be permitted, but it was worth it. It was the right thing to do. And maybe, just maybe, between now and next year, I can make something good out of this mess I've gotten into."

She took his hands and held them, looking into his eyes and seeing worry fade and pride take its place.

"Diana thinks I can do it, Papa . . . She's helping me sort things out." She bit her lip, not bothering to blink back the tears she knew would soon begin to fall. "I wish I'd known her all these years, Papa . . . She is so clever, and so wonderful. I know now why you love her so . . . and I am more sorry than I can tell you for not making it easier for you. Please forgive me . . . It should never have taken this long for Diana and me to be friends. We both love you so much . . ."

Father and daughter sat silently, both in tears, both in total understanding of one another. It had been a long time since they had been in such accord, and Athen berated herself for denying them both this closeness. Diana had been right. It was all in Ari's eyes.

"And something else, Papa," she told him as she wiped first his wet face and then her own, "if I had known about Dan, I never would have gotten into this . . ."

Ari's eyes narrowed at the sound of his old enemy's name.

"Diana told me that . . . that there'd been problems between you and Dan, but he never let on . . . I guess he thought if I didn't know, it would serve his purposes just fine," she thought aloud, still digesting this recent news. "I wish I knew what you know . . . I wish you could tell me. But maybe, before all this is over, maybe we can piece it together, Diana and I." She smiled broadly. "And wouldn't that be something, Ari's girls ganging up on Dan to bring him down . . ."

Ari's eyes filled with anxiety.

"No, Papa, don't worry," she quickly assured him, "we

will be very careful, I promise. I may have been very foolish over the past few months, but I promise, I will be very cautious."

She deliberately changed the subject then, bringing him up to date on Callie's latest scholastic and athletic accomplishments. Before long she found herself talking about Quentin, how confused she was about him, how a part of her wanted to trust him, and yet at the same time, feared the hand offered in friendship might be a ruse to use her, as Dan had, for his own purposes. On the one hand, she told her father, she respected Quentin—he had, after all, come to her to apologize, and when pressed, he told her very honestly he could not promise to never write an unfavorable story about her. If he'd been trying to win her trust at any cost, would he not have simply agreed to write only articles that would cast her in a favorable light? It could all be so confusing sometimes, she confided, knowing who and what to take chances on.

"In case you are wondering," she told him as she was leaving, "I will be back in my office tomorrow morning. My office, Papa. And if Dan wants me out of there before next year, he will have to take it from me . . ."

28

Athen dressed more carefully than usual the next morning, deciding on a black and white linen dress and high black leather heels which made her appear even taller than she was. She slipped on large gold button earrings, and her gold watch. Standing back to inspect her appearance, she tried to put her finger on what, exactly, was wrong with the picture.

"It's the hair," she said aloud, standing in front of her dresser mirror. "I have too much hair. Long and straight may be fine for Callie, but it doesn't do much for me."

She tried wrapping it in a bun, but there was simply too

much of it. Never having been much of a hair stylist, she was all thumbs, but eventually decided to braid it and wrap the long braid at the nape of her neck.

"Not perfect," she told herself, "but neater . . . and certainly more professional."

She was in the building by eight o'clock, at her desk with coffee she'd prepared by 8:10, long before anyone else would arrive. As she'd suspected, the mail, which should have been piled ceiling high after a week's absence, was nowhere to be seen. Her desk was perfectly clean, and she steamed with every minute that passed until Edie arrived at 9:30.

Hearing Edie's banter with Rose at the other end of the hall, Athen went to the door of her office and leaned back against it.

"Good morning, Edie." She forced herself to be pleasant.

"Oh, Athen . . ." The secretary was visibly rattled to see her. "What are you . . . I mean, when did you . . ."

"Yes, I'm much better, thank you, and it's good to be back." Athen attempted to smile though her jaws were clenched. "Edie, where's the mail?"

"The mail?" Edie repeated nervously.

"My mail, Edie, the mail which comes addressed to this office every day . . ."

"I—I took the mail home . . . to answer it for you . . ." the woman stammered.

"Then I trust you brought it back." Athen fixed her gaze on Edie's face, which had developed a sudden tic of sorts.

"I . . . no . . . I guess I forgot it . . ."

"Then I guess you'll have to go home to get it." Athen turned towards her office with much greater confidence than she felt. "I'll just be in here waiting, Edie. It shouldn't take you more than, what, twenty minutes, thirty at the most, to bring it back . . ."

Athen closed the door behind her, congratulating herself on her performance. She glanced at her watch. By now Edie would be in Jim Wolmar's office, calling Dan and asking him what to do. And what instructions would he give her . . . Ignore Athen? Tell her it was stolen? Tell her the truth?

Athen began to pace. She wanted to call Ms. Evelyn, wanted to sit down and talk to her as soon as possible. Of course, Dan would know immediately—Edie would make sure of that the minute Ms. Evelyn arrived and the door closed behind them. Maybe I should call her now, and meet with her tonight . . . but if she's not there and I have to leave a message, Edie will answer the phone when she calls back and report the call . . . Damn, Athen all but exploded, this is ridiculous. I have a secretary who is working for the enemy, who will without doubt be reporting every move I make . . . just as she has been doing all along.

She sat down at her desk and tapped a thoughtful finger on the leather blotter. Maybe it's time Edie got a transfer . . .

Searching her desk for the inter-office phone list, she scanned the names and circled the number she was seeking. She lifted the receiver and dialed.

"Veronica? This is Athen Moran . . . Much better, thank you." Athen smiled and leaned back in her chair. "Veronica, I want you to clean your desk of all your personal belongings and come up here as soon as possible . . . Of course you're not being fired. You've just been promoted . . ."

Edie had squawked like a wounded crow when she'd arrived upstairs—without the mail—to find her things in a box on a chair near the elevator and Veronica happily unpacking her family photos at Edie's old desk. She'd been even more incensed when Athen told her she'd arranged for Edie's transfer to the Public Works garage, where she'd have a nice desk right next to the storage room. Edie stomped and cursed and ran, no doubt, directly to Dan. Athen wondered how long it would take before the phone rang . . .

Exactly seven minutes had passed before Veronica appeared in the doorway to announce that Dan was on the phone, and "he don't sound happy."

"Good morning, Dan," she said evenly, hoping to hang on to the confidence she'd felt since she'd awakened that day.

"You think Edie's the only person I have to rely on?" he skipped the pleasantries and cut to the chase.

"Certainly not," she replied calmly, "but at least now I know I'll get my phone calls and my mail . . ."

He laughed. "It won't be that easy, Athen . . ."

"I don't expect it to be easy, Dan."

"Pack it up, Athen, there's nothing for you in city hall," he taunted, "and just what do you think you're going to accomplish, besides pissing me off even more than you already have. I'd quit while I'm ahead, if I were you . . ."

"Mary Jo Dolan." She took a deep breath and went for the throat.

"What about her?" he asked cautiously after a long moment had passed.

"By noon today I want her car keys on my desk." Closing her eyes, she took another deep breath. "And I want her at her desk in personnel at 12:03."

She waited. There was no pretense offered. It was clear he knew exactly what keys to which car she had referred.

"What do you intend to do?" Momentarily thrown off guard at the unexpected sound of the girl's name, he attempted to affect a jaunty manner.

"I haven't had time to think about it," she told him with more nonchalance than she felt. She was still waiting for the other shoe to drop, as she knew eventually it would.

"I would suggest you think very long and very hard, Athena. You may well be lighting a fire you will be unable to put out." The menace was undisguised.

"By noon, Dan," she repeated coolly, "and certainly the city will expect to be reimbursed for the premiums paid out for this vehicle's insurance for the past four years, as well as the mileage." She mentally patted herself on the back for her clear thinking. "And of course, we'll want reimbursement of the wages she was paid beyond the normal six-month short-term disability she was entitled to."

Athen twirled a paper clip on the end of a pencil, suddenly feeling a bit jaunty herself.

Dan swore a blue streak. She ignored him.

"And it goes without saying that if she fails to report for work, she will no longer be paid . . ."

He muttered one last obscenity before slamming down the receiver. The gauntlet had hit the ground.

It was then she realized she was sweating, the palms of

both hands as well as her face clammy in the air-conditioned room.

I did it, she said to herself, and waited for a bolt of lightning to crash through the wall and strike her down.

Oh, my God, I did it. She paced the room anxiously on trembling legs. What will he do to me now?

Rossi had been incensed, enraged . . . but at exactly twelve o'clock noon, Veronica walked into Athen's office, two keys dangling from a chain held between her thumb and her index finger, a silly grin on her face.

"Yo, Mrs. Moran, you won't believe this, but guess who just turned in her car . . ."

29

"Well, Athen, it's good to see you up and about and looking fit again. Though your coloring could be a bit better . . ." Ms. Evelyn squinted in the bright glare of the early morning sun. "And aren't you up early for a Saturday morning . . . Where's that young gal of yours today?"

"She had a girlfriend over to spend the night, and I suspect they stayed up quite late," Athen explained, "since they were both out cold when I left the house."

"You be sure to tell her I was asking after her." Ms. Evelyn removed her glasses, wiping them clean on the tail of her red-and-white striped shirt. "And be sure to tell her in another month I'll have some choice plants for her garden. Right from my own fields." She pointed to the area behind the greenhouse. "Second-year plants, so they won't be too expensive. There's a bumper crop of some varieties I know John was partial to."

"I'll be sure to bring her back," Athen promised.

"Now then, what would you be needing today? Too early for perennials, guess you know that . . . unless of course you're looking for some primrose, or maybe some pansies . . ."

Ms. Evelyn pointed to the flats of gaily colored flowers which sat outside the greenhouse door.

". . . and I do have some flowering bulbs left over from Easter—tulips, daffodils, hyacinths—but other than that . . ." She stopped to ponder what else she might have to offer.

"Umm . . . maybe some of those gold, ah . . . primroses." Athen hoped the plants she pointed to were, in fact, the primroses. "And some of those dark blue and yellow . . ."

"The pansies?" Ms. Evelyn asked and Athen nodded. "They've always been a favorite of mine . . . you go on, now, and pull out the ones you want, Athen . . ."

Ms. Evelyn waved a friendly greeting to another customer who had pulled into the small lot.

"Good morning, Mrs. Stephens," she called as the woman exited her car. "I have those red azaleas you were looking for . . . right this way . . ."

Athen poked around the flats, making her selections slowly, all the while anxiously debating within herself as to the best way to approach Ms. Evelyn as Diana had suggested. When Mrs. Stephens had departed, Athen casually made her way to the counter over which an ancient cash register presided.

"I think I'll take four of the primroses, and four of the pansies," she announced.

"Now, when you say four, do you mean four plants each, or four flats?"

"Four flats," Athen told her.

Ms. Evelyn nodded and pulled a pencil from her shirt pocket. "So now," she said as she began to tally up Athen's purchases on a small piece of paper, "how are we doing with our shelter?"

"Not very well, I'm afraid, at least for now." Athen took a deep breath and plunged into the business of politicking for the first time. "You know I'm behind it one hundred percent, Ms. Evelyn. Unfortunately, there is very little support for this on council . . . I guess you've already heard that. Outside of George Konstantos, upon whose support I feel I can rely, I just don't see anyone else coming over to our side . . ."

"Athen, honey, were you not aware when we took our little walk to Fourth Street that this problem existed?" Ms. Evelyn continued writing small numbers in her neat, even hand, but never looked up.

"I suspected there would be some resistance," Athen replied carefully, "but I really thought that when the other members of council saw how much support there was in the community, I assumed they'd come around. Unfortunately, that has not happened." She shook her head sadly. "You may have seen Councilman Wolmar's press conference this week?"

"I certainly did." Ms. Evelyn sniffed indignantly. "And I can tell you that the UCC did not appreciate his comments. Not one bit . . ."

"Then you know where council stands," Athen ventured.

"I know where Jim Wolmar says it stands." Ms. Evelyn flashed a look of anger.

"Well, right now I don't see any sense in bringing this before council, Ms. Evelyn. George Konstantos is perfectly willing to introduce the issue, but since no one else is willing to vote with him . . ." She shrugged her shoulders and held her hands in an I-don't-know-what-else-we-can-do gesture. "Council always votes together, Ms. Evelyn. There's never been a split vote . . . at least, not since I've been mayor. I've never been called upon to cast a tie-breaking vote. Right now, I just don't see any way to pry one more vote from the three remaining council members . . ."

"That'll be thirty-two dollars," Ms. Evelyn finished her computation. "Let me put them in a box for you."

The spry little woman disappeared into the greenhouse and emerged with a cardboard box.

"It's a sad day when Woodside Heights can't see fit to take care of the unfortunate in its midst." Ms. Evelyn's white-haired head shook slowly, side to side. "A very sad day, indeed . . ."

Athen was all but holding her breath, waiting for Ms. Evelyn to "get creative," as Diana had assured her she would do. Ms. Evelyn was seemingly engrossed in packing Athen's primroses.

"We need another box," Ms. Evelyn muttered as she returned a second time to the greenhouse.

They carried the boxes of flowers to Athen's car with no further conversation. Athen tried not to panic, tried to stifle the growing urge to grab Ms. Evelyn by the shoulders and yell, "You're supposed to be my ace in the hole. Diana said you'd know what to do!"

Ms. Evelyn offered a hug before Athen got into her car, but no words of wisdom were forthcoming. Disappointed and depressed, Athen took the long way home.

Her secret weapon appeared to be a dud.

The hoped-for game plan not having materialized, a downcast Athen poked about the house, looking for something to do. Remembering the plants tucked into the trunk of her car, she decided now was as good a time as any to put them in the ground. She changed into jeans and a sweatshirt, pulled up her sleeves and set about the task of looking through the garage, rebuilt after the storm, for a garden tool.

"Wow," Callie had exclaimed as she rounded the side of the house, "Mom . . . you're digging . . ."

"How very observant of you," Athen replied dryly.

"Where'd the plants come from?" She walked closer to peer into the boxes.

"Ms. Evelyn's."

"You went to Ms. Evelyn's without me?" Callie protested.

"You were out like a light and I didn't want to wake you," Athen told her, "but she did say she'd have some things you'd like in another month or so . . ."

"Oh, boy, what things?"

"I didn't ask," Athen shrugged, "but I'll take you back in a few weeks and you can see for yourself. What are you and Nina up to?"

"We want to go to Carolann's house. Her mom said she'd take us to the movies and let us go back to her house to order pizza . . . Is it okay with you, Mom?"

"What's the movie?" Athen asked.

"It's the one about the dog on the airplane who gets sent

to one airport while his humans go someplace else," Callie told her.

"I guess that's okay." Athen put her trowel down and sat back against the tree. "Do you have money?"

"My allowance," Callie said, nodding.

"How will you get there, how will you get home, and when can I expect you?"

"Mrs. McGowan, Mrs. McGowan, and the three of us wanted to sleep over at Nina's." Callie ticked off her responses on her fingers. "Nina's mom said it was okay."

"Stop out here before you leave so I can kiss you goodbye," Athen instructed.

Twenty minutes later, Callie announced she was packed and ready to go, just as Athen finished placing the last primrose in the firm ground.

"Not bad, Mom," noted Callie, "actually, it looks pretty good, for your first flower bed. See you in the morning."

Athen kissed the top of her head, refraining from hugging her child with her dirt-encrusted hands. When Callie and Nina had departed, Athen sat down on the top step to admire her work. She had placed the new plantings between the clumps of daffodils that were just coming in to bloom. She walked to the end of the flagstone walkway near the street for a different perspective. "Not bad," she repeated Callie's praise. The colors of the flowers were bright and added a splash of cheeriness to the still gray-green grass that surrounded the small bed.

Hands on her hips, she surveyed her little domain. Her eyes followed the walkway to the front of the red brick Tudor-style house. Elongated arms of forsythia covered with masses of golden blossoms reached upwards to the second-floor windows from their places on either side of the front steps. I should find one of John's shrub books, she told herself, and figure out how to prune those. This is the second spring they've not been cut back, and they're out of control.

She strolled up the walk, inhaling deeply as a light breeze bore the scent of magnolia from the side yard. She plopped herself on the steps again, relishing the first sense of contentment she'd felt in . . . how long? When was the last time she'd felt this quiet pleasure in her own company? Too long, she acknowledged, and she permitted herself the luxury of savoring the minutes of peaceful solitude.

All in all, she had to admit, things could be worse—had, in fact, been worse. This time last year she had truly been a lost soul. Granted, her job was now in jeopardy, the most powerful man in the city would cheerfully break her neck, and she had all but promised a homeless shelter that she could not deliver. But there were other things to consider, other things that, in her life, had proven to carry greater import than the state of Dan Rossi's disposition.

Returning to the Greek center three weeks earlier, she had been humbled by the warmth with which she had been greeted. She had not realized how much she had been missed, or the value of the service she had provided. Helping the elderly to fill out medical forms, translating mail, teaching the basics of this foreign English language to those who could speak or read only Greek, she had filled a real need. She was grateful to be needed again, grateful to once more find something within herself to give. Returning every Wednesday night had become a priority.

The warming weather, too, had drawn her out of the house, and she could no longer resist the pull of the new bike. She rode early each morning for thirty minutes, and found her enthusiasm for this once-favorite pastime returning. She had forgotten how much she enjoyed the quiet streets, nearly empty just after dawn, when the fragrance of a new day was in the air. The regular exercise had renewed her energy as well as her spirit.

And I've even planted my first garden, she mused, yet again admiring her handiwork. Recalling that John had always watered immediately after planting, she went around the side of the house and returned with the hose. She had just finished dousing the newly planted flowers when she heard a car door slam. Glancing towards the curb, she recognized the small dark blue sedan parked in front of her house from which Quentin Forbes was emerging.

"Hi," he called as he walked up the flagstones that led to the front door.

"Unexpected visits are becoming a habit with you," she said, surprised to realize how happy she was to see him.

"Didn't Callie tell you I called?" he asked. "I told her perhaps I'd stop by . . ."

"I guess it slipped her mind." Athen wondered if it had in fact been an oversight on the part of her daughter, who was usually reliable when it came to messages.

"Where is the little general?" he peered up the driveway.

"Off with her girlfriends for the night." She turned off the hose. "What brings you out this way?"

"Timmy had baseball practice this afternoon. I dropped him off at his friend's house over on Falmouth. I thought since I was just a block away, I'd stop in and see if you would be free for dinner . . . and apparently you are."

"Ahhh, well . . ." She was suddenly befuddled.

"Look, it's just a casual night out. There's a new Thai restaurant I've been wanting to try. And it's not often I'm footloose and fancy-free on a Saturday night. I'd venture to guess you get out without Callie about as often as I get out without Timmy."

"Quentin, I don't think it would be a good idea," she said, shaking her head.

"Why not?"

"Well, let's start with the fact that I'll be afraid to open my mouth for fear that anything I say will end up in print . . ."

"I promise you that will not happen," he assured her. "As a matter of fact, we can agree not to discuss your job, city hall, anything you feel uncomfortable with . . ."

"You really feel you can stick with that?" she asked skeptically.

"Absolutely," he said, his blue eyes fixed on her without blinking. "Scout's honor . . ."

"Well, I guess we could." She remained unconvinced, but his manner was so sincere . . . his dimples so deep . . .

"Great. I'll pick you up at—what's a good time—seven?"

"At least seven." She held out her hands and arms, which were caked with dirt from her fingers to her elbows. "It will take me at least that long to get cleaned up."

The sun had almost set and the street lights came on to signal the approach of evening. Standing with her back to the light, she cast a shadow over his face.

"I'll see you then," he said and, smiling, headed for his car.

No wonder Meg and her college friends had hung out the window just to watch him walk by, she mused. He certainly has a great . . . walk.

30

Attempting to apply makeup with increasingly trembling hands, Athen tortured herself endlessly, questioning the wisdom of having accepted the casual invitation. How long has it been since I've had a date? Sixteen years? Seventeen? Whatever possessed me to say yes? What will we talk about? I'm not good at small talk. I haven't even had male companionship—on a one-to-one basis—in eighteen months. Other than my father, of course, or Dan . . .

Opening her closet, her fingers tiptoed from one hanger to the next . . . too matronly . . . too dressy . . . too old, why do I still have this? . . . too casual. One by one, she rejected everything she owned. She started over again.

She finally settled on a pair of loden green slacks and a short-sleeved shirt of a pale sage hue she'd bought on sale but never worn. She frowned at her reflection. Too . . . plain. She rummaged through a drawer until she found a scarf of gold, red, green, and light blue paisley, which she tied around her neck. She frowned again. Too '70s. She fretted with her hair. The bun was too severe. She removed the pins and let it fall straight down her back. Too young. She gathered it with the scarf, which she tied in a big floppy bow at the back of her neck. Better.

"I'll bet men don't go through this," she grumbled aloud to Hannah. "I'll bet Quentin just got out of the shower and pulled on the first thing he saw . . ."

Eyeing herself critically, she decided the peach-toned blush was a mistake. Returning to the makeup kit Meg had sent her for her birthday, she scanned her choices. Maybe the plum . . . she eradicated the peach with a tissue and gently stroked on the darker blush. That's better. Softer. She studied her eyes. I should have used some shadow . . . something light . . .

She contemplated the choices displayed on the little wheel of colored powders. The soft greenish-gray shade looked appealing, so she dabbed it across her eyelids, then, on a whim, she put a little more on the small spongy brush and added a little extra to the outer edge of her eyelid as she had seen someone demonstrate on TV. Pleased with her appearance, she slipped into a pair of flats and ran downstairs.

"Come on, Hannah, it's dinnertime," she called, and the big yellow dog ambled into the kitchen as Athen poured dry dog food into the hard plastic crater that served as a dinner dish.

She glanced anxiously at the clock: 6:45. Tapping nervously on the countertop with her fingers, she watched Hannah inhale her dinner, then opened the back door to let the dog out. Noting the air had cooled, she raced upstairs. She slid a muted plaid jacket from its hanger and pulled it on, pondering her reflection for the hundredth time. The colors of the jacket—eons old—were perfect, but it looked dated. She rolled up the sleeves. Great, she assessed. Ooopps. No earrings.

She fumbled through her jewelry, searching for a pair of silver and malachite earrings that Meg had given her, with their matching ring, for Christmas the year before. She opened the box that still held all three pieces and put the earrings on. In the bottom of the drawer she spied a silver bangle bracelet and slipped it onto her wrist, her eyes momentarily resting on the ring finger of her left hand, upon which her plain gold wedding ring still wound its endless circle.

Slowly she removed the symbol of what she had come to think of as another lifetime, rolling it around and around in her right hand. So long reluctant to part with it, she now placed it in her jewelry box, acknowledging the time had come. Ringless after so many years, her finger felt naked. She replaced the thin gold band with the silver ring that matched her earrings as the doorbell rang.

"Hi," she greeted him at the door. "Come in."

"You look wonderful." He smiled as if he meant it.

"Thanks." She could feel a faint blush creeping its way from her neck to her face. "I just have to let Hannah in . . ."

She all but ran into the kitchen to escape his presence, her heart pounding in her ears. This was a mistake . . . maybe I could tell him I'm sick . . . I probably will be by the end of the evening if I put food into this stomach . . .

She opened the back door and Hannah bounded in, searching for the stranger she knew was there. Quentin held his hand out, and the tail began to wag the dog.

"You remember me, girl?" Quentin bent down to pet her. "I think she remembers me," he told Athen, obviously pleased.

"Ummm," she said, nodding from the kitchen doorway.

"Well, I guess we should get going." He motioned towards the front door.

Athen nodded, trying to display something that could pass for a smile. He opened the door for her and she forced her feet in that general direction, shoving her hands into her jacket pockets to hide their shaking fingers. Closing the door behind them, he took her elbow and she almost jumped out of her skin at the slight touch. If he noticed, he hid it well.

The restaurant was a ten minute ride away, though it seemed to Athen she had been trapped in his car for hours. The ride had been marked with mostly silence, Quentin making some effort at small talk to which she had given brief responses. Once seated at their table, however, the conversation flowed more easily, and before too long, her nerves had calmed enough for her to respond in full sentences.

"Don't order any of the starred dishes unless you like really spicy food," he cautioned.

"Ummm . . . I haven't had Thai food before." She bit her lip. "Maybe you could recommend something that's not too heavily seasoned . . ."

"Try the Thai beef salad," he suggested, "you might like that."

"I thought you said you hadn't been here before," she said after their orders had been taken by a doll-like woman wearing a brightly colored, heavily embroidered dress.

"I haven't." He smiled across the table. "But I've heard this place serves authentic Thai dishes, which I am very partial to. I was delighted to hear such a restaurant had found its way to Woodside Heights."

"Where did you develop such exotic tastes?" she asked.

"My dad used to go to the Far East on business. Thailand was one of his regular stops. I accompanied him on a number of trips."

"What did your father do?"

"He ran the family business. Actually it was my mother's family's business," he explained, leaning back from the table as the waitress placed a dish of shrimp lanced through with long wooden spikes between them on the table. "Here, try these with the peanut sauce, it's wonderful . . ."

"What kind of a business was it?" She bit into a shrimp which she'd hesitantly dipped into the small sauce bowl. "Mmm. You were right, this is good . . ."

"Well, my mother's father was a bit of an entrepreneur," he told her. "He bought several small businesses that he thought had some potential back in the thirties when everything could be bought dirt cheap. As those businesses did well, he bought others—all sorts of things—real estate, restaurants, hotel chains, manufacturing plants, you name it. He was not a man to put all his eggs in the same basket. Over the years, he had accumulated quite extensive and diversified holdings."

"And your father worked for him?"

"Worked with him, actually. My uncle Stephen, my mother's only brother, had worked for him for years, with the understanding that one day he'd take over the whole thing. Unfortunately, Uncle Stephen hated it, he simply wasn't cut out for it, I guess. After years of trying, he had a severe breakdown. My grandfather recognized that his son would never be capable of taking over, so he turned to my father . . ."

"Your father liked it?"

"He loved it. He thrived on the stress, the travel, the long hours, the wheeling and dealing required to keep that big ball rolling . . ."

"And you?" She speared a piece of roast beef with her fork, having passed on the chopsticks which she noted he handled adeptly.

"I was into it for a while." He looked down at his plate, as if concentrating on what to eat next. "Being the only son, I was expected to take the reins someday."

"What happened?" she asked.

"Well, I guess I wasn't really cut out for it either," he grimly acknowledged. "I did try, for my father's sake, to find something I liked about it, but I couldn't. My mother, bless her soul, realized early on that it was not my cup of tea, so to speak—maybe she saw some of her brother in me—and she was more than willing to release me from the burden after my father's death."

"So did she sell the company?"

"No, she appointed a board to oversee the entire conglomerate. Each company is sort of self-contained, but reports to the board on a quarterly basis. The only stipulation Mother made when I resigned was that I stay on the board and attend all the quarterly meetings. Other than that, I could do as I pleased."

"How long did you work there?" The extent of her curiosity was beginning to surprise her.

"Until I came here," he told her. "After Mother married Hughes, and with Cynthia gone, there seemed to be little reason to stay in St. Louis. And since it is important to me that Timmy knows my mother, I thought I'd come out here for a while."

"What is it you wanted to do?" she asked, wondering how long a while would be.

"Write," he confided.

"Well, you're certainly doing that," she noted.

"Journalism wasn't exactly what I'd intended. That was Brenda's idea to keep me off the streets and keep me from getting lazy." He smiled. "I've always dreamed of writing a series of history-oriented books . . . I'm a history buff, particularly the Civil War era. I'm fascinated, for example, by the Underground Railroad, the concept of a whole network of people putting their lives on the line for strangers simply because it was the right thing to do. When I came out to visit my mother, Brenda took me on a tour of the city and pointed out a few homes that had been part of it—honest to goodness stops on the way to freedom. And she introduced me to Ms. Evelyn, who is a veritable fountain of knowledge on the subject." He paused to chew, then swallowed and said, "You know she grew up on the hill?"

Athen nodded, her mouth full of lettuce glazed with spicy peanut dressing.

"Well, she's sort of an unofficial historian. She has agreed to work with me on a book I'd like to do on the subject. As a child she listened to the stories told by some of the old folks about their experiences as they fled north. She's been meeting with me, retelling the tales, which I've been recording. I promised her that once the book was completed, I'd give the tapes to the library, so that none of it will be lost. I'll play some of the tapes for you sometime if you're interested . . ." he offered.

"I'd like that," she accepted.

The waitress refilled their cups with more of the pleasant, aromatic tea, then seeing they had finished, sent another tiny woman to clear the table. Quentin requested a cup of coffee in place of the tea.

"Ms. Evelyn is quite a character." Athen sipped at the flavorful tea.

"She's a fascinating woman," he agreed, "a true renaissance woman, if you will. She is involved in virtually every aspect of this community, from running literacy classes in the housing project to singing in the church choir. She runs a taxi service of sorts all the way to Elizabeth twice a week to the medical center there, for everyone from senior citizens needing their prescriptions filled to young mothers from the inner-city whose babies need medical care . . . been doing it for years."

"I had no idea." Athen set her cup down on the table and held her hand up, signaling "No thank you" to the overly attentive waitress who rushed to refill it. "I've known her since I was a child—she was a friend of my father's and worked actively for him when he campaigned—and John knew her well because he always bought plants from her . . . but apart from her involvement with the UCC, I didn't know the extent of her activities . . ."

"Ms. Evelyn is a one-woman redevelopment task force. Have you heard about her latest project?"

"Her latest project?"

"She has very quietly tracked down the owners of several vacant adjacent lots on Third Street and conned them into entering long-term leases with the UCC to establish an enormous community garden where people from the housing project can grow vegetables and flowers and fruits."

"The lots that border on Schyler?" Athen asked. "The ones that look like they've been used as dumps for the past twenty years?"

"They have been used as dumps for the past twenty years," he told her, "but she has enlisted volunteers from each of the churches to haul out the debris for her. She has also gotten someone she does business with at her nursery to donate soil—talked him into delivering free of charge when she's ready for it—even got a few of her suppliers to donate fruit trees . . ."

"Where did you hear about this?" she asked curiously.

"From Ms. Evelyn." He chuckled, his dimples suddenly appearing to dance in the light of the candle which sat between them in a black lacquered holder. "I stopped to see her this afternoon, and she told me she was looking for more volunteers to clean the lots next weekend and did I know how to operate a backhoe . . ."

"Do you?" she asked.

"I guess I can learn." He grinned. "There's no saying no to that lady. She showed me the sketch she made for this garden, Athen, it's amazing . . . She even has a sort of, I don't know, like an old-fashioned town green with a sort of platform in the middle . . ."

"What kind of a platform?" she asked.

"Sort of what you'd see at the turn of the century, a sort of bandstand, right in the middle of this huge garden. It will be absolutely wonderful if she pulls it off . . . which, of course, she probably will."

"Is she planning on running concerts?" Athen pondered the need for a platform in the middle of an inner-city garden plot.

"Anything is possible with her." He smiled at the waitress as she delivered the check on a red enamel tray and awaited the bills which he handed to her.

"Thank you, Quentin," Athen told him, "I'd forgotten how enjoyable adult dinner conversation can be."

"Well, there's no lack of adult conversation at my mother's." He helped her on with her jacket. "But this certainly beats a replay of Hughes's golf game any day. I'm looking forward to doing this again."

"Will we ever both be temporarily childless on the same night again?" she wondered aloud as they walked out of the restaurant and into the night air.

"Maybe we can arrange to be." He held her arm as they walked to the car.

"A penny for them," he offered, noting her engrossed silence as he stopped at the red light two blocks from her house.

"I was just thinking how nice it was that you kept your word. Do you realize you didn't mention city hall one time?"

"That was the deal." The light changed and he made the turn onto Harper Avenue. "Although I have to admit I had to bite my tongue several times to keep from asking you how you got rid of old Edie and how you wound up with that character who sits outside your door . . . interesting accent she has, by the way."

"Veronica?" She laughed. "She is one of a kind, isn't she? And that accent is one hundred percent pure South Philadelphia. She was working in the personnel department. As far as Edie is concerned, I just arranged a transfer for her . . ."

"Why'd you choose Veronica?" he asked as he parked in front of her house.

She hesitated, wondering if she could trust him. Something inside her drove her towards the truth, but something else warned her against disclosing that, in tipping her off to Rossi's little arrangement with Mary Jo Dolan, Veronica had presented Athen with the only weapon she had against Dan. As much as she was beginning to like Quentin, he was still a reporter. Was he, as she was beginning to suspect, more interested in her as a woman than in a good story? There was one way to find out.

"Quentin, if I told you something in complete confidence, would you promise that you would never use it? In the paper, I mean." She turned to look him full in the face, watching his expression.

"Of course," he replied without hesitation.

"Even if it was something that would make a truly great story? Could you still keep your word?"

He pondered this momentarily, stroking his chin. "You mean the type of story that would make your average reporter salivate?"

"Just that sort." She was testing him, and they both knew it.

"If it was that important to you that I not write about it . . ." He nodded slowly. "Yes, I would keep my word."

Athen took a deep breath, and told him how she had met Veronica, how Veronica had blown the whistle on Dan and Mary Jo.

"Whoa, are you serious?" He leaned forward. "Dan had an underage mistress, had her paid by the city for four years, gave her a car . . . ?"

She nodded. The light in his eyes flooded her with concern. "Quentin, you promised . . ."

"Didn't I tell you this guy was a crook? Good lord, Athen, you could bring this guy down in a flash with this . . ."

"No, Quentin, I can't," she said quietly.

"What do you mean, you can't? Athen, this is precisely the type of thing that could . . ."

"You don't understand, Quentin." She shook her head slowly. "I can't. I can threaten Dan with it, I can hold it over his head, but I will not publicly use it. Of course, Dan doesn't know that."

"You've lost me. I can't think of one reason why you would sit on something like that." He held his hands palms up in bewilderment.

"Mary Jo's father ran off about ten years ago . . . he just left town and never came back. Her mother has been holding down three jobs to keep her family together. She has nine children. Mary Jo is apparently the only bad apple in the bunch." Athen's voice was a faint whisper in the small car. "Her mother cleans houses and cooks for the rectory at St. Michael's. She cleans offices at night. She doesn't know about Mary Jo and Dan."

"Who told you all this?"

"Diana Bennett."

"Where does Mrs. Dolan think Mary Jo got her car?"

"Mary Jo told her she won it in a raffle."

"And that's why you won't use this, to protect her mother?" he asked incredulously.

"I think the woman's been through enough, without having her daughter's name dragged through the papers."

"Even though this could rid the city of Dan Rossi?"

"There has to be another way," she told him, "without stooping to that level. Nothing good is gained by hurting someone else."

He reached over in the darkness and sought her hands, threading his fingers through hers.

"You are quite a woman, Athena Moran," he said, his voice revealing more than simple respect.

"And that is why Veronica is my right hand. She is the only person in city hall that I can completely trust."

"It must have been hard for you, knowing that every move you made was being watched."

"It was only hard after I realized it. For a long time, I didn't know. Ignorance was bliss." She smiled. "But it's not so bad. Veronica keeps her ear to the ground. It's amazing how much she hears from the other secretaries."

"She certainly is in a class of her own," he chuckled, "with that sixties hairdo and those earrings."

Athen laughed, and the solemn mood began to lift.

"Don't let her appearance fool you. Under all that hair

and behind all that makeup is a very bright young woman. She is funny and straightforward—a real breath of fresh air."

"And she is one hundred percent loyal to you," he observed.

"Yes. I believe she is."

"Well, then, not to be outdone by Veronica, I guess I will have to prove myself just as loyal." He leaned over and whispered in her ear, "Your secret is safe with me. I will keep my promise."

"Thank you, Quentin."

His face was so close she could see, even in the dark, the tiny laugh lines around his mouth. Disconcerted by his proximity, she said, "I think I should go in now."

His reluctance was evident, but he withdrew and got out of the car. Opening the door for her, he took her arm as they strolled up the flagstone path to her door. She wondered if she should invite him in.

"Thanks for spending the evening with me," he said, leaning casually against the doorframe. "After all that's happened over the past few months, I'm really happy that we are having a chance to start over. And thank you for trusting me. It means more to me than you know."

Before she could reply, he had leaned over slightly, taken her chin in his hands and kissed her square on the mouth. Gathering her into his arms, he kissed her again, and she felt herself drifting into the warmth he offered, being swallowed whole by it.

"I've been wanting to do that since the first time I saw you, Fourth of July last year . . ." he whispered as he released her.

Her shaking fingers dropped her keys and they clattered on the concrete steps. Amused, he bent to pick them up and handed them to her. She found the door key and turned it in the lock.

"I'll call you soon." He planted one small kiss on the top of her head and swung the door open for her.

"Okay," she managed to squeak as Hannah pounced upon her to show her delight in Athen's return.

She watched through the curtains as his car left the curb, the headlights hazy under the streetlamp's glow. Sighing, she sat down in the darkened living room, unexpectedly grateful to have the house to herself. The evening had left her with a lot to think about. Quentin aside, there was this news of Ms. Evelyn's latest project. What was she up to? And could it somehow tie in to some creative plan Diana still insisted Ms. Evelyn would devise to garner support for the shelter? Or had Ms. Evelyn given up on that entirely, choosing to put all her energies into the community garden, which would require no approval from council?

She touched her fingers to her lips where Quentin's mouth had been, acknowledging that she was more attracted to him than she had wanted to be. Grateful they had been able to put their animosity behind them, she questioned the wisdom of having told him about Mary Jo. Should she have trusted him? It had been so easy to confide in him. Would she later regret it? Would his journalist's desire for a story be stronger than his loyalty to a promise? Would he knowingly take from her the only thing she had to hold over Dan's head?

She wondered when, or if, he would call her. She smiled ruefully, trying to recall just how long it had been since she had waited by the phone for a man.

31

"Mom!" Callie made a face. "Mr. Forbes is on the phone for you."

Athen took the receiver, and tried to talk, feed Hannah, and make dinner for Callie and herself at the same time. The call had been brief and to the point.

"Why's he calling you?" Callie asked suspiciously when Athen had hung up.

"I guess because we're friends," Athen replied.

185

"You have to be friends with him just because he brought you flowers when you were sick?" Callie's hands rode high on her hips as she interrogated her mother.

"No, Callie, we're friends because we . . . we like each other." Athen avoided her daughter's eyes. "We had dinner together last night."

"You had dinner with Timmy Forbes's father?" Callie asked incredulously. "Mom, how could you?"

"Callie, Quentin Forbes is very nice. He is very nice to be with."

"You didn't used to think he was so nice," Callie jabbed.

"Yes, that is true. I didn't used to like him."

"But now you do?" The statement, delivered flatly, was an accusation.

"Yes," Athen openly admitted, "I do."

"Is he the same Quentin Forbes who used to work for the newspaper, the same one who embarrassed and humiliated you?" Callie asked pointedly.

"Yes." Athen tried to ignore Callie's sarcasm. "And he still works for the newspaper."

"How do you know he won't embarrass you again?" the child taunted.

"Well, I guess I don't know that for sure, Callie, but sometimes you just have to give people a chance." She set the baking pan of moussaka on the table.

"Grampa used to make this better," Callie told her.

They ate in silence. Athen knew how sensitive Callie was as far as her father's memory was concerned. Did Callie think she was being unfaithful to John because she'd shared the company of another man?

Before she could think of a way to approach the subject, Callie asked, "Are you planning on seeing him again?"

"He asked me if I'd be at the Spring Concert at school on Wednesday night," Athen told her, "and I said I would be."

"If he asks you out again, will you go?"

"Yes. I will."

"Oh God." Callie pushed her plate away and left the room, moaning loudly. "My mother is dating the butt-head's father. I hope this doesn't get around school . . ."

* * *

For the first time since she had taken office, Athen found herself actually looking forward to the Wednesday morning press conference, knowing Quentin would be there.

"How do I look?" she asked Veronica before she set out for the large conference room.

"Beautiful," Veronica told her, somewhat startled by the unusual inquiry. "You always look terrific . . ."

"Thanks." Athen took a deep breath and headed for the elevator.

She'd worn a lightweight knit dress of the palest dove gray adorned with a white lace collar, which she smoothed as she stepped off the elevator. He was there, in his usual spot in the front row, when she entered the room. She had some difficulty sticking to her agenda, feeling his eyes all over her. At one point he had smiled at her, and the sight of his deep dimples had caused her to momentarily lose her place. She cleared her throat and admonished herself for acting like a schoolgirl.

There were few announcements that day, and so the question and answer session was uncommonly brief. He caught up with her in the hallway.

"Will I see you tonight at school?" he whispered.

"Yes." She nodded.

"Can I pick you up . . ."

Recalling Callie's horror at her mother's having had dinner with him, Athen thought it best to pass on the ride.

"No, thank you. I may have to rush from work. I have a meeting at four which may run a little late," she told him, avoiding eye contact since she knew the meeting would only last about five minutes.

She had not been surprised, she realized, to find him waiting for her in the school lobby.

"Want to sit with me?" he asked.

"Sure," she replied, knowing that being onstage, Callie would never be the wiser.

The band performance was an exercise in discipline for the audience, which tried desperately to restrain from open laughter at the unharmonious renditions of "My Old Kentucky Home" and something that Athen simply could not identify. They finished up with a version of "Yesterday" that none of the Beatles would have recognized. The auditorium filled with cheers of gratitude when the instrumental nightmare had concluded.

"God, that was bad," Quentin whispered, shaking his head. "I'd say Timmy needs a few more lessons on that trumpet . . ."

"They're just kids." Athen stifled a giggle. "They'll get better as they get older."

"Lord, I hope so." He moved his leg so that it rested against hers. "We have, what, seven, eight more years of concerts to endure?"

The choral group was much better, though it appeared that some of the younger members got off track a time or two and sang from the wrong page.

She couldn't stop herself from watching Quentin out of the corner of one eye, cautioning herself to take this all very slowly. Keep your feet on the ground, her inner voice lectured, you both have a lot to overcome from the past. You both have jobs to do and children to raise . . .

All true, she sighed softly. But he was handsome—just look at the way those dark curls tumble onto his forehead, how those little lines crinkle around his eyes when he smiles. And those dark lashes that define those blue eyes, and the way his mouth curls slightly just before he laughs. Shoulders big enough to stand on. She recalled a time when Ari, too, had had such shoulders. In her mind's eye she could see herself as she had stood, a foot upon each of her father's shoulders, like Colossus. A fleeting glimpse of a happy, willful, stubborn child skipped briefly through long forgotten passages . . . the child she had been before her mother had become ill and her world had become irrevocably jumbled.

She squeezed her eyes tightly, erasing the vision of her mother seated in the big chair by the front window, her face aglow as she watched Athen's attempts to master her new roller skates, while her own legs hung useless, encased in metal braces.

"Athen." Quentin leaned close to her ear, his breath soft upon her face, and covered her hand with his. "Are you all right?"

188

"Yes . . . of course." She nodded, unaware that she had drifted momentarily. She made herself smile to prove she was just fine.

She could feel his eyes on her, watching, and she sat up a little in her seat. She'd been holding her breath, she realized, and so she forced herself to exhale in a long, slow stream of warm air, as if to compel the lingering dark thoughts back to whatever small corner of her being they inhabited.

"It can't go on too much longer." He squeezed her hand, thinking her restless, bored with the length of the performance.

"It's okay," she whispered, "but it does make me wonder what they were doing, all those days Callie stayed after school for rehearsals."

Then, finally, the finale came, with a beaming Mr. Halterman bowing at center stage to the cheering audience—the cheers reflecting gratitude for the show's conclusion.

The smiling parents were invited to the reception room following the concert to share refreshments as well as to await their offspring. Athen and Quentin were standing somewhat apart from the others, deep in conversation, when Callie and a few of her friends joined them. Callie rolled her eyes when she recognized her mother's companion.

"Well, that was some show," Quentin told her as she approached.

"It stunk and you know it," she said flippantly.

"Callie . . ." Athen protested.

"Would it make you feel better if I told you you were terrible?" Quentin asked matter-of-factly, unruffled by her impertinence.

Her efforts to get a rise out of Quentin having failed, Callie shrugged her indifference and addressed her mother impatiently. "Can we go home now?"

"In a minute." Athen's ire was beginning to rise at her daughter's ill manners. "Why don't you get some punch?" It was a command, not a suggestion.

"Yech. School punch. How appealing," muttered Callie as she walked off to get a cup.

189

"Quentin, I'm sorry . . ." Athen began.

"Don't mention it." He smiled good-naturedly. "Callie's a good kid, but I seem to bring out the worst in her. Which is perfectly understandable. Timmy was the same way the first time I went out with someone after his mother left. He got over it. In time, she will too . . ."

"I hope so." Athen watched her daughter, who was sharing some whispered secret with her girlfriends.

Timmy joined his father, and Athen could not help but compare his courteous greeting to Callie's rudeness. *Maybe Quentin is right, maybe it's just because he is the first man I've gone out with since John died . . .*

"Mom, I have a history test tomorrow." Callie pointedly ignored the boy's presence. "Can we please go?"

"Yes, Callie, we can go." Athen sighed.

"We're leaving too," Quentin said, "we'll walk out with you . . ."

Callie rolled her eyes to the heavens for the second time in just under ten minutes.

"Do you have a history test tomorrow too?" Athen asked Timmy as they walked through the parking lot. "Aren't you in Callie's class?"

Before he could answer, Callie snapped, "No, he is not. He's in the brainy section."

"I thought you were in the top section," Athen said, following her daughter towards their car.

"I'm in the smart section," Callie told her with great exasperation, "but Timmy's in the super-smart section. He takes classes with the upper grades."

"Not in everything," Timmy said in his own defense, Callie having made the issue of his intelligence an accusation. "I only take history, math, and science with that section . . . everything else I take with you."

Callie ignored him and leaned against the car door, waiting for her mother to open it. When she saw that Athen was in no hurry, she called, "Keys, please."

"Just a minute, Callie," Athen told her.

"How about dinner Friday night?" Quentin whispered. "You think she'll let you out?" He nodded towards Callie with more good humor than Athen would have had any right to expect, considering her daughter's churlishness.

"Let me see what the agenda is," she said, attempting to smile in spite of her anger over Callie's behavior.

"I'll call you tomorrow." He waved goodbye to Callie, who stood with her arms folded across her chest.

"Callie, you really embarrassed me," Athen said the minute the car doors had been closed.

"Well, you embarrassed me, too," Callie grumbled.

"How did I embarrass you? Was I rude to your friends? Did I insult anyone?"

"You did not have to go off in a corner with Mr. Forbes," Callie snapped.

"We were not off in a corner." Athen negotiated the turn onto the main road.

"You're my mother," Callie said, struggling with her temper, "and you know how I feel about Timmy . . ."

"Callie, what is wrong with Timmy? He's nice, he's polite . . ."

"Oh, please . . ." Callie groaned dramatically.

"Then what is it . . . ?"

"Timmy is the smartest kid in the school. He's the best at every sport. He gets to ride horses everyday 'cause his grandmother owns a lot of them. And he's rich . . ." Callie rotely ticked off the litany of Timmy Forbes's offences.

"Sounds like jealousy to me," Athen said quietly.

"I am not jealous!" Callie slammed the car door even before Athen had turned off the ignition. "He is this perfect kid, Mom. He never gets anything wrong on tests, he never swears . . ."

"Do you?" Athen interjected.

"Do I get things wrong on tests or do I swear?" Callie turned the outside light on over the back door so that Athen could find the keyhole. "Sometimes, to both."

Athen pushed open the door and Hannah, aroused from sleep, barked as she ventured into the kitchen to investigate.

"Mom, Timmy doesn't really talk to anyone, or go out of his way to be friends with anyone," Callie told her.

"How can you try to make friends with people who make fun of you?" Athen tossed her purse halfway across the room to the counter. "And has it occurred to you or your friends that maybe Timmy is shy? It isn't easy coming in to a new school where everyone already knows everyone else. And he's had a hard time these last few years, Callie. His mother left them . . ."

"Left them for what?" Callie's head shot up from her bookbag where she searched for her history notes.

"For a job," Athen told her softly.

"At least his mother is still alive," Callie retorted, "at least maybe he'll be able to see her again someday."

"Do you think it would make him feel better to tell himself that when maybe he needs her now?"

"You are only taking his side because you like his father," Callie whined.

"I'm taking his side because I think he's a nice kid who is lonely and has had to deal with a great loss in his life, a loss that is every bit as big and every bit as real as yours has been—maybe worse because your father did not choose to die, but *his* mother chose to leave. I don't think you are being fair to him and that makes me feel badly. I don't think he deserves the treatment he's gotten. And I'm ashamed to know that you are a party to it, Calliope Moran."

Callie dropped her eyes, picked up her bookbag, and fled to the sanctity of her room.

32

"Well, there're six different movies playing here tonight," Quentin told Athen on Friday evening as they entered the multiscreen theater. "Do you have any preference?"

"No." She shook her head. "You choose."

She stood slightly to the side while he bought the tickets.

"I hope 'Silver Mornings' is to your liking," he told her as he ushered her behind door number four. "It's gotten excellent reviews."

"I haven't kept up with movies," she said, taking his arm to keep from getting lost in the crowded lobby.

They took seats midway down the aisle as the lights began to dim. The previews of coming attractions were just rolling when he decided to go for popcorn. Returning to his seat as the feature was about to start, he handed her a cup of syrupy soda and placed the enormous box of popcorn between them. The rippling notes of the piano played the theme song as the scene opened onto a moonlit beach, where a woman paced anxiously in the sand, rubbing her hands together in obvious distress. The camera moved in on the woman until the lovely face of Dallas MacGregor filled the entire screen. Athen choked and Quentin patted her on the back.

"You okay?" he whispered. "Got popcorn stuck in your throat?"

She nodded dumbly and sunk back into her chair. She squirmed uncomfortably through the movie, to the extent that Quentin, assuming her view was obstructed, asked her if she'd like to sit somewhere else. Yes, she had wanted to reply, the lobby would do nicely.

She endured what she had considered to be sheer torture. The camera had appeared to be devoted to Dallas, never showing her at a bad angle—if indeed there was such a thing—lingering on her face so that every expression was viewed up close and personal on the wide screen. Athen thought she would be ill. Quentin put his arm around her and she was tempted to bury her face in his shoulder to blot out the lavender eyes, the pouting smile, of her late husband's first love.

An hour and a half later, they emerged, holding hands, Athen grateful that the film had finally ended.

"Good movie, don't you think?" he commented as they walked towards the car.

"Umm hmm," she replied from between painfully clenched jaws.

"Where do you want to have dinner?"

Dinner? Who could eat when one's insides are doing a line dance towards one's throat?

"I don't care." She shrugged.

"Let's try Scotties across the street . . ." He led and she followed quietly.

They placed their orders for sandwiches and he noted, "You didn't seem to enjoy the movie very much."

She did not reply.

"Athen . . . ?" He peered across the table, leaning his head slightly to make eye contact with her. "What is it? Were you terribly bored?"

"It's just that Dallas MacGregor is not my favorite actress, that's all." She glanced away, pretending to watch the antics of a group of teenagers, two of whom had shaved heads, and one of whom had purple hair.

"I think she's terrific," he told her nonchalantly, "and I thought she was wonderful in her role in this film. And she's certainly one of the most beautiful . . ."

"Quentin," she couldn't hold it in any longer, "John was in love with her."

"So are ninety-percent of the men in this country," he said with a shrug, "including yours truly . . . so what?"

"No, Quentin, I mean they were in love with each other," she explained.

"John actually knew her?" His jaw was dangerously close to dropping clear off his face.

"Intimately. They dated all through college," she confessed.

"Boy, John must have been something," he said, sipping at his coffee, "to have had the two most beautiful women I ever saw in love with him."

"Very gallant, Mr. Forbes." She could not disguise the peevish undertone.

"Very true, Mrs. Moran," he told her pointedly. "You are every bit as lovely, every bit as fascinating, and certainly every bit as sexy as the woman who appeared on the screen tonight. I tip my hat to John Moran, who, besides being a selfless hero, had impeccable taste in women."

The fingertips of both hands tapped out the staccato beat of her agitation on the tabletop.

"Oh, come on, Athen, don't tell me you're still jealous of her after all these years . . ." His eyes narrowed with skepticism.

"A few months ago, I found a box of letters she'd written to him, hidden in the back of his closet," she said softly.

"Recent letters?" His eyebrows raised. A married cop from some small city in northern New Jersey having an affair with one of the world's most glamorous film stars?

"No. From years ago," she acknowledged. "Letters she had written after she'd graduated from college and moved to California."

"I don't understand the problem," he stated, adding, "particularly if he had stopped seeing her before he started seeing you . . ."

"I guess . . . I guess I just hadn't realized what she had meant to him." Athen unconsciously began to tear tiny pieces from one end of a paper napkin. "John never talked about her. From the time we began dating, I don't remember him ever mentioning her name."

"Why should he have? It was obviously a closed subject by then."

"But he kept her letters all those years."

"Everyone keeps mementos of their past, Athen. And I would think that he declined discussing her with you because she was, in fact, the past. You were his present, and his future. Besides, only a totally insensitive man would have reminded his wife that his first love had been one of the most celebrated beauties of our generation. From all I've heard about John Moran, he was a pretty decent fellow."

"Yes, he was." She nodded.

"So why would John, who loved you, want you to harbor any doubts that you are as beautiful, as desirable, as she is, when he knew without question that you are?" His sincerity almost seemed to embarrass him. "In any event, I suspect John simply put it behind him when it was over, and went on with his life and probably considered himself the luckiest man on the face of the earth when he married you. Which he was."

"Thank you," she said softly, "that's very sweet."

"I am, you should know," he told her in a mockingly serious tone, "one supremely sweet guy."

"I've said that very thing about you many times over the past few months," she said with a smile.

"Now I thought we were going to let that dead dog lie?" He grinned as the waitress passed by the table and handed him the check.

"Well, maybe it wasn't such a bad picture," she conceded as they strolled arm in arm to the car.

"And the acting was exceptional, wasn't it?" he goaded her.

"Yes," she replied hesitantly, "I guess maybe it was."

"That's the spirit." He winked as he opened the car door for her.

She had hesitated only momentarily before asking, as he pulled into her driveway, "Would you like to come in for a few minutes?"

"Sure." He nodded. "It's still fairly early."

Athen shushed Hannah who met them at the door, her tail thumping loudly against the wall. Having decided that Quentin was her friend, Hannah made joyful noises as they attempted to get past her large self into the foyer.

Tossing her jacket onto the back of a chair, Athen motioned Quentin to do the same and to follow her into the kitchen.

"What can I get you?" she asked. "Coffee, tea, metaxa . . ."

"What was that last one?" He pulled a chair out from the table and sat down.

"Metaxa," she said with a smile. "It's Greek wine."

"I'm game," he told her and she went into the dining room, returning with a tall thin bottle and two small glasses.

"I used to keep this for my father," she told him as she poured small amounts over ice. "Would you like me to water yours down a bit? It's somewhat strong, if you're not accustomed to it . . ."

"I'll try it without." He studied her as she poured small amounts into each glass, then added water to one, telling him, "I can't drink this undiluted."

"Whoa." He choked as he downed the first sip. "It is a bit heady, isn't it . . . ?"

She laughed and reached for his glass, but he waved her hand away, saying, "No, no . . . I've handled heartier stuff than this . . . I just didn't expect the bite . . ."

She watched his face as he took another more cautious sip. "It has an interesting flavor. If you hadn't told me this was wine, I would have suspected some type of whiskey, perhaps . . ."

The muffled sound of the front door quietly closing sent Hannah to welcome Callie home from a birthday party. Athen wondered how Callie would react at finding Quentin Forbes alone with her mother.

A slight movement at the doorway caught Athen's eye. Callie stood with her hands on her hips, surveying the scene.

"Did you have a good time at the party, sweetie?" Athen said calmly, well aware of her daughter's frame of mind as clearly evidenced in the brown eyes which narrowed as they went from mother to guest and back again.

"I guess it was okay," Callie said. She seemed to be awaiting an explanation for the tableau.

"Can you at least say hello to Mr. Forbes?" Athen tried not to glare at her daughter.

"Hello, Mr. Forbes," Callie replied flatly.

"Hi, Callie," he said softly, not wounded by her hostile attitude and understanding of its source.

"We saw a really good movie tonight," Athen told her.

"You didn't tell me you were going to the movies," Callie accused.

"Well, I didn't know when you went to Julie's that I would be going out," Athen said without apology.

Callie remained at her post in the doorway.

"Well, I should be getting on home." Quentin stood up. "I've got an early date with Ms. Evelyn in the morning . . ."

"Ms. Evelyn . . . ?" Callie asked, her curiosity piqued.

"Yes," he replied casually, "I promised to be Ms. Evelyn's mule this weekend."

"What do you mean?" Callie kicked off her sneakers, intrigued in spite of herself.

"I mean she has some heavy work to do, and I told her I

would do it for her," he explained, while Athen marveled at the effective means by which he calmly diffused Callie's anger and drew her into conversation. "She needs help cleaning up some vacant lots she's planning on transforming into the Garden of Eden."

"A real garden?" Animosity was rapidly being upstaged by curiosity.

"Absolutely," he assured her, "and from what she tells me, she's planning on growing a little bit of everything. She even started a lot of the plants in her greenhouse."

"Who's the garden for?" Callie's stockinged feet padded softly into the room.

"It's for the people who live in the city, who can't afford to buy a lot of fresh things in the market, or who don't have spare money to buy a bunch of flowers to brighten up their home." He became serious. "Some people don't know how to grow things, so Ms. Evelyn offered to teach them, so they could learn how to grow vegetables and fruits for their families."

"Why did she ask for your help?"

"Well, actually, I volunteered," he told her.

"Why?" Callie wanted to know.

"Because we're friends, and she has a big job to do, and friends help friends when help is needed." He turned to Athen and said, "Maybe if you have a few hours to spare tomorrow, you can come down and give us a hand . . ."

"I don't know how much help I'll be," Athen said with a laugh, "I never planted anything before last weekend."

"Planting!" he exclaimed. "I suspect we'll spend the entire weekend just clearing the ground. It's overgrown with weeds, litter, trash . . . no, right now, we're talking strictly dirty work. You game?"

"What time?" Callie asked before Athen could respond.

"Anytime," he told her. "We'll probably be there all day."

"Can we, Mom?" Callie begged. After all, wasn't Ms. Evelyn her special friend, too?

"I guess we can drive down and see what we can do," Athen readily agreed.

"Great!" The twinkle had returned to the girl's eyes as

she hugged her mother. "Let's get up real early . . . what time are you going, Mr. Forbes?" It was the first time she had spoken rather than spit his name, and he was not oblivious to the fact.

"Probably around seven, but you don't have to worry about going that early." He made a point of addressing Callie, rather than her mother. "There's some equipment that's being delivered—small tractors, some Dumpsters, stuff like that—but if you come around ten or so, I'll bet there'll be plenty for you to do."

"Thanks, Mr. Forbes." Her smiling face was evidence that he had gone from suspect to ally, all in the course of a brief conversation.

"Well, if we're all going to be working hard tomorrow, I guess it's time to say goodnight." He winked at Athen and headed for the front door, stopping to pick up his jacket from the chair.

"Mr. Forbes, will you tell Ms. Evelyn I'm coming to help?" Callie had followed close behind him, climbing two steps up the stairwell to bring herself to his eye level.

"Of course," he assured her. "I'm sure she'll be delighted. I know you're a big favorite of hers."

"She told you that?" Callie bit her bottom lip to conceal her pleasure at his pronouncement.

"On more than one occasion." He slipped into his brown tweed jacket and adjusted the sleeves.

"She's one of my favorite people, too," Callie said, sharing this bit of herself with him, "she's always so good to everyone. She always makes me feel good when I talk with her, and she never makes me feel like a pesky kid."

"Well, I think that's her way of showing her respect for a fellow gardener," he told her.

"Hmmm . . ." Callie considered this. Just as she turned to go up the steps, she glanced towards the kitchen where her mother stood slightly inside the doorway. Pausing only briefly before she ran up to her room, she admonished with a certain amount of exasperation, "Mom, the least you could do is walk Mr. Forbes to the door . . ."

33

"What do you think, Mom," Callie asked over breakfast the next morning, "jeans and sweatshirts?"

"Hmm?" Athen had glanced up from the newspaper. She'd been trying unsuccessfully for ten minutes to read the same article, her mind insisting on dragging her back to the night before, to long deep kisses in the darkened doorway that had rattled her soul and had kept her riveted to the spot even after he had closed the door behind him.

"I said, maybe we should wear jeans and sweatshirts," Callie repeated. "It's a little chilly this morning."

Athen nodded. "Jeans and sweatshirts it is."

"Let's leave a little early and stop and see Grampa." Callie poured herself a bowl of corn flakes, the only cereal she could ever tolerate.

"Sounds like a good plan." Athen folded the paper, and reaching for her coffee, sighed. It had seemed a lifetime since she had been kissed that way . . .

"This will be fun." Callie sprinkled sugar into her bowl, "I wonder what Ms. Evelyn will want me to do . . . Mom, why are you grinning like that?"

"What?" Athen, shaken from her reverie, covered quickly. "Oh, I was just thinking about . . . how nice it is to help a friend . . ."

"I agree." Callie rinsed out her breakfast dishes and stacked them in the dishwasher. "It was sure nice of Mr. Forbes to let us help. Maybe he's not so bad, Mom. I mean, he was really pretty nice to me, even though I hadn't been real nice to him . . . I'm going to run up and get dressed so I can take Hannah for a walk . . ."

Callie disappeared from the room in a flash, leaving her mother to shake her head in wonder. Sometimes being a parent to a preadolescent child is like doing penance. One day they are sullen and moody, the next day they are responsible and resourceful, then suddenly they are four year olds again, dependent and demanding . . .

"You are amazing," she had whispered to Quentin the night before, "you totally turned her around in a flash. How did you know how to do that?"

"Kids like to be treated with respect and like to be recognized for their accomplishments," he said with a shrug. "Callie admires Ms. Evelyn and that admiration is returned. I thought it wouldn't hurt if I let her know."

"Callie hasn't treated you with much respect lately," Athen had reminded him.

"Sometimes kids need to know that you respect them first." He had started to nibble on her bottom lip, and if there had been further conversation after that, she could not seem to recall it now . . .

"Mom, you'd better get dressed." Callie breezed through the room, Hannah's leash over her shoulder, the dog bouncing and hopping merrily behind her. "Come on, girl . . . Mom, try to be ready when I get back, okay?"

The visit to Ari was more abbreviated than Athen would have liked, her father appearing somewhat pale and distracted. Athen had checked with Lilly on the way out, who confirmed that Ari seemed to be coming down with a cold, but Lilly assured her that she would make certain that the doctor checked in on him before the day was over.

"Wow!" exclaimed Callie as she and her mother approached their destination on foot, having had to park almost three full blocks away due to the large number of cars parked by other volunteers who had arrived before them.

"Wow indeed," Athen had repeated.

Scores of workers filled the vacant lots, bustling about like ants on moving day. Some carried old tires and broken pieces of furniture to the Dumpsters which lined the Schyler Avenue side, some were carefully picking up broken bottles, some removing rocks so that those who sat upon the large lawn mowers could begin to cut down the high grass. Along the Third Street side awaited the tractors, which would turn over the long-neglected hard ground, into which another army of volunteers would work truckloads of top soil and cow manure, the pungent aroma of which was just beginning to drift on a slight breeze.

"Hey, Ms. Evelyn!" Callie's face lit at the sight of the old woman in overalls and sunglasses who was directing the activity.

"No, no, Joe, you have to finish clearing that side section before you can bring that mower in there." Ms. Evelyn pointed a long thin brown finger towards the back of the lot, "and you, Thomas, go see Ms. Adeline for a Band-Aid for that cut . . . I told you to watch out for broken glass. Callie, I heard you and your mother would be helping out today. I'm so happy that you came by to give us a hand."

"What would you like us to do?" Callie asked eagerly.

"Well, Callie, I see Timmy is still moving rocks over there by the back fence. I'm sure he'd appreciate your help . . ." Ms. Evelyn suggested.

Athen closed her eyes and held her breath, awaiting Callie's protest.

"Sure," Callie agreed with only the slightest hesitation as she drew heavy canvas work gloves from the back pocket of her jeans. She took off in the designated direction, without a backwards glance at her somewhat drop-jawed mother.

"And you, Athen . . ." Ms. Evelyn smiled and patted her arm. "Let me see if I can find something suitable . . ."

"No, no," Athen shook her head, "I'm here as a friend. Like everyone else. I'll do whatever it is you need done now . . ."

"Well, then," Ms. Evelyn said as she surveyed the work in progress, "why don't you join Georgia—she's the young lady in the green sweatshirt over there—and Mr. Tate . . . they're picking up bottles and such . . . there's a basket right by the sidewalk there . . ."

Athen picked up a basket and headed towards her assigned work crew, unsuccessfully seeking out Quentin's tall form among the crowd. She introduced herself to old Mr. Tate, who appeared more than slightly hard of hearing, and to the green-shirted Georgia, a slender, pretty young woman with skin the color of cocoa and eyes like chunks of coal, who proved to be an amicable work companion. Georgia hummed and sang softly in a lovely lilting soprano as they carried out their chores. Athen found herself wishing she could carry a tune so that she could join in. At some point a photographer from *The Woodside Herald* snapped a picture of Athena as she lifted a load of glass.

Carrying yet another basket of bottles, Georgia had suggested they dump cans in one box, bottles in another so they could be recycled. Athen looked over her shoulder to locate her daughter in the ever-growing crowd of workers. As she scanned the throng, she found not only Callie, standing next to Timmy, but Quentin as well. He was speaking to both children, and seemed to have the absolute attention of both. She smiled to herself as she watched him place a hand on his son's shoulder.

What an incredible man he had turned out to be. She shook her head in wonder. Far from being the wisecracking reporter she'd thought she'd known, she could see in him strength and humor, gentleness and sweetness. She sighed inwardly. Not to mention that he'd awakened something inside her she'd assumed she'd never feel again . . .

"Well, I see you've met the boss," Riley Fallon said, exchanging a loving look with Athen's companion.

"Oh, you're Georgia's fiancé?" Athen was startled from her musings.

"Riley and I will be married in August." Georgia beamed.

"Well, my best to you both." Athen smiled with genuine pleasure, sneaking a peek over Riley's shoulder. The children were back to work carrying rocks. Quentin was nowhere to be seen. "I wish you every happiness."

"Thank you, Athen," Riley said as a loud whistle pierced the din created by a hundred or so chattering voices.

"What was that?" a startled Athen asked.

"The signal for lunch break," Georgia told her.

"Gosh, it didn't occur to me to pack lunch," Athen thought aloud. "I'd better grab Callie and run out to pick something up . . ."

"That's all been taken care of," Georgia assured her. "When you work with Ms. Evelyn, you don't have to worry about going hungry. I'd better go see if I can lend a hand . . ."

The young woman followed a path worn through the high

grass to the sidewalk, where tables were being set up in a highly organized fashion. The tables were quickly covered with white cloths upon which boxes were neatly stacked. The ladies of the AME Church of the Brethren were about to serve lunch.

"Ugh!" Athen studied her dirty hands, wondering how she could eat anything these fingers had touched. She waved to Callie as her daughter and Timmy approached her.

"Isn't this fun, Mom?" Callie's eyes sparkled.

"Let me see your hands," Athen demanded, and the child held out two blackened paws for inspection.

"Not to worry, Mom," Callie assured her, pointing to the line which had formed to the right of the tables.

She should have known Ms. Evelyn would think of everything. A hose hooked up to an outside faucet on the front of a row house across the street spewed water, and one of Ms. Evelyn's ladies offered liquid soap in a large pump container. Rolls of paper towels were stacked in the back of a nearby station wagon, large trash cans standing by for the discards.

"Hey, this is great stuff," Callie exclaimed as she opened her box lunch. "Look, Mom, ham sandwiches, apples, brownies . . . neat!"

They sat on the ground under a tree, surrounded by others seeking shade from the warming sun. Athen gratefully propped herself against the rough bark, happy to give her aching back a respite from bending over countless times to retrieve discarded bottles in the high grass. She popped open a can of icy cold soda and explored the contents of the white box.

"Hey, Timmy, over here!" Callie waved, turning to her mother to caution, "Don't say it, Mom . . ."

"Don't say what, Callie?" Athen asked innocently, suppressing a smile.

"Don't say 'I told you he was a nice kid,' okay?" Callie whispered.

"Never crossed my mind." Athen grinned as both dark-haired Forbeses approached.

"Hey, Timmy, I got brownies, did you?" Callie leaned over to open Timmy's box to peer inside.

"You look comfortable." Quentin smiled down at her. "Mind if I join you?"

"Pull up a rock and sit down." She smiled back. "But the tree trunk is mine and I'm not sharing it."

"A little out of shape, are we?" He plopped to the ground next to her.

"Sadly so." She nodded, unwrapping a ham sandwich on what appeared to be a freshly baked biscuit. "I haven't bent over this much since Callie was a baby and made a game out of pitching toys from the high chair . . ."

"Well, you know, some men find a woman covered in dry dust very sexy." He leaned towards her, a glint in his eye, whispering, "I myself find those grimy smudges across your face irresistible . . . and those little pieces of dried leaves in your hair . . ."

"You're a sick man, Quentin Forbes." Her hands probed around her head until she found the foreign matter and pulled the crunchy brown leaves from the tangle of her long tresses.

"Well, would you look at Himself," Quentin sat up suddenly and motioned towards the center of the clearing, where Dan Rossi, accompanied by Jim Wolmar, Harlan Justis, and Angelo Giamboni, strode through the crowd like visiting royalty.

"What do you suppose he's up to?" Athen wondered aloud, her eyes narrowing as she watched her former mentor shake a hand here, pause to give a pat on the back there.

"Giving this effort his blessing, my dear." Quentin grinned and took a bite of his apple. "And creating a photo op for himself at the same time. Look, there's the Channel Seven news van, just pulling up . . ."

The mobile newsroom set up quickly, the street reporter and camera crew seeking out first Ms. Evelyn, then Dan Rossi, who seemed to be doing a lot of gesturing and smiling. Athen observed in silence from her place at the back of the clearing, hidden from the cameras by the sea of workers in whose midst she went unnoticed.

"What a charade," Quentin scoffed as Rossi prepared to take his leave minutes after the news van had departed.

"What good timing on his part," Athen noted.

"Good timing, my foot." Quentin laughed derisively. "You don't really think it was a coincidence that he just happened to arrive right before the cameras, do you?"

"Of course not." She shook her head. "But to watch him, you'd think he was campaigning . . ."

"Certainly he's campaigning," Quentin told her. "A good politician never misses an opportunity to shake a few hands and make the people feel like he's one of them." He scrutinized her expression, then asked, "That doesn't bother you, does it . . . ?"

"Why would it bother me?" she fairly snapped. "He knows the job is his to take back next year. It just seems a little . . . early, that's all."

"Never too early," he replied, "especially since there's bad blood between the two of you. I suspect he knows you're here, and just wanted to remind everyone that he's still around. There are a lot of votes out here today."

"So?" Athen gathered up the wrappers from her lunch and stuffed them into the box.

"So he's just letting them all know he's on their side, so to speak."

"Whose side would they be on? There is no 'side' but his," she churlishly reminded him.

"Maybe," he muttered, "maybe not . . ."

"Want me to take that, Mom?" Callie reached a hand out for Athen's empty lunch box. "I'll throw it in the trash can over there . . ."

Callie and Timmy collected a stack of white cardboard containers from the adults sitting around them and headed for the trash receptacles which had been placed throughout the crowd.

"Guess it's time to get back to work." Quentin stood and offered a hand to Athen, who groaned as he pulled her up.

"What are you working on?" she asked. "I tried to find you earlier, but didn't see you."

"Well, I was helping Cal Greene and Reverend Davison with the tractors." He appeared pleased that she had admitted to looking for him. "And now I get to load cow manure onto wheelbarrows . . ."

"Better you than me." She grimaced, heading back in the general direction of her work basket.

"Well, now . . ." Ms. Evelyn observed them with genuine pleasure, noting the casual manner in which Quentin's hand rested on Athen's shoulder. "Isn't this nice?" Athen blushed scarlet as Quentin winked at Ms. Evelyn and went back to work.

If the morning had been long, the afternoon was endless. By four o'clock, however, the lots were devoid of debris, the weeds cut down, the ground plowed, and the new soil mixed in with the old. Ms. Evelyn was delightedly tearful as she surveyed the acre and three quarters of fertile ground. One by one the work crews departed, Ms. Evelyn hugging each of her laborers and thanking them for their efforts.

"Your father would be proud of you today," she told Callie, "you worked like a trooper . . ." Callie beamed with pride at the compliment. "As would Ari be," she added, holding Athen's hand. "God knows the man would have been right in the thick of things . . ."

"We'll be sure to tell him all about it," Athen assured her.

"Okay, Ms. Evelyn," Quentin said as he leaned down to place a fond kiss on the small woman's forehead. "Tomorrow morning, same time, same place?"

"Bless you, Quentin." She patted his arm.

"Tomorrow . . . same time, same place?" Athen asked in disbelief as they walked up Schyler Avenue. "You mean there's more . . . ?"

"Just for the carpentry crew," he said, laughing at the look of horror that had frozen to her face, "to build the platform I told you about. I told her I'd bring a hammer."

"Mommy, Timmy said I could come over and ride with him." Callie's delight at the prospect shone in her eyes. "Can I go? Please? I haven't gone riding in soooo long," she pleaded.

"Now?" Athen beheld the filthy urchin who stood before her. "I think you should go home and get cleaned up and have dinner . . ."

"She can have dinner with us, Mrs. Moran," Timmy offered.

"That's a great idea," Quentin said, taking hold of Athen's

207

elbow, "why don't you both plan on a ride with us, then stay and have dinner . . ."

"Quentin, this body is no match for a horse," she said with a groan, "my knees are sore, my back is sore . . . all I want is a long hot bath. Sorry, guys, but a nice brisk ride is not on my agenda. And Callie is not fit for polite company until she gets a shower."

"Well, then, why don't you two just go on home, get cleaned up, then drive out when you're ready?" he pressed. "We can sit and relax while the kids have their ride, then we can all have dinner together . . . Come on, Athen," he lowered his voice, "Callie and Timmy are getting along great, and she hasn't snarled at me once all day . . . I think we're making real progress here . . ."

"Okay," she agreed, "but I'll need at least an hour, if not more."

"Whenever." He unlocked his car and Timmy jumped in. "You remember where the house is, at the end of Pond Lane?"

She nodded, and steered Callie, who chattered incessantly, in the direction of their car. Dinner for the four of them would be interesting, she mused, but right now, nothing was more appealing than the thought of a hot bubbly tub and clean clothes. The Forbeses would have to wait.

34

Driving up the long lane which lead to the Chapman mansion, Athen recalled the one and only other time she'd been there, the night of the rally when Dan had announced her candidacy. She inwardly shuddered at the memory of that entire evening.

She parked at the side of the house and she and Callie proceeded to the front door. Brenda Chapman responded to the bell, greeting them with much more warmth than she had on the previous occasion of their meeting.

"Timmy's out back in the ring," Brenda told Callie. "I'm glad to see you wore long pants to protect your legs. Have you ridden before?"

"I used to take lessons," Callie told her as they proceeded through the enormous hallway, "but I stopped last year."

"Well, let's see just how much you remember." The young blond woman winked at Athen as they passed through a banquet-sized dining room and into a smaller one—probably the family breakfast room, Athen thought. French doors at one end of the room led onto a wide porch which spread the length of the house.

"Lydia," she addressed her stepmother who was seated on a high-backed white wicker chair, looking for all the world like a duchess, "Athen and Callie are here."

Lydia Chapman welcomed them as if they had been the oldest and dearest of friends.

"Do sit with me, dear." She motioned for Athen to take the chair to her left. "Quentin tells me you're not up to riding this afternoon. Brenda, take Callie down to the stable and let her choose a horse, will you? And tell Quentin our guests are here." Turning to Athen with a charming smile, she added, "Quentin took a walk down to see the new foal."

"A foal?!" Callie all but jumped for joy. "Can I see too?"

"Of course." Brenda laughed. "Right this way, miss."

"Quentin tells me you and Callie worked very hard today," Lydia said as she pressed a button on the wall. "Wonderful project. If Hughes and I were younger and less arthritic, we'd have been working right alongside of you. We're big believers in backing community efforts . . . Rose Ellen," she addressed the woman who appeared in the doorway in response, Athen surmised, to the push of the button, "we'd like some tea . . . you do drink tea, Athen? Good. A small pot would be lovely, Rose Ellen."

"You have a beautiful home, Mrs. Chapman," Athen told her.

"Thank you, dear, but do call me Lydia." She leaned back

into her chair and said, "Hughes bought this place at auction, years ago. It had been the home of a robber baron or Mafia person, I forget which. In any event, he spent years bringing it up to snuff. So much had to be done to it, it had been vacant forever." She paused momentarily as Rose Ellen produced the requested tea tray. "Thank you, dear . . . and we've had such fun buying antiques these past two years, though of course I had many of my own things shipped out from St. Louis—family pieces—no point in leaving them in storage with this wonderful house waiting to be filled up."

Lydia seemed to possess the ability to speak indefinitely without pausing for breath. Athen's head was beginning to swim when she noted Quentin's approach from across the vast lawn where, last Labor Day, tents had stood.

"Ah, there's my son now." Lydia smiled at the sight of him. "I can't tell you how delighted I am to have him and Timmy living here with us. They've had a bad time of it, what with Cynthia abandoning them like that . . . No one was more surprised than I was when she pulled up stakes with little more than a fare thee well and left them . . . How any woman could walk away from such a good man and such a darling child . . ." A cloud crossed Lydia's face. ". . . He's such a joy, my grandson . . . my only grandchild, you know . . . so like his father as a boy . . . Hello, darling, we were just talking about you."

"If I know you, you were talking and Athen was politely listening." He grinned, then said to Athen, "Feeling better now?"

"Much." She nodded, sipping at the hot tea.

"Not too late for a ride," he offered, perching himself on the railing that surrounded the porch.

"You let her relax," Lydia instructed, "and besides, she's not dressed for riding. That blue-green color is wonderful on you, by the way, Athen." Lydia indicated the sweater Athen wore. "Just right with those heathery colored slacks . . . I always loved those heather shades . . ."

"Mother," Quentin interjected, "I think Hughes just pulled up."

"Oh? Perhaps I should dash down to tell him we've

company for dinner." Lydia rose and bustled off into the house.

"My mother will talk you deaf, dumb, and blind if she likes you," Quentin said with a laugh, "and obviously she likes you. She'll have you dizzy before the night is over."

"I don't think it will take that long." Athen shook her head, wondering what had caused Lydia Chapman's apparent change of heart. The older woman's clear blue eyes, tranquil as a gentle sea today, had, on their last meeting, dismissed Athen with their frosty stare.

"Quick, let's walk down and watch the kids before she comes back." He held out his hand to her.

"Good idea." Athen placed the delicate porcelain teacup carefully back into its saucer, and together they strolled down towards the riding ring where Timmy and Callie appeared to be receiving some instructions from Brenda.

They hung over the fence for a while, quietly observing their respective offspring walk, trot, and canter at Brenda's command.

"Have you any interest in meeting the newest member of the family?" he asked.

"Who's that?"

"Right this way." He took her hand and led her down the hill.

The air was warm and close inside the stable. He turned a light on, disturbing a fat and sleepy cat who'd perched atop a bale of hay. The cat stretched long straight front legs, her eyes still closed. Athen followed Quentin down the dirt passage between the stalls. An occasional horse stuck an inquiring head over its gate.

"Here we are." He stopped in front of a double wide stall and opened the gate. "Hey, Jassie, good girl. We came to see your baby . . ."

He dug in his shirt pocket and retrieved a lump of sugar which he offered to the chestnut mare.

"Athen, grab an apple out of that basket behind you and give it to Jassie to show her you are her friend," he directed, stroking the horse's muzzle.

"A peace offering, is that it?" she asked, doing as she was told.

"Right. No, no, don't hold it like that, she'll take your fingers along with the apple," he instructed. "Hold your hand out flat with the apple on your palm . . . that's better."

Athen extended her hand and the horse leaned down to sniff at the offered treat. Large lips, soft as velvet, caressed the palm of her hand as the horse gently accepted the snack. Athen reached her hand up to the mare's head and ran her fingers along the white streak between Jassie's ears.

"She's lovely," Athen exclaimed.

"Don't you ride?" he asked.

"Callie does," Athen said, shaking her head, "but I never have."

"Want to learn?" he offered.

"Someday maybe, but certainly not today." She laughed. "I think my body's taken quite enough abuse for one day."

"Anytime you want, I'll be happy to give you a lesson or two. Now," he told her, "step on in here and see who's hiding in the corner."

Athen peered behind him, where a tiny foal tottered on rail-thin legs.

"Oh, how adorable," Athen whispered.

"Come here, Sophia," Quentin told the little one, "and meet my friend."

"Sophia?" Athen asked.

"My mother named her." He shrugged, coaxing the foal towards him.

"I had an aunt named Sophia," Athen told him as she petted the little animal. "She was my mother's sister. I only met her one time."

"When was that?" he asked, crossing the stall to give the required attention to Sophia's mother, who was warily watching the stranger. Quentin's voice seemed to calm her, and Athen was permitted to continue to stroke the newborn.

"When my mother died. Aunt Sophia came . . ." Her voice trailed off. "She and my father argued terribly. She blamed my father because my mother had polio . . . because my mother died. She wanted to take Mama back to Greece to bury her there."

"Did she?"

"We did. My father and I. It was the only time I ever went there. I never wanted to go back."

"Not to visit her grave?"

"I don't have to go to Greece to visit with her."

He looked at her quizzically.

"How much time before dinner?" she asked.

"Probably an hour."

"Come on." She took his hand, "I'll show you."

He drove through the park and out along the river as she directed.

"Go right," she told him, "now here, to the left through the gates of the cemetery . . . then follow the road back towards the river . . . slow down . . ." She peered past him, looking to the left. "Stop here."

He followed her from the car, crossing over a ridge where a well-worn path led to the river. They passed a grove of trees, beyond which was an embankment which stood thirty feet above the riverbed. A stone statue of a woman seemed to grow from the very rocks upon which she sat.

The woman sat back against a bench, holding in her arms a small girl. Both carved faces bore the traces of unspeakable sadness, and both faced in the direction of the sea, far from the embankment on which they perched.

Athen translated the inscription, which was written in Greek.

Melina Olympia Stavros.

Rest in peace, beloved.

"I thought you said she was buried in Greece," he said.

"She is," Athen told him. "My father had this sculpted the year after she died. It was his way of keeping her here with us, even though she rests so far away."

"The child is you, of course," he noted, stepping closer to inspect the features.

"The sculptor was my father's cousin." She nodded. "He knew my mother well, and was able to capture her delicacy quite nicely."

"She was lovely," he told her.

"More lovely than you could imagine." Athen stepped back to a small stone bench that stood nearby and sat upon it. "She was so tiny, so fragile. Her face could just about fit"—she held up one hand—"in your palm."

"What caused her death?"

"She had polio when she was young. It left her lungs very weak," she said softly. "She died of pneumonia."

He joined Athen on the bench and they sat wordlessly in the setting sun.

"I used to come here almost every day," she told him. "I couldn't bear it, not having her. I missed her so terribly for so long. The first few years after her death, I'd walk out here after school . . . I'd sit and pretend I was talking to her while I did my homework."

"You walked all the way out here?" His eyebrows raised. "It must be several miles."

"Two miles and seven-tenths," she said, smiling. "But I never minded. I always felt she was here, waiting for me. It changed my life, my mother dying when I was so young . . . it took away my sense of . . ." She groped for words.

"Security . . . ?" he ventured.

"It went deeper than that." She shook her head slowly. "My father always tried to make me feel secure and safe, but I had lost the ability to believe that he would always be there for me. For a long time I had the feeling that he, too, could be taken from me, and I would have no one . . ."

"And you wonder sometimes if Callie feels the same way?"

"Sometimes," she confessed, "but it's different because Callie was older than I was . . . I was five when my mother died. At least Callie was old enough to have had some understanding of what had happened to John. And she has a wealth of memories that I didn't have."

Quentin moved closer and put an arm around her, leaning over to kiss her forehead right at the hairline. He pulled her towards him, so that her back rested against his chest. She relaxed, and let her full weight lean upon him.

"When I found out about my father and Diana Bennett, I came up here and cried," she confessed. "I couldn't understand how my father could replace my mother in his life, with her watching from up here."

"And now . . . ?"

"Now I'm beginning to see how Diana filled all those empty places inside him, and it embarrasses me that it took me so long to accept it."

The shadow of the stone woman began to settle over them as the sun sagged behind the trees. A cool breeze blew across the embankment, and Quentin caressed her arm to warm her.

"I guess we should get back." Athen stood, taking his hand and pulling him up with her. "Callie will wonder where we've gone . . . I just wanted to show you . . ."

"I'm pleased that you did," he told her, "that you shared this bit of yourself with me."

She glanced back towards the statue, the features of which were in darkness.

"Which word is 'beloved'?" he asked as they turned to go.

"Agapemou," she said, pointing to the weathered wording, "means 'my beloved.'"

He repeated the word to himself softly, as if to memorize it, as they walked back to the car.

Dinner was a relatively informal affair. Informal, because Lydia had wanted to dine on the porch, but only relatively so because a staff of three had served them.

Hughes Chapman was affable and sweet, obviously adoring of his loquacious wife, indulgent of Brenda, his only child, and totally taken by Timmy, who, if Brenda had her way, would be as close as Hughes would ever come to experiencing the joys of grandparenthood.

"So, Athen . . ." Hughes smiled pleasantly at her as the salad was being served. "What's that scoundrel Dan Rossi up to these days?"

Athen all but choked on her water.

"Hughes, dear, Quentin said we're not to talk about Athen's job, or politics, or any of the articles he's written on either topic," Lydia told her husband from the opposite end of the table, under which Athen wished she could disappear.

"Well, then, that sort of narrows the field, doesn't it?" he noted. "Callie, Timmy tells us you're a crackerjack athlete . . ."

Athen chose to listen, rather than to participate in the conversation throughout dinner. From time to time she would glance across the table at Quentin, who ate quietly, an amused look on his face from salad through the main course of perfectly broiled lamb chops to the lemon mousse that completed their meal. At ten, when she could no longer keep her eyes propped open, she thanked her host and hostess, promising Lydia she would, indeed, love to come again, and motioned to Callie it was time to call it a day.

"Please bring Callie back next Saturday," Brenda pressed her, "she has the makings of a superb rider. Oh, I almost forgot . . . I wanted to get in touch with Meg. Would you happen to have her number with you?"

Athen scratched the number down on a piece of paper, wondering why Brenda would want to call Meg but was too tired to ask. Quentin and Timmy walked them to the car, Quentin promising to call her at some point over the next few days.

"Wake me when we get home." Callie yawned and Athen watched enviously as her daughter pushed the button to recline her seat.

Athen rolled the window down to let the cool night air flood the car, hoping it would keep her awake long enough to make the ten minute drive to their home. She pulled in the driveway, woke Callie, and together they walked on wooden feet to the house.

"Can you carry me?" Callie laid down on the steps, Athen dimly noting that where once her daughter could stretch from the first to the third steps, she now took up six.

"I am not certain I can carry myself." Athen stepped over her. "So unless you want to wake up in the morning with a horrendous backache, I suggest you drag your little self to bed."

"Waaa . . ." Callie protested weakly before getting up. "It was a fun day, Mom. Thanks for taking me. And for letting me ride with Timmy . . ." She yawned again. ". . . we had fun. And Brenda is so neat . . . and Sunny—that was my horse—is the best horse I ever rode . . ." She blindly kissed her mother's cheek and stumbled to her room. "'Night, Mom."

"Sweet dreams, baby," Athen replied, stripping off her sweater and her slacks as she passed into her room.

She grabbed a nightshirt and had barely pulled it over her head before all but crashing face forward onto the bed. Blurred images drifted behind her closed eyes . . . baskets of discarded bottles faded into mountains of rocks, which gave way to a parade of sorts, Callie and Timmy on horseback, Quentin on a backhoe. Scores of people lined up to wash their hands from a hose, and the church ladies dispensing lunch to everyone who had given up a day to help. Georgia Davison's hauntingly lovely voice drifting over the weeded lot. Ms. Evelyn's smile of pride and triumph at the end of the day as she had surveyed their accomplishments. Her mother, watching it all, from her place high on the ridge over the city.

Faces spun around and around, borne on the confused winds of a twister that blew through her semiconscious. Dizzy with fatigue, she stretched stiff arms and legs and sought to find a comfortable spot for her neck on the pillow, recalling suddenly what it had felt like to have rested against Quentin earlier that evening as they had sat overlooking the river. His body had been hard as a rock and yet as comforting as a feather bed. For the first time in her life, she fell asleep wishing she was wrapped in the arms of a man who was not her late husband.

35

"So," Meg's cheery voice sang through the phone, "is my room ready?"

"I'm working on it." Athen silently vowed to do exactly that this week. "Are you planning on a trip back East soon?"

"Possibly very soon," Meg announced in a rush of excitement. "Athen, the most incredible thing has happened . . . Brenda Chapman called me at nine o'clock this morning . . . you will never believe this . . . it seems Daddy Bigbucks, aka Hughes Chapman, just purchased a cable TV station . . . and he's looking for a news anchor . . ."

"Are you serious?" Athen bit her lip in gleeful anticipation. Brenda certainly had wasted little time between last night and this morning . . .

"Am I ever," Meg rhapsodized. "Brenda asked me to send her some tapes by overnight delivery . . . If they like them, they'll want me to come out to talk to them . . . Is this the best?"

"Meg, that would be wonderful." Athen all but danced at the prospect.

"You know, Brenda and I had talked briefly at Chapman's Christmas party last year—the one Buddy took me to—but I never dreamed that casual conversation would lead to something like this." Athen could visualize Meg's blond curls dancing as she shook her head. "And speaking of Buddy, what's this Brenda's telling me? What is going on?"

"I'm not sure that I know . . ." Athen hesitated.

"Brenda tells me you're pretty tight," needled Meg. "Why the change of heart?"

"It's a long story." Athen sighed.

"One I trust you'll relate in minute detail the very second I step off the plane," Meg prompted. "I did, by the way, tell you that he had eyes for you, did I not?"

"Yes, Meg, you did." Athen laughed at the memory.

"Well, he's a darling man, I've said that all along, and I think you could be very happy together," Meg told her.

Yes, he is darling and I am happy when I'm with him, Athen had wanted to confess. Knowing Meg would likely hop onto that like a flea onto a dog, Athen decided to spare herself Meg's investigative inquiries. For now, at least.

"I think you're being a bit premature," Athen said levelly, "since I've only seen him socially a few times."

"But you really like him, don't you?"

"Yes." Athen sighed. "I do, but . . ."

"Good," replied Meg, "it'll be good for you. If for no other reason than to remind you that you have a whole life ahead of you. I'm glad you're seeing someone, and I'm particularly happy that it's Quentin. He's still quite a catch."

"I'm not so sure I want to catch him or anyone else, but I will admit that I've enjoyed the time I spent with him."

"You make me crazy," Meg chided, "he's bright and funny and you may have noticed that he's adorable and handsome and . . ."

"Can it, Meg." Athen laughed. "We'll talk about it when you get out here."

"Well, hopefully that will be very soon. I'll let you know," Meg promised. "Give my love to Callie."

"Will do," Athen said as she hung up the phone.

What fun that would be, she mused as she washed up the lunch dishes, having Meg here. And I will call someone to come in and finish that wallpapering. What was the name of the man who had done all that work for Mrs. Kelly earlier this year? Parker? Pepper?

She dried her hands and went through the yellow pages. Here we go . . . Parsons. Norman Parsons. She dialed the number listed. Mr. Parsons answered the phone, and after listening to her description of what she needed, agreed to stop over on Tuesday evening.

She gathered up the Sunday paper and took it to the back porch. Opening the front page out flat, she was surprised to see her picture, bold as life, gracing the front page. "Woodside Heights Mayor Athena Moran was one of many enthusiastic workers at yesterday's kickoff of the UCC's new community garden. Story on page 3." Page three highlighted a series of photos, Ms. Evelyn waving a tractor onto the lot, a group of workers leaning on their shovels, Reverend Davison greeting several volunteers . . .

"Hey, Mom." Callie poked her head out the door. "I'm going to Carolann's for a while, okay?"

"Sure." Athen nodded, absorbed in the text of the article.

She scanned the paper, then folded it over, making mental notes of several articles she'd read in depth later, maybe after dinner. She thought of taking her bike out, but she was still tired from yesterday's exertion. What to do, she pondered. Impulse led her up the steps and into the attic, across a creaking floorboard or two to the alcove that overlooked the side yard.

The sheet covering the easel was gray with dust, and she carefully removed it, dropping it in a heap on the floor. She studied the canvas before her with a critical eye. Turning on the lights, she leaned closer. The tall spikes of the pale pink flowers rose against a background of faintest blue. White roses twined around a half-finished arbor. In the foreground, a branch of magnolia bent to frame the garden beyond. The painting, intended as a gift for John, had remained incomplete for over a year.

She stared at it, wondering if the image of the garden that had been destroyed by the storm remained full enough in her mind's eye to finish what she had begun. What a wonderful present for Callie, she thought. She went back downstairs and gathered the tools she would need. Some of her paints had dried and would need to be replaced, but there was enough to begin. Though the brush at first felt slightly awkward in her hand, soon she was lost in the colors, carefully shading here and adding light there. She was immersed in concentration, totally absorbed in her craft. When her stomach reminded her that she had not eaten in hours, she looked at her watch and was surprised to find that the afternoon had passed without notice. Callie would soon be looking for dinner.

She stepped back to look at her work. Not bad, she thought. I've done better, but after a long hiatus, this is pretty good. Gathering her brushes to clean them, she realized she was humming. How good it had felt, she acknowledged as she all but skipped down the steps, to shape color into form again. Bringing that form to life had once been a source of joy to her. Finding she could still transmit to canvas with her hands that which her eyes had seen filled her with a sense of peace. She was beginning to feel whole again.

She cleaned her brushes and changed her spattered shirt. Callie still was not home. She sat on the sofa and leaned her grateful back against the cushions. Perhaps just a short nap, she thought as she pulled a light afghan up to her chin.

It was after six when she was awakened by the ringing telephone. Dumbly following the shrill sound to its source, she stumbled into the kitchen and lifted the receiver.

"Did I wake you?" Quentin asked. "You sound as if you're half asleep."

"There's a reason for that." She yawned mightily.

"We need to build up your stamina," he admonished with a chuckle.

"Ummm . . ." she replied, then asked, "Did you get Ms. Evelyn's platform finished?"

"Yes, we did," he told her, slight static from the car phone cutting him off briefly. "Of course, we had a lot of expert assistance. Mr. Rossi showed up, hammer in hand, smiling for the cameras so that tomorrow's paper can show him participating in manlier-than-thou work. No sir, no sissy stuff like filling baskets with bottles for old macho Dan."

Athen laughed, and he told her, almost as an aside, "He invited me to interview him."

"What?"

"You heard me," he said.

"What's he want to talk about?" she wondered aloud.

"If you'll open the front door, I'll come in and tell you in person."

She peered out the side window. The little blue sedan was parked at the curb.

"I'm on my way," she laughed as she hung up.

He was dirty and sweaty and, she thought, positively adorable. A yellow baseball cap sat on the back of his head, the dark locks of hair stuck to his forehead with perspiration, and his Mets T-shirt bore the same smears of grime as did his arms and face.

"So what's Rossi up to?" she asked, wishing she had the nerve to put her arms around him, maybe kiss that little smudge that ran across his upper lip . . .

"Beats me, but I thought it was really interesting that he sought me out," he said with a grin. "I'm to meet him out at his club for dinner. Curious, no?"

"Curiouser and curiouser." She led him by the hand into the living room.

"No." He shook his head as she approached the sofa. "I'm much too grimy to sit on your furniture. I just thought I'd stop and see how your aching back was faring."

"Much better, thank you." She smiled as he leaned back against the wall and drew her to him.

"Perhaps a quick massage . . ." He ran his hands up and down her back, kneading her muscles with his strong fingers.

"Ouch . . ." She winced and he softened his touch. "We had fun last night, Callie and I . . ."

"So did we." He watched her face as his fingers made their way more slowly from her neck to her waist and back again. "Mother made me promise to bring you back. And of course, Timmy and Callie have made plans for next Saturday to ride."

"Well, I certainly don't want her to impose . . ." His proximity was beginning to make her dizzy. She wondered if he could tell.

"Tim loved the company, and Brenda enjoyed working with her," he assured her, rubbing her shoulder blades gently.

"Brenda called Meg this morning, did you know?" Maybe if she could keep a conversation going she could regain control of her breathing . . .

"I knew she was going to." He paused before asking, "What do you think of the idea?"

"Of Meg working back here? Are you kidding?" . . . then again, maybe not.

"That's what I thought, too." He tipped her face up slightly and kissed her as she had hoped he would do. His lips were warm and soft and drew her deeper and deeper towards a place she had thought she'd never find again. Forgotten emotions surged through her, and she felt her hands moving on their own to his face, her fingers touching his cheeks, moving upwards slowly to wind their way through the damp curls at his forehead.

It took a moment for her to realize he had stopped kissing her, that his lips were merely resting upon hers. She opened one eye and looked up at him, then opened the other, confused. His gaze was locked onto something beyond her.

She twisted around in his arms to see what was distracting him from what she had considered to be some world-class kissing.

"What?" she asked. The room was as it had always been.

"I feel as if I'm defiling a shrine," he told her, nodding towards the mantel where John Moran watched from a row of photos which spanned the entire fireplace.

She could feel his hands losing their hold on her until they barely rested around her waist. She raised her eyes to meet his, and they stared at each other for several long minutes.

"I think I'd better get going." He cleared his throat, as if mildly embarrassed, then glanced thoughtfully over her head to the photographs once again, "I'm supposed to meet Dan at seven"—he peeked at his watch—"which doesn't give me much time to clean up."

She nodded, confused and at a loss for words. She walked him to the foyer, watching his face even as he bent to kiss her lightly before opening the screen door and stepping onto the landing. He turned and hesitated, as if about to say something.

"I'll call you later, if I get in early," he said, and she knew the words he spoke were not the ones he'd wanted to say.

She leaned against the spot on the living room wall where his body had been, studying the opposite wall, trying to see it as he had. The array of photos, the row of framed commendations for John's acts of bravery which lined the nearby wall, all stood as testimony to the man who had once lived in this house, the man who had loved her and fathered her child. Quentin had felt John's presence and had been spooked by the thought of kissing her beneath the eyes of her dead husband.

Her back followed the wall to the floor and she sat, Indian style, as the clock ticked on towards evening.

"Oh, John . . ." She sighed, the words barely audible in the heavy stillness of the room.

Soon the daylight moved from the open windows and shadows began their soft advance across the carpet, and still she sat, caught between the past and the present, and taunted by a future that threatened to slip away from her.

* * *

Running late the next morning after a sleepless night, she grabbed the paper from the front steps on her way to the car. Her first glimpse at page one came at her desk as she had opened it and sputtered half a mouthful of coffee onto the headline, "Rossi blasts Moran," then below that, in only slightly smaller print, "Calls present mayor 'the only political error I ever made.'"

White knuckles grasped the edges of the paper to hold it in front of her disbelieving eyes. "In an exclusive interview with *The Woodside Herald,* former mayor Dante Rossi admitted he had committed a major "error in judgment" in backing political novice and current mayor Athena Moran for office. "Athen Moran is a lovely woman, and she means well, I'm sure," Rossi said, "but the fact is that she hasn't a clue about running this city, except maybe to run it into the ground by trying to give away parcels of valuable land that should be used to increase tax revenues, not to add to the burden which our taxpayers are already shouldering."

On and on it went for almost half the page.

"That—that son of a bitch," she sputtered, "when I get my hands on Quentin Forbes I will kill him!"

Pacing the length of the room on trembling legs, she waged war with her emotions, jousting with the rage which threatened to overpower her. She was incensed that Quentin would do this to her, infuriated with herself for having let her guard down, for believing he could be anything other than what he had proven himself to be in the past. She was too angry to even acknowledge that he had not broken his promise. The article contained no reference to Mary Jo Dolan.

"Mrs. Moran," Veronica buzzed through the intercom, "Mr. Forbes is on line seventeen."

"Tell him I'm not in," she seethed, "not today, not any day. If he has something to say to me, he can address it at the next press conference."

"Excuse me, Mrs. Moran," Veronica teetered in on high heeled red shoes that matched the color of her dress, "but I don't think I heard . . ."

"You heard, all right." Athen's eyes blazed. "You tell that son of a bitch . . ."

Veronica calmly picked up the receiver on Athen's desk and announced in a slightly nasalized monotone, "Sorry, Mr. Forbes, but Her Honor is supremely pissed off and doesn't want to talk to you . . ." She covered the mouthpiece with her hand, asking Athen, "How was that . . . ? What? Okay, hold on . . . Mrs. Moran, he said it's really important that he . . ."

"Not now, not ever." Athen launched into a string of bilingual curses.

"No go, Mr. Forbes," she told him. "I'll give her the message, but it won't do any good, I can tell ya, she's really steamed . . . yeah, cursing in English and in Greek."

"Hang up the damned phone!" Athen hissed.

"Sorry," Veronica sang blithely as she hung up. Turning to Athen, she asked, "What'd he do?"

Athen pointed to the newspaper which now lay in a crumpled ball on the floor. Veronica picked it up, scanned it, then whistled long and low.

"Wow," she said, "Rossi's got it in for you, all right . . . what an ass . . . but don't worry, Mrs. Moran, it's obvious he's just trying to make you look bad 'cause you pissed him off."

Veronica headed for the door, thinking a cup of tea might calm the boss lady down. She had gone as far as the hallway, when she turned back to Athen and said, "Ya know, I can see you wanting to lynch Rossi for saying all those things about you . . . but why're you mad at Mr. Forbes?"

"He wrote the article." Athen stated the obvious through tightly clenched jaws.

A look of mild confusion passed over the young woman's face. "But . . . isn't that his job . . . ?"

"Out," whispered Athen, clinging to the very last shred of her patience, "and close the door."

Athen remained holed up in her office all day, taking no calls and accepting no visitors. Veronica brought her some lunch, which she could not eat, and when she left a half hour early, Veronica told her, "He called seven times, Mrs. Moran."

"I don't want to hear about it," snapped Athen.

"I promised him I'd tell you."

"And you have. Goodnight, Veronica."

It did nothing to improve her state of mind to walk into her kitchen and find him waiting there, calmly talking to Callie.

"Hi, Mom." Callie brightened as her mother came through the back door.

"What are you doing here?" she asked him coldly.

"I want to talk to you," he replied.

"I don't have anything to say to you." She walked past him into the hallway.

"Fine. I'll talk and you listen."

"Guess now's a good time to take old Hannah for a walk," Callie announced uneasily. "Come on, Hannah . . ."

"Athen," he said, following her.

"You really have a lot of nerve, coming into my house, after what you did to me." She spat out the words.

"What I did to you?" he asked incredulously. "Look, Athen, I can see you being angry that Rossi's come out swinging, but . . ."

"I didn't expect you to help him."

"What's that supposed to mean?" He grabbed her arm as she tried to breeze past him. "Athen, I didn't put words in his mouth."

"You promised me you'd never come after me in print again." She swallowed back the tears. "So much for your word."

"Athen, I promised I'd be fair to you, but that doesn't extend to not reporting on what someone else says about you, particularly when that someone is Dan Rossi," he explained as calmly as he could.

She ran cold water in the sink and filled a glass, taking a long deep drink.

"I want you out of my house." The tears welled up and she fought to keep them from rolling down her face.

"Athen, do you honestly believe I'd deliberately write something with the intent of hurting you?" he asked softly.

"You gave him a forum to openly criticize me."

"What are you saying, Athen, that I should have used everything he said except what he said about you?" He leaned back against the counter and crossed his arms. "Do you really expect me to censor what is printed so that only the nice things that people say about you get into the paper?"

She glared at him, but did not respond.

"Athen, I'm a reporter," he said with a sigh, "not your personal press secretary."

"You could have at least warned me it was going to be so . . . ugly."

"Athen, it was so late when I got home last night . . . and I tried to call you this morning . . . Athen, what would you expect him to say about you, given the circumstances?" He ran his fingers through the curls which drooped on his forehead. "For Christ's sake, Athen, if you'd read the article all the way through, you'd have seen that he's using you as an excuse to run again . . . 'I feel honor bound to take the city back from the misguided few who would create a fiscal nightmare' . . . That's a story, Athen. The fact that I wanted to put the SOB's lights out because of what he said—and that it killed me not to dangle his little sweetheart in his face—has nothing to do with the fact that I have a responsibility to report what he says—as he says it. I can't pretty it up because of our relationship."

"Well, you won't have to worry about that anymore," she said quietly.

"What's that supposed to mean?" He eyed her cautiously.

"You said it best, Quentin. 'Fool me once, shame on . . .'"

"Athen, please . . ." The two words, whispered, were a prayer.

"I want you to leave now." She avoided his eyes.

"Athen, I'm more sorry than you know," he told her from across the room, his heart very much visible, right there on his sleeve.

They stared glumly at each other, the silence widening the distance between them. He appeared to be searching for words, his lips moving slightly, though nothing came forth. Finally, he shook his head numbly, then turned, shoulders slumped, and walked out the back door.

Athen was still standing near the sink, the glass of water in her hand, when Callie came back into the house.

"You're not happy with Mr. Forbes right now, are you, Mom?" Callie seemed to choose her words carefully.

"No, Callie, I'm not." Athen turned her back on her daughter and emptied the water glass into the sink.

"Does this mean I can't ride with Timmy on Saturday?" Callie asked wistfully.

"Of course not," Athen assured her, "this has nothing to do with you and Timmy."

"Good." The child sighed with relief. "Brenda said she'd teach me how to jump."

36

"Life Sucks" announced the bumper sticker on the car stopped in front of Athen's at the red light. No argument there, she wryly noted. At least, not this week.

The congestion of cars fleeing the city at five o'clock normally did not bother her. Tonight, the maze of vehicles, the pouring rain, the honking horns, all served to aggravate her already morose mood which had been with her since the alarm had gone off that morning and only deepened as the day progressed. Veronica wisely had kept Athen's door closed to all, not intruding into the big office herself other than to deliver phone messages that she quietly slipped onto her boss's desk, or to bring in an occasional cup of coffee. For the better part of the day, Athen sulked in solitude.

It can all turn sour so quickly, she had noted bitterly, looking out the window to the view up Third Street. In the distance she could see the open brown plot of newly turned soil at Ms. Evelyn's garden, the trace of a white structure rising from its center. She turned her back on it and went back to her desk, rattling through the stack of mail that she barely read, feeling the woes of the universe on her shoulders.

Everyone had let her down. Ms. Evelyn had not pulled

through for her, Rossi has made her look like the village idiot . . . thanks to Quentin. Quentin. She shook her head, wondering how she could have believed for one minute that she would ever be more than a potential story to him, how she could have trusted him. But he did not betray that trust, a tiny voice inside reminded her.

At least Meg will be home soon and I'll have a sympathetic shoulder to cry on, she comforted herself as she slowly rounded the corner onto her street, avoiding the wide slashes of water, remnants of the brief but heavy downpour. A strange pickup truck was parked in her driveway. Curious, she pulled up to the curb and approached the man who sat in the driver's seat.

"Norman Parsons. Paint & Paper" read the sign on the truck. Of course. Mr. Parsons . . .

"Hi," she called to him, dodging a puddle at the end of the drive, "am I late?"

"No, actually I'm a bit early." He turned off the radio talk show and hopped out of the cab. He was a very small man, half a head shorter than Athen, with the face of a gnome and white hair upon which sat a painter's white cap, speckled with multicolored bits of confettilike paint, the evidence of recent jobs performed.

"Come on inside." She motioned him to follow her.

Hannah sniffed intently at his shoes as they entered the house, Athen telling Mr. Parsons to ignore the beast whose nose began to inch up his pants leg. Athen banished Hannah to the backyard.

"I can see you need a lot done here." He nodded, looking from the entry into the living room. "I'd say your whole first floor . . ." He followed the faded walls right up to the second-floor landing. "Yep, all the way up . . . How long's it been since you painted in here?"

"Umm . . ." She tried to recall when John had last tackled the job. "Maybe eight years . . ."

"I'd say you're due," he told her, "but I'd have to schedule that for maybe August, booked solid through July . . ."

"Well, this wasn't what I'd called you about," she said.

"There's a bedroom upstairs that's partially papered that I'd like completed . . ."

She went up the stairs, the gnome in the painter's hat stopping to check the wood moldings. "This should all be redone," he told her, a bit too cheerfully, she thought.

"Yep." He surveyed the job which John's death had interrupted, "not a whole lot here to do . . . you got enough paper?"

She pointed to the brown wrapper wherein three double rolls of pale yellow paper were bundled, explaining, "My husband started this . . ."

"A shame that was." He shook his head slowly. "Met him a time or two. Had all the tools stolen off my truck once, your husband responded to the call. Nice young fellow he was. A real shame."

"Yes. Thank you." Athen nodded, wondering how she'd tell Meg she would be stuck in the room with the bunny paper again. "Do you think you could fit this in before August?"

"Well, it's a real small job . . . maybe half a day, having the table and all set up will save a little time . . . Did you need this done anytime special?"

"Well . . ." She paused, trying to judge when Meg would most likely be back. "As soon as possible, actually. My sister-in-law will be here for a visit within the next week or so . . ."

"Hmmm . . ." He studied the project. "How 'bout Thursday morning . . . that soon enough?"

"That'd be great," she said, relieved that she would not have to endure another one of Meg's lectures about putting things off, "but I thought you were booked up?"

"This job is nothing . . . the big jobs get booked, but this I can fit in." He smiled pleasantly. "I can probably do this myself. Seven-thirty too early for you?"

"Not at all." She was pleased. Something went right for a change.

"You really should think about doing the rest of the house before too long, Mrs. Moran," he told her as they marched back down to the first floor. "Bright, pretty lady like you should not be living in such drab rooms."

But they are perfectly coordinated with my life, not to mention my state of mind, she had been tempted to tell him.

"I had thought about repainting, but I haven't gotten around to it," she said as she led him to the front door.

The phone rang once and Callie answered it in the kitchen. Judging by Callie's shriek of laughter, it was one of her girlfriends. Athen went upstairs and changed into slacks and a light sweater, the evening air being brisk with the passing of the storm. She had to do something about feeding them both, but had no inclination to cook.

"Callie, want to go for pizza?" she asked as she strolled into the kitchen.

"Wait, hold on Tim." Callie put her hand over the phone. "What, Mom?"

"Pizza?" She frowned. Timmy. I had to encourage her to befriend him.

"Sure. Just a minute . . . go on, Timmy . . . yes . . ." She giggled.

Athen sighed and went out onto the back porch to sit with Hannah, waiting for her daughter to finish her conversation with the enemy's spawn.

Mr. Parsons had, indeed, finished the room on Thursday, which, as it turned out, was not a day too soon. Returning from work at five-fifteen on Friday afternoon, Athen opened the back door to let Hannah out and found Meg camped on the back porch.

"For heaven's sake, what are you doing out there?" said a delighted Athen, hugging the new arrival.

"I forgot my keys." Meg shrugged nonchalantly.

"How long have you been here?"

"The cab dropped me off maybe forty minutes ago." Meg lifted her suitcase and carried it into kitchen, Athen following with the smaller overnight bag. "I thought Callie'd be home."

"Ordinarily she would be," Athen told her, "but she has a big softball game on Saturday, so they had an extra practice. I take it you're here at Ms. Chapman's request . . . ?"

"She called me at the station yesterday." Meg's eyes

glowed. "She loved my tapes, showed them to her father, he loved them . . . so they wanted to meet with me. Needless to say, I could not get out of Tulsa fast enough."

"When's your meeting scheduled?" Athen put water on for tea.

"Tomorrow. Brenda said you and Callie would be out in the afternoon, that Callie will be riding, so I will get to talk to Hughes, providing, of course, that I pass the test with Brenda. Great, huh? You get to shmooze with a handsome man, Callie gets a riding lesson, hopefully I'll get a job offer . . ."

"Two out of three ain't bad." Athen opened the cupboard and removed two cream colored mugs.

"What's that mean . . . two out of three?" Meg frowned.

"Callie will be riding, and you will be interviewing, but yours truly will not be shmoozing or anything else with your future employer's stepson."

"What?" Meg dropped her purse on a chair. "Four or five days ago this was a promising romance. What the hell happened?"

"This happened." Athen pulled the offending news article from beneath a stack of papers on the floor near the back door. Meg sat down and read through it, occasionally uttering a curse on Rossi's head.

"He is one nasty critter," Meg noted, reading a particularly odious phrase or two aloud, causing Athen's eyes to fill with tears all over again.

"Can you believe he did that to me?" She broke down and sobbed the way she'd wanted to do all week. "And I trusted him, Meg . . ."

"I told you before," Meg said, shaking her head slowly, "Rossi is not a man to be trusted."

"I'm not talking about Rossi." Athen sniffed. "I'm talking about Quentin."

"What about Quentin?" Meg stared at her blankly.

"What do you mean, 'what about Quentin'?" Athen blew her nose. "It's his story . . ."

"It has his byline, but he didn't say all those things about you, Athen, Dan Rossi did." Meg pointed out the obvious. "So what's the problem . . . ?"

"The problem is that a man I was starting to care about and trust . . ."

"Stop right there." Meg held up a hand, her eyes widening. "Are you telling me that because you had something going with Quentin, he should not have gone ahead with this story? Is that what this is all about?"

"Meg, Quentin promised me he'd be fair to me . . ."

"Don't you understand that this article has nothing to do with you?" Meg asked incredulously.

"It has everything to do with me," Athen protested, blowing her nose into a tissue. Where was the sympathetic shoulder, the comfort of her best friend . . . ?

Meg scanned the article again, shaking her head. "I just don't believe this . . ."

"I didn't believe it either." Athen sniffed again and reached for a tissue.

"It's your attitude I don't believe." Meg's eyes began to smolder the way they always did when her ire was aroused. "Your expectations are way out of line, Athen. You have no right to think that because you're cozy with the press . . ."

"He promised he wouldn't hurt me," Athen protested.

"And he hasn't," Meg nearly shouted, "Dan Rossi has. Can't you tell the difference?"

"You sound just like Quentin!" Athen glared at Meg.

"I should hope so." Meg nodded vigorously.

"I thought he cared about me," Athen tried to explain.

"I'm sure he does," Meg shot back, "and I'm sure this"—she grabbed the paper—"has nothing to do with the way he feels."

"It hurt me that he wrote those things about me." Why did she need to defend herself to her best friend?

"Then develop some thicker skin." Meg poured herself another cup of tea. "Athen, if you take this type of thing personally, you and I could have some real problems. If I get this job—which I hope very much to do—there may be times when the news doesn't put you in a particularly favorable light. Are you going to expect me to only report on the positive and ignore the negative? Because if you do . . ." Meg shook her head emphatically. ". . . the next year will be a very long one . . ."

The lump in Athen's throat had grown as Meg spoke.

". . . and we should get one thing clear right here and now," Meg told her bluntly, "don't ever expect me to compromise myself for you the way you expected Quentin to. It won't happen, Athen."

They sat in stony silence, staring at each other.

"Are you angry with me?" Meg asked quietly.

"No," whispered Athen. "I guess I expected you to be more supportive of my feelings, but I'm not really angry. I just didn't want to hear it from you . . ."

"I am—now and always—supportive of you," Meg said and sighed. "You're one of the most important people in my life, Athen. I love you and I'm very sorry you feel wounded. But you're wrong this time, and I can't lie and tell you I think Quentin is a cad for not refusing to print what Dan had to say. What you need to understand is that he had no choice . . . that's his job, and I'd be willing to bet he wasn't particularly happy about doing it."

Fingers tapping on the table, Athen stared into her cup of cold tea.

"And here's something else you won't want to hear," Meg said without rancor, "you owe him a very big apology, regardless of how you feel about him . . ." She paused, then asked, "How *do* you feel about him?"

Athen shook her head to indicate she didn't know. She was having trouble separating her emotions, and wasn't too sure of anything right at that moment.

"Yea! Aunt Meg!" Callie flew through the door and engulfed Meg in a bear hug.

"The Woodside Slugger has arrived," Meg said and laughed. "Big game on Saturday, so I hear."

"Will you come?" Callie pleaded.

"Wouldn't miss it," her aunt assured her.

"Come on, Aunt Meg." Callie grabbed the flight bag with one hand and Meg's arm with the other, pulling her towards the door. "We have a surprise for you upstairs . . . You coming, Mom?"

"In a minute." Athen tried to force a smile at her exuberant offspring.

"You think about what I said," Meg whispered as Callie dragged her from the room.

Mr. Parsons had done a fine job on the wallpaper, but unfortunately, the bed in which Meg was to sleep was still in pieces in the attic. After dinner, the three Morans carried the components down to the second floor, and assembled the bed, then folded up the work table, and removed it and the ladder to the garage. By ten o'clock, a guest room had emerged.

"This is wonderful, Athen," Meg said with a smile, "my own room . . . temporarily, of course."

"For as long as you need it."

"Thanks." Meg held out a hand to her. "Am I forgiven?"

"There's nothing to forgive." Athen took Meg's hand. "But you're right, you know. I behaved like a bratty child. And what do I do about it now?"

"Well, the shortest distance between two points is still a straight line." Meg sat down on the edge of the freshly made bed. "Why don't you just call him?"

"I don't know what I'd say." Athen leaned against the doorway.

"How 'bout, 'Quentin, I'm sorry. I was wrong'?"

"I think I'll have to work up to it," Athen told her.

"Well, don't take too long." Meg unzipped her suitcase, searching for a nightgown and her toothbrush. "I'm sure you're not the only woman in Woodside Heights who knows a hunk when she sees one."

37

"Here, Callie, give me that." Meg reached for the picnic basket which Callie had single-handedly filled with God only knew what.

"Thanks, Aunt Meg." Callie straightened her baseball cap

and grabbed her glove and cleats. "Mom, you ready? I want to stop and see Grampa before the game."

"I know, Callie." Athen bent down to tie her sneakers. "I will be just one minute . . . What's the picnic basket for?"

"Oh, see, I thought since you and Aunt Meg would be at the game," Callie closed the door behind them as they headed out, "you could have lunch together."

"That's very thoughtful, Callie." Athen rubbed a hand across her daughter's back fondly.

"Judging from the weight of the basket, I'd say you could probably feed the entire team," Meg said with a laugh.

"Well, there are a few extra sandwiches and stuff," Callie explained, "in case I get hungry too."

"Hey, look!" Callie all but jumped from the car as Athen slowed to park in the Woodside Manor lot. "Mrs. Bennett's up on the porch with Grampa . . ."

Diana waved as Callie flew up the slight incline, and turned Ari's wheelchair so he could watch his grand-daughter's approach. She folded the newspaper she'd been reading to him, and pulled three more chairs over to accommodate his visitors. They laughed and chatted for almost an hour, Ari seemingly pleased to be surrounded by those he loved most.

"Mom, it's almost ten," Callie noted with alarm, "I have to be on the field in fifteen minutes."

"Then we'd better get you there." Athen leaned over to kiss her father, telling him, "Your granddaughter is the designated slugger, Papa. You should see her hit that ball."

"I for one can't wait." Meg stood up and stretched. "And since I remembered my camera this trip, we'll have lots of pictures to show you, Mr. Stavros."

"Mrs. Bennett . . ." Callie stood before Diana's chair. "Would you like to come to my game too?"

"Why, I'd be delighted." A broad grin spread over Diana's face, obviously grateful to have been included.

Callie gave her directions to the field, reminding her not to have lunch, "'cause I packed lots of stuff."

"You and Diana seem to be getting along well these days," Meg noted as they spread an old blanket on the ground behind the fence that ran the length of the first-base line.

"We are, I am pleased to say." Athen nodded. "I was so wrong about her, Meg. She is so devoted to my father . . ."

"That's obvious." Meg anchored one end of the blanket with the picnic basket. "What the hell could that child have stuffed in here? This damned thing weighs a ton."

"Let's take a peek." Lifting the lid, Athen began to laugh. "Take a wild guess how many sandwiches . . ."

"Six?"

"Try eight." Athen poked a finger inside the lid, counting. "And a dozen juice boxes packed in plastic bags filled with ice. That accounts for the weight."

They settled down on the blanket, Meg popping up every few minutes to snap a picture of her niece. Diana joined them within the hour, sitting between the two of them, and immediately asked, "Have I missed lunch?"

"Not by a long shot." Athen opened the basket and rattled off the contents. "Let's see . . . peanut butter and . . . this looks like grape jelly. Peanut butter and what . . . Raspberry? Cherry? Hard to tell—let's call it red stuff. Peanut butter and maybe peach or apricot . . ."

"I'll have one with the red stuff." Meg reached out a hand. "And one of those juice things."

"Apple juice or berry punch?" Athen asked.

"Apple." Meg peered inside. "What else has she got in here . . . ?"

"Doritos . . . grapes . . . a bag of little candy bars, and two packs of sugarless gum."

"Child thought of everything," Diana said with a laugh. "Pass over one of those sandwiches . . . yes, that one's fine. Mystery jelly was always my favorite."

"My juicebox is missing its little straw." Meg held up the box wrapped in cellophane. She pitched it back into the basket and reached in and grabbed another.

"Have you had an opportunity to speak with Ms. Evelyn?" Diana asked.

"Yes, I did." Athen frowned. "But there's no sign of life there."

"What do you mean?"

"She didn't seem to have any ideas at all," Athen said and shrugged.

"Be patient." Diana fought with the tiny straw, trying to force it into the even tinier hole in the top of the box. "She'll come up with something."

"I don't know, Diana." Athen unwrapped her sandwich. "I'm not certain that she hasn't given up on the shelter and just put all her energy into the community garden."

"Not a chance," assured Diana, "I see that garden as part and parcel of some master plan of hers. Besides, it's not in her nature to give up."

"Well, she certainly didn't offer much encouragement." Athen dabbed at a glob of jelly that had plunked onto the front of her shirt.

"What did you expect her to say?" chided Diana good-naturedly. " 'No problem, Athen. I'll just get ahold of Riley Fallon and influence him to change his vote' . . . ?"

"I guess I thought she'd, I don't know, maybe be more forthcoming," Athen admitted.

" 'These things must be done delicately,' " Diana effectively mimicked the wicked witch from *The Wizard of Oz*. "But don't worry, she will come up with exactly the right approach, trust me. And when she does, you will be struck dumb by her ingenuity. I've seen her do some pretty amazing things over the years."

Callie came up to bat, and Athen stood near the fence to cheer her on. On the third pitch she hit a double, her mother jumping up and down and yelling, her aunt whistling between two fingers. Three batters later Callie rounded third base towards home, and after crossing the plate to score, putting her team ahead, she raised a fist and pumped her arm in the air in the general direction of her mother.

". . . but I sure wish I had a handle on what he's up to . . ." Diana was saying to Meg when the proud momma sat back down.

"Did you see that kid run?" Athen was out of breath from yelling. "What who's up to?"

"Diana was filling me in on Rossi's curious attachment to

those vacant houses on Fourth Street." Meg tossed the bag of Doritos across the blanket to Athen.

"Diana thinks whatever it is, it's something Dan has been sitting on for the last three or four years."

"Why?" Meg asked, picking through the grapes and wrinkling her nose. "Do you think Callie thought to wash these? The last few tasted a bit gritty."

Athen laughed and picked up the bag of grapes, taking them to the water fountain to wash them off. She sat back down as Meg asked Diana, "Then you think something Ari saw that morning was somehow connected . . . ?"

"I feel certain of it," Diana said, nodding emphatically, "and I think that whatever it was, Ari had words with Dan about it, particularly since Dan rushed to the hospital practically within minutes of Ari's admission. He waited there all night, as if he had to know what condition he was in and couldn't wait for the reports."

"So he goes to the hospital and finds out that the fates have intervened by sealing Ari's lips, so to speak," Meg murmured, obviously intrigued.

"Throw me one of those little Snickers bars, will you, Athen?" Diana caught it in her right hand.

"What could Ari have seen?" Meg wondered aloud. "Something through the window?"

"Impossible," Diana said and shook her head. "The only window in Ari's office was at the opposite side of the room. The phone didn't reach."

"Something out in the hall, then . . . something outside his door . . ." Meg mused.

"No. Ari had put the phone down and closed the door . . ." Diana told them.

"Something he saw before the phone call?" suggested Athen.

"I don't think so," Diana said as she unwrapped the miniature candy bar and took a bite, "because we were talking about something else . . ."

"And what was it he said?" Meg asked.

"He said, 'I see he's gone too far this time,'" Diana recited.

"If he couldn't see out the window, and he couldn't see out into the hallway, what the hell could he have been looking at?" Meg scratched her head. "A memo? A letter . . . ?"

"The newspaper," whispered Athen.

Diana's head shot up. "Of course. It was the first thing he did every day . . ."

"What was the date of your father's first stroke, Athen? Do you remember . . . ?"

"Late September, early October . . ."

"October 9, 1990," Diana said quietly.

"Look, my interview with Brenda is at her office at the *Herald* at two . . ." Meg told them.

"I thought it was at the house," Athen said, munching a grape.

"That's the interview with Poppa Bear at four." Meg rumbled around in the basket for another box of juice, noting, "These things don't hold much, do they? In any event, maybe if there's time after the interview I can go through the archives, see what's on microfiche for that day . . ."

"It's certainly worth a shot." Diana nodded.

"Callie's up again." Athen went to the fence, her companions following.

The three women shouted encouragement, to which Callie responded by slamming a long ball into right field. The runners on second and third both scored, ending the game in favor of the Woodside Heights Girls Club. The jubilant winners lined up for the traditional handshake with the opposition, after which they threw their hats into the air and jumped up and down hugging each other, Meg in their midst snapping one photo after another.

"You guys save me any food?" The business of winning the game having been tended to, Callie plunged into the open picnic basket with both hands.

"Eat quickly, kid." Meg tapped her on the head. "I have an interview in exactly one hour and fifteen minutes, and I'm not showing up in Brenda Chapman's office in jeans and sneakers . . ."

* * *

At three twenty-five, Meg called from the office of *The Woodside Herald.*

"Did you find anything?" Athen asked immediately.

"First you have to ask me how my interview went," Meg instructed.

"Of course." Athen laughed, knowing there wasn't a snowball's chance that Meg had not wowed Brenda. "How did your interview go?"

"It was great," Meg told her confidently. "Brenda Chapman is one very savvy young lady. Forget the fact that she's the daughter of the man who owns the paper. This gal can hold her own with anyone. We hit it off famously. Now you can ask me if I found something."

"Did you . . . ?"

"I don't know," she replied slowly.

"What do you mean, you don't know? You either found something or you didn't." Athen frowned.

"I found a photograph—I did get a copy of it, by the way—Rossi is in it, supposedly some fund-raiser . . . There are a few other people in the photo, but I don't know who they are."

"Chances are I won't either," Athen said, frowning, "but maybe Diana will."

"Look, tell Callie I'll pick her up in fifteen minutes," she told Athen, "that will give me just enough time to get to Chapman's to meet with the mister. Are you sure you don't need your car for the rest of the day?"

"Positive." Where would I be going? Athen thought glumly.

Meg blew in long enough to hand Athen an envelope and yell for Callie to hurry up. They flew out the front door in a flurry, promising to be back around six or shortly thereafter.

Athen sat down at the kitchen table and opened the envelope, and held the photocopy of the picture up to her eyes. She slid on her glasses and studied the black and white image carefully. A tuxedoed Dan Rossi gripped the arm of a tall white-haired man, both of them smiling broadly for the camera. Immediately to the left of the duo and slightly in the background stood a third man whom Athen thought looked vaguely familiar. The caption referred to a fund-raising event—"Woodside Heights Mayor Dan Rossi greets the party faithful at weekend fund-raiser"—but gave no clue as to whom either of the others in the picture might be.

She went outside and watered her plants, coming back in just in time to answer the phone. The Chapmans had invited both Meg and Callie for dinner . . . Athen, too, of course, if she'd care to join them. Meg would drive back to pick her up, to which Athen had responded, "Are you crazy . . . ?"

"Would you be upset if we stayed?" Meg asked tentatively. "Callie's having a riding lesson . . . God, but she's good, Athen . . . is there anything that child can't do well? . . . and Hughes and Brenda and I were just discussing the format for the new show. They have some great ideas . . ."

"Of course you should stay." Athen bit her lip. "I don't mind at all. I'll see you when you get back."

"Traitors," she mumbled as she hung up the phone.

Fighting a sense of increasing annoyance, she made herself busy cleaning the kitchen, grumbling to herself the entire time. It did not take her long to recognize that the person she was most annoyed with was Athen Moran. If she had called Quentin and apologized the way she knew she should have, she wouldn't be home alone, she reminded herself.

She changed into sweatpants and took her bike out of the garage. Maybe a ride would put her in better spirits. She pedaled out along the river road to the cemetery and pulled some errant weeds from the base of her mother's memorial. Hands on her hips, she stood at the top of the ridge overlooking the river and inhaled deeply. Scanning the view, she noted that from where she stood the back of the barn on the Chapman estate was visible. Grumbling to herself that even here she could not be rid of him, she rode home like one being pursued.

Callie and Meg were probably sitting at one of those lovely wicker tables on the veranda at that very minute, enjoying a beautifully prepared supper while she was fishing in a near empty refrigerator deliberating between leftover pizza and yesterday's tuna salad. She flipped a coin. The tuna won.

Was Quentin having dinner with them, or, she wondered, had he a date with someone, one of those other ladies Meg alluded to who knew a prize when they saw one. Maybe he'd taken her to that little Thai restaurant . . . she could almost see him urging his faceless companion to try the shrimp with spicy peanut sauce . . .

Hannah scratched at the back door, and Athen let her in. She sat down on the hard kitchen floor and leaned back against the wall, the dog gazing up at her in adoration as she plunked her huge head in Athen's lap. She was still sitting there in total misery when Callie and Meg returned home shortly after eleven.

"Sorry we're so late," Meg apologized, "but . . ."

"It's okay," Athen assured her, "I took a long bike ride, and then Hannah and I just hung out for a while."

"I'm going to bed, Mom." Callie kissed the top of her head in passing. "I'm pooped . . ."

Meg leaned back against the sink and sighed. "It went great, 'Thena. Chapman really seems to like me . . . he wants me to meet with one of the candidates for station manager and see what I think of him . . . can you imagine? He wants my input on something like that . . . it's unheard of . . ." She shook her head in wonder.

"I take it they offered you the job?" Athen smiled.

"There're some details that need to be worked out, but essentially, yes," Meg said, a look of amazement on her face. "Brenda says as she walks us to the car, 'Dad and I both feel there's no need to look for anyone else. We'd like you to think about how soon you'd be able to come on board . . . we'd like you to work with us as we get this thing rolling' . . . Can you believe it . . . ?"

"Meg, that's wonderful." Athen got off the floor and hugged her.

"I can't wait to go back to Tulsa and stick this in Cal Robbins's smug face . . ." Her eyes narrowed, mirroring total satisfaction at the prospect. "He has been jerking around with my contract for the past two months."

"When does it expire?"

"October first," Meg said with a grin, "after which time I will belong to CCN—that's Chapman Cable Network—body and soul."

"Will they make you work through September?" Athen inquired.

"Probably not," Meg told her, "Cal doesn't really like me any more than I like him . . . I should have sued the SOB for sexual harassment when I had the chance, the old lecher."

Athen recalled Meg's complaints of someone at the station "hitting on her" when she'd first gone to Tulsa.

"You probably still could," Athen suggested.

"Naw," Meg said, shaking her head, "that sort of thing stays with you wherever you go. I don't want to bring that kind of baggage to CCN . . . Cal will get his, eventually. It just won't be at my hands. I just want to leave, quick and clean."

"How was dinner?" Athen asked casually.

"Wonderful," sighed Meg, "what a cook they have . . . and what a lifestyle . . . cocktails on the veranda . . . dinner in that lovely dining room . . ."

"The big one?" Athen pressed.

Meg nodded. "The one with the enormous Waterford chandelier and the Degas on the wall . . ."

"Were there a lot of people there?" The Chapman's "big" dining room was cavernous, not suited, Athen thought, for a small gathering.

"A larger group than I would have expected, considering we were supposed to be conducting a job interview," Meg noted. "The formality of the house aside, I take it the Chapmans are pretty loose, you know? There was some cousin of Lydia's there, from St. Louis, with her husband and four children. And Lydia's daughter, Caitlin."

"Lydia's daughter?" Athen's eyebrows raised. Quentin had never mentioned a sister.

"She's wrapping up her residency at a hospital in Chicago." Lowering herself wearily into a kitchen chair, Meg kicked off her high heeled shoes. "Caitlin is quite a gal. She wants to work in an inner-city hospital or clinic, working with low-income families . . . with their money, she could probably build her own damned hospital. Did you know that Lydia Chapman's father founded Bradford International? And that she controls the trusts? We are talking major Yankee dollars . . ." She shook her head.

"What's Caitlin like?" Athen wondered aloud.

"She is the very image of her mother, except that she's a strawberry blonde, and taller." Meg studied her sister-in-law's face carefully. "Aren't you going to ask if Quentin was there?"

"No, I . . ."

"Of course you were, stop acting like you're not interested," Meg teased.

"Okay, was he?"

"Yes, he was." Meg lifted her legs onto the seat of the chair next to the one in which she sat. "Handsome and charming as ever."

Looking for something to distract herself with, Athen picked up Hannah's water bowl, rinsed it out in the sink and refilled it.

"Athen, I love you dearly, you know that, but you're a fool," Meg said levelly, ". . . don't interrupt me . . . Quentin Forbes is one mighty miserable man, though not, perhaps, any more miserable than you are. If you do not straighten this out, you will regret it for the rest of your life . . . and deservedly so."

"I know," Athen replied softly.

"You know?" Meg sat up straight in the chair, her feet wrapping around its lower rungs. "Then what are you going to do about it?"

"I guess I'll have to call him . . ." she said.

"Don't 'guess,' Athen, do it." Meg reached down and scooped up her discarded shoes. "I suggest you start rehearsing what you're going to say . . ." She yawned widely. "God, I'm tired . . ."

"Let's lock up, then." Athen bolted the back door and turned off the light over the sink. "Come on, Meg, we can talk more tomorrow."

Meg dragged herself up the steps, Athen following thoughtfully behind, mentally searching for an opening line.

38

"Damn!" Meg erupted into the kitchen at ten the next morning. "I overslept . . . damn! Brenda said she'd pick me up at eleven . . ."

"Calm down." Athen shoved a mug of hot coffee in Meg's general direction. "You still have an hour."

"An hour to shower, find something to wear . . . I only brought home the one suit I wore yesterday, I can't show up in the same thing." Meg tried to untangle her hair with her fingers. "And anyway the skirt's wrinkled . . ."

"I'll iron the skirt while you're in the shower, and you can borrow a blouse from me." Athen opened Meg's fingers, stuck the mug into her hand and directed her back up the steps. "Go take your shower . . . I'll find something for you to wear . . ."

Forty-five minutes later, Meg was trying on shoes pulled from Athen's closet.

"It's amazing, you know," she said as she walked to the mirror, spinning on black leather heels, "as tall as you are, and as short as I am, that we wear the same size. Of course, what looks like a tiny, delicate foot at the end of your long leg looks like a tugboat on me. It's the Moran curse, you know," she said and sighed dramatically, "big feet and short stubby legs . . ."

"Your legs are not stubby." Athen laughed. "You're petite . . ."

"A marketing term for short and stubby," insisted Meg as she draped a belt around her hips.

"Blouse the front of the shirt a little," Athen suggested. "That's better . . ."

"Oh, God, there's Brenda." Meg poked her head out the window. "Thanks, Athen, for the blouse, the ironing job, the shoes, the belt, the earrings . . ." Meg sang off the list of borrowed items as she ran down the steps.

Athen collected the empty coffee mugs and took them down to the kitchen. On the counter lay the reprinted newspaper photo Meg had given her the day before. The name of the man in the background would not come to her. After searching unsuccessfully for the phone book, she lifted the receiver and called information.

"I'd like the number for Diana Bennett on Rosedale, please . . ."

The house at 417 Rosedale Avenue looked exactly like a house that Diana Bennett would choose to live in. Small and compact, little more than a cottage built in the '20s, it had charm and beauty and an air of romance about it. From the rose-covered arbor that framed the neat front door to the airy and light interior, it had Diana's name all over it. It was, Athen thought, the perfect subject for a painting.

The entire first floor was white, providing a simple background for Diana's collection of beautifully painted pottery.

"They're all American pieces," Diana volunteered when Athen had admired the pastel vases that paraded across the deep windowsills, "Weller, Rosewood, Van Briggle . . . I'm partial to the Weller, though, since I grew up in Zanesville, Ohio, where it was made . . . my mother was a painter there. From time to time I've been able to find some pieces with her initials."

Diana lifted a pale green vase draped with white flowers and held it, base up, to Athen to show her the letters scratched in the bottom, as Athen's eyes screeched to a halt abruptly and lingered on the portrait that stood importantly at the center of the small stone mantel. Ari and Diana beamed—no, glowed—in full living color, Ari handsome as an aging movie hero, Diana soft and beautiful in a champagne colored lace dress.

"What a lovely photograph." Athen quickly masked her embarrassment at having been caught gaping at this glimpse into a life Ari had shared, without having shared any of it with his daughter.

"That was taken two weeks before Ari's stroke," Diana said quietly.

"It's beautiful," Athen told her, unable to take her eyes from it, "you look so happy . . ."

"We were . . ." Diana whispered.

"I guess now is a good time," Athen swallowed hard, "to apologize to you for . . ."

"For thinking I was just a good time for a lonely old man?" Diana smiled gently.

"I don't know that I'd put it that way." Athen squirmed uncomfortably.

"Sure you would have." Diana jabbed with more good humor and grace than Athen thought she could have mustered under the circumstances. "At least, once upon a time you might have. But you don't owe me an apology, Athen. Neither Ari nor I gave you any reason to think otherwise."

"All those years, I should have made things easier for him, I should have included you in our holidays . . ."

"Don't be so hard on yourself." Diana patted her hand. "I probably wouldn't have come anyway."

"You wouldn't?" Athen had never considered this possibility.

Diana sat on the ottoman in front of the oversized, overstuffed chair and shook her head.

"We'd made such a happy little world for ourselves here, I just didn't want to share him. So on Christmas, he'd spend the day with you and John, and come home to me, and we'd have our own holiday together." Diana wiped a slow tear from her face and looked around the room. "The only truly happy birthdays, the only joyous Noels I've ever had, have been here, with Ari. This is the only place I've ever felt safe."

"Safe?" Athen asked cautiously.

Diana went into the kitchen and returned with a box of pale green tissues, telling Athen, "I have the feeling I might need these," as she sat back down.

"I suppose the simplest way to explain is to say that I went from being an abused child to being an abused wife," she said bluntly. "I married Donald Bennett right out of high school. I thought he'd take me far away . . . and he did. He'd gotten a job with a pharmaceuticals company about eight miles from here and went to graduate school at night. I got a job as a clerk in the finance department at city hall. One of the girls in the office invited me to go with her to a campaign workers meeting one night . . . Sam Tarbottom was running for mayor that year, you remember?"

Athen shook her head. "Not really . . ."

"Well, I had nothing else to do. Donald would be at school, we'd made no friends, I guess I was lonely, so I went. Ari was one of the organizers of Sam's campaign. I thought he was so wonderful . . . so . . . European and suave and handsome . . ." Diana laughed, just a hint of blush rising to her cheeks. "Everyone was so nice to me. It was the first time in years I felt that I had a place to go, a place where I had friends. I didn't care who the candidate was—I'd still have gone every week, just for the companionship, you know?"

Athen silently nodded her understanding. She too had felt isolated once.

"And so I went back, every week. I knew Donald would have a fit if he knew, he was so jealous." She swallowed a hard lump. "But I almost didn't care. For those few hours, I could be like everybody else, out for an evening with friends. We'd laugh and talk and drink beer—once your father brought bottles of metaxa and Tarbottom got drunk as a skunk . . ." She laughed at the memory. ". . . but mostly it was stuffing envelopes and laughing. That's what I remember most about those nights. Then one night I got back a little late and Donald was already at the apartment," she said, her tongue flicking across her upper lip nervously, "and he was not happy. When Donald was not happy, no one was happy. And I paid for my nights out with two black eyes and a couple of broken ribs . . ."

Athen sniffed and reached for the tissue box, stunned at the thought of anyone striking this gentle soul, marring the perfect skin on Diana's sweet face.

"Of course, I had to call in sick the next day, and the next . . . until the bruising subsided a bit. And I had to plaster makeup on my face before I could appear in public. And I didn't dare attend next week's meeting. Or the next few. But three weeks later, when Donald had exams, I went back.

Carol Parker—she was my friend in the office—I know she knew, but she never asked . . . she promised she'd get me home early, but her car broke down. And Donald was waiting for me again . . . I decided that maybe I didn't need friends after all." She paused and blew her nose. "The following week, when we were moving the finance offices from the second floor to the third, we all had to stay late, to move our own areas. Ari helped us pack up. He kept looking at my face, and I knew he wanted to ask, but wouldn't. He carried my boxes for me," Diana's voice was almost a whisper. "Donald came to the office, looking for me. He thought we were alone, since everyone else had gone upstairs . . . I'd gone back to get my jacket . . . Your father came in as Donald was winding up for the second punch . . ."

"Oh, my God, Diana," Athen whispered in horror.

"Ari just about put him through the file cabinets. He picked up the phone and told Donald if he didn't agree to leave the city by nine o'clock that night, he'd have him arrested." Diana's eyes began to glow softly. "And Donald left. Ari took me home with him and cried as he put ice on my face. By the next morning he'd arranged for surveillance of my apartment in case Donald had not left town and he got me a lawyer to start working on my divorce. He was my hero, Athen. No one had ever defended me before."

"I always wondered why someone so young and beautiful . . ." Athen struggled with what she realized was an inappropriate thing to say.

". . . fell in love with a man old enough to be my father?" Diana chuckled. "Ari is the only person who ever really loved me, ever really believed in me. My life began that night, and I thank God every day for having brought him to me. He's given me the only joy I've ever known."

"But even now, when he's . . ." Athen bit her tongue.

"I will love that man with my whole heart . . . in sickness and in health, as the saying goes . . . until the day I die," Diana told her solemnly. "No one could ever mean to me what he has meant. He taught me how to laugh, and how to love . . . and how to believe in myself. He talked me into going to college, and later for my CPA. He is the one and only love of my life."

Athen openly wept, Diana passing the tissue box to her across the small space formed by their parallel knees.

"So," Diana said, "now you know. And maybe you understand why I had no interest in sharing him, with you or anyone else. He was all I had. I did want to be your friend, though, I will admit that. Especially after Ari's stroke . . . and when John died, I wanted to be there for you. Ari would have wanted me to."

"I'm sorry we didn't talk sooner." It was Athen's turn to blow her nose. "It must have been hard for you, when Dad was in the hospital, and only John and I were allowed in his room those first few days."

"Sharing the waiting room with Dan Rossi was a test of my mettle, I will tell you that," Diana said grimly.

Athen suddenly remembered why she had come here in the first place. "Oh, speaking of him, maybe you can help me with something."

"What's that?" Diana's eyebrows rose with curiosity.

"Meg found this photo on microfiche at the newspaper yesterday." Athen opened her purse and took the paper out, folding the creases flat onto her lap. "This man, the one in the background, looks somewhat familiar."

Diana leaned over for a better look. "Philip Harper. He's an estate attorney from down around New Brunswick someplace. Or at least he was."

" 'Was' . . . ?"

"He retired last year. I heard he moved to Florida or Arizona, someplace warm," she continued. "He was a real heavy hitter. He had a lot of money, and I think he thought of political contributions as a sort of investment. I didn't know him well, but I met him a few times."

She studied the details of the picture silently. "We were at this party . . ."

"You were?" Athen's eyes widened.

"Sure. It was at Wynn and Ellen Thomas's house in Saddlebrook. I remember every detail of that night . . . It was quite the society bash—tickets were a thousand dollars a head, which is one way of separating the wheat from the chaff, as they say." She sighed at the memory. "Everything was perfect—the caterer, the band—we danced until I could barely stand up. The ballroom was decorated to look like a Hawaiian grotto, complete with waterfalls, and there were flowers absolutely everywhere."

"Do you recognize this man, the one in the front with Dan?" Athen tapped on the photo.

"No," she said slowly, "I don't think so . . . I knew everyone there that night. I mean, it's the same people, all the time. State pols . . . county people . . . but only the wealthiest contributors and the candidates. This was the last big fund-raiser before the election, as I recall . . . but I don't think I remember this man," she said as she shook her head. "I wish I did . . . especially if this was what Ari was looking at that morning."

"It has to have been," Athen told her. "Meg said she scanned the paper end to end and found nothing about Rossi but this."

"Well, I guess the key to it all," Diana said, handing back the piece of paper, "lies with the mystery man. I wish I knew who he was."

"So do I." Athen folded the picture and returned it to her purse. "I wonder if my dad knows."

"I'd put money on it." Diana nodded vigorously. "But then again, if Ari could speak, we'd know the whole story, wouldn't we . . . ?"

What a difference a year makes, Athen mused as she dressed for the Memorial Day outing. This time last year I was praying for gale-force winds. Today I can't get there fast enough.

She'd tried for the past week to make the call she knew she had to make, but each time she'd lifted the receiver, she'd returned it to its cradle without dialing. After torturing herself for days, she'd decided to wait until the press conference on Wednesday, where she'd nab Quentin on the way out of the room and nonchalantly ask him to stop into her office before he left the building. That plan had to be scrapped when he'd blown out of the room as if pursued by demons.

She would have to go with Plan B. She guessed he wouldn't pass up an opportunity for a story, and so she suspected he'd make an appearance at some point today. She'd be ready for him. She'd corner him and give him her best, her most sincere apology. With any luck, maybe by tonight she'd be back in his arms again.

There was no need this year for Callie to urge her mother to hurry. Athen was downstairs and dressed before Callie had awakened.

"You look nice, Mom," Callie had told her as they got into the car. "I like that outfit on you."

It had been chosen carefully, black and gold checked pants, a pale gold cotton pullover, black and gold sandals, a chunky gold bracelet and a gold scarf to tie back her hair. She'd fretted over her makeup and had done her nails the night before. The picnic be damned—she was dressed for an impromptu dinner invitation, with maybe a stop at the park to feed the ducks. Her words of apology well-rehearsed, she and Callie headed off for the day's events.

Diana had insisted on accompanying them, telling Athen on the phone the night before, "Dan will be attempting to hold court as he has for the past sixteen years. We're going to be there to remind him that he's just another ex-employee, just like the other old-timers."

When pressed for an explanation, Diana merely smiled. "Just follow my lead," she told Athen.

"I just love Diana's little house, don't you, Mom?" Callie sighed as they pulled up to the front door to pick up Diana for the Memorial Day festivities.

Diana waved from the front window, and within minutes, had locked the door and walked briskly to the car.

"Shall we stop and see Dad?" Athen asked when they were back on the main road.

"He wasn't feeling well earlier this morning." Diana frowned. "His cold seems to be getting worse. He was sleeping when I left."

"Has the doctor been in to see him?" Athen turned to her with concern.

"Yesterday. He gave him some medication that seems to make him tired," Diana told her.

"Maybe we should put off our visit," Athen thought aloud.

"Maybe for today," agreed Diana. "Have you spoken with Meg since she left on Monday?"

"She called last night," Athen said and laughed. "Everyone at the station out there is buzzing about her new job. And of course, she can't wait."

"When will she start?"

"Officially, she goes on Chapman's payroll October first, though the station won't kick off till December first. Of course, Brenda wants her as soon as the good folks in Tulsa will release her from her contract." Athen pulled into the already filled parking lot at the park.

Callie went off in search of her friends as Diana and Athen walked towards the gathering under the trees.

"Now stay close, Athen," Diana instructed, "because today I'm going to teach you something you should have learned from your father."

"What's that?"

"How to work a crowd."

Athen marveled at how fluidly Diana floated through the throng, never matching the wrong name to the wrong face. Dressed all in white—a white cotton dress with a full skirt, a wide-brimmed white hat, flat white shoes—she could have been hostessing at a garden party.

"Mrs. Amory!" Diana exclaimed, taking the hand of a plump woman who was headed for the food table and turning to Athen. "Athen, of course you know Mrs. Amory . . . she worked side by side with me eight years ago when your father ran for council. Oh, and wasn't that election night one to remember." She turned back to Mrs. Amory. "Did you ever see such rain? And how is your daughter? Did I hear she was engaged . . . ?"

Next it was, "Mrs. Simpson." Diana bent to place a kiss on the face of an elderly woman perched on the edge of a picnic bench. "What a coincidence! I was just telling the mayor about that pothole at the end of your street. Athen, Mrs. Simpson is the lady I was telling you about . . . the most dreadful pothole . . . perhaps someone from Streets could go out tomorrow and take a look . . . ?"

"David Gilmartin," she said, hugging a thin, bald-headed man as if he were her long-lost cousin. "I was devastated to hear about your wife . . . what a loss to us all. Athen, David's wife passed away in March."

And on it went until Athen whispered in her ear, "What in God's name are you doing? And when can we stop and sit down for a minute?"

"A cold drink would be wonderful, yes, thank you. Athen? Something cold?" Diana swooped two cans of ice-cold soda from a huge cooler. "You are doing what the mayor is supposed to be doing at things like this, and we don't stop till we leave," she said out of the corner of her mouth, handing one of the cans to Athen and popping open the lid of the one in her hand.

"Before this day is over, you will have shaken every adult hand, kissed every baby, and said something endearing to every child in attendance." Diana grinned.

"That's what you do when you're campaigning," Athen grumbled, searching the throng for the only person she was interested in saying anything endearing to, "which I am not."

"Dan certainly is," Diana said with a nod in the direction of the small crowd that had gathered around the former mayor.

"He can do whatever he wants." Athen made a face. "And he doesn't need to campaign. The job is his."

"Now, Athen, didn't your daddy ever tell you there's no such thing as a sure thing?" Diana turned to the couple approaching them from the left. "Ann . . . Mike. How good to see you again . . ."

Athen scanned the crowd for a tall, dark-haired man with broad shoulders and a killer smile. She found him over by the ball field where the children were being divided into teams.

"Excuse me, Diana . . . Jim, Nancy, it was wonderful to see you," she echoed Diana's smooth tones in making a graceful exit. "I think my daughter is in the softball game, and I don't dare miss a play."

She took a deep breath and headed across the field, rehearsing what she'd say to him. With each step closer, her heart pounded a little louder. She came up behind him and fixed a smile on her face. She touched his right arm and he turned around, obviously surprised she had sought him out.

"I thought that was you." She smiled at him as calmly as possible. "How are you?"

"I'm fine." He looked around to see if her pleasantries were for the benefit of some third party.

"Is there a score?" she asked, nodding towards the playing field.

"Not yet."

The awkward silence was her cue.

"Quentin . . ." She took a deep breath. "I want to apologize to you. I had no right to interfere with the way you do your job. And I do understand that you were doing exactly that when you wrote the Rossi story . . ."

"Do you?" he asked, not looking at her.

"Yes, Quentin, I do." She tried to sound as contrite as she could.

"Did Meg have anything to do with your change of heart?" He seemed to be looking at her from the corner of one eye, but the dark glasses made it tough to know for sure.

"We discussed it," she acknowledged, "and she told me I was dead wrong. Which I was. My feelings were hurt and I guess it was difficult for me to look beyond that at first."

"Athen, I would never intentionally hurt you," he said softly.

"I know that." She smiled, relaxing. The worst was over. "You were right, of course. If Rossi says something, Rossi being who he is in this city, you have to print it. Especially if it's about me. Whether I like it or not."

"I'm glad that you understand." He looked down at her, his eyes shielded by the dark glasses. "And I'm very sorry that something I did upset you. But I can't promise that it will never happen again."

"I realize that," she told him, "it's all right."

She waited for him to say something else, and when he did not, she took a small side step to better study his profile. There was no smile on his face, no dimples to dazzle her, no banter forthcoming. He looked distracted at best, uncomfortable at worst.

"Well," he said, turning to her, "thank you for the apology. It means a lot to me to know that you understand."

She smiled her biggest smile, happy that it was behind them now. They could pick up where they'd left off . . .

"Well, then," he said awkwardly, "I guess I'll see you next week at the press conference."

He nodded to her as if she were a casual acquaintance and she watched, dumbstruck, as he abruptly strode off across the field towards the parking lot without a backward glance. Her cheeks flushed with embarrassment at his apparent disinterest, her mind numb in the wake of his sudden dismissal.

Her disbelieving eyes followed the yellow cap as it wound through the rows of cars, her stunned heart clanging dully on the macadam as it dragged behind him, all the way across the parking lot.

39

The night Callie had left for Florida, Athen had rambled aimlessly from one room of the house to the next, unable to shake the anxiety that had engulfed her as her daughter's plane had become a shining silver dot that, seconds later, was devoured in one gulp by a monstrous cloud. Her only child having disappeared into the sky, beyond her control, beyond her reach, Athen had somberly returned to the empty house, second-guessing her decision to allow Callie to fly—alone—to spend the last two weeks of summer vacation with the elder Morans. John's parents had every right to expect Callie to make the trip, Athen reminded herself repeatedly, they haven't seen her since John's funeral. They need the connection with her, need to see how like their son she had become, Meg had pointed out, and Athen had agreed. She simply had not anticipated the degree of angst she would experience as she watched a buoyant Callie, primed for adventure and savoring her independence, disappear through the tunnel into the plane.

Vulnerability, thy name is parenthood.

Athen fed Hannah and tried to stop pacing, tried not to watch the clock. Callie was supposed to call as soon as she arrived at her grandparents. The plane ride was little more than an hour. She should be there by now. Why hadn't she called? The knot inside her grew and twisted until the phone shook her out of a mild frenzy shortly after seven.

The plane had been on time. Grandma and Grandpop had been at the gate waiting for her. They had stopped for dinner on the way back from the airport. The flight had been completely uneventful, she was fine, tomorrow they were taking her to DisneyWorld and don't forget she wanted her room blue blue, not pale blue.

Relieved that her precious daughter was safely delivered by USAir into the waiting arms of her adoring grandparents, Athen relaxed as she hung up the phone. Callie would have a whale of a good time. John's parents would guard her with their lives, spoil her rotten, show her off to all their friends, devote every waking minute to her every whim, photograph every move she made, and send her home with a whole new wardrobe to start school.

Athen made herself a light supper, afterwards taking her coffee outside to accompany Hannah on a stroll around the yard. The garden was almost spent now, the end of summer being upon them. A few flowers remained in bloom, some phlox, palest lavender against the brooding dark blue monkshood, and some roses, deep red climbers, their fragrance still heady this late in the season. The side garden, given over to annuals, was still happily ablaze with the sharp hues of the zinnias Callie had planted. Delicate cosmos, pink and white, swayed gracefully on tall, thick stalks, their feathery leaves neatly framing the bird bath, the base of which was encircled with red impatiens. Athen bent over to remove a weed, careful not to shake its seeds back into the flower bed.

She wandered around to the front of the house where a

single yellow daylily, bright as the July sun, stubbornly continued to bloom in defiance of the calendar. Hemerocallis, she smiled as she repeated the name aloud, fondly touching the golden petals as she passed by. She had made a point to learn the names of all the flowers she and Callie had chosen, and was pleased that she remembered them all. Knowing their names had made them hers. Knowledge was indeed power, she mused.

Returning to the back of the house, she sat down on the porch steps and drained a few drops of cold coffee from the cup that dangled from the fingers of one hand. The setting sun draped a pinky glow behind the trees and the warm evening air was thick with the scent of sweet autumn clematis. She leaned against the step behind her and inhaled deeply, thinking it might be good for her, after all, to have some time to herself. Meg always said that everyone should live alone for a while. Athen never had. Now, for two short weeks, she would have time to think about things she'd been avoiding. First thing tomorrow morning she would go to the paint store—hopefully she'd find a blue to match the one Callie had her heart set on. She'd put her house in order, try to put her life in order.

Hannah thumped into a huge half-moon at her feet, and Athen leaned down to scratch behind her ears.

"Miss your playmate, do you? I miss her, too," Athen confided. "But we will be very busy while she's gone . . ."

She made a mental list of things she wanted to do. Clean the attic—that would be a weekend project. Redecorate the house. Organize several boxes of photographs into albums—she could do a little each night. Not think about Quentin, or who he's seeing now, or how she missed him more than she'd ever expected to. How her hands still shook slightly when he entered the conference room on Wednesdays, how she still harbored a faint hope that one day, when she'd least expect it, he'd hang around after everyone else had left instead of bolting from the room the minute the press conference had ended . . .

Face it, she told herself sternly, that is a closed chapter. For whatever reasons, he wanted nothing more to do with her, and that was a fact she would have to live with. It surprised her to realize the thought still brought a lump to her throat.

"Come on, Hannah." She stood up and stretched. "Let's go inside and put some of this free time to good use . . ."

"No, I don't think that's quite the shade she had in mind." Athen leaned across the counter, one finger sorting through the pile of colored chips spread before her by the young man in the paint store. "More like this one." She nudged the chip from its place in the pile.

"That's sort of a strong blue for a little girl's room," the young man noted.

"She's a strong little girl," Athen said with a laugh, "and that's what she wants."

The young man, Ed, as proclaimed on the front of his shirt, retrieved a can of the chosen blue and set it upon the counter. "Anything else I can get you?"

"Well, I need something for my hallway. I've been thinking maybe something like this creamy color, with maybe a bit more gold in it." She nodded slowly as he tapped a finger on a sample which had been hidden towards the back of the pack. "Yes, that color. That's exactly it. And now something for my bedroom—a green. No, that's too yellow. I want something soft, like a sage—yes, that one right there . . ."

She purchased rollers and brushes and dropcloths, writing a check while one of young Ed's helpers loaded up her car. On the way out, a display of stencils caught her eye, and she stopped to inspect them. She'd never done stenciling before, but loved the look. How difficult could it be? She bought three—a grapevine, ivy and a rose border—along with the requisite brushes and jars of paints. It would be a huge undertaking—repainting the inside of the house—but it would give focus to the days, with Callie gone for two weeks. Maybe she'd take a few days off herself, she thought, and finish it all before Callie got home.

She strolled leisurely across Harmond Avenue towards her car, which she'd parked at a meter on the street. A sign in the window of the fabric shop two storefronts from the car caught her eye. She hesitated only briefly before redirecting her steps to the small shop.

"Your sign says you make slip covers," she said to the young woman behind the counter.

"Yes, ma'am, we do." The clerk barely looked up from her paperwork.

"Great." Athen smiled. "Here's what I want . . ."

Having selected fabric to re-cover the living-room furniture and dining chairs, and made an appointment for measurements to be taken, Athen whistled as she walked back to her car. Over the past twenty-four hours, she'd not only come to terms with herself, but had laid the groundwork for revitalizing her home. What else needed to be done?

What else indeed, she mused, pausing in front of the pink stucco storefront closest to her car. She stood for a very long minute, pondering the thought. Grinning broadly, she slipped another quarter into the meter.

"May I help you?" the perky receptionist asked.

"Do you take walk-ins?" Athen inquired.

"Yes," the woman said with a nod, "did you have anything particular in mind?"

With her right hand, Athen reached to the back of her head and gathered her hair into a stream that cascaded almost to her waist.

"Shoulder length, I think," she told her.

"Are you sure?" The receptionist raised an eyebrow.

"Absolutely," Athen replied confidently.

"Have a seat." The young woman motioned to a row of chairs near the window. "I'll see who's free . . ."

"Oh, my God!" Callie had exclaimed as she did a double take at the woman who had reached out for her when she got off the plane. "Mom! Your hair!"

"Like it?" Athen hugged her daughter, grateful to have her home again.

"I . . . I don't know." Callie's expression was somewhere between horror and admiration. "I mean, you look gorgeous . . . but it's so different. Why did you do that?"

"It was time for a change," Athen told her.

"Do you like it?" Callie was still staring at her mother's head.

"Very much so." Athen grinned.

"It sure is different."

"I admit I didn't recognize myself the first few days." Athen laughed. "But I'm used to it now and wonder why I didn't do it sooner."

Her mother's hair was not the only thing that had undergone a drastic change while Callie was in Florida. She had walked wordlessly through the house when they arrived home.

"Well," Athen finally asked, "what do you think?"

"Everything's changed," Callie said slowly. "I went away for two weeks and now everything's changed."

"Do you like it?" Athen cautiously asked.

"It's beautiful, but it doesn't look at all like our house anymore." She sat down on the sofa, observing, "This sofa doesn't go with the room now. And neither do the chairs."

"The new slipcovers will be done in about two more weeks," Athen told her.

Callie nodded and looked around, taking it all in.

"Did Mr. Parsons do all this?"

"No." Athen smiled with satisfaction. "I did."

"The stenciling, too?" Callie's eyes widened, following the tendrils of ivy which led from the front hallway through the living room.

"Yup." Athen beamed. "Go see the dining room."

Callie peaked her head in through the opening, wandering behind the trails of grapevine which wound around the top of the walls into the kitchen.

"Was it hard?" Callie pointed to her mother's handiwork.

"Harder than I thought it would be," Athen admitted, sparing her daughter the details of her frustration the first day she had wrestled with the stencils, all of which had had three or four parts to the designs. It had driven her crazy until she had gotten the feel for it.

Callie came back into the living room, focusing on the watercolor that hung over the mantel.

"Did you paint that?" She nodded to the painting, studying the splashes of color which depicted a summer's garden as seen through a garden gate.

"It's one I did a long time ago, one of the first big paintings I ever did." Athen slid into a chair, wondering if perhaps she should have been a little less zealous in her drive to refashion her surroundings. "I had done that for Grampa one year. I found it in the attic and decided to bring it down."

"Where are Dad's pictures?" Callie asked uncertainly.

"In your room. I thought you might like to have them." Callie nodded without comment.

"Are you all right?" Athen leaned towards her slightly.

"It's just that everything's so different." Callie frowned.

"Change is not necessarily bad," Athen told her quietly, "as a matter of fact, it can be very good. Nothing can, or should, always stay the same, Callie. The house looked tired and gloomy, and I felt tired and gloomy. I wanted someplace pretty and bright for us to live in. And I felt that it was time to change the way I look, too. Do you understand?"

"I think so." She looked around the room again. "It is very pretty, Mom. And so's your haircut. Did you do my room, too?"

"Of course." Athen laughed. "Blue blue. Not pale blue. Go take a look."

Callie shot up the steps and Athen held her breath.

"Wow!" exclaimed Callie. "Wow!"

Athen smiled to herself when Callie leaned over the second-floor railing and called down to her, "It's just right. It's just the color I had in my head. Everything looks great, Mom. It's just like getting a new house without moving. Boy oh boy will Aunt Meg be surprised . . ." Her voice trailed off as she went to inspect her mother's room.

Leaning back against the chair, Athen relaxed. Callie would adjust to her new surroundings just as Athen had become accustomed to her own new look. Putting a bit more of the past behind had somehow made the future seem a little closer. She could not foresee what it would bring, but she knew with certainty that she was ready for it.

40

An early fall had led into a glorious Indian summer, followed, inevitably, by the first touches of frost. Athen and Callie had spent a long weekend cleaning up the flower beds and preparing them for winter. They cut back the perennials and mulched the beds and treated themselves to a night out for pizza and a movie when they had completed their work.

Rossi had laid low throughout September and early October, much to Athen's relief. She wanted nothing more than to serve out her term and step aside, leaving Dan to his devices. The voters who reelected him would only get what they deserved. The city seemed unusually quiet, and she began to wonder if the UCC had abandoned its efforts to obtain their shelter, or if perhaps they were considering alternative sites.

She was musing over just this thought one morning when Veronica stepped into her office to announce that Ms. Evelyn would like a minute of her time. Athen greeted her warmly, telling her, "I was just thinking about you."

"Well, it's been some time since I saw you, and I thought since I was in town . . . I wanted to check on those fruit trees we planted last summer up in the green . . ." She motioned towards the window, beyond which she had transformed ugly empty lots into a haven of beauty and abundance. ". . . and I thought I'd stop and see you first and deliver my invitation in person."

"Invitation?" Athen asked, her curiosity piqued.

"Well, now, Athen, you know that fall has always been the time to celebrate the harvest, and this year we have much to be thankful for. We fed dozens of families with what we produced in our garden. The ladies of the churches gathered what was left over and showed the young women from the housing project"—she gestured towards the city's one high-rise—"how to put up green beans and tomatoes . . . my, what a time we had." She chuckled at the memory, then added, "There are families who'll have food this winter who last year had less, and plenty put aside for the kitchens where we feed the hungry." Her voice softened, and she told Athen, "It was the first time most of those young women had had an opportunity to give to those less fortunate than themselves . . . being poor, they didn't realize that others had even less. We all learned a little something from working together . . ."

As always, Ms. Evelyn's generous spirit and true love of humanity humbled Athen.

"I thought we should celebrate our good fortune in some special way," Ms. Evelyn continued in her slow, precise voice, "that perhaps we as a city should unite to give thanks for the harvest we have been able to share with so many. I was thinking of a community day of prayer, a day when the churches could unite in a common service of worship, perhaps to be held at the green. It seems right to give thanks in the midst of God's bounty, don't you think?"

"It's a lovely idea, Ms. Evelyn," Athen agreed.

"It occurred to me that you, as mayor, as well as one who had volunteered her time to help with the project, might like to be a guest at the service." Ms. Evelyn looked at Athen from across the big desk. Something seemed to play behind her eyes, giving Athen just a hint of speculation as to what, besides prayer, Ms. Evelyn might have in mind.

"I am honored that you have thought to include me," Athen told her sincerely, "and I would be delighted to attend."

"Wonderful." Ms. Evelyn smiled. "Two P.M., the Sunday after next. Pray the weather holds. It so often turns cool the end of October."

She rose to leave and Athen walked her to the door.

"Do bring Callie," Ms. Evelyn said as she walked to the elevator and waved.

Something is afoot, Athen told herself as she opened the drapes to give full view to the lush green spot just three blocks from city hall. The autumn sun danced off the few trees which grew along the perimeter of Ms. Evelyn's garden, the russets of the oaks and the yellows of the maples forming a brilliant outline along the back border. Athen thought back to the day she had spent there early in the summer. It had been the best weekend she'd had for as long as she could remember.

She had tried her damnedest not to think about Quentin. She still could not look at him without feeling confused. He had set in motion feelings she had believed she'd never feel again and then quietly walked away from her without explanation. He was gracious to her at the weekly press conferences, yet avoided speaking to her outside the conference room, other than once to mumble "great haircut" as he passed by her. He avoided making eye contact with her, yet she could feel his eyes on her from the moment he entered the room until his speedy exit. There were times when she wished she could grab him by the collar and shake him silly and yell, "What is wrong with you?" But of course, she never would, and so they continued to meet once each week within the confines of a public press conference.

Secretly, their mutually professional and forced polite demeanor drove her crazy. She wondered what he felt, what he was thinking, as he watched her from his seat in the first row. This Quentin was new to her and she could not read him at all. He looked the same, but the fire he had once displayed was gone. He had even, on several occasions, uncharacteristically passed on opportunities to grill her on one topic or another, and his daily news stories lacked his old spice. She wished he would talk to her, if only as a friend. She still missed him, even after all these months. His presence in her life took on the aura of an unfinished sonnet. Someday, she knew, they would have to write the last verse.

"These are perilous times, friends, and we are in the midst of a perilous journey," Reverend Davison's voice boomed across the immense crowd that had gathered for the UCC's Community Day of Prayer. "Mankind stands on the brink of destruction of the spirit. Only by gathering together in a common cause can we triumph over the forces of despair. The path before us is clear, sisters and brothers. We can, as a community, set in motion the means to care for those among us who, through no fault of their own, need a hand to help them along . . ."

Athen bit her bottom lip and arched her foot inside her shoe, trying to distract herself so that she would not openly grin. Ms. Evelyn was, in fact, a genius. She had personally visited every member of the city's clergy to invite them to attend this event, and as a result, every church and synagogue in Woodside Heights was represented on the dais. As mayor, Athen had been seated in the first row. Next to her sat Riley Fallon and his wife, Georgia, Reverend Davison's daughter. Clearly, the seating arrangement had been deliberate. As the good reverend launched into his plea for community support of the UCC's efforts on behalf of the homeless, he was backed on the platform by the mayor, a member of city council, and every religious leader in the city. Brilliant, Ms. Evelyn. Simply brilliant.

". . . and so we ask you to support us as we strive to do His work, to feed the hungry in our midst, to shelter the homeless, to clothe those whom the bitter winds of the coming winter would chill . . ."

Looking out across the sea of faces, black and white, Hispanic and Asian, Greek and Irish and Polish, Athen knew that the battle was won. Hundreds of people jammed the garden and spilled onto the adjacent street and sidewalk. She glanced sideways at Ms. Evelyn, seated at the end of the row, marveling that the spirit of this one small woman had proven to be greater than the forces of power that had opposed her for so long.

She sought Dan Rossi in the crowd, wondering what thoughts were going through his mind. She had not seen him arrive, but knew that he would be there. To have avoided the event would have been a political error he would not have made. The press had built the Day of Prayer into a happening that no one of standing within the community would have missed. Athen would have bet her last dollar that before the day was over, Dan would have arranged to have his picture taken with Ms. Evelyn.

". . . just as our hard work has resulted in this beautiful garden wherein we now gather, so can we banish the blight from this city. Let us pray."

As the closing prayer commenced, the clouds that had hidden the afternoon sun all day shifted, allowing the warming light to cover the crowd. Athen suppressed a giggle. If anyone could have arranged for so dramatic a touch to end the ceremonies, it could only have been Ms. Evelyn.

Walking through the dispersing crowd, Athen realized that Callie was no longer at her side. Peering around, she found her walking towards the sidewalk with Diana. Heading in that direction, she found her way blocked by a solid form dressed in khaki pants and a brown tweed jacket.

"Hello, Athen." He smiled.

"Hello, Quentin." She smiled back.

"Quite a gathering Ms. Evelyn put together," he said.

"I doubt anyone else could have pulled it off," she agreed, hoping he could not hear her sudden, erratic heartbeat.

"I guess she'll get her shelter built," he continued.

"I'd bet on it."

They'd been walking slowly, small steps through the maze of people, neither paying attention to which way they were going. She realized they'd headed back towards the garden, away from the sidewalk and Callie. Athen stopped, and so did he.

"Brenda tells me Meg will be home next week," he said.

"Yes. Tuesday." She was becoming annoyed with the small talk.

"Callie is doing exceptionally well with her riding, did Brenda tell you?" He still avoided her eyes.

"Yes, she did," Athen replied. "It's been really wonderful of Brenda to pick her up on Saturdays and bring her home."

"Well, it's not out of her way, and both Callie and Timmy really have a great time. They've become best friends, almost like sister and brother. You should come out to watch some afternoon. You're always welcome."

A tense silence began to build and she struggled with a response. Deciding that she'd been polite long enough, she said pointedly, "I don't feel welcome, Quentin. For some reason that I don't quite understand, I seem to make you extremely uncomfortable. I can accept the fact that you don't care to continue . . . well, pursuing a romantic relationship. But we're both grown-ups and given the fact that our children are such close friends, I can't understand why we can't be friends as well. This polite but distanced attitude of yours is very annoying. Could we just forget about everything else and just be friends?"

For the briefest of moments he permitted his eyes to meet hers before looking away. In those few seconds she saw a flash of longing so defined that her knees all but shook.

"I'm afraid it isn't quite that simple, Athen," he said softly, avoiding her eyes once again, as if realizing he'd already given up more than he'd intended.

"Quentin . . ." She laid a hand on his arm just as Callie grabbed her from behind.

"Mom," she said, tugging on Athen's sleeve, "I've been looking all over for you . . . Hi, Mr. Forbes."

"Hello, Callie," he said with a smile, his fondness for the child as apparent as his gratitude for the interruption.

"Can we go?" pleaded Callie. "I'm starving and I have a math test to study for."

"I was just leaving," Athen told her. She turned to Quentin and said, "It was good to see you. I'm sorry if I . . ."

"You have nothing to be sorry about," he said, cutting her off and holding her elbow gently. "It was good to see you, Athen."

"I don't understand you, Quentin," she said bluntly.

"Someday . . ." he hinted cryptically, his lips attempting a slow half smile, ". . . I'm hoping someday you will."

"You make me crazy," she told him from between clenched jaws.

"Good," he whispered. The smile having faded wistfully, he squeezed her elbow before turning to search for his son in the crowd.

It had not taken a political genius to figure out that at the following week's council meeting, a motion would be made to lease the houses on Fourth Street to the UCC. Although

Wolmar and Giamboni voted against it, George Konstantos voted with Riley Fallon to hand the properties over. Athen cast the deciding vote, and the deed was done.

"This is your first clear victory since taking office. How do you think the opposition will react?" she was asked at the press conference that afternoon.

"First of all, I do not see it as a victory for anyone other than the people who have worked for this so hard and so long," she said. "People like Ms. Evelyn Wallace, Reverend Davison, and the other leaders of the UCC . . . it is their victory, not mine. And as far as the opposition is concerned, I would hope that Councilmen Wolmar and Giamboni would respect the wishes of the people of Woodside Heights."

"And Dan Rossi?" A voice from the middle of the first row asked pointedly.

"Dan Rossi does not sit on council, Mr. Forbes," she reminded him.

"It is my understanding that after the first of the year, Mr. Rossi will announce that he will, once again, be a mayoral candidate in the May primary," he continued. "Since he has been an outspoken opponent of a shelter at that location, do you foresee any problems in getting the project off the ground before you leave office?"

"Do you mean, will the shelter be open before my term expires?"

Quentin nodded.

"I have another year in office, Mr. Forbes. I cannot imagine that it would take a year to complete this." She tapped her foot in agitation. "The fact that last month's amendment moved the primary up to May does not affect this project. I fully expect the shelter to be open well before next November."

"Then are you conceding that you will not run against former mayor Rossi in the primary?" Dave Higgins from one of the local network affiliates asked her, as the TV camara lights flashed sharply.

"I never intended to seek reelection, Mr. Higgins," she told him bluntly.

"But if the shelter was delayed," he persisted, "or in jeopardy between now and May, would you consider . . ."

"The shelter will not be delayed in any way," she cut him off shortly, seeing the line of questioning beginning to drift towards waters she had no interest in treading. "There are plans in place to move this forward as quickly as possible. Perhaps Councilman Fallon would be good enough to fill you in on the timetable . . ."

"Congratulations, Athen." Quentin had hung back at the end of the conference, and had edged himself towards her.

She had watched him out of the corner of one eye, wondering if today he would elect not to make his usual dash for the door. She was pleased to see that he was slowly gathering his things, seeming to time himself so that they would be heading for the door at once.

"Congratulate Riley." She turned to him and smiled. "Or better still, Ms. Evelyn. She's the one who made this happen."

"You cast the deciding vote," he reminded her.

"Only because there was no one else there to do it."

"Do you really think Dan will let this happen?" They had moved into the hallway.

"I can't see how he can stop it, Quentin," she told him confidently. "What could he possibly do?"

"It just isn't in his nature to back off graciously." He ran a hand through his hair and his leather binder, held in the other hand, began to slip forward from his grasp. She reached out and caught it before it could fall. Their fingers touched, and they stood frozen for a long minute, politics and old hurts briefly forgotten. A current passed from one to the other and back again.

For a moment she forgot that she was the elected mayor of the city and that she was in the middle of a jammed hallway teeming with reporters in city hall. Their fingers instinctively entwined, and neither made an effort to disengage from this small unexpected connection. The air between them crowded with questions that could neither be asked nor answered. When she met his eyes, he did not avert his gaze as had become his custom.

"Excuse me, Mrs. Moran." The photographer from *The Woodside Herald* approached her from behind. Quentin juggled his binder up under his arm and the spell was broken as their fingers slid apart. "We'd like a picture with you and Councilmen Fallon and Konstantos . . ."

She scrambled to regain her recently departed wits and turned to face the camera, smiling as she stood between the two councilmen. When she turned back, Quentin had vanished.

41

"Good lord, Meg, the only thing I've ever worn that was cut this low was a nightgown." Athen tugged at the front of the evening gown.

"Leave it alone." Meg slapped at Athen's fingers. "You're throwing off the lines of the dress."

Meg stood back to assess the fit. "It's perfect, 'Thena. Gorgeous. The color is perfect . . . the dress is perfect. Oh, and with your mother's garnet necklace . . ."

"I don't know, Meg." Athen shook her head uncertainly. "It shows a lot of skin."

"But it shows it so very well." Meg grinned.

"Would you wear this in public?"

"If I was tall and built like you?" Meg's eyes rounded. "In a heartbeat. I hate to sound corny, but you do, in fact, look like a Greek goddess."

Athen anxiously studied her reflection in the dressing-room mirror. The dress was beautiful, she admitted. The softest shade of red wine velvet, it had wide shoulder straps and just skimmed her body all the way to the ankles. And Melina's garnets would be spectacular. She looked back at Meg, undecided.

"I'm not used to being this dressed up."

"Look, this will be a very fancy party. Hughes has invited everyone he knows to this bash to celebrate the kickoff of his new toy. People from the entertainment world, business people, politicians from three states," Meg reminded her. "Everyone will be dressed up. You want to look spectacular . . . and in that dress, you do."

"Which dress have you decided on?" Athen asked her.

"I think the cream one, it's lace over satin."

"Go put it on and let me see." Athen shoved Meg through the dressing-room door.

She reached around behind her to pull the zipper down and caught her reflection in the mirror. She turned and looked at herself from all directions. The dress was more beguiling than overtly sexy, she decided. Maybe she should . . .

"For pity's sake, Athen, get that finger out of your mouth and stop biting your nails. You'll ruin your manicure." Meg stretched to fasten the wide gold strand of garnets around her sister-in-law's neck.

"I'm nervous."

"Get over it." Meg popped earrings into her own lobes and checked in the mirror to make sure they were straight. "Maybe I shouldn't wear these, they always turn around. What do you think?"

"I liked the pearls better." Athen handed Meg the box holding the pearl earrings.

"You're right." Meg slipped the gold earrings out and replaced them. "They look better with my hair back . . . Will you please get that glum look off your face?"

"What if he ignores me?" Athen tapped her fingers on the dresser top.

"How could he ignore you?" Meg shook her head, exasperated. "You look spectacular. If I could look like you for just one week of my life I'd die a happy woman. Now come on. If we leave now, we can make an entrance."

"Oh, God, Meg . . ." Athen rolled her eyes to the ceiling and Meg laughed.

"Leave the dress alone," Meg commanded as she pushed Athen towards the step. "That dress is precisely the reason God invented cleavage. Now put your cape on and walk your little velvet butt out to the car. I'm driving. You just sit back and compose yourself. I have a feeling this will be a night to remember . . ."

The Chapman mansion was decked from top to bottom for the holidays. White Christmas lights illuminated every tree lining the drive and defined each window and doorway of the immense house. The illusion was, Meg noted dryly, of a crystal palace, plucked from the pages of a children's fairy tale and dropped into the upper regions of northern New Jersey.

The valets approached the car, one to each side, and assisted the ladies from the vehicle. Meg grabbed Athen by the elbow and steered her towards the front door.

"Smile nice," she ordered, "and be prepared to have a wonderful time . . ."

The entrance hall, festooned with trees trimmed in burgundy velvet and gold lamé, was mobbed with partygoers who, like Meg and Athen, had just arrived and were awed by the grandeur of the holiday decorations that met the eye at every turn. Thick green garlands, draped with huge bunches of dried hydrangea and gold mesh ribbon, wound lavishly up the huge staircase. The chandeliers bore gold lights and enormous burgundy bows. The effect was stunning.

The throng of guests drifted in the direction of the music beckoning from the ballroom off the entrance hall. Uniformed waiters offered delectable goodies from silver trays, and served fluted glasses of bubbly champagne. Couples took to the dance floor and swayed to the music played by a band from New York generally reserved for society bashes. Athen peered around for their host and hostess just as Lydia came up behind them and placed a bejeweled hand on each of their shoulders.

"How lovely you both look . . . so glad you could join us." Lydia was draped in a green satin gown, chosen, no doubt, to set off the incredible emeralds which rested around her neck. "Hughes, darling, look who's here . . ."

"Ah, ladies, how delightful to see you . . ." He kissed them both on the cheek. Turning to the good-looking blond-haired man beside him, he said, "Jeff, have you met Athena Moran? Our honorable mayor here in Woodside Heights.

And Meg Moran . . . our lead anchor on the new network. Ladies, Senator Thompson . . ."

"It's Jeff Thompson . . . and Mrs. Moran, I've certainly heard about you. Threw a curve or two at Dan Rossi, I understand." He chuckled and turned to Meg. "And of course, I recognize you, Ms. Moran. I've not missed a broadcast since you went on the air a few weeks back. You have a marvelous delivery, if I may say so. You're a delight to watch, just the right balance of intelligence and humor and beauty. An irresistible combination, in my book. Hughes was a genius to hire you, as I just finished telling him."

"Why, thank you, Senator." Meg was actually blushing for the first time Athen could ever recall.

"Jeff . . ." he reminded her, signaling for a black-tied waiter. "Champagne, ladies?"

Meg's eyes sparkled as the well-known bachelor senator from Pennsylvania proposed a toast to the success of the Chapman Cable Network. Athen took a step or two backwards, trying to ease out of the picture while at the same time scanning the room for Quentin.

"Athen Moran?" A lanky man with light brown hair touched her elbow.

"Yes?"

"Donald Moore. The state attorney general's office? We met a few months back at the New Jersey Today conference . . ."

"Oh, yes, of course, Donald. How are you?" She smiled, having no recollection of ever having seen his face before.

"Fine. Fine." His Adam's apple bobbed up and down along with his head. "I must say you look absolutely stunning this evening."

"My thoughts exactly." Quentin appeared out of nowhere and offered her another glass of champagne.

"Thank you both for the compliment." She shook her head to decline the drink.

The band began to play a soft, slow ballad, and Athen watched as couple after couple headed towards the dance floor. Quentin opened his mouth to speak but before he uttered a word, Donald had a hand on Athen's arm.

"Dance, Athen?" he asked, and before she could respond, he steered her towards the center of the room. "Excuse us, Quentin," he said over his shoulder.

Don was an accomplished dancer, and she tried her best to keep up with him. The song ended as another began and then yet another. She begged off the fourth, having long since run out of small talk.

"How about a cool drink?" Donald suggested.

"A club soda or something along those lines would be fine," she told him, surreptitiously scanning the room for Meg and the senator, for Quentin, but they were nowhere to be seen.

Donald returned bearing a crystal goblet filled with shaved ice and wafer-thin slices of lime.

"Perrier okay?" He handed her the glass.

"Just right, thanks." She sipped at it thirstily.

"Would you like to make a stop at the buffet?" he asked, obviously charmed by her company. "They have some lovely things . . . Lydia always finds the most wonderful caterers . . ."

"In a bit," she said, suddenly feeling closed in by the crowd. "I think I'd like to wander and ogle the decorations."

"Great idea. It's quite something, this house, don't you agree? Let's poke into the library here . . ." He led the way through the huge wooden door with the arched top. A fire burned brightly, and they stopped to chat with several small groups gathered around it. Donald seemed to know just about everyone there.

Strolling into the dining room, he whispered, "I see the esteemed Dr. Logan is here with his latest wife. Let's see, is she number five or number six . . . I seem to have lost count."

"Seriously?" She giggled. "Five or six?"

"That I know of, anyway. There, the couple right there in front of the punch bowl."

"You mean the thin man with the white mustache . . ."

". . . and the bad toupé, you're too polite to say it."

"His latest wife, you said?" Athen tried not to stare. Dr. Logan, short, tanned and clearly in his sixties, was overshadowed by the tall, shapely, bleached blonde hanging adoringly on his arm. She wore shiny red stiletto heels and a red and silver beaded dress which barely covered her on either end, the skirt as short as hot pants and the top as revealing as a bikini. And Meg thought I had cleavage, Athen mused.

"Mindy. The others, in order, were, let's see, Candy, Lisa, Cherie, Samantha, and Cindy. That's six. And they all looked exactly the same. As soon as they hit thirty, he dumps them and finds another look-alike." Donald shook his head in wonder.

"What?" Athen sputtered. "That's outrageous . . ."

"But true. What do you think, this one has maybe, what, six more years to put up with him?"

"I don't know, she seems awfully young." She frowned as a vision of Dan Rossi with the very young Mary Jo Dolan flashed suddenly before her eyes . . .

Donald shrugged, "All that alimony . . . but then again, he can afford it. Let's take a peek at the drawing room and see what Lydia's decorator has come up with in there . . ."

He guided her across the hall along with several other guests who also could not resist taking a tour of the Christmas wonderland. Athen paused momentarily to permit another couple to exit the room when Donald grabbed her arm playfully.

"Why, Athen, you've stopped right under the mistletoe," he said, grinning meaningfully.

She looked straight up overhead to where the white berries and green leaves were suspended. As she lowered her head, he leaned towards her slowly.

Good lord, was he going to kiss her?

"Ah, Athen, there you are." Quentin's hand slid onto the small of her back. "Excuse us, Donald. I believe this is our dance."

"Why did you do that? I was having a good time," she protested as he led her by the hand through the entrance hall to the ball room.

Ignoring her question, he took her in his arms and hummed along pleasantly with the band before asking, "Would you have let him?"

"Would I have let who do what?"

"Would you have let Donald kiss you?" His breath was warm against her ear and neck.

"How do you know Donald was going to kiss me?"

"It was written all over his face," Quentin said, "not that I blame him, of course. However, dragging you from one room to the next, from the dining room to the library, to the drawing room . . ."

"He wasn't dragging me," she protested, then laughed. "Quentin Forbes, you were following us."

"Every step of the way," he admitted.

"Why?"

"You think I'd let you disappear into the night with a womanizer like Donald Moore? Especially after Brenda had the florist tack mistletoe up over every doorway?"

The music stopped and several of the dancers in the crowd applauded enthusiastically.

"And what if I had, Quentin? I haven't seen you beating much of a path to my door lately. As a matter of fact, everytime I see you, you take great pains to run in the opposite direction. Don't deny it, you've been doing it for months."

"I don't deny it," he said, embracing her as the music began again. "Speaking of which, have I told you how beautiful you are tonight?"

"Yes." She was beginning to steam and wanted no more of his flattery. "Quentin, I have had enough of this. I don't understand you. First you're my friend, then you turn on me and make my life just one long run through Hades. Then you like me again and you take me out and we get along splendidly . . . I didn't imagine that, did I? I mean, I thought we were . . ."

"Splendidly is exactly right," he readily agreed, "you didn't imagine anything."

"Then the next thing I know, you come to a screeching halt and take off like a bat out of hell everytime I get within five feet of you . . ."

"Ten feet," he muttered, "I tried to keep it to about ten feet . . ."

"Why?" she demanded, weary of his playful quips. "Why, Quentin?"

He was silent, holding her close and slowly rubbing her cheek with his. When the song ended he took her by the hand and led her to the small morning room off the kitchen. He turned on a light and bent down to stoke the fire before placing another log into the fireplace.

She leaned back against the table in the middle of the room, her arms folded across her chest. He turned to her, walked slowly to where she stood, and ran his hands slowly up and down her arms, staring deeply into her eyes. He kissed her gently, his hands warm on her bare skin. He kissed her mouth and her chin, her cheeks, her neck, and her shoulder, before moving back to her mouth again.

"Why, Quentin?" She would not be put off. She wanted an answer, even while her knees buckled and her heart pounded and she wanted him to keep on kissing her.

"I thought things would be easier for you . . . and for me . . . if we put our relationship on hold for a while," he said with a sigh.

"Why?" she repeated.

"When I did that interview with Rossi . . . even though I wanted to put his crooked little face through the wall, I had to be objective." He paused and sat next to her on the table, taking her hand. "When the interview ran, you were so hurt—not because someone said unflattering things about you, but because I wrote the story. You thought I cared about you—and I did, very much—but that I hurt you anyway for the sake of a story."

"Quentin, I told you I understood . . . at least, after I thought it through, I did . . . It's okay."

"It's not okay, Athen, because it's bound to happen again and again between now and the primary."

"If it's any consolation, it didn't hurt so much after the first time."

"The article I did on Wolmar, when he called you an inexperienced embarrassment to the city . . ."

"I had to consider the source. Anyway, I am inexperienced, though if I've embarrassed anyone from time to time it's only been myself."

"And the one where Rossi said the city will be lucky if it doesn't go into bankruptcy between now and next November?"

"Rolled right off my back," she said with a shrug.

"How 'bout the one where Rossi . . ."

"Quentin, this is silly. Yes, I lost my head after that first article, but since then, I've come to understand that it's your job, and what you think and what you report are not necessarily the same thing. I thought I made that clear to you. At least I tried to."

"I figured once Rossi wins the primary, he'll forget you're alive. So I thought if I backed off for a few months, it would be easier for both of us. Then maybe we could pick up where we left off."

"Did it help? Backing off?"

"God, no." He ran his fingers through his hair. "It was as close to insanity as I've ever come. I'd sit there in the press conferences, maybe only hear one-tenth of what you'd say, because I was so busy taking in your every move, what dress you wore, studying your face, your gestures . . . pathetic, isn't it?" he confessed.

"Quentin, you had no right to decide for me if I could take the heat and continue to see you," she told him.

"Could you have?"

"I think so. I would have appreciated your giving me a chance to try. But I don't see that your keeping your distance has accomplished anything other than making us both miserable."

"Were you miserable?" He turned to her, their noses almost touching.

"Yes," she admitted, "I was. I couldn't figure out why you dumped me."

"I did not dump you," he protested, "I merely put you on hold."

"Call it what you like. It still hurt."

"Ah, Athen . . ." He slid off the table and pulled her to him. "I could not continue falling in love with you at the same time I felt that, on any given day, something I would have to print would hurt you . . ."

"Were you?" She arched her eyebrows. "Falling in love with me then?"

"A little bit more every day since I met you." He leaned closer until they were forehead to forehead.

"Want to try again?" she asked with a grin.

"I think that's supposed to be my line." He kissed her nose and nibbled on her bottom lip.

"That was your line last time." She kissed him back, feeling their bodies mold together through the soft velvet of her gown. They kissed long and deeply, the hunger which had lain dormant in them both seeming to explode.

"Quentin . . ." The door swung open and Brenda appeared. "Quentin . . ."

He reluctantly disengaged his lips and looked over his shoulder in obvious annoyance.

"I'm sorry to disturb you," she said, coming towards them in a rush, "but I just got a call from downtown. There's a fire . . ."

"Where?" he asked, only mildly interested.

"Fourth Street," she said meaningfully, looking past him to Athen.

"Fourth Street . . . ?" Athen repeated, then understanding fully what Brenda was telling them, cried, "Oh, God, no . . ."

"Come on, Athen." He grabbed her hand and led her from the room. "Brenda, see if you can find Athen's wrap and meet me at the front door . . . I'll get a car and drive around."

42

The orange flames that filled the entire sky above Woodside Heights were visible from the end of the Chapmans' drive. They rode in tense silence, Quentin taking the winding curves on two wheels, yet neither Brenda nor Athen appeared to notice.

Fourth Street was blocked off at Schyler Avenue and a uniformed police officer directed them to turn left, away from the fire. Athen rolled down her window and called to him.

"Officer Townsend . . . it's Athena Moran. I need to get through."

"Oh, hi, Athen," he said, turning to the car. "What a mess, eh?"

"How bad is it?" she asked anxiously.

"'Bout as bad a fire as I've ever seen." He leaned into the car slightly and said, "They got trucks up there from every company in the city and every surrounding town, but it ain't doin' much good."

"How far can we drive?" Quentin asked impatiently.

"Well, the fire marshall doesn't want any cars up there, 'count of all them pumpers, but you could probably go a block up, then park . . ."

Quentin was off in a shot, turning briskly at the next corner and pulling into the first empty spot on the street.

"How fast can you move in those shoes?" he asked, gesturing towards Athen's high-heel-clad feet as he put the car in park.

Ignoring him, she opened the door and began to run towards the three houses that were clearly engulfed in flame. The fire marshal met her a block from the conflagration and refused to let her go any further.

"Any one of those walls could go at any moment, Athen. I can't let you get any closer. I'm worried enough about the men, without having to worry about you too," he told them. "We're trying our damnedest to keep it from spreading to the other side of the street. We've already evacuated two blocks in every direction, sent folks to their churches to wait this out."

Quentin and Brenda caught up with her moments later. Quentin put an arm around Athen and drew her near, his chest absorbing the sobs that wracked her slender form.

"That son of a bitch," she cried from her very depths. "He will not get away with this. That son of a bitch . . ."

"Hold on there, sweetheart, you don't know . . ."

"Oh, yes, I do know," she choked angrily, pounding on

his chest for emphasis. "I do know. And I will not let Dan Rossi get away with this."

"Athen, before you start making accusations . . ."

"Are you going to try to convince me that this is a coincidence?" She turned wild eyes upon him, her fists clenched in fury.

Quentin watched the fire burn out of control, watched as the facade of the first house crumbled, sending red-hot bricks in a blazing shower to the street below. The heat and smoke surrounded them even at this distance and he pulled her back another twenty-five feet. He knew that more than old buildings were being destroyed that night, and he knew that she was right.

"No," he said gruffly, pulling her back to rest against him as they watched in helpless disbelief as the second, then the third house fell, shaking the ground beneath their feet and filling the night with smoke and thunder. "No, Athen, I do not think this is a coincidence . . ."

They stayed, frozen to one spot, till there was nothing left to burn but the rubble. He led her gently from the scene, and they walked wordlessly back to the car. Brenda had caught up with the photographer from *The Woodside Herald* and was herself interviewing the fire marshal as they passed. She waved to them, indicating she'd get a ride home.

At some point during the drive to Athen's house, she began to cry again, not tears of anger now but of futility. He parked the car in front of her house and took her inside, placing her gently on the sofa. He sat down next to her, pulling her half onto his lap and rocking her in his arms.

"How could he do this to Ms. Evelyn? To all the people who have worked so hard . . . ?" she cried, her eyes filled with a terrible sadness. "How could he care so little . . . ?"

"Athen, it is a sorry fact of this life that there are people who truly believe they are above the rules that everyone else follows." He stroked her hair and tried to comfort her. "They feel that, for whatever reason, what they want is more important than what others want, and that somehow they are justified in doing whatever it takes to get what they want."

He paused thoughtfully for a very long minute, then said,

"It really makes you wonder, though, doesn't it?" He rubbed his chin and she twisted her head around to look into his face. "Just what is it that Dan wants so badly that he'd risk setting an entire neighborhood on fire to get it . . . ?"

Somewhere around six, Athen had fallen asleep, still wrapped in the warmth of Quentin's arms. He sat motionless, though wide awake, so as not to disturb her troubled slumber. A weary Meg, her lovely cream lace gown wrinkled and limp, arrived home around eight-thirty, accompanied by her senator. Quentin placed a finger to his lips when she poked her head into the living room. Meg nodded and tiptoed into the kitchen.

Athen roused slowly, almost dully, from her sleep shortly thereafter.

"I smell coffee," she murmured.

"Right here." He helped her to sit up and handed her the mug which Meg had brought to him a few minutes earlier.

"What time is it?" She yawned.

"A little before nine," he told her.

She sipped at the warm liquid and handed it back to him.

"It wasn't a dream, was it?" she asked woodenly.

"No, sweetheart," he replied, "it wasn't a dream."

She sighed deeply and leaned back against the sofa, unconsciously combing her hair with her fingers.

"Guess that's the end of that," she said sadly.

"Only if you let it be." His jacket, which earlier he had removed and draped over her, had slid off her shoulders, and he reached out and pulled it back up to cover her.

"What's that supposed to mean?" she asked peevishly.

"It means that you have a lot of thinking to do, my darling," he told her.

"About what?" She frowned. "How to nail Rossi's butt to the clock on top of city hall?"

"That," he said with a nod, "and how to use this little setback to your advantage."

"Quentin, what the hell are you talking about?" She gazed at him quizzically. "This is no little setback. The shelter went up in smoke."

"Only those buildings went up in smoke."

"Those buildings were the shelter," she reminded him archly.

"Then look for another site," he said.

"There isn't another site." She wanted to smack him.

"Then find a way to use the one you have."

"You aren't making any sense." She did smack him then, with the small pillow from the end of the sofa.

"I can't believe you'd give up so easily." He shook his head. "Athen, there are grants you can apply for from the government for this type of thing. All you need to do is track them down and apply . . ."

"I thought I heard voices." Meg came slowly into the room, her shoes long discarded and her hair hanging in disarray. "I'm so sorry, Athen. I know what this meant to you."

"It's not me I'm concerned about," Athen said, shaking her head, "it's all the people who needed that space to live in . . . where will they go this winter? Riley told me on Thursday that the renovations would have been completed by the middle of January, the first of February at the very latest. Now there's nothing . . ."

She stood up on stiff legs and attempted to stretch a kink from her neck. She sipped from Quentin's coffee and made a face. "It's cold," she mumbled.

"Come on in the kitchen," Meg said, putting an arm over her shoulder, "and I'll get you a fresh cup . . ."

Senator Jeff Thompson sat at the kitchen table, his tie hanging from his open collar, the first few studs of his tuxedo shirt undone. He looked tired, though his eyes brightened slightly as the trio slouched into the room and he focused on Meg's disheveled appearance.

"My condolences, Athen," he offered as he pulled a chair out for her. "Meg's been filling me in on recent history with those properties. You will, of course, request a full investigation . . . ?"

"Immediately," she said vehemently, accepting the coffee Meg offered with a wan smile. "I want the county fire marshal and the state fire marshal in on this now."

"How far up does Rossi's influence stretch?" Meg asked.

"I guess we'll find out soon enough," Athen grumbled, "though I know he has friends in very high places."

"Jeff," Quentin said, stirring cream into his cup thoughtfully, "isn't there money available at the federal level for projects of this sort?"

"You mean like community development grants, inner-city renovations, that sort of thing?"

Quentin nodded.

"I think HUD has some programs," Jeff replied, "though I'm not certain of the requirements. I have a friend with the agency. I can give him a call first thing in the morning, if you'd like."

"Could you do that?" Meg asked.

"Would it put you forever in my debt?"

"Absolutely," she said with a laugh.

"Consider it done," he assured her.

"That would be wonderful, Jeff." Athen managed a smile. "I'd really appreciate any help you could give me."

"Well, I have to admit that knowing the background of the situation, then listening to Rossi's sorrowful little dissertation last night about what a shame it all was . . ." Meg began.

"What are you talking about?" Athen's head shot up sharply. "Where did you see Dan . . . ?"

"He was at the scene when we arrived," Meg told her.

"I didn't see him," Athen noted. "Which side were you on?"

"The city hall side," Meg replied. "Where were you?"

"We came in off Schyler." Athen plunked her cup down loudly onto the tabletop. "I can't believe he had the nerve to show up there."

"Complete with crocodile tears and words of the most heartfelt condolences to the UCC." Meg leaned back in her chair. "I even got him on tape . . ."

"What?!" Athen fairly shrieked.

"I called the station from Jeff's car," Meg told her, "and asked for a camera crew. They had already gotten a call and were setting up when I arrived." She peered over her shoulder at the clock on the wall. "They'll probably run the tape around nine. We can catch his little performance in the living room in about five minutes. Come on, let's tune in so that we don't miss a minute of it."

"I can barely wait." Athen bit her bottom lip, her anger rising again, making a face as Meg left the room followed closely by her new suitor. "That son of a bitch . . ."

Quentin rose to place his empty cup on the counter. As he passed the refrigerator door, he paused, then leaned closer to inspect something held by a magnet.

"Athen," he asked, a look of puzzlement on his face. "What is this . . . ?"

"What? Oh, that." She waved a hand to dismiss its immediate importance. "Meg found that picture in the *Herald* archives. We were looking to see what had appeared in the paper the day my father had his stroke. I was trying to find out who the man in the background was but couldn't . . . it's a long story, Quentin."

She got up from the table to move towards the living room, grabbing his arm to divert his attention from the piece of paper which he intently studied.

"Paul Schraeder," he said without looking up.

"What did you say?" She ceased tugging.

"It's Paul Schraeder," Quentin told her.

"You know him?" she asked in disbelief.

"He was corporate counsel for Rest America about five years ago."

"Rest America?" She was suddenly all ears.

"It's a company which owns several hotel chains, franchise restaurants, that sort of thing," he explained.

"So?"

"So Rest America is owned by Bradford International."

"Your mother's company . . ." she stated flatly.

"May I borrow this?" Quentin held the picture up and she nodded.

"What would he be doing with Dan Rossi . . . ?" she wondered aloud.

"That, my dear Athen, is a very good question." He folded the paper and tucked it into his pocket. "Now, let's go see if we can catch Danny's little performance on the morning news."

Meg and Quentin both spent most of Sunday interviewing the parties central to the issue, Ms. Evelyn and Reverend Davison, Riley Fallon, and Edward Snipe, who as chief cook and bottle washer at the nearby UCC soup kitchen, spoke of the somber demeanor of those who had filed in for a breakfast that morning. Face after face, each stunned by the unexpected turn of events, was photographed to appear either live on Meg's evening broadcast or in print to grace the next day's coverage by the *Herald*.

Athen spent the afternoon in her office, meeting with Ms. Evelyn and several others to commiserate. She had tried unsuccessfully on several occasions to reach the state fire marshal. She did manage to get through to the county marshal, Ted Boyd, but despite his assurances that a thorough investigation would be launched, she held little hope that any conclusive evidence would be forthcoming—particularly after Ms. Evelyn pointed out that Boyd was a longtime supporter of Dan Rossi.

Quentin had called from his car phone shortly before five to tell her he'd swing by her house in twenty minutes to pick her up. Lydia, realizing how busy they'd all been that day, had dinner prepared for the group and expected them all by six. Athen reached the house just as Quentin pulled up. It had taken them both several minutes to rouse Callie, who, suffering from sleep deprivation following Carolann's slumber party the night before, had crashed on the sofa.

Although still festively bedecked, the Chapman house seemed somehow more somber, the import of the events of the past eighteen hours overshadowing the holiday air of the previous night. Dinner was postponed in order that they might watch the six o'clock rebroadcast of Meg's coverage of the fire.

"This is Meg Moran for Chapman Cable News." Meg appeared on the larger-than-life sceen in the Chapmans' den, dressed in her lace gown, "reporting from Woodside Heights at the scene of one of the worst fires in northern

New Jersey's history. The buildings burning behind me had only recently been leased to the United Community of Churches, a grass roots organization that was formed to help the unemployed and homeless of Woodside Heights. I'm here with former mayor Dante Rossi . . . Mr. Rossi, it's my understanding that you have been an outspoken opponent of this project since its inception . . ."

"Now don't you think for one minute that this"—he waved his hand behind them towards the burning buildings—"gives me any pleasure. It saddens me more than I can tell you to see a portion of this city I've loved and served for twenty years go up in flames." He dabbed meaningfully at his tear-filled eyes, pausing for effect. "As far as the shelter was concerned, that issue had been decided by a majority of city council. But I would like to remind you, Miss Moran, of two things. One, I was in opposition of using these old properties to shelter human beings because I feared exactly what you see here tonight. I feared a loss of life and God knows how many lives we would have lost had anyone been in those buildings when the fire broke out. And two, I have felt all along that taken in its entirety, that whole area could—make that should—be used to generate badly needed income for the city. I still believe that. Now why don't you go on home," he said, his eyes narrowed to shining little beads and focused on Meg, "and ask that sister-in-law of yours what she intends to do now that she has several acres of empty ground on her hands."

"Mr. Rossi refers to the fact that Athena Moran, my late brother's widow, is currently the mayor of Woodside Heights," Meg told the camera, not missing a beat in spite of her certain embarrassment.

"Ouch!" Brenda, seated on the edge of a sofa, winced.

"Ouch indeed," Meg nodded grimly.

"You handled it very well, dear." Lydia patted her arm.

"That won't happen again, I assure you, Mr. Chapman," Meg told him apologetically, "and I had someone else interview Athen."

"You go with what you've got," he muttered.

"Hey, there's Mom." Callie brightened as Athen appeared on the screen, taped earlier that afternoon in city hall.

". . . and of course, everyone's still in shoek," Athen was telling Helena Gables, who'd been sent by Meg to cover this part of the story. "I'm grateful that no one was injured, and I would commend the firemen who did such an outstanding job in rousing the residents nearby and getting everyone to safety. I've had a report of several firemen who were overcome by smoke, but other than that, I'd say we were extremely fortunate."

"Is arson a possibility?" Helena stepped closer to Athen and the camera zoomed in.

Of course it's arson, you nitwit, Athen had wanted to scream. Cautioned, however, by Quentin to watch what she said publicly, she appeared to pause thoughtfully before responding. "I think it's a bit premature to speculate. We'll have to wait to see what the fire marshal finds . . ."

"Do you have any plans now for the use of that area?" Helena asked.

"The ashes are still smoldering, Ms. Gables," Athen told her wearily. "No one's had time to consider where to go from here. We will, over time, look at several options . . ."

"Good job, 'Thena." Meg leaned over and patted her on the back.

"You have no idea how hard it was for me not to have grabbed that microphone and spoken my mind," she said, shaking her head.

"Well, I would caution you to keep biting your tongue," Brenda pointed out. "And Meg, I'd suggest that you continue to have Helena cover this from here on out. I understand that you were the one on the scene and I think you handled yourself well under the circumstances. But it should not happen again. We must avoid the appearance of a conflict of interest through this. And while I'm thinking of it, Quentin, I think you should keep your distance as well. I'm reassigning you to the state desk. I'll have Anthony cover the city from now on."

"I had planned to suggest exactly that to you," he told

her, "but you'll need someone else to cover the state news, since I'll be taking a little trip to St. Louis this week."

"What for, dear?" Lydia asked, noting Rose Ellen's signal that dinner was ready to be served.

"I just thought I'd pay a visit to the Bradford home office and see what was doing." He winked at Athen.

"Well, the board meeting isn't until the end of January, dear." Lydia motioned everyone towards the dining room.

"I know, Mother," Quentin said, taking her arm, "but I thought I'd check in on a thing or two before the meeting, so I could be better prepared this year."

"Really, Quentin . . . ?" Lydia beamed as he seated her, then took his place next to Athen at the table. "You've no idea how pleased I am that you're finally taking an interest."

"Oh, I'm certainly interested," he said, kicking Athen lightly under the table.

"Well, dear, you know that, this being the holiday season, there's not likely to be too many people in the office next week."

"That's okay." He smiled. "I think I'd like to just poke around a little . . ."

"Well, then, I'll call Stafford's office in the morning and make sure that he and his staff give you full access to everything." Lydia sipped at her wine, thinking how pleased her late father and husband would have been that the heir apparent was finally gravitating back towards the family business.

Certain that her son's obvious infatuation with Athen had something to do with his sudden concern for family affairs, she smiled to herself. If it took a woman in his life to get Quentin back into Bradford International, she would encourage the relationship in every way she could. "Callie, dear," Lydia patted the chair to her left as Callie and Timmy approached the table, "sit next to me and tell me all about the play you're in at school. Timmy says you're absolutely wonderful . . ."

"Jeff said that you should consider forming an agency within the city to deal with HUD," Meg told her Tuesday evening as she reheated the dinner she had missed earlier. "He spoke to a friend of his who told him that if you had some sort of redevelopment authority, things would move more quickly."

"Hmmm . . ." Athen considered the news.

"Jeff is having someone from HUD call you this week." The timer on the microwave alerted her that her leftovers were ready. "Isn't he an ace?"

"An ace," Athen agreed with a grin.

Meg grinned back. "Speaking of adorable men, have you heard from Quentin?"

"He called right before you came in." Athen plunked down in a chair and fiddled with the small centerpiece Callie had made for the kitchen table. Dried holly berries fell and ran the length of the table, small red balls that bounced onto the floor. Knowing their poisonous qualities, Athen bent to retrieve them before Hannah did. "Stafford Banks, who heads Bradford International, is in London with his family until the second week in January. It appears there's but a skeleton crew in St. Louis this week, which is certainly to Quentin's advantage. He can pull any records he wants without anyone asking questions."

"How lucky can you get?" Meg shook her head and laughed, adding, "And to think if you'd cleaned off the refrigerator door, as I'd been harping at you to do, we'd never have a lead on this."

"I don't know that we have a lead on anything," Athen reminded her, "but Quentin seems to think that somehow this Paul Schraeder may be a player in whatever it is that Rossi planned to do on Fourth Street."

"What do you think?" Meg asked, twirling strands of spaghetti around her fork.

"I think it's terribly curious," Athen admitted, "that someone in Schraeder's position would show up at a fund-raiser for a little local politician in the wilds of northern New Jersey. If that is the photograph my father was looking at that morning, he must have known who Schraeder was and why he was there. And whatever it was that he knew, it sent his blood pressure sky high . . ."

43

"So tell me," she begged, "what did you find out?"

"All in good time, my dear." Quentin grinned mischievously and slammed the car door. "This is New Year's Eve, and we are going to have a perfectly lovely evening, Athen. We are going to leave this damned city and the UCC and Dan Rossi and even—dare I say it?—our beloved children behind us and head off for a romantic getaway at a very private little spot I know of on the ocean."

"A romantic evening?" She raised a curious eyebrow, thinking of the woolens and sweat clothes packed in her bag. "You told me to bring my warmest clothes. What is your idea of romantic, might I ask?"

He pondered the question as he headed towards the turnpike. "Having a sense of the moment," he told her as he peered past her to make sure no other cars were turning onto the ramp.

Quentin's "private little spot on the ocean" was the Chapman summer home in Bay Head on the New Jersey coast. Athen's eyes widened as the car pulled into the drive of the rambling weathered house overlooking the Atlantic. A stream of smoke drifted from the chimney, and lights burned invitingly inside.

"Quentin, it's breathtaking," she exclaimed as they climbed the tiered steps to the deck overlooking the sea.

"I knew you'd love it." He dropped the overnight bags he'd carried from the car and draped an arm over her shoulder to share the view with her.

The beach was deserted save for a foraging gull whose call was all but lost in the sound of the pounding surf. The air was crisp and cold and smelled of salt and the dunes below the deck.

"It's wonderful," she told him. "Thank you for bringing me here. It's been forever since I've been to the beach."

Pleased that his choice of a getaway was the right one, he hugged her. "Come on inside and let's see what Mrs. Emmons has for us . . ."

"Mrs. Emmons . . . ?" she asked, ducking inside the door he held open for her.

"She's the housekeeper," Quentin explained. "I called her from St. Louis and asked her to freshen things up and prepare one of her devastatingly wonderful dinners . . ."

"She lives here all year round?" Athen inquired. "By herself?"

"Her husband takes care of the grounds and the cars and the boats, that sort of thing . . . Ah, there she is." He smiled as a pudgy woman with salt and pepper hair and a pleasant round face toddled into the kitchen.

"Hello, Quentin," she greeted him, happy to have something to do to earn her keep besides dust empty rooms.

"This is my friend, Athena Moran," he said, introducing the two women. Athen extended a hand, trying to guess how old Mrs. Emmons was. Late fifties? Sixties? "She'll be staying with us for a few days."

"A few days?" Athen poked him as they walked into an enormous living room, presided over by a stone fireplace in which a healthy fire burned. A large Christmas tree, devoid of decorations, stood in one corner of the room. She eyed it curiously but said nothing.

"You need a few days away," he said as he rubbed her shoulders, "specifically, a few days away with me."

"But Callie . . ." Athen protested.

". . . will be fine. Mother and Hughes are taking her and Timmy to New York where they will see shows and take in the sights and have a wonderful time before they have to go back to school. They will hook up with my sister Caitlin and have a ball . . . Cait is a barrel of fun, when she's not working, which she all too often is . . . You don't mind, do you?" He turned her to face him, his hands on her shoulders. "I know I should have asked you first, before I allowed Mother to make her plans, but I really wanted to surprise you with a little vacation. And Meg thought it would be all right. If you object, we can call the Plaza and have Mother cut the trip short."

"Of course not," she told him. "I'm sure Callie will be more than adequately looked after, and I'm sure she'll have a wonderful time. It's very nice that your mother wanted to include her . . . or was that your idea?"

"A little of both," he said. "Mother has grown very fond of Callie, and when I told her I'd like to come down here with you for New Year's Eve, she suggested that perhaps you'd have a better time if your daughter had a little holiday of her own."

"That's very sweet." She nuzzled into his chest, the soft wool of his sweater tickling her nose. She moved to pull his head down to kiss him. His eyes brightened and she closed her own, leaning up to where she thought his lips should be just as he said, "Yes, Mrs. Emmons, right there would be fine."

He disengaged himself, seemingly oblivious to the fact that Athen's lips were left suspended, skyward. She frowned slightly and followed his gaze to the sofa next to which Mrs. Emmons had stacked several large brown boxes.

"I'll have your refreshments in just a minute," Mrs. Emmons announced as she returned to the back of the house.

"Come sit, Athen." He motioned to her to join him on the floor. "Let's see what we have here . . . Oh, these will be just fine . . . what do you think?"

Athen peered over his shoulder as he opened the lid to allow her to gaze inside.

"They're seashells," she said aloud, slightly puzzled.

"Of every variety and size and color." He grinned like a small child. "Just exactly what I wanted."

"Wanted for what?" She sat down on the floor and opened another box. More shells.

"Let me put this down here for you." Mrs. Emmons stepped around her and placed a tray bearing mugs of mulled wine and a huge bowl of popcorn between them.

"Oh, great." Athen smiled, "My favorite snack." She reached her hand into the bowl and lifted out a handful.

"Go easy on that," Quentin cautioned, "Mrs. Emmons has a way with shrimp you won't believe . . . ah, there they are."

295

He took the platter of shrimp wrapped in bacon from Mrs. Emmons's hands as she placed yet another huge bowl of fluffy white popcorn on the table. She returned in seconds with an equally large bowl of cranberries and a leather envelope which she handed to Quentin with a wink.

"That should do you," the woman said cheerfully. "I'll have dinner for you in about an hour. Would you like me to set up in the dining room, or would you prefer a table in here?"

He glanced about the room, then nodded to the windowed alcove off to one side.

"How about over there?" he gestured.

"Fine," she replied and disappeared once again.

"Quentin . . ." Athen leaned back against the sofa, "who do you expect to eat all this?"

"I expect you and I to eat the shrimp." He grabbed one from the tray and offered it to her. "And the other goodies we will string." He opened the leather pouch and withdrew a card of long thin needles and several spools of thread. "Because as you can see, our tree has yet to be properly dressed for the season. And a tree by the ocean should be turned out . . ."

". . . in shells," she concluded.

". . . precisely." He laughed and handed her a box. "The Emmons's son owns a concession on the boardwalk down the coast a bit, in Ocean City. Of course, this being the dead of winter, he doesn't have too much business right now. I asked Mrs. E. to get some of his best shells, and Mr. E. drilled holes in them . . . Where's that little bag with the tree hooks . . . Here we go . . ."

He stood up and reached a hand down to pull her along. Handing the bag of hooks to Athen, he carried a box of shells to the tree. He speared a shell with the wire and gave it to her, saying, "As guest of honor, you should hang the first one."

She studied the tree for a moment and placed the first shell, a pearly oyster that glistened with luminescence in the fire's light, near the top. They worked side by side, taking turns hanging shell after shell, until they had gone through all the boxes. Then they sat back on the floor and strung popcorn and cranberries on long sturdy threads, trading memories of long-ago holidays, until Mrs. Emmons appeared to set up for dinner.

They ate perfect Caesar salad and grilled swordfish marinated in wine and vegetables sliced into slivers barely wider than the hooks they'd used to hang the shells upon the tree, and drank wine at the little table that overlooked the ocean. For dessert, Mrs. E. produced superb creme caramels and bowls of raspberries laced with Grand Marnier and a pot of freshly brewed coffee. Athen felt she'd been transported magically from the life she had known to some distant place that was strange and yet somehow comfortably familiar at the same time.

Languid with food and wine, she tried to beg off when he'd thrown her parka at her and said, "Let's take a little walk on the beach while Mrs. E. cleans up."

The night air was sharply cold and fragrant with the sea, the sky ablaze with a thousand stars. "Diamonds on black velvet, as they say," he noted as they trudged across the sand. The wind kicked up off the ocean as they walked, and the breaking waves scattered a salty mist. She leaned her head back and filled her lungs, taking in as much of the night and the sea as she could.

"This is," she announced as they strolled back to the house, "the most perfect night."

"Umm," he agreed as he led her up the steps and held her arm as she unlaced her low rubber boots and shook out the sand.

The house was warm and cozy. Mrs. E. had laid several more logs on the fire and set out a carafe of wine and two crystal goblets before disappearing for the evening.

"I truly love this room," she told him as she sank to the floor in front of the fire and gazed around at the simple but comfortable furniture. Overstuffed chairs and sofas, all in peach and dark green on cream, florals and plaids and stripes, stacks of cushions and casual appointments, bid one to sit and to stay.

"We don't use this room much in the summer," he noted

as he sat next to her and leaned back on one elbow, "and unfortunately, no one comes down much in the winter. But it is a wonderful room . . . Hey, we forgot something . . ."

"What?" she asked, turning to look behind her at the tree, to see what he was doing.

"We forgot the star at the top." He grinned. "Now, let's see, where did I put that?"

"You brought a star for the tree?" She lay back and rolled over on her stomach to watch him.

"Of sorts." He opened a small bag. "Would you like to put it on the tree?"

"You do it." She smiled, and leaned up on her elbows.

With great ceremony he placed the object at the tree's uppermost branch.

"Why, it's a starfish," she said with a laugh.

"Of course." He joined her on the floor and laid next to her before the fire. "What did you expect . . . ?"

"Quentin, it's perfect," she told him. "A bit unconventional, perhaps, but perfect all the same. However did you get the idea?"

"I wanted to do something that was just for us," he told her quietly, "something that just you and I could share. Athen, we both bring a lot from the past with us. I wanted to start to make memories that were only ours . . ."

He leaned down to kiss her and she pulled him to her with a fervor which surprised them both. They blended into each other as they both had known they would do.

"Furry sweaters are wonderful against the cold," he said as he raised his mouth from her neck to comment, "but they are, at this moment, impeding progress somewhat . . ." He removed little bits of fuzz from his mouth and she laughed, sitting up slightly and grasping the bottom of her sweater, as if to pull the purple garment over her head, a soft blush rising to tint her cheeks as she looked into his eyes.

"That first big step always seems to be the hardest, doesn't it?" He smiled gently, sensing her hesitancy, stroking the side of her face with his fingertips. "I guess only you can decide if you want to take that step, and see where it leads us."

298

His quiet assurance gave her confidence, and she pulled the sweater over her head and lay back against his arm.

"Agapemou . . . Did I say that right?" he asked, and she nodded that he had. "I've been rolling that word around in my head for months, since the night you showed me the statue of your mother, waiting for the time when I could call you my beloved. Athen, I would have waited forever if I'd had to, just to be with you now . . ." He caressed her gently, whispering her name over and over, leading her slowly and patiently onward towards a place where they could, indeed, begin to make memories that only they would share . . .

"Come on, sleepyhead." He nudged her from a most peaceful sleep. "Wake up."

"Why?" She tried to turn over but he refused to let her bury herself in the pillow.

"Because you have the opportunity to watch the sun rise over the ocean on not only a new day, but a new year." He kissed her ear. "So get up and come outside . . ."

"Outside?" she grumbled. "It's eighteen degrees and I'm wrapped in a blanket and you want to go outside . . . ?"

"Here," he said, handing her a pair of flannel pajamas and a heavy woolen robe, "these will help."

"Not by much." She pulled the flannel over her legs and arms and wrapped herself in the robe. She joined him at the French doors, which opened onto a porch that ran the entire length of the second floor. He flung a heavy blanket over the cushions of a settee and pulled her down to sit next to him.

"Better?" he asked, pulling the ends of the blanket around her shivering form.

"Umm . . ." She snuggled next to him and fixed her eyes on the horizon as the first stray shards of light broke through the morning sky. As the minutes passed, the light spread slowly over the dark ocean, turning the brackish water into glowing greenish gray and gold beneath the mist.

"Oh, that's beautiful." She sighed. "Thank you for making me get up to see this."

He smiled with pleasure, watching her eyes sparkle as the

sky continued to unfold and the morning of the new year spread out around them. Soon the show ended as daylight reached the shore.

"What a lovely thing to share with me." She kissed his chin.

"You warm enough?" he asked.

"It's warmer inside." She nudged him. "Let's go back to bed . . ."

His eyes widened in mock surprise. "Are you the same woman who only last night wasn't sure she remembered what to do?"

She stood up to her full height and flung the end of the blanket over her shoulder. "It did, as you suggested it might, come back to me . . ."

"I'll say it did," he mumbled, following her towards the open door. "Great idea, leaving the door open for twenty minutes. It's like a meat locker in . . ."

She dropped the robe and started to unbutton the pajama top.

"Close the door, Quentin," she instructed with a mischievous half-smile, "and let's see what else I can remember . . ."

"Now," Athen said pointedly over breakfast, "I want to know everything that happened in St. Louis."

Mrs. E. had set the small table where they'd dined the night before with a tray of scrambled eggs, bacon, English muffins, and delicate home-fried potatoes promptly at eight-thirty as Quentin had requested.

"Well, to make a long story short, I discovered that our old friend Paul Schraeder is now the guiding light at Clover Inns," he told her, "and has apparently set his sights on Woodside Heights for a convention center and luxury hotel."

"A luxury hotel?" She almost choked on her words. "In Woodside Heights? Who would want to stay in a hotel in the midst of all that urban blight?"

"Well, the idea is to dispose of the blight and start with a blank slate, more or less." He buttered a muffin as he spoke.

"Once the hotel has a foothold in Woodside Heights, they would offer to purchase the homes in the immediate area."

"Since those homes aren't worth much, I doubt the neighbors would sell," she told him, "I mean, they wouldn't get enough for their houses to be able to afford to go anywhere else."

"That's where having a friend in local government comes in handy," he said, "someone who could put pressure on the residents to move . . . There're all sorts of methods. Listen, two years ago in Georgia, Clover Inns was building a hotel and wanted to buy up a block on the opposite side of the street for a park. The residents didn't want to sell. So Clover Inns got the local pols to pass an ordinance that extended the construction hours in the evening and permitted the work to begin earlier in the morning. After months of listening to the racket well into the night and have it start at the break of dawn the next day, one by one, the company got its hands on every piece of property it wanted."

"How could they get the city to do that?"

"By crossing the appropriate palms with the appropriate amount of silver would be my guess," he replied.

"How did you find out about all this?"

"I called Schraeder's successor at Rest America," he explained, "and asked him what was new, what was on the drawing board, that sort of thing. He said we're getting some stiff competition from Clover Inns. Word has it that Schraeder has plans to get a strong foothold in the East, to try to establish his chain beyond their traditional midwest holdings, and that he has some very promising sites in New Jersey and Connecticut."

"Do tell." She leaned her elbows on the table, all ears.

"The location outside Greenwich is in the bag but apparently there's a bit of a snafu in the New Jersey site," he said, smiling meaningfully. "However, Schraeder apparently is confident that will be resolved within six months."

"Why would he want to build in Woodside Heights?" She frowned.

"It's actually a good location." He sipped at his coffee. "Close enough to get in and out of New York City in a short amount of time, and land is comparatively inexpensive. It's not a bad idea, from a strictly business standpoint."

"So what's the deal with Rossi?"

"I suspect that Schraeder offered Rossi cash to secure the properties for him," Quentin said bluntly. "Probably paid him a sort of finder's fee . . . so much cash to agree to help Schraeder, with a bigger bundle when Clover Inns took title. It's not the first time Paul has engaged in such dealings, and is exactly the reason why he and Rest America parted company a few years back."

"So then Dan had to obtain the properties for the city so he could in turn sell them to Clover Inns." She nodded thoughtfully. "The city confiscated those properties a few years ago for nonpayment of taxes . . . two elderly brothers owned them, as I recall."

"Two elderly, senile brothers," he pointed out. "Both in a nursing home in Arizona."

"How do you know that?"

"I had Brenda check the tax records, then followed up with Social Security to track them down." He shook his head. "Neither had any recollection of having received any notice of a sale, but neither seemed to care too much, either. They're both in their eighties and that was ancient history to them."

"Well, if Dan has had those properties for three years, why didn't he sell them to Schraeder back then?"

"Because the Greenwich deal came through faster than Schraeder had anticipated. I suspect he paid Dan a little extra to sit on the Fourth Street site for him until the company had the cash flow to proceed in Woodside Heights," Quentin surmised.

"I wish I could nail Dan for taking that money," she sighed.

"Well, short of a signed confession, there's no way to prove any of this. Schraeder's not likely to admit that he's paid local authorities in exchange for their cooperation any more than Dan's going to admit he accepted the bribe," he reminded her, "but there's no doubt in my mind he promised Dan a bundle to sit on those lots for him. There's no other explanation for Dan's resolve to keep control of them."

"I wonder if my father knew," she murmured, "I wonder if that's why he hit the ceiling when he saw the picture in the paper . . ."

"Maybe Schraeder approached Ari first," Quentin suggested.

"You mean offered my father a bribe . . . ?" Her eyes widened in horror at the thought.

"It's very possible," he continued. "From all I've heard, Ari Stavros was a very influential man . . . Schraeder may have made a mistake in judgment and offered to make a deal with him."

"It would certainly explain Dan's actions after my father had his stroke," she told him. "But none of it really matters, since it can't be confirmed." She shook her head dejectedly. "I mean, Dan will run again and he'll be elected. He'll find a way to get those leases back from the UCC and the city will sell the property to Clover Inns. Dan will make a tidy sum on the deal. And he'll get away with it."

She got up from the table and paced, her arms folded over her chest.

"God, it makes me mad." Her anger continued to rise. "What he's done to all those good people . . . just to line his own pockets. Damn . . . what I wouldn't do to trip him up now."

"How far would you go?" he asked quietly.

"As far as I had to." She leaned over the back of his chair. "Unfortunately, without Schraeder admitting that he offered the bribe . . ."

". . . which will never happen . . ." he interjected.

". . . obviously . . ." she said as she wrapped her arms around him from behind and rested her chin on the top of his head. "There doesn't seem to be any way to beat him. He's sure to win."

"Well, as long as he runs unopposed, he's a sure thing." Quentin reached up to stroke her arm.

"I can't think of anyone who could defeat him," she murmured, "'cept maybe Ms. Evelyn."

"Do you think she'd run?" he asked.

"I can't think of anyone else who'd have even a ghost of a chance . . ." She shook her head. "I'll talk to her when we get back home . . . maybe she'd consider it."

"Well, for someone who professes to have no interest in politics," he said, pulling her down onto his lap, "I'd say you're getting pretty close to the heart of the matter."

"This isn't about politics," she protested, "it's about doing what's right and keeping a crook like Dan Rossi from carrying out his personal agenda at the expense of the city."

Quentin laughed out loud.

"What is so funny?" she asked stonily.

"When I expressed exactly that sentiment to you, it started a feud that lasted for months," he reminded her.

"That was different," she said, sniffing indignantly.

"How so?" He nuzzled her neck and she tried not to smile.

"Because I didn't know then what I know now." She snuggled closer. "God, if I had . . . to think that I'm the one who made it possible for that rat to regain office . . . that all these months I've done this job just so he could carry on . . ."

"Do you regret it?" he asked.

She thought about the past year, all she'd done and all she'd learned. The big room was very quiet, the occasional crackling of a log in the fireplace the only sound for several long minutes. "I'm sorry I let him use me, and I'm sorry that I will have to give the office back to him. But the truth is I'm not the same person I was before I had to deal with the man he truly is, before I saw the faces of the people he was hurting, and before Ms. Evelyn showed me what people could do when they work together. And besides, the woman that I was before I took this job would never . . ." She paused and bit her lip.

"Would never what?" he asked quietly.

". . . would never be here with you," she said simply.

"Then, if for no other reason, I am in the debt of Dante Rossi," he whispered as he drew her closer. "I never wanted anyone the way I want you, Athen. I've spent many a night dreaming about you, wondering what it would be like to wake up with you in my arms, to share my days with you and to fall asleep next to you so that I could wake up again the next morning and find you still there. I have been haunted by you since the first time I saw you at the footraces in the park. Remember . . . ?"

She nodded, mesmerized by his declaration, loving every word he spoke.

". . . and if somehow I have Rossi to thank for bringing you into my life, I'll give the devil his due, and gladly. You are the light of my life, sweetheart, and I'll do anything I have to do to keep you right where you are . . ."

"I'm not going anywhere," she told him, leaning down to kiss him hungrily.

". . . except maybe over by the fire . . ." He stood up and lifted her in one movement.

"But only because it's too cold to venture down to the beach . . ." She smiled as he laid her back on the soft carpet in front of the fireplace.

"Next summer, I promise you," he said as he covered her slim body with his own, "we will make love on the beach in the moonlight at least once every weekend."

"Well, since I can't wait that long," she pulled his lips to hers, "let's just make do with what we have . . ."

44

"So," Meg prodded, her eyes twinkling.

"So, what?" Athen dragged her overnight bag into the hallway and dumped it by the bottom of the steps.

"So how was it?"

"It was heaven, Meg." Athen sighed, sitting down on the step, her chin in her hand.

"Oh, my." Meg laughed and plunked herself down on the next step up. "This does sound serious . . ."

"It was wonderful. Three days of walking on the beach and laying by the fire . . ." Athen leaned back dreamily.

"Laying by the fire . . . ?" Meg repeated, her eyebrows arching. "That certainly sounds romantic . . . Did you behave yourself?"

"No, I did not." Athen closed her eyes and rested against Meg's knees.

"I'm so glad." Meg sighed happily.

"Glad about what?" Callie skipped into the hall and sat down at her mother's feet.

"Glad that your mom had a good time," Meg told her.

"Did you?" Callie turned to ask.

"Lovely," Athen assured her. "And you? How was New York?"

"Lovely," parroted Callie, leaning back against her mother's knees. "We stayed at the Plaza Hotel, Mom, and I shared a room with Timmy's Aunt Caitlin. She's a doctor in Chicago and she met us there. We saw a show at Radio City Music Hall and skated at Rockefeller Center and ate at restaurants two times a day. Caitlin is really neat. She's Mr. Forbes's sister and she talks real fast. We ordered ice cream from room service last night and stayed up to watch a spooky movie and she asked a lot of questions about you."

"Like what?"

"Like what you do, that kind of stuff." Callie shrugged it off.

"What did you tell her?" Athen was curious.

"I told her you had a job, that your job was to make sure that things were done right in Woodside Heights because you were the mayor," recited Callie, "and that this year I taught you how to plant flowers and that we had a big garden and that you were a fast learner."

"Thank you, Callie." Athen suppressed a giggle.

"Did I say something wrong?" Callie turned her earnest little face to her mother.

"Of course not." Athen bent down and kissed the child's chin.

"Good." Callie grinned. "Can we go food shopping? We have no snacks . . ."

My job is to make sure that things are done right in Woodside Heights, Athen mused after she had turned her light out that night. Out of the mouths of babes. And to that end, I will ask Ms. Evelyn to meet me for lunch tomorrow.

She turned over and stretched her hand out to the emptiness on the other side of the bed. She closed her eyes and wished she could open them and find herself back in the house overlooking the ocean, where the bed had never been empty and the world had not extended beyond the one that they had made for each other. For just a few short days, the hours had been filled with love and warmth and a kind of peace she'd forgotten existed.

That first big step had not been so difficult after all. Now she looked forward to the rest of the journey.

"Papa, there's someone I want you to meet." Athen knelt before her father, her eyes sparkling, still holding on to Quentin's hand. "This is Quentin Forbes . . ."

"Mr. Stavros," Quentin said as he pulled a stool up close to the wheelchair, "I have heard so much about you from Athen. I am honored to meet you."

"Quentin and I have been . . . seeing a lot of each other, Papa," Athen told him. "I wanted you to know. And I wanted him to know you."

Ari's eyes softened as they went from Athen's face to Quentin's and back to rest on his beloved daughter.

They made small talk for a few minutes, Athen reading a short story Callie had written in school for which she'd won an award. When she'd finished, Quentin suggested she take a walk down to the pond.

"I'd like a few minutes with your father, if you don't mind," he told her, and she complied.

Almost a half hour had passed before Quentin had joined her on the bench overlooking the pond.

"What on earth were you talking about all this time?" she asked, not happy at having been left so long on the cold bench.

"Guy stuff." He shrugged and zipped up his jacket. "They just brought your dad lunch, or I'd still be there. It's getting nippy. How 'bout I drive you back to work before we both freeze our butts off."

"Oh, fine," she said, not needing to be coaxed into the

warm car, "when it's your butt that's at risk, we get to leave. When it's my butt . . ."

"I'll be more than happy to warm it for you." He grinned, rubbing her bottom briskly.

"Quentin!" She laughed while trying to protest. "What if someone sees you . . ."

" 'Mayor mauled by newsman.' " He opened her car door. "Film at eleven . . ."

"You're so lucky, Mrs. Moran," Veronica said with a sigh as Quentin had given her a wink on his way out of Athen's office. "I swear if my Salvatore was not the natural hunk that he is . . ."

Athen peered over the rims of her glasses, thinking how amused Quentin would be to have been compared to that natural hunk who was the apex of Veronica's young life.

"You want me to set this up over here, by the sofa?" Veronica was carrying a tray to set up for Athen's lunch with Ms. Evelyn. "Mr. Forbes isn't staying? You said to order three of everything."

"Mrs. Bennett will be here too," Athen told her.

Thinking perhaps the occasion called for a little more political savvy than she herself possessed, Athena had, as an afterthought, called Diana to discuss her plan. As suspected, Diana agreed that Ms. Evelyn would be a perfect opponent for the Rossi forces, and had volunteered to help convince Ms. Evelyn of the fact.

"As much as I hate to see him run unopposed," Ms. Evelyn had said after Athen had made her plea, "if Dan is going to build that hotel, he'll at least be bringing jobs into the city. I can't even offer the voters that much. The very idea of building a luxury hotel while folks are sleeping in doorways," she said, shaking her head, "makes me see red, thinking about that whole expanse of the city going to some damned fool hotel instead of it being used for what the city really needs . . ."

"What's that, Ms. Evelyn?" Diana asked.

"Well, the shelter aside, let's start with the fact that this city has no true medical center, no emergency facilities." The old woman jabbed an index finger in the air for emphasis. "And we need a community center, with a job training center and a place where folks can learn basic skills . . . things that could help folks learn to help themselves."

"I doubt any of those things were part of the deal that Dan made with Schraeder," Diana said softly. "But the UCC does still hold the leases, Ms. Evelyn. You could refuse to turn them back to the city."

"And be accused of blocking the jobs that would result from the development of the area?" She raised an eyebrow. "I don't think so, Diana. Tempted though I'd be, at least some folks would be working. I just don't see the point in opposing him without having anything better to offer the city."

"And she's right," a glum Athen told Quentin over dinner that evening. "Ms. Evelyn may be the best person to beat Rossi one on one, but he's holding all the cards. Some jobs are better than no jobs."

"What if she had something to offer as a choice?" Quentin asked thoughtfully.

"Something like what?" Athen frowned.

"Like her medical center," he suggested.

"Right, Quentin," she snapped sarcastically, "they grow on trees . . . do you have any idea what that would cost?"

"Roughly." He smiled at the waitress as she placed a huge steak on the table before him. "What happened at your meeting with the HUD people?"

"Not encouraging." She shook her head. "We'd have to hire someone just to fill out the forms, complete the applications . . . It would be so far down the road Rossi would have the hotel built and operational before we could even get the preliminary work done."

"Hmmm . . ." He dug into his dinner, lost in thought.

"What are you thinking?" she asked curiously after he'd sat wordlessly for several minutes.

"Oh, I was just thinking about Ms. Evelyn," he told her. "If ever there was someone whose dreams should come true, it's that lady's, don't you think?"

"Well, unless we can find her a fairy godmother within the next few weeks, it won't matter." Athen picked at her salad.

"A fairy godmother . . ." he repeated, his mouth sliding into a slow grin. "Yes. Exactly. A fairy godmother . . ."

On Valentine's Day morning, Quentin showed up at her office bearing not the expected bouquet of roses or a satin encased box of chocolates, but a long cardboard tube tied with a big red bow.

"Happy Valentine's Day, sweetheart," he whispered as she wrapped her arms around his neck and kissed his mouth.

"What is it?" she said, examining the cylinder.

"Open it and find out," he said with a grin. "Here, put it on your desk . . ."

She tugged at the rolled-up papers inside the tube, casting mystified glances in his direction. Finally she withdrew the contents and opened them flat across the surface of her desk.

"Oh my God!" she exclaimed as she realized what lay before her. "Oh my God . . ."

"It's something, isn't it?" He grinned.

"How did you ever get this done so quickly?" she gasped.

"Actually, I didn't. These were the plans for the medical center Caitlin wanted to build outside Chicago," he told her, his eyes twinkling, "but the deal on the site she wanted fell through. So I called her and asked her if she'd consider moving her operation to Woodside Heights."

"How can she afford to do this?"

"With a generous donation from the Bradford Foundation." He rubbed her back, and found her shoulders to be trembling.

"The Bradford Foundation," she repeated blankly.

"Mother controls the funds," he said, leaning over slightly to whisper in her ear.

"Do you think she would . . . ?" Athen was positively wide-eyed.

"She already has, my sweet," he said, grinning.

"Oh, Quentin . . ." The full import of his words dawned on her. "Oh, Quentin, I truly love you . . ."

"Well, if I'd known this was what it would take to pry those words out of you, I'd have called Caitlin sooner."

"You are unbelievable!" She all but danced gleefully into his arms. "Quentin, do you know what this means?"

"Yes." He kissed her soundly. "It means Evelyn Wallace will be the next mayor of Woodside Heights."

By the end of March, the campaign had turned into a hotly contested race. Ms. Evelyn, to Dan Rossi's utter amazement, had found a plan that spoke to the voters in a way he could not. Though still favored in the polls, Dan's margin had clearly begun to slip. Athen had worked tirelessly with her candidate, vowing to do whatever was necessary to ensure a victory for the tiny woman who would save the city from itself.

Confident of a win, Athen spent a long weekend with Quentin in Bay Head, the first time they'd been alone for more than a few hours in weeks. They walked on the beach and made love in front of the fire, winding more and more deeply into each other's hearts. They savored every minute of their forty-eight-hour respite, and returned to Woodside Heights refreshed and renewed, ready to resume the battle.

A sobbing Callie met them in the driveway.

"Mommy . . . Mommy," she choked.

"Oh, God, Callie." Athen jumped from the car and grabbed her daughter. "What's happened . . . ?"

"Mommy, Ms. Evelyn . . ." The weeping child flung herself onto her mother.

Meg rounded the side of the house.

"She had a heart attack," Meg answered the unspoken question, "she didn't make it, Athen . . ."

"Oh, no . . ." Athen collapsed backwards onto Quentin's car, holding Callie's shaking form. "Oh, no . . ."

"When?" Quentin asked.

"About two hours ago," Meg told them. "Riley called from the hospital."

Quentin put an arm around both Callie and Athen and led them wordlessly into the house, where they all sat in stunned silence, no words capable of expressing the sorrow they all felt for the dearest of women who had so touched all their lives.

In accordance with Ms. Evelyn's own wishes, a memorial service had been held in the once vacant lots that less than a year ago she had reclaimed. The clergy for the UCC, as well as family members, rose to give testimony to the meaning of Ms. Evelyn's life, and one by one, they had shared their memories. Reverend Davison had asked Athen to offer her thoughts, and she had prayed she'd have the strength to address the gathering with dignity.

"I have known Evelyn Wallace since I was a child, but came to know Evelyn Wallace as an adult through the plants she sold to my family," Athen spoke clearly from the podium, "and the first thing I learned about her was her endless capacity for warmth and love and friendship. She was friend to my father, to my late husband, to my daughter, and to me. She was a woman whose life was filled with joy and filled with hope . . . a woman whose love for this city was boundless, whose vision of what this city could be was an inspiration. She was the only truly selfless person I've ever known, and in her complete devotion to others I learned what public service truly means. The people of Woodside Heights have lost their strongest advocate and their greatest friend . . . and so have I . . ."

There had been more she had wanted to say, but the words choked off in her throat. She descended from the podium and as she crossed to stand between Callie and Quentin, her eyes strayed to the opposite side of the crowd. Dan Rossi stood in the front row, his hands clasped in front of him, his somber demeanor appropriate for the occasion. His gaze locked on Athen, and she could see even from the distance between them how his eyes gleamed. Diana's description of how Dan had fled to the hospital after Ari's stroke came suddenly to mind, and Athen knew instinctively that Dan had worn the same malevolent look of triumph then that he wore now. How fortunate for Dan that fate had intervened not once, but twice, sparing him from engaging in a final fight.

Not this time, Athen told him wordlessly as she lifted her chin defiantly, her eyes narrowing as she met his. They stared at each other openly, he silently issuing a challenge, she accepting it. Quentin had sought her arm at the close of the service, and seeing her distraction, followed her intense gaze. He recognized the resolve in her face, and knew what was to come.

"Quentin . . . ," she said when they had returned to the house and Callie had gone upstairs to change.

"I know, sweetheart." He pulled her next to him on the sofa and drew her to him, kissing the top of her head thoughtfully.

"I can't let him win, Quentin," she said quietly.

"No." He sighed. "You cannot."

"And there isn't anyone else who could step in this late in the race," she told him softly, "at least, I can't think of anyone . . ."

"There isn't anyone but you," he readily agreed.

She curled up in his arms, staring at the floor. Finally, she turned to him and asked, "Do you mind?"

"Do I mind that you are willing to go through everything that a contested campaign entails for the sake of keeping alive the dreams of friend?" He caressed her arm pensively. "I don't have the words to tell you how proud of you I am . . ."

"Really?" she asked.

"Really," he assured her. "But do you understand that Dan will come after you with everything he has . . . that it will be as ugly as it can get between now and May? Are you certain you can handle it?"

"I'm sure." She nodded without hesitation. "But can you? Can you be objective and write all the awful things he's going to say about me . . . ?"

"Absolutely not," he told her vehemently, "I'll end up killing him."

"You're not going to suggest we stop seeing each other until this is over, are you?" she asked grimly.

"Are you crazy?" He laughed. "What would that accomplish?"

"Well, I was thinking of how before you felt compromised . . ."

"Athen, there is nothing in the world that means more to me than you do." He pulled her closer to his face. "But you are right, I cannot cover this campaign. I think the best thing for me to do is to leave the paper . . ."

"Quit your job?" She sat up. "You'd quit your job?"

"I'd already decided to." He shrugged.

"When?"

"When the service for Ms. Evelyn was over and I saw that Dan could not make you blink," he said. "I knew without a word being spoken what you had to do. And I knew that there would be a more important job for me."

"What's that?"

"Well, I figured you'd need a good press secretary . . . someone who believed in you and who could skillfully spread the word that you would be dedicated to accomplishing all Ms. Evelyn set out to do." His fingers drifted across her lips. "There's no one who believes in you more than I do, Athen. Whatever I have is at your disposal—time, energy, money . . . whatever you need to win."

"I might not win, Quentin," she reminded him softly.

"Win or lose . . ." He kissed her deeply. ". . . I will be there with you every step of the way."

"I love you very much, Quentin," she told him softly, knowing that in winning this man's heart, she had won the greatest prize of all. Her life had come full circle over the course of the past year. She had found the bits and pieces of herself that had scattered when John died, and had found the strength to put herself back together again. In Quentin's love she had found all the peace and joy she would ever need. She had regained her self-confidence and had found self-respect when she had defied Dan. There was nothing Rossi could take from her now but her job.

"I love you, too, Athen." He smiled, happy to be on her side this time, happy to be with her through the fight that lay ahead. He would give his all for her, regardless of the final outcome. "Now get on the phone and get Diana over here. We have a lot of work to do."

Diana had made an excellent choice for campaign manager. She had been with Ari through all his campaigns, and knew all the old stalwarts and all the new blood. They had worked late into the night, plotting their strategy and making up lists of the ward leaders and committee people they would be calling on. Athen would announce her decision to run the following Wednesday, and they had many weeks' worth of work to accomplish in a very few days.

True to his word, Quentin worked around the clock on the literature and posters with which he would plaster the city. Posters bearing the replica of the new medical center and community center asked the residents to "Keep the dream alive." Full page ads in the local papers carried Athen's promise that the vision of a new Woodside Heights offered by Evelyn Wallace was still within reach, that her work would be carried on as a testament to her memory.

Rossi had swiftly retaliated, dismissing Athen as no more than an opportunist who would fight to keep her office even if it meant stepping over the "still warm body of a woman she had called friend." Think, he crooned, of what a hotel, a convention center would mean to the city, of the revenue it would bring in. Think of how the city could grow and prosper once the center of town had been cleared of the blighted neighborhoods, he urged the voters.

"Put Dan Rossi back in office," he promised a wildly supporting crowd, "and I'll put Woodside Heights back to work!"

"Dan Rossi means he'll put Woodside Heights back to work for him," Athen had responded. "Ask him where he was when all those jobs were leaving Woodside Heights."

"Ask Athen Moran what she's done for this city in the past two years," Rossi taunted.

"Ask Rossi what he accomplished in the previous eight," she replied calmly, then grinned, adding, "I think getting a commitment from the Bradford Foundation to fund not only a badly needed medical center but a true community center as envisioned by Evelyn Wallace was a pretty big accomplishment."

"She's a novice," Rossi sputtered upon hearing Athen's remark. "An amateur. The hard-working taxpayers of Woodside Heights want to see this city soar in the nineties, want to see this city become a mecca here in the northernmost part of the state."

"If that's what the citizens of this city truly want, that's what they'll vote for on election day," Athen had told the reporter from the *Herald.* "They will choose. All this harping from Mr. Rossi is a smoke screen. For eight years he sat back in his chair and smoked his big cigars and watched this city fall apart. For the first time, someone is offering Woodside Heights a choice, and the choice is greater than him or me. It's an opportunity to decide the direction in which this city will grow. Until the first Tuesday in May, no one will know for certain what that direction will be. We'll all just have to wait, and we'll find out together . . ."

"More wine, Ms. Moran?" the waiter offered solicitously.

"No, thank you, Henry." She shook her head. "Quentin, don't you think this is odd, the entire room is deserted . . ." She surveyed their surroundings, clearly puzzled. They were, as she had observed, the only diners in the small, elegantly appointed side room of Etienne's, the lavish restaurant that just months ago had opened in a lovely old mansion on a hill overlooking the city. "Where do you suppose everyone is?"

"Probably at the polls, doing their civic duty." He shrugged nonchalantly. "Besides, this is a Tuesday night . . . and the night of the hottest election this city has ever seen. I'm sure people will begin to filter in later."

"Maybe we ought to get back." She shifted nervously in her seat. "Maybe we ought to check the returns . . ."

"Sweetheart, the polls don't close for another hour." He entwined his fingers with hers. "Just sit back and relax a little. We've plenty of time."

"I didn't expect to be this nervous," she confided. "I never thought a day could be as long as this one has been."

"Well, it's almost over and we'll know soon enough," he reminded her. "I think I'd like some coffee. How about you?" He signaled for the waiter.

"Quentin, I have had about ten cups past my limit." She sighed. "I'm positively wired."

"Two decafs," he told Henry.

"Quentin, I feel like I should be back at headquarters with everyone else."

"Nonsense." He moved his chair closer to hers and massaged one of her tired shoulders with his right hand. "It's going to be a long evening, sweetheart, and after the ordeal of the past six weeks, I think you have earned the right to sit and have a peaceful hour or two . . . Here's our coffee . . ."

He leaned back as Henry placed their cups on the table, then pushed Athen's back slightly and placed a large goblet filled with raspberries and whipped cream before her.

"Henry . . ." She frowned. "I didn't order dessert."

"Etienne made it special for you, madam," Henry told her, beaming. "He ordered the raspberries only for you."

She managed a smile, and as Henry left the room, said to Quentin, "If I eat another bite, I'll be sick . . ."

She passed the goblet to him. He passed it back.

"Of course you won't be sick." He smiled. "Eat your dessert."

"Quentin, I don't want . . ." she protested as he lifted the spoon towards her mouth. "Oh, honestly, Quentin . . ."

"Athen, you don't want to offend Etienne." He leaned forward. "He's the best chef in town."

"Oh, all right, I'll eat some of it," she said with a shrug, "if you'll finish it . . ."

He watched closely as she dipped her spoon into the frothy cloud of whipped cream, playing with it, unconsciously raising small peaks here and there.

"You know, it's funny." She put the spoon down on the plate beneath the goblet. "The last election was just an exercise. I hadn't the faintest idea what was going on, nor did I really much care, and I won so easily. Of course, that time I was unopposed and had Rossi's backing. This time, when it means something, when there's really something at stake, it's so difficult. I want so badly to win, Quentin. Not just to beat Dan, but for Ms. Evelyn . . ."

"She would have been immensely proud of you, as I am," he said softly, "as everyone who loves you is. Not just for taking on Dan, but for the way you've conducted yourself all through this. And Dan should thank you for not throwing Mary Jo Dolan in his face."

"You know I couldn't do that."

"Weren't you even tempted, just a tiny bit?" he teased.

"Maybe a little." She laughed, adding, "But then, that would make me just as bad as he is."

"You are a most admirable and amazing woman, my sweet." He leaned over and kissed her ear. "Now, finish that little confection and let's get going."

"Quentin, I feel like a whale," she moaned.

"Well, you haven't been eating regularly these past few weeks. At least polish off the whipped cream . . ." He handed her the spoon.

"I can see you won't be satisfied until I explode." She grimaced, taking the spoon. "Maybe if I just move it around a bit it will look as if I've eaten more than . . ."

She stopped in midsentence, her attention on the bowl of the spoon, her mouth half-opened in surprise.

"May I clean that up a bit for you?" he asked softly.

Her eyes filled with tears as they moved from the spoon to his face.

"Athen . . ." he whispered, holding out his hand. She passed the spoon to him and he dipped it into his water glass. Retrieving the ring from the bottom of the glass, he dried the diamond with his napkin.

"I guess having gone this far, I should go the whole nine yards." He smiled and pushed back his chair.

Her eyes never left his face, even when he dropped before her on one knee.

"Athena Stavros Moran, will you marry me?"

Still stunned and speechless, Athen sat wide-eyed, barely blinking.

He cleared his throat.

"Athen, this is no time to go mute," he told her in a mock stage whisper, "this is supposed to be a big moment, you know . . ."

She nodded her head slowly.

"Was that an affirmative yes, you know it's a big moment, or yes, you will marry me?" His eyes twinkled as he rested an elbow on his raised knee.

"Both," she whispered.

He took her hands in his and slipped the ring on her finger. She hardly seemed to notice.

"Don't you want to see it? It's almost four karats, Athen, at least look at the damned thing," he said with a laugh.

"It's gorgeous." She leaned over to hold his face in her

hands. He kissed the trail of tears which had streaked down her face. "Are you sure you want to do this? If I get elected, things could be pretty hectic . . ."

"Nothing could be more hectic than the past few weeks have been," he told her, "and yes, I want to marry you. I've never been more certain of anything in my life, Athen. I love you more than I thought it could be possible to love anyone. Your future is my future. Whatever happens tonight, we'll celebrate together or we'll lick our wounds together. Whatever the future brings, we'll deal with it together."

She leaned over and kissed him again, the election forgotten for a few long minutes. Finally, she tugged at his lapels. "You can get up now." She laughed, realizing he was still kneeling on the carpeted floor.

"Quentin, I do love you." She sighed as he moved his chair to within an inch of hers and draped an arm around her shoulders. "I would marry you this minute if it was possible. These past few months have been murder, making Meg take Callie out so we can have the house to ourselves on Friday nights until we can fit in a weekend away . . . I feel like a kid sneaking behind her mother's back, only I'm the mother and she's the kid . . ."

"We can be married as soon as you like." He laughed. "And yes, I think poor Meg has seen enough movies and spent enough Saturday afternoons at the roller rink to last her a lifetime."

"I always wanted to be a June bride," she told him wistfully.

"June it will be," he agreed.

"That's barely a month away." Her eyes widened at the thought.

"Then we'd better enlist my mother," he said. "She's a whiz at that sort of thing."

"What do you think the kids will say?" she wondered aloud.

"Guess there's only one way to find out." Quentin signaled for the waiter to bring their check. "By the way, you're thirty-seven votes behind with three more precincts to be counted."

"How do you know that?" Her jaw dropped.

"Henry's been checking in with Diana all night." He grinned. "And he's been giving me an update every time you turned your head . . ."

Quentin pulled into the drive at the carriage house on the Chapman estate that had been converted into Athen's campaign headquarters and turned off the car lights. They sat in the dark for a few moments, savoring the last few minutes of calm they would know for the next few days. He ran his fingers lightly through her hair, and she rested back against his shoulder.

"Ready?" he asked.

"Quentin, I just want you to know that, whatever the final outcome is, I will never be able to thank you for everything you've done. I don't mean just the material you wrote or the money you raised. You always made me feel that this was as important to you as it was to me . . . that you believed in me," she told him.

"I do, sweetheart." He kissed the side of her face. "And I always will. Win or lose."

"Let's go see which it is." She took a deep breath and slid across the seat to open her door.

They could hear the shouts before they had reached the door. Mayhem greeted them as they walked into the carriage house and her jubilant supporters welcomed her wildly. The tally from the final precincts had just been announced. Athena Moran had defeated Dante Rossi by seven hundred fifty-three votes.

45

Athen leaned upon the top railing of the deck and watched the gulls as they swayed in graceful circles above a serene blue sea. The morning sun danced a dazzling ballet of endless, glittering arabesques across the water for as far as the eye could see. She shaded her eyes with one hand to dim the glow to see beyond the shoreline, out to where the fishing boats had already dropped anchor. The warming sand lay before her seductively, and she was unable to resist its invitation.

Kicking off her sandals, she set off across the beach, startling a red-winged black bird who'd landed on the outstretched arm of a lone scruffy shrub at the top of the dune. The bird took off in an agitated flurry, one short dark feather spiraling down to rest upon the sand. Athen picked it up as she passed and followed the wooden boardwalk down towards the shore.

She ventured a hesitant toe into the white froth of water left behind by a gentle wave. Even the sand so close to the water line was still cold, the early summer sun not yet quite strong enough to have warmed the sea, and she stepped backwards, her feet seeking a dry, warm spot on the shore where the low tide had not reached. A glint in the sand caught her eye and she reached down to it, wiping the object on her sweatshirt to clean it off. The sun's light radiated off the bright green piece of sea glass, bestowing upon the once humble piece of broken bottle the luster of an emerald. She turned it over and over in her hand to study it before slipping it in the pocket of her shorts with the feather. On her way back up towards the house, she kicked the sand up a little, revealing an occasional shell which she added to her treasures.

Halfway up the beach she plunked herself down in the sand and leaned back on her elbows, squinting as she glanced up first one side of the beach then the other, not seeing a soul on either end. She dug her toes beneath the sand and hung her head back, her face lifted to the sky, savoring the moment's solitude and the joy of being exactly who and where she was. There is something so primitive in being on a deserted beach, she mused, something peaceful in lying on the sand with the cry of the gulls and the soft lapping of the ocean as musical accompaniment to the rhythm of your inner thoughts.

"There you are." Quentin followed the path of narrow boards, then stopped to remove his shoes. From her vantage point, he took the form of a giant striding across the sand.

"Come join me." She patted the space next to her. "Pull up some beach and sit down."

He lowered himself to the sand, waving a fat white bag to taunt her.

"Guess what I have?" he teased smugly.

"Wedding pictures?" Her eyes lit up and she reached for the bag.

"Not with those sandy hands, my dear." He laughed and pulled a pack of photos from the bag. "I will hold them and we can both look, but you may not touch."

"Stop teasing, Quentin, I can't wait to see . . ." She leaned over his shoulder. "Now whose film was this?"

"Meg's, I'd guess, since Brenda's in this first shot." He held the picture up. "Although it could be Jeff's . . ."

"Your mother looks positively flustered." Athen giggled.

"That must have been right before the wedding, right after Mother discovered that the florist had placed the topiaries at the wrong end of the garden." He chuckled.

"Look how beautiful everything was." She sighed as he placed the next photo before her. The Chapmans' grounds had been transformed into a bower of roses for the wedding only the Saturday before. Lydia Chapman had insisted that only a rose garden wedding would do for the marriage of her only son, and it had taken several florists to bring her vision of clouds of roses to life. "Was there ever a more beautiful wedding . . . ?"

"Never. It was spectacular," he agreed. "Everything was perfect, wasn't it?"

"It still is." She nudged his shoulder with her nose.

"Oh, and just look at my father," she exclaimed, leaning closer for a better look. Ari sat proudly in his wheelchair, Diana behind him, smiling happily, her hands resting on Ari's shoulders. "Wasn't he handsome? And Diana, how beautiful she looks. I'll have to have that one enlarged and framed for them both. And Callie . . . look how serious you both look, Quentin. What were you talking about?"

"Miss Callie was informing me in the gentlest possible terms that while she was in fact delighted that I was marrying her mother," he smiled at the memory, "I had better not be harboring any thoughts of becoming her father, because she already had one, thank you, even if he was dead."

"Leave it to Callie." Athen grimaced slightly. "What did you say?"

"I told her that I had great respect for her father and I am very much aware of how close they were and that I would never try to step into his place in her life," he said, "but that I would always be there for her if she ever needed me."

"We should have spent more time talking to the kids about what this will mean," she thought aloud.

"I think we handled it well, before the wedding." He shook his head. "There's a lot we haven't anticipated, Athen, but we'll handle their concerns as situations arise."

"I guess Timmy must feel the same way." She hugged her knees. "I mean about me not being his mother."

"I don't think it's quite the same," he told her, "I don't know that he has any glowing memories of Cynthia. Timmy might like to be mothered just a little."

He shuffled through the pack of photos, Athen peering over his shoulder. Meg—a beautiful maid of honor in pale rose silk—with her senator. Veronica on mile-high spikes—dyed baby blue to match her dress—her hair newly piled skyward and freshly lacquered for the occasion, clinging to the arm of her husband, the stalwart Sal, who, all muscle, was almost as wide as he was tall. Brenda, in a yellow silk sheath, with her man of the hour, a film producer from California. Caitlin Forbes, in a green suit, her hair short and casual, her arms around her beloved brother. Athen had met her for the first time the week before the wedding, and they had sat for hours talking like old friends.

"I will never forget the way you looked when you came through the doors onto the veranda," he said in a soft voice, holding a picture of his bride as she had walked into the sunlight, stunning in a simple ankle-length sheath of deep ivory satin and lace with a high Victorian choker, a lace picture hat trimmed in satin roses framing her face. "I have never been so touched by a single moment, Athen, as I was when I looked up and saw you walking to me . . ."

He seemed to struggle for a second, collecting the right words.

". . . and it seemed to me right then and there that I knew what it felt like to be reborn. That after all the pain of the past few years there was something so wonderful waiting for me." He rubbed the side of his head gently against hers, his voice all but a whisper across the dune. "I would have endured a thousand heartaches to have had that one moment, when I knew that I would be spending the rest of my life with you."

Athen's eyes filled with tears and she sniffed quietly.

"If I could ever tell you what you have given me." She swallowed hard in hopes of gaining control of her voice. "When John died, I really thought my life was over. That there would never be another truly happy moment, or a day when I would ever be filled with the sheer joy of being alive. I honestly believed that my only purpose on this earth was to raise my daughter, that my own life had no meaning beyond Callie, and that there would be no reason to laugh or feel pain or watch a sunset. No joy, no wonder—nothing to make me feel alive, just a dull ache inside me from the minute I opened my eyes in the morning until I closed them again at night . . ."

"And then along came Dan Rossi," he whispered in her ear.

"How can you mention that man's name at a time like this?" She glared indignantly.

"Because he was the devil who prodded you back into the world, my darling," Quentin reminded her, "and as much as I'd like to take the credit, Athen, it was Dan who coaxed you into taking that first step."

"I'll give him that much, the scoundrel." She leaned back against him, shaking her head. "It all seems so long ago now. I look back on those first days in city hall and it seems like another lifetime."

"It was," he said and nuzzled her. "And we have yet another lifetime to discover together."

"Funny how it worked out, isn't it?" she asked, drawing circles in the sand with one finger. "You coming east when you did . . . ?"

"Everything that happened before was leading me here." He kissed her. "To this moment, to this place."

He studied the circles she had drawn, then kissed the top of her head, and stood up. She watched as he walked across the sand, looking down as if searching for something. He picked up a large clam shell, then began drawing something in the sand, about ten feet from where she sat. Amused, she stood to watch him, then walked closer.

"Quentin . . ."

"Watch it," he playfully admonished, "you're standing on the 'S'."

"What 'S'?" She backed up and looked down to the marking in the sand.

"There you go." He grinned and stood back to admire his work.

Quentin loves Athen.

They both laughed, and she draped her arms around his neck.

"And I love you, Quentin . . ." She kissed his mouth. ". . . With all my heart."

"Ah, that's what's missing." He smiled down into her eyes, kissed her neck, then pulled the shell out of his pocket. Bending over, he enclosed his message inside two swooping arches.

"What do you think?" He grinned, draping an arm over her shoulder and pulling her very close.

"I think it's perfect," she told him. "As perfect as this morning, as perfect as this week has been."

"And as perfect as the rest of the day will be." He pulled her along towards the boards which lead to the house. "Let's go upstairs and open up those doors." He nodded upwards to the French doors off their bedroom balcony. "And let the sun and the sea air in our room and take an early siesta . . ."

"What will Mrs. Emmons think?" She nudged him as they walked clumsily, their hips and shoulders gently colliding from time to time as their feet sunk into the sand.

"We're sending Mrs. Emmons to Manasquan to do some shopping and as many other errands as we can come up with," he whispered.

"Ah, I forgot the photographs," he told her as they reached the bottom of the steps. He sprinted across the dune to where he'd left the white bag laying on the sand.

Athen climbed the steps and stood at the railing, watching as Quentin returned the pictures to their envelope and stuffed it back into the bag. He turned and walked back towards her, a smile of deep contentment on his face. They would have today and the rest of this week to enjoy each other, before returning to Woodside Heights and its turmoil, before taking the first steps into the unknown waters of stepparenting and blending their families under one roof.

For now, it was enough that they were here and alone and had these days. Behind Quentin on the sand she could see the outline of the heart he had drawn. The message it held was all she needed to know.